SOMEDAY IN PARIS

SOMEDAY IN PARIS

Olivia Lara

An Aria Book

This edition first published in the United Kingdom in 2020 by Aria,
an imprint of Head of Zeus Ltd

Copyright © Olivia Lara, 2020

The moral right of Olivia Lara to be identified as the author
of this work has been asserted in accordance with the Copyright,
Designs and Patents Act of 1988.

A CIP catalogue record for this book is available from the
British Library.

ISBN 9781838933142

Typeset by Siliconchips Services Ltd UK

Cover design © Charlotte Abrams Simpson

Aria
c/o Head of Zeus
First Floor East
5–8 Hardwick Street
London EC1R 4RG

www.ariafiction.com

For anyone who ever doubted themselves:

Believe in yourself, listen to your heart and always – I mean ALWAYS – follow your dreams.

DOMINIQUE

COLMAR

What makes people fall in love? Truly in love? What makes them believe they've found the one, their soulmate? And why that person and not someone else?

What draws us in and never lets us go? Is it their eyes, their smile, their voice? The way they fit into our world? Is it because our parents like them and our friends think we'd make a great couple? Or maybe they make us laugh, have a good job, and want two kids like we do?

What if it has nothing to do with that? What if it is something else entirely?

I was fifteen the first time I asked myself this question. It was then that I had my first dream that didn't feel quite like a dream. My mother said women in our family are special. She said I should listen to my dreams, but I was young, and I didn't believe her. Or maybe I didn't understand.

I am eighty years old now. I don't pretend to have all

the answers. But I've lived through enough to know people don't believe you until you show them. And they shouldn't. They should make up their own minds, listen to their own hearts, and follow their own dreams.

My story, the one I've been waiting to tell for so long, the one I never thought I would get to share until Valerie was born – my youngest son's daughter – will not answer questions. Not even the question. But it will ask them.

Ever since Valerie turned fifteen, I have been waiting for the day she would say, 'Mamie, I had a dream.' And then I would have to tell her. To show her. When she turned sixteen, seventeen, eighteen and nothing happened, I started to worry. What if I'm not around when it happens, or I am around but too senile to remember everything? That's when I wrote it all down. That way, no matter what, she will know what happened and how it all came to be. And when the story's done, she can make up her own mind about the dreams, the connection and what her soul is trying to tell her. She might believe me, she might not, but I have to try.

A few days ago, she celebrated her twenty-first birthday. Still no word of the dreams. But there is a young man in her life, although she's reluctant to talk about him. I don't know if today of all days I should ask, but something tells me it might be time. There's a spark in her eyes. A familiar spark. I might be wrong; it might be nothing, but it might be everything.

'How are things with you, darling?' I ask as we get close to Reims. The plan is to drop her off to meet some friends at the university in Reims while I go to Paris. Every year, on 9 December, I go to Paris no matter what.

'Fine,' she says, too busy with her phone to look at me.

'Anything interesting happening?'

'No, not really.'

As usual. Either Valerie has a painfully dull life or a secret one.

'Ugh, perfect,' she scoffs and throws the phone in her bag. Then she picks it up again like she can't decide what to do.

'What's wrong?'

Silence.

'It might help if you talk about it,' I say.

'It's nothing really. Just this guy.'

'What guy?'

I think I already know the answer.

'Someone I met online. We've been chatting every day for a while now, but for the last two days, he's been completely ignoring me. No email, no text, nothing. I'm so naïve. It's my fault, really, for getting worked up about a man I've never even seen. Isn't it stupid?'

I smile. No, no, it's not. Not at all.

'He's clearly ghosting me. This is so embarrassing.'

'What does ghosting mean?' I ask.

'Ghosting? It's when someone disappears without an explanation. I've sent him tons of messages since Friday and nothing. Look,' she says, shoving the phone in my face.

'Can't see while I'm driving, darling,' I say calmly.

She seems frustrated with me. 'Anyway, my friends say he's a catfish; otherwise, why wouldn't he talk on the phone or Skype?'

'First ghosts, now catfish. Everything used to be much easier when I was your age.'

'A catfish is someone who pretends to be someone else online,' she says.

I don't see the connection between that and a catfish, but what do I know?

'Online as in on the internet?'

She laughs again. 'Everyone is on Facebook and Twitter these days. He could very well be a twelve-year-old Parisian having fun with his playmates.'

'As opposed to?'

'A twenty-six-year-old actor on a movie set in Sydney.'

Today is probably not the day I tell her about the dreams. Even to me, an actor who avoids showing his face seems fishy.

'He won't even send me a photo. All the signs are there. Why did I even think there could be something between us? This whole thing is stressing me out. I can't eat. And ever since he stopped responding I've been having the strangest dreams.'

'What are the dreams about?' I ask. A dream can be just a dream. Even in our family.

'Don't know. Stupid stuff.'

'Please, tell me.'

'Why?'

'Please, Valerie.'

She looks out the car window. 'I dreamed about a man with a gun. He was pointing it at me, and I was scared, terrified. But the strange thing is, although it was me in the dream, it wasn't me. I'm not sure how to explain it. It's as if I saw it through someone else's eyes.'

4

I slam on the brakes.

'Are you okay, Mamie? What's wrong?'

'Valerie, what do you really feel about this man?'

'What do you mean? I told you. I don't even know him.'

'That's not what I asked.'

Her eyes fill with tears. 'I feel I can't breathe without him, that's what I feel. Happy now? If I don't talk to him for a few hours, I miss him. I want to share everything with him. I feel I was somehow meant to meet him. And it's like, no matter who he is, what he looks like, I wouldn't care because—'

'Because you love him.'

'That's impossible. You can't love someone you've never met.'

I take a deep breath. Of all the days. It had to be this one.

'You will have to meet your friends some other day, darling,' I say as I take a sharp right back onto the highway instead of driving into Reims.

'Where are we going?' asks Valerie and I hear the concern in her voice.

'You'll see when we get there.'

She keeps asking me all the way to Paris, but I don't say a thing. I have to do this right. There's an accident on the highway, and we get caught in a lot of traffic, but we finally make it.

'Why are we stopping here?' asks Valerie and follows me out of the rental car.

'Button up your coat, darling. It's freezing.'

I open the trunk, grab the flowerpot and tuck it into my coat.

'Slow down,' she says, rushing to catch up with me.

The fresh snow crunches under our boots and the wind blows through the naked trees.

'I don't like to keep people waiting. It's disrespectful.'

'You're meeting someone in the cemetery? Mamie, are you sure you're alright?'

They are waiting at the end of the alley.

'Sorry we're late,' I say and hug each of them.

'Who's this?' asks Hugo, staring at us.

'My granddaughter, Valerie.'

'This is the first time in fifty-five years Dominique has brought someone along,' he says. 'How in God's name did you convince her?'

'I'm not sure I did,' says Valerie.

'Shall we?' I ask. I lead her through untouched snow, to a row of identical stones. The names and the dates of birth are different, but the date of death is the same.

9 December 1964

Valerie steps closer. 'Mamie? Who are all these people and why are we here?'

I caress her face. 'In the beginning, they all came. Over a hundred people. Through the years, some died, some moved away, others just couldn't make the trip anymore. It's only the eight of us now, and I can't abandon them.'

The group spreads out, each of them stopping in front of a stone. I do the same.

'I don't understand. Why do you all come here and whose grave is this?' she asks, reading the name engraved on the stone. 'Who is Alexander Roberts, did you know him?'

I clean the snow off and carefully place the small pot of lilies.

'I dreamed about him once.' I smile. 'Now, let's go home. We'll make hot cocoa, and I'll read you a story.'

'I'm too old for stories, Mamie.'

'You're never too old for stories. Definitely not for this one.'

'You're very mysterious. Does Grandpa know about this story of yours?' she asks.

'Your grandfather and I have no secrets.'

A few hours later, we're sitting on the couch, our feet warm under a plush blanket.

Sixty-five years to the day. I feel a hand on my shoulder and my heart smiles.

'What is the story about? Is it about this man? This Alexander Roberts?' asks Valerie.

I open the leather-bound notebook. 'It is about the three identical paintings on the wall you've been asking about and the book with lilies on the cover. It's about dreams and taking chances. Missed opportunities and mistakes. Loss and sacrifice. But above all, it is about love. The kind of love that survives time, distance. Even death. The kind of love I wish for you.'

I take a deep breath, clear my voice and start reading.

PART I

'Life is a long sleep
and love is its dream.'
— Alfred de Musset

ZARA

COLMAR

The guard pushed a metal cart through the museum's main gallery and into the minuscule art library. He took a piece of cardboard out of his pocket and wrote something on it before placing it on one of the many empty shelves. Zara squinted and counted. 'One, two, three... seven.' The last time she had seen that many new art books in Colmar's library was over a year ago when Madame Martin, the lonely old lady on Rue Rapp, passed away. As much as she lived for the days when new books arrived, she hoped nobody had died this time.

When the cart's wheels screeched again on the hallway's marble floor, she sneaked out of her hiding place and rushed to the shelf. The note said 'December 1954. New,' and the books were all about architecture, sculpture, and art restoration. All except for one book with no visible title. A big, shiny tome with water lilies on the cover. She was sure she had never seen it before, but somehow it looked familiar. It felt familiar, and she was drawn to it, inexplicably.

Zara went back to her safe place, in the east corner of the library, holding the book tight, and carefully opened it. *Monet's Impressionism*. Limited First Edition. 1954. On the inner cover were two initials in ink: '*L.P.*' Below, two more: '*A.P.*'

'Whose story is this? I thought maybe you'd tell me all about your past since you've always been so secretive. But who's this Zara girl? I've never heard you mention her. And what does she have to do with the cemetery and 9 December 1964 and that Roberts man?' asks Valerie.

'You have to wait. And listen. Above all, listen. And when your ears get tired, listen with your heart,' I say before turning the page.

Zara wondered what it was about that book that got her so interested. Inside there were lilies, more lilies, tens of variations, trees, forests, a thousand angles.

She flipped a few more pages, and her eyes rested on a ghostly painting. A lonely boat in the middle of the ocean, a red ball of fire in the sky. She stared at it; hypnotized. *Impression, Sunrise*. Claude Monet, 1872.

The dream she had the night before. The reason she was there that afternoon, looking for the first time for an art book about paintings, rather than sculpture, architecture, and art restoration. She closed her eyes, trying to remember all the details in the dream.

It was a room full of people. The men were dressed in nice suits and the women in long, sparkly dresses. And she was standing right in the middle of them all. They had glasses of champagne in their hands and talked loudly. Music played quietly in the background. Someone said something to her, but she didn't understand. Or maybe she didn't hear. Where was she? It seemed to be her museum in Colmar, but different. Bigger, brighter. The walls were covered in paintings. Paintings she knew so well. But how and why did she know them? She had never cared for paintings.

Zara walked towards the corner of the room and found herself in front of a mirror. Who was that woman looking back at her? It wasn't her. Not the 'her' she knew. She was old, well, not old but her mother's age perhaps. Her hair was long and wavy. She never wore her hair like that. A tiara-like headband? A long, flowy emerald-green dress and high heels? It could only be a dream. A fantasy. She would never look like that, no matter how many years passed.

She closed her eyes and started humming Edith Piaf's 'Hymne a l'Amour', almost unwillingly. When she opened her eyes, in the mirror, behind her, she saw someone. A man. Her pulse quickened, her legs felt weak, and she had to hold on to a chair, afraid she would fall. She couldn't see his face, yet she knew what he looked like. She knew who he was. She just knew.

'I don't know if in this life or maybe in my dreams,' she heard. It was him, wasn't it? His voice. Almost like a whisper.

Zara turned around, but he wasn't there. She turned to her right, to her left. He was gone. Like he'd vanished. That's when she saw it. Covering an entire wall. More impressive than all other paintings. Breathtaking. The Monet.

Yes, the painting in the dream was the painting in the book. She had found it. Now what? What did it all mean? Who was the woman in the mirror? Was it her? What about the man?

Zara felt even now that sensation she couldn't describe. In the morning, she woke up with tears in her eyes and now she was almost crying again. What in that dream had made her so emotional?

The lights in the library flickered for a moment then went off. It wasn't the first time the old museum had had a total blackout. Zara checked the pockets of her cardigan for her flashlight. It wasn't there. She'd been in such a rush when she left the house, she must've forgotten it. That dream had completely dazed her.

Never mind. With or without her flashlight, she could return the book to its place, then sneak out like nothing happened.

She got up when the wall clock chimed loudly six times in the main gallery. Six o'clock? Was the museum closing? Had she really been staring at the painting for that long? What would she do now? Every day, five minutes after six o'clock, the museum's guard and curator – the watchdog as she'd nicknamed him – always did his rounds.

'Oh, no, this is bad.' It was bad. The watchdog had warned her mother time and time again to keep her out of the rare books section of the library, or she'd lose her job: 'This is for scholars only. Fifteen-year-old girls should read Jules Verne and Alexandre Dumas, not art history. There is a kids' section in the town library, a couple of streets away. Go there,' he'd said to her a few months before when he caught her browsing through an eighteenth-century tome. 'This is your last warning.'

That's when she decided to hide. What else could she do? She had already read all the books about Frédéric-Auguste Bartholdi and Eugène-Emmanuel Viollet-le-Duc she could find. There was nothing left for her in the public library. But here, inside the rare books section, she had discovered a hidden treasure. Albums, notes, drawings and photos of their work, even le-Duc's own books. Facsimiles of their handwriting. Bartholdi's drawings and plans for the statue. She had to see them. This was all she had been interested in for years. While other kids were outside playing, she was sitting in her room reading. Teaching herself art. Hiding inside the museum was the least she could do for her passion.

Why did I do this? It was just a dream. I wasn't supposed to be back here until Saturday morning. None of this would've happened if I had just let it go.

Footsteps. Coming her way, echoing through the empty hallway. They closed in then slowed down until they stopped right next to her. She couldn't see anything. It was pitch black. She held her breath, pressing her back against the wall while trying to tuck the book behind her. 'Hello?' she heard next to her.

It wasn't the curator. Zara didn't move a muscle and held her breath.

He repeated. 'Hello?' and this time it sounded even closer.

'The museum is closed,' she said bravely.

'It wasn't closed when I walked in. What happened to the lights? Can you turn them on?'

He was trying so hard to sound French, she snickered.

'I wish. The power went out.'

'I don't really know what I'm doing here,' he said in a low voice.

'That makes two of us,' said Zara. 'I wasn't even supposed to be here today.'

'Is this your museum, mademoiselle?'

Zara burst into laughter.

He was quiet for a moment, and Zara felt terrible for laughing at him. She knew better.

'I'm sorry. My French isn't so good. I'm trying to find a painting. It might not even be here but, for some reason—'

'Which painting?' she interrupted.

'Monet's *Impression, Sunrise.*'

Zara gulped. The one in the dream. The one in the book. She got so flustered, she forgot she was holding the book and let go. It fell to the floor with a loud thump.

Startled, she stepped to the left but stumbled onto something, losing her balance. Just as she almost hit the floor, he caught her with a strength she didn't expect. He let go of her arms and their hands touched accidentally. Her heart beat fast. She wasn't scared of him or the dark. It was just a strange sensation. Zara pulled back, embarrassed. What she felt in that moment for this boy she couldn't even see, this boy she didn't even know, was quite impossible and it both scared and fascinated her. A familiar, warm sensation. A tingling in her fingers, a fluttering in the pit of her stomach. Why was it familiar if she had never felt it before?

'Sorry,' he said. 'Are you alright? I was just trying to help.'

'I'm f-fine,' she stuttered.

'I found it,' he said, a moment later. 'What book is this? It's so heavy.'

She hesitated. '*Monet's Impressionism.*'

'Really? Now that's what I call a coincidence. I have the exact same book. Well, I used to. My father gave it to me, but unfortunately, I left it on the train when I returned to school in September. I think there are only fifty copies in the entire world, and they're all numbered, and every sale is recorded. It's a pretty special book. How amazing you have it too, right?'

'I guess,' she said.

'So, you like Monet?'

'I don't know anything about Monet.'

'Why do you have the book then? Do you like art?'

'I like Bartholdi and Viollet-le-Duc if that counts.'

'Never heard of them,' the boy said in a low, timid voice.

'I'm not surprised. They're not as famous as painters are, for instance.'

'Yes, I love painters. Well, I mean I love paintings. Mostly by Monet. I like Cezanne too. Degas, sometimes. Pissarro. Manet less. Renoir is okay too. And Toulouse-Lautrec—'

He spoke so fast. She stopped him. 'Can I have it back now?'

'What?'

'The book.'

'Oh, sorry, of course.'

Zara stretched out her arms just a bit and felt the edges of the book. He let go of it.

'Thank you,' she said. 'You're not from around here, are you? Your accent—'

'I'm from New York. But I go to school in Switzerland.'

Apart from Paris, New York was her favorite city in the whole world even if, just like Paris, she had never seen it.

She knew everything about it. New York was every artist's dream. The skyscrapers, the fantastic architecture, the bridges, the statues, the parks. She had read many books about the city and even more about the statue.

'You're lucky. I've always wanted to visit New York. Maybe one day. I'm fascinated with *Liberty Enlightening the World*,' she said in one breath.

'Enlightening what?' he asked tentatively.

'The statue. The Statue of Liberty. That's what it was initially called. Did you know the mastermind behind it lived here, in Colmar? The old town is filled with his sculptures and fountains. They're magnificent.'

'No, I didn't know that,' he said.

'Yes, Colmar is not just a pretty small town on the Alsatian wine route. But let's keep it between us because if word gets out, this place will be swarming with tourists.'

He chuckled, and her heart fluttered. She tried imagining what the face of a boy with such beautiful laughter looked like. She wondered if you could like someone without seeing them, without knowing anything about them. There was something about him. Something that made her feel things she'd never felt before.

'Too late. I'm a tourist, so your secret is out. Tell me about this man who built the statue.'

'He didn't build it; he designed it. You know who built it? Gustave Eiffel, the same man who made the Eiffel Tower in Paris. Don't feel bad, not a lot of people know this.'

'But you do,' he said. 'Hey, you never answered my question.'

'What question?'

'The painting. Is it here?'

'I'm afraid not,' she said. 'In Paris, perhaps. Like I said, I am not that good with—'

'Paintings,' he said and chuckled. 'Apparently neither am I.' He sounded disappointed. 'Well, at least I tried.'

'Did you come all the way from Switzerland for this? What's so special about it?' Maybe there was something about *Impression, Sunrise* that would explain her dream.

'It belongs to my family.'

'Really? Then how come you don't know where it is?'

'It's complicated.'

'My mother says that everything worthwhile is at least a little bit complicated. Besides, I'm in no rush. Tell me,' she said, sitting on the floor next to him.

She forgot about the watchdog, about getting caught. It didn't seem to matter anymore.

'Alright then. Claude Monet made four identical *Impression, Sunrise* paintings. One he signed, the other three he kept secret and gave to his closest friends – among them, my great-grandfather. Years later, during World War II, the painting was stolen from our family's house in Newport.'

'And someone told you it might be in Colmar?' asked Zara.

'Not exactly. No. I just – I felt I had to come here. Not sure why. I saw the signs pointing to the museum, and here I am.'

'I'm sorry you didn't find what you were looking for,' she said.

'I...' Silence.

'Yes?'

'I wouldn't be so sure about that,' he said quietly.

Zara's pulse quickened.

'Well, now you know why I am here. What about you? Why are you hiding in the dark?'

'My mother works for the museum, but I'm not allowed inside. Not in the art library at least. You must be an adult and even then, you need the curator's permission.'

'What does she do? Is she in charge of the collections? Is your father into art too? They sound like my family – collectors of everything, keepers of nothing. Paintings, drawings, sketches, sculptures. Anything they can get their hands on. Our summer house in Newport is filled with them. And our apartment in New York.'

He was speaking very quickly again, not even stopping to take a breath.

'I doubt our families are alike, although yours sounds lovely. My mother cleans the museum. Sometimes she also takes care of the books. Puts them all back on shelves, in order. Back in Romania, she was a literature teacher at the university,' she said.

'You lived there too? My father went there once; he said it's pretty.'

'I wouldn't know. I was born in Romania but only lived there for a few years.'

'Why?'

'My father died when I was little, and then we moved here.'

Talking about it always made Zara feel sad, although she barely remembered him.

'I'm sorry,' he said. 'I didn't know.'

'Not your fault. Not anybody's fault, I guess. Well, except for the war.'

'Why isn't your mom a teacher in France too?'

'For years now, she has been trying to go back to teaching, but it's hard to do that in a small town like Colmar. There are plenty of universities in Paris though, and she just took her last teaching exam so now she can get a job there. I really hope it will happen soon. She wants this so much.'

'I hope so too. Paris is amazing. Or so I've heard.'

She chuckled. 'You've never been to Paris?'

'Not yet. You?'

She shook her head then remembered he couldn't see her. 'Me neither.'

'Is that why you're into art? Because your mom works in the museum?'

'Not really, no. I think that's from my great-aunt, my grandmother's sister. She was the artist in the family.'

'Was?' he asked.

'Unfortunately, she died a few years ago. But when I was young, I used to stay home with her while my mother was at work. She was in her nineties and could barely see, but she still found her way around the house, and I remember her gathering a huge pile of art books every morning and making me read them to her. Page by page. And in the afternoons, she would take me around town to show me the sculptures we had just seen in the books and tell me their stories. I didn't understand much, but I was fascinated. When she died, I kind of carried on her passion and I continued reading and learning. And when I finished all the books in the public library, I discovered the museum.'

'I'm sorry to hear she passed away. She sounds amazing.'

'Thank you. She was.'

'Now it's just the two of you alone here?'

'Pretty much. Alone, but not lonely. Colmar is a special town.'

'I believe you,' he said. 'Too bad I didn't get a chance to see much of anything in Colmar. Like those sculptures.'

'I could show them to you later. It's not a big town and it won't take us long. And not just the sculptures. There are a few places unlike anything you've ever seen.'

'Like what? Tell me.'

'I could take you to see the winding waterways and the medieval streets to understand why Colmar is called "Little Venice". Then there's my favorite bakery that sells kugelhopf and the best croissants in all of France. And the little Statue of Liberty – yes, we have that too. The French Neo-Baroque and German Gothic architecture, which I can't let you miss. And you must see three fountains that have Bartholdi's statues as centerpieces. Words can't describe them. Colmar is just—'

'Magical.'

'Magical.'

They were both quiet for a few moments.

'Why the Monet book?' he asked suddenly.

'Excuse me?'

'Why were you holding the Monet book earlier? Why that one of all the books?'

She took a deep breath. 'I – I'm not sure. I really don't know anything about painting.'

'Really?' he said. 'Let's see. Do you know, for instance, who the most prolific painter is?'

'Dead or alive?'

'Whichever.'

'Picasso?'

'Seriously? You said you don't know anything about painting.'

'It was just a lucky guess. Try again.'

'Fine. Do you know the name of the town in *Starry Night*?'

'In what?'

'Vincent van Gogh's *Starry Night*. The blue and yellow painting.'

'Oh, yes, wait. I know this. The mayor visited the town. It's in France.'

He was quiet.

'Remy? Saint-Remy?'

He scoffed, amused. 'You're making fun of me.'

'No, why? Am I right?'

'Of course you are right.'

'It was just a coincidence.'

'I don't believe in coincidences.'

'Try again.'

'Last time. Do you know why some painters are called Impressionists?'

'Because they painted their impressions of... no, I don't know.'

'Finally, something you don't know.'

They both chuckled. 'Because of Monet and his most famous painting. The one I am looking for. *Impression, Sunrise*. Get it? Impression. Impressionism.'

'See? You know things I don't.'

'Barely. Truth is, I never met anyone interested in art before. Anyone my age, I mean.'

'How do you know we're the same age?'

'I don't know, you just sound my age, I guess. How old are you?'

'Fifteen.'

'I just turned sixteen,' he said and paused. 'You and I, I think we'd make a great team. Maybe you could help me find the Monet.'

'What will your father do with the painting after you find it? Is it worth a lot?'

'Millions. But he'd never sell it. I'm sure he'll donate it to the Monet museum in Paris.'

'There's a Monet museum in Paris?'

'Yes. The Marmottan.'

'I don't know many people who would give up millions of francs.'

'Millions of dollars you mean. That's a lot more than francs. It's probably worth a few houses in Paris, yachts in Newport and then some change to last someone a lifetime. He doesn't need it though. He's a successful businessman in New York. I hope one day I'll be just like him.'

'Like him, how? Rich? Successful?'

He laughed.

'I bet if I told him I met you and you're going to help us find the painting, he'd be excited. Maybe one day we could both go to Paris and look for the painting. Or to Giverny. That's where Monet lived. My great-grandfather visited him there often. He used to go with him by the entrance to the forest and watch him as he painted. Isn't that something? Le Havre too. I know all the places where he lived and painted. We could do a tour.'

'I would love to—' she started, but was interrupted by the guard's baritone voice from a way away.

'You can call for him, but I seriously doubt he's here. The

museum has been closed for over an hour. I was just doing my final round before locking up for the night.' There was a metallic noise then silence. 'What did you say his name is?'

Another man responded. 'It's alright, I'll do it.'

'Suit yourself,' said the watchdog.

Zara didn't move. They sounded close. Probably at the library's entrance. She could see the light from the guard's flashlight.

'Leon, I know you're in here. Vincent saw you running this way. If you're not back at the bus in ten minutes, I'm calling the police. You give me no choice. You hear me?' he bellowed.

'Leon? Is that your name?'

'Yes.'

'Who is the man looking for you?'

'My teacher. We're all on a field trip here. At the public library. I kind of sneaked out.'

'Then you're in trouble. You should go.'

'Big trouble probably. It was worth it though,' he whispered.

Zara wasn't used to such directness and didn't know how to react at first. What she did know was that without her help, he'd get caught.

'Come on, I'll take you out. Where's the bus parked?' she asked.

'In the town square.'

'Alright. If you make a run for it, you'll get there before him. When you exit, take the first street to your left then run all the way to the end and turn right. That's the square.'

'Uh huh,' he said, sounding a bit lost and unconvinced.

'Let's go,' she said.

'Where? I can't see anything,' he grumbled. 'Give me your hand.'

The moment their hands touched, this time on purpose, she felt that sensation again. It was more powerful now. Almost like a bolt of lightning went through her body.

They tiptoed out, walking carefully along the walls and stopping at corners. She saw the light from the guard's flashlight going up the stairs. Here was their chance. 'Let's run,' she said when they arrived at the exit sign before she realized she was still holding the Monet book.

'I can't. I wish I could, but I have to put the book back, or I'll be in trouble too.'

'I'll wait for you,' he said.

'Don't. You have less than five minutes to get back. You heard your teacher.'

He moved in closer. Their faces were inches away. 'I don't want to go.'

She didn't want him to go either.

'I wish we had more time. I wish we could talk more.' He took a deep breath. 'Could I maybe write to you when I get back to Switzerland?'

She gulped.

'You want to write to me?'

'If you want me to, of course. But if you don't, and you think I'm—'

'I'd like that very much,' she said, not letting him finish. Her face was on fire.

Heavy footsteps. The watchdog was coming.

'You have to go,' she said shortly.

He turned to leave, then stopped short.

'Where's my head? How can I write to you if I don't know where to send the letters?' He chuckled. 'I never asked you what your name is. Silly me.'

'Zara. My name is Zara Ionesco.'

'Zara,' he repeated.

She loved the sound of her name coming from his mouth.

'24 Rue des Jardins. That's my address.'

'I'll write as soon as I get back. Promise.'

A door opened then closed. Two sets of footsteps were approaching. They were now dangerously close. 'We can look here as well if you want,' said the watchdog.

'I have to go. I'll be seeing you, Zara,' Leon said and ran towards the door.

Standing in the middle of the pitch-black corridor, ignoring all sounds and shadows, she watched him leave and wondered if he was right. If she would ever see him again.

LEON

VAUD

They'd missed the play in Strasbourg because of him. The teacher had almost called the police. And on their way back to La Rolande, on the school bus, everyone gave him nasty looks. Some even said nasty things. Vincent, who would jump at any opportunity to just be Vincent, shoved him and pushed him to the back of the bus. Leon would've pushed back under any other circumstances, but now he didn't care. His mind was elsewhere. Busy with her. And how interesting she was, so unlike anyone else he ever met. How he would've listened to her talk about green beans if that was what she was interested in because she made everything sound like a story, a fairy tale almost. Magical.

And it was magical, wasn't it? He'd seen the sign for the museum and felt drawn to it, not knowing why. Then he'd run faster and faster like he was running for his life, desperate to get there. But what he found wasn't at all what he expected. A small museum and no sign of the Monet. And then darkness. And in that darkness, magic happened when he heard her voice. When their hands touched. When they sat next to each other on the cold floor, in the dark, and time stood still. He had never felt that way before. She smelled like jasmine, and her laughter was the most beautiful thing in the world. Leon closed his eyes, trying to picture what she looked like, how she smiled. He wondered if she had blonde hair and blue eyes like his best friend, Nicole. Even her name was unique. Zara. Zara and Leon. Leon and Zara. Magical.

Back at school, Leon ran to the girls' dorm and up the stairs to Nicole's room. Luckily there were no teachers around to see him and tell the headmaster. He was in a lot of trouble anyway because of what had just happened in Colmar. One more stunt like that – not his words – and he would get detention and lose his privileges for all eternity. But he had to tell Nicole what happened. They always told each other everything.

He knocked on her door and when she opened, he lunged forward and pushed her in, quickly closing the door behind them.

'Sit down. No, let's both sit here,' he said in one breath as he pulled her by the hand and pushed her shoulders down until she sat on the bed.

'What's going on?' she asked. 'I haven't seen you this agitated since you told me about your father's Monet. I hope it's not something about that.'

Leon ignored her snarky remark because he was too

busy smiling from ear to ear. Nothing could dampen his happiness. He got up and walked to the window then back and, stopping in front of her, slapped himself on both cheeks. Not hard, but hard enough to make them red probably. He could feel them burning now.

'What's gotten into you? Are you okay?'

'I'm just – I can barely sit still.'

'Obviously.'

Now it was her turn to pull him by the hand and force him to sit next to her.

'Tell me,' she said as she was holding both of his hands in hers.

'I met someone.'

'You met someone. Okay. That sounds interesting. Who is this someone?'

'Her name is Zara and she's just – oh God, Nicole, I don't know how to explain. She's like me... but a girl. No, I'm lying. She's better than me. She knows so much about art. She's so interesting and—'

Nicole let go of his hands and slowly pulled hers back and placed them in her lap. She looked down for a moment.

'What?'

'Nothing,' she said. 'Go on, tell me. Where did you meet her? Who is she?'

Without stopping to breathe, he told Nicole every detail of his one hour with Zara. When he finally looked up, Nicole looked like she wasn't even listening to him. Absentmindedly playing with her fingers, she seemed totally disengaged, staring out the window.

'Am I boring you?'

She didn't respond.

'Nicole,' he said a bit louder.

Almost startled, she turned to him. 'Yes. I'm listening.'

'You're not saying anything. What do you think?'

'About what?'

'What do you mean about what? About Zara. Isn't it incredible?'

'Yes. Incredible,' she repeated.

'Hey, I listen to all your Vincent stories,' Leon said, frowning. 'And I never complain, though you know what I think of him.'

Nicole tilted her head to the side and looked at him for a moment. 'What does she look like? Is she pretty?'

'I don't know what she looks like. Have you been listening to me? I couldn't see her. But I'm sure she is. I'm sure she's the prettiest girl ever.'

Nicole snarled. 'But she could very well be a three-headed monster with hairy legs and a big wart on her nose, couldn't she?'

'That's not funny,' he said, stung by her tone.

'It is, in a way,' she said. 'You've been talking nonstop about a girl you haven't even seen. I find that funny. Ridiculous, even.'

Leon and Nicole had shared everything through the years, with one condition: he didn't judge her and she didn't judge him. That was Vincent's job and he had been doing it impeccably since they were kids. Perhaps Nicole had been spending so much time with Vincent lately, she was turning into him.

'Does it matter what she looks like? I like her for who she is, not how long her hair is or how blue or green her eyes are.'

She looked away.

'This all sounds—' She suddenly stopped.

'What?'

'I don't know. Childish.'

Leon got up. He was hurt. 'Why childish?'

'Because only kids have fixations like this. You barely talked to her, you don't know what she looks like, and you're acting like she's the best thing that's ever happened to you. You did the same with that silly quest of yours. It was childish then and it is childish now.'

'You're wrong! I thought you of all people would understand. You're my friend. I thought you'd care,' he said, his voice raised. 'You want to see childish? I'll show you childish,' he said and stormed out of the room.

'I do care—' Leon heard her say but he didn't turn around.

He was mad. So mad, he didn't talk to her at all for two whole days, which was the longest they'd ever stayed away from each other since they first met.

In the summer of 1945, when Leon was seven, his father, Leonard Price, moved his family from a small house in the suburbs of New York City to the Upper West Side, in one of the three apartments on the top floor of Manhattan's most coveted and newest high-rise: 'The Diamond Tower.'

The other two apartments were occupied by the D'Angers – Jean Jacques, Demetria and their seven-year-old daughter, Nicole – and the Saint Germains. Leon didn't know anything about the Saint Germains, but he knew Jean Jacques D'Angers, his godfather and his father's best friend;

Jean Jacques had visited them many times on his way back home from his travels, always bearing gifts.

While his parents were busy unpacking, Leon wandered out into the hallway and from there to his godfather's apartment, where he was invited in by a blonde girl with pigtails and a sparkly red dress.

'I'm Nicole,' she said as soon as he walked in. 'You're Leon, aren't you? Papa told me you were coming. Come to my room – I have lots of toys. Want to play with my dollhouse?'

Leon wasn't sure he wanted to play with dolls, but he was happy to finally have a friend. Where he'd lived before, the kids were older, and he had been spending most of his time alone.

That same afternoon, Vincent Saint Germain, the boy next door, showed up too. He was eight, taller and stronger than Leon. And because he had met Nicole before Leon did, he seemed to think he had some sort of right over her.

Vying for Nicole's time and attention seemed to be a constant in their lives, even now, nine years later, although one thing had changed: their group's dynamic. In time, Leon and Nicole became best friends, while Vincent was now her boyfriend.

Nicole and Vincent made sense as a couple and Leon had known from the beginning he was the odd one out. Even when they were small, he was merely 'accepted in their world'; he didn't truly belong. His family was 'new money', not like the Saint Germains and the D'Angers, whose noble names carried a lot of weight on both sides of the Atlantic.

In 1946, Demetria D'Angers died of influenza, leaving JJ a young widower with a small child. Taking pity on him,

Vincent's parents, Margaux and Francois Saint Germain, sometimes allowed Leon and Nicole to play with their son in their apartment.

Soon though, both Leon and Nicole regretted accepting the invitation, especially after overhearing Margaux Saint Germain talking to her friends about JJ.

'He says he's grieving, and his work is the only refuge he has... but traveling the world and leaving the girl alone for months on end is preposterous. Poor child. Can you imagine? What she must be feeling knowing her father doesn't love her and wishes she didn't exist! How can you not feel sorry for her?'

'Don't listen to her,' Leon comforted Nicole when she started to cry. 'Your father loves you. He works a lot and he's sad because your mother died. It's hard for him. I would be sad too.'

But the damage had been done, and Nicole never forgot what she had heard that day. Or how she felt. And that was only confirmed one year later when her father informed her he'd made arrangements for her to live in Europe. Without him.

JJ and Francois had both studied at La Rolande, Europe's most prestigious school, so it came as no surprise to anyone – except for the children, perhaps – when they both made plans to send Nicole and Vincent to Switzerland when they turned ten, the minimum age to be accepted into the elite establishment. Vincent left first, and then, a year later it was Nicole's turn. Afraid it might jeopardize their status in New York's high society if Leon attended a regular private school, Leonard proceeded to enroll his son at La Rolande too, despite his protests.

Now, six years later, La Rolande was the children's second home. It was where they lived and learned, laughed and cried, celebrated their birthdays and even their Christmases.

And while Vincent and Leon, too fundamentally different to bond as friends, were never close and didn't even try to pretend they liked each other, they were still part of each other's lives because of their relationships with Nicole.

Two days after their fight, Nicole knocked on Leon's door.

'Are you still mad at me?'

Leon opened the door and leaned against the frame. 'It depends. Are you going to apologize?'

'I'm sorry. I didn't mean it.'

He let her in.

'I missed you. Let's not fight again,' she said earnestly.

'I missed you too. I got bored of talking to myself.'

She laughed, then looked around at his messy room and picked up a crumpled piece of paper. 'What is this?'

'Nothing,' he said, yanking it out of her hand.

'I thought we didn't keep secrets from each other.'

'We don't,' he said, 'but I don't want you to start again.'

'Start what?'

'It's a letter to Zara.'

Nicole rolled her eyes.

'See? I knew it!'

'Is that what you've been doing for the last two days, locked up in your room?'

He nodded, feeling a bit embarrassed.

'How about we do something together instead?'

Leon looked at her blankly.

'Everyone is going skiing,' she said in a singsong voice. 'You know how much you love skiing.'

'I don't want to go,' he said stubbornly.

'Why not? So you can continue scribbling notes you're not even sending?'

Leon shrugged.

'Fine. If this is what you want, I'll leave you to it,' she said, walking to the door. 'I'll go see where Vincent is. I bet he won't say no.'

'Don't go,' he pleaded. 'I don't know what to write. Please help me! What do I say?'

'You want me to tell you what you should write to another girl?'

'Why not?'

She crossed her arms. 'Because.'

Leon had never written to a girl before. He'd started the first letter fourteen times and torn it apart fifteen. The last one he'd double ripped out of sheer frustration.

'Just write something already. This is torture,' said Nicole, exasperated after a while. 'It's going to be dark soon and we'll miss the whole day.'

He quickly wrote a silly note and put it in an envelope.

Do you remember me?
Leon

'That's it?' she asked and started laughing.

'It's better than nothing,' he mumbled.

'I would never respond to this. It's a waste of time anyway. You have plenty of friends here; you don't need a new one.'

ZARA

COLMAR

It didn't matter that she'd had to wait one more hour, hidden in the library until the guard finished his evening round. Nor that she had to walk home in the freezing rain and go to bed hungry after telling her mother she was too tired to eat. What Zara felt in that short time she'd spent with Leon, she had never felt before. She didn't regret anything except not telling her mother about him, but they had never talked about boys before and she didn't know how she would react. Or whether she would understand. For now, he was her little secret. Her magical little secret.

Days passed and there was no word from him. She started doubting her memories of that evening. What if he had forgotten her? What if he had written the address incorrectly and his letter was lost? What if he'd just said he would write, but never planned to?

She would watch from her window to see when the

postman arrived and before he even got back on his bike to go to the next house, she was standing in front of the mailbox, rummaging through the envelopes. Not for her, not for her, not for her. No. Nothing.

Almost a week after their meeting, as she was going through the daily mail as usual – although now a bit less hopeful – she got to the last one in the pile and couldn't believe her eyes. A simple, small white envelope addressed to Zara. She turned it on the other side to check the sender. It simply said, 'Leon Price, La Rolande, Vaud, Switzerland'.

She squealed excitedly.

'Good news?' asked the postman, smiling.

'The best,' she said, beaming back. After running back upstairs to her room, she closed the door behind her and placed the envelope carefully on the small desk. She wasn't just excited, she was also inexplicably nervous. Zara kept circling the desk, looking at the letter, but not daring to open it. Then, all of a sudden, she grabbed it and ripped it open.

Getting that first letter, it was as if nothing else mattered. Even if he'd only said hello, he had remembered her and kept his promise. And maybe that meant he was thinking about her, which was good, because she couldn't think of anything else *but* him.

Zara wrote back that same day and mailed it the next morning.

LEON

VAUD

After five days of waiting and pacing and obsessively checking the mailbox, a letter came for him. A letter from her.

> *I remember you, Leon from New York.*
> *Zara*

Leon couldn't wait to tell Nicole, but she wasn't in her room, the library, the tennis court, or the cafeteria. Where was she? After thinking for a moment, Leon dashed to the boys' dorm, walked up to the top floor and stopped in front of room 165 for a moment before knocking.

There were few reasons he would ever visit Vincent's room. But now, he was willing to ignore Vincent's presence. He needed his best friend. Even if that meant having to endure Vincent's mockery, which was sure to come.

Vincent opened the door and twisted his mouth in a grimace.

'What is it, trouble?' he asked in his usual mocking tone. That was his nickname for Leon. Trouble. 'You couldn't last ten minutes without her?'

'Is she here?' Leon asked and peered inside.

'Where else?'

Nicole must've heard his voice, because she showed up in the doorway. Vincent wrapped his arms around her and pulled her closer to him.

'Leon, hi. Something wrong?' she asked, seeming a bit uncomfortable.

Ignoring Vincent, Leon pulled Nicole by the hand and into the hallway.

'She wrote back,' he whispered in her ear.

Nicole looked at him, then back at Vincent. 'Why don't you come in?' she said, loud enough for Vincent to hear.

'Is that a good idea?' Leon said.

'Not really,' said Vincent. 'You're kind of interrupting us.'

'It's fine,' said Nicole.

Vincent had just moved into his 'senior' room and Leon hadn't been in yet. The room was bigger than his, with large windows on both sides overlooking the back garden and the lake.

'Nice view,' said Leon.

'What do you have? The inside court?' Vincent sneered.

Leon ignored him, pulled the letter from his pocket and gave it to Nicole to read.

He was used to this exchange with Vincent. He'd had years of it and it rarely affected him anymore. Vincent wasn't a bad guy. He just had a big ego and an even bigger mouth.

Nicole took the letter from him and walked to the side window.

'What is that?' asked Vincent.

Nicole didn't say anything as she took the paper out of the envelope and Leon wondered what he should do. Tell him? No. Why would he tell Vincent about Zara?

'Just a thing I wanted to show Nicole.'

'It looks like a letter,' Vincent said, staring at Leon for a second. 'Can I see it? Let me see it,' he insisted. 'Wait a minute. Are you sending letters to Nico now? In front of my face?'

Nicole hated to be called Nico, and she and Leon gave each other a look.

'Calm down, Vincent,' said Nicole. 'It's not for me.'

'Then who is it for?'

'Leon.' Her face was expressionless, and Leon didn't know if she'd read it or not.

'Aww, a letter for my little friend. Make my day and tell me it's from a girl,' he said and batted his eyelashes.

Leon shoved him but it did little to budge Vincent, who was a year older, a head taller and well built.

'It's none of your business,' said Leon. But he knew sooner or later Vincent would find out. Nicole wasn't very good at keeping secrets.

'You're in my room, giving letters to Nico, so I'd say that makes it my business.'

Leon sighed. Without going into all the details, he told Vincent the truth.

The more he talked, the more Vincent's face relaxed.

'Hallelujah,' he said when Leon finished.

Leon and Nicole looked at each other, confused.

'You like a girl. Other than Nico. This is a big day – we should celebrate.'

'But I...' Leon tried to say something, but there was no way to stop Vincent. He seemed truly excited. It was weird.

Leon would've said he didn't like Nicole that way, but he had already said it many times before, defending their friendship when Vincent accused him of trying to separate them. 'Don't you think I know what you're doing?' he used to say. 'Always around her, like a little mouse? You are waiting for me to make a mistake so you can swoop in. In your dreams, trouble!'

'Don't start with that again, Vincent,' Nicole said now. 'If Leon liked me that way, he had plenty of opportunities to do something about it. But he never did.'

The way Nicole said it, it seemed like Nicole was angry with Leon, rather than Vincent. He shrugged. Girls were complicated and Nicole more than others.

'Fine. I'll stop. But it's not my fault I want you all to myself,' said Vincent and kissed her. Nicole smiled at him lovingly, then turned to Leon. 'It's nice you have a pen pal,' she said. 'Not much of a letter, but at least now you have someone to talk art with, right?'

She knew very well Zara was much more than a pen pal. And it wasn't just about art.

Realizing he'd made a mistake coming over, Leon headed for the door. 'Thanks. I have to go. I have a letter to write.'

He waved goodbye and rushed out.

For hours Leon walked around the campus, reading

those eight words again and again like they were the world's biggest love declaration. After the initial euphoria passed, he panicked. What should he say next? That night he wrote back.

Dear Zara,

Have you ever had so much to say but found it impossible to say anything? Like you don't know where to start or what's most important? I want to tell you everything, you know? And I want to know everything. I wish I was there with you; it would be much easier. I keep thinking of our time together and how fast it went.

Can you tell me more about Colmar? My grandparents lived in a small town in Normandy, and I have some vague recollection of it. In a way, I think Colmar reminds me of it. My favorite spot was a square in the center of the town. It was surrounded by a park and in the middle of it there was an ice cream place. I loved their chocolate banana ice cream. Still miss it. What's your favorite place in Colmar? Aside from the museum, of course.

You know, it might sound strange, but I envy your freedom to walk wherever you want, come and go as you please, discover new places and see all those marvelous things you told me about. Our campus is pretty big, it's almost like a village so I can't complain about that, but I can't go beyond the gates. Not without an adult anyway. And we have a curfew at night. To be honest, if they opened the gates now, I don't even know where I would go. Maybe I could make my way to the train station... and accidentally end up on a train back to Alsace.

Talking about the train station, remember I told you about my Monet book and how I lost it? Well, I have decided to write a letter to SNCF in Paris and ask them if they found it. They must have a lost and found desk there. I keep thinking what an amazing coincidence it was that you had the same book and how nice it would be if we both had a copy, especially since there are so few of them in the world.

Leon

ZARA

COLMAR

A few days later, a second letter arrived. And she responded again, right away. She didn't know where to start or how to end her letters. She wouldn't stop writing if she didn't have to. She didn't want to keep him waiting.

Dear Leon,

I don't know anyone who's at a boarding school besides you. It must be so different from my school. I imagine a big building where everyone studies and then there are rooms, maybe twenty or thirty of them, with three to four in one room. Am I close? Our school is an old brick building with maybe ten classrooms. At the end of the eight hours, everyone goes home. I sometimes wish I had someone to share my room with. A best friend. Eh. Oh, and we also have a small yard and an even smaller garden we take care of.

Do you have a garden at your school? I don't know if you even like flowers, but my absolute favorite is jasmine. Have you ever seen a jasmine shrub in the spring? You have to.

Why won't they let you leave the campus? Are there many kids there? Perhaps it's hard for the teachers to keep an eye out for all of you. When do you get to go home? It's a long way to New York.

You must miss your parents terribly. I couldn't imagine my life without seeing my mother every day. We are very close. In a way, she is the best friend I said I wish I had.

Zara

P.S. I went back to the museum the other day, and into the library when the guard wasn't paying attention, and I sat where we sat. But this time the lights didn't go off and you didn't show up. Let me know when you're going to take that train back to Alsace. I'll be waiting for you in the museum.

P.P.S. Almost forgot to tell you about my favorite place. I have a few. But I think the closest to my heart is a bit similar to yours. It is in the town square as well, but it's not an ice cream place. It's a small boulangerie. Sometimes, as a treat, my mother and I take a walk around town, then stop for croissants and hot cocoa in the winter, or ice-cold lemonade in the summer. You can sit there for hours, in the sun, watching people pass by and listening to a street performer. It is the perfect place.

Dear Zara,

Next time, maybe I can go with you to the boulangerie. I would love that.

Our campus is pretty different to what you've imagined, though I like the picture you created better. La Rolande is home to over a thousand students from all over the world. It's like a small village. I don't share my room with anyone, although I used to in my first few years. There are over sixty classrooms. Then there are science laboratories, a few music rooms, and a massive library – my favorite place here. We have a garden too, but I don't go there often, although now I will, so I can see if we have any jasmine.

It does get lonely out here and we don't go home that often. Some students are luckier and spend all their vacations with their families. I don't. My parents are very busy and travel a lot; I see them for maybe three or four weeks during the summer. But even that doesn't happen every year. Luckily, I do have a best friend here, and just like you with your mom, I couldn't imagine what my life would be like if we weren't so close. We grew up together in New York before moving here. We're like family.

What will happen when your mom gets a job in Paris? You'll go with her, right?

Leon

This letter was followed by another one, and then and another. Zara responded to each of them the very same day and mailed them to Switzerland the morning after, on her way to school.

Even the mailman knew she was waiting for letters from Switzerland, so he'd place Leon's letter on top of the pile.

Zara would've written to him every minute of every day if she could, as if they were continuing a conversation.

47

Because that was it exactly how it felt and there was always something to tell him.

Sometimes it was something she'd read.

Dear Leon,

I found an article in Le Figaro *about Monet. It's from a few weeks ago, but I don't know if you've seen it, so I cut it out for you. See where it says the original* Impression, Sunrise *is on tour through Alsace museums? Maybe you weren't so far from it when you came to Colmar. Maybe you read it and it was in the back of your mind.*

Zara

P.S. I forgot to tell you that when I went back to the Unterlinden, I looked for the book but couldn't find it anymore. It made me sad. For some reason, it felt important to me.

I know I put it back, but after that, I don't know. And I can't ask the curator because then he will know I was in there. I wonder what happened to it. Now we've both lost our copies of the book... I hope at least you find yours.

Sometimes it was something she'd heard.

Dear Leon,

Have you ever been on the Metro? I didn't even know what it was until my mother explained they have one in Paris too and they've had it for over fifty years. I have just heard on the radio they recently opened one in Rome. I've never been to Rome and I've never been

*on the Metro either but everyone seemed so excited, it
must be something fascinating. It is like a train, Mama
said, but in the city and underground. It sounds a bit
scary to me.*

*I've been on a bus, on a train and I think on a boat
when I was little. That's all. Have you been on the Metro?
Maybe I'll try it when I go to Paris.*

Zara

Sometimes it was something she'd listened to.

Leon,

*You said there was a music room at La Rolande and
there must be a record player or a radio there. I'm hoping
they will play this song on one of the channels. I've only
recently discovered it, but it must have been released a
few years ago. It's called 'Sous le Ciel de Paris' by Jean
Bretonnière. It's my absolute favorite song.*

Zara

Every little thing. She wanted to share every small detail
with Leon. Zara never thought she would feel so much for
someone in such a short amount of time. She and Leon had
become friends instantly. Maybe the best of friends. He
didn't get bored with her stories, and she was fascinated by
his. They liked the same things, the same books, even the
same food, although they came from such different worlds.

If she had the money, she would've asked her mother
to take her to Switzerland. Zara had never even seen his
face, yet he was in her every thought, in every little thing
she did. She woke up thinking about him, went to school

imagining they walked hand in hand. Sometimes she wrote their names together in her journal, side by side. Zara and Leon. Leon and Zara. How perfectly they fit together. Like they were meant for each other.

But would she ever see him again?

LEON

VAUD

Leon started every day with a letter to Zara and ended it the same way. She had become his first thought in the morning and his last whispered word before he finally fell asleep at night.

Dear Zara,

I was sorry to hear about the book. Maybe you could ask your mother to talk to the curator.

I wrote to SNCF, although I didn't hear back yet. But there's hope.

Thank you for the article! No, I hadn't read it before. Now it is glued in my scrapbook with all things Monet, next to a map of Alsace where I'm circling all the museums and seeing where it might go next. Wouldn't it be something if Colmar was on the list?

You know, sometimes I dream that after I find this

painting, I'll start looking for others. I would travel the world, going from museum to museum and from collector to collector, asking questions, spending a ridiculous amount of time just staring at beautiful art. Now that's a sweet dream, isn't it? Leon, the painting detective, at your service. Lost your Degas? Someone stole it? Leon will find it for you. The problem is I'll have to learn everything about all the painters, not just Monet. Hard work. But I think I would love it.

Leon

P.S. What is your dream?

Dear Leon,

My dream? I've never really thought about it. It must be something to do with art. I wish I could... breathe art, walk in the footsteps of the big and famous artists in Montmartre, live surrounded by all that beauty. My mother and I have been talking about moving to Paris for years now, but it's hard. She can't seem to find a job there. She doesn't give up though. I dream about it too, but I also don't know if I'm ready. I told you how much I love this small town. It's home. Paris is a dream, yes.

Zara

He was more and more in awe of her. So many times, he thought of asking her for a photo but he didn't want Zara to get the wrong idea, and he didn't want to scare her away.

Excited to talk to someone about her, since Nicole avoided the subject, he wrote to his father about how they'd met, how special she was and how excited he was about going after the painting together. The three of them. Even the four of them, with Nicole's father JJ.

But his father didn't react as he'd hoped. 'I don't want to hear such nonsense from you again. You're a young man now. Those were just childhood fantasies. You have better things to do than dream about paintings. As for this girl, she doesn't sound like someone your mother would like to have over for dinner. You know how she disapproves of these kinds of people.'

His mother. Yes. She did, in fact, disapprove of almost every kind of 'people', except for the ones in her circles. Although Leon didn't understand her desperate need to fit into the snobby groups she and his father frequented, he tried not to judge her too harshly. Just like he tried not to judge the ease with which she had sent him away, or her lack of contact throughout the year. He knew she loved him in her own way, and he loved her too. And watching Nicole's pain, even when she tried to hide it, over not having a mother, made him appreciate his even more. But that didn't mean she didn't exasperate him sometimes or disappoint him. Like now. Even if he'd expected some resistance from his parents, he hadn't thought they would be so obtuse and unwilling to give Zara a chance. No, she didn't have Nicole's money or Vincent's titles, but she had Leon's heart.

From that day, Leon stopped talking to his father about Zara or Monet. The two things that meant so much to him – he would keep them to himself. At least until he was older, happy with Zara and had the Monet in his possession. Then he would go back to his parents to prove them wrong.

He also stopped mentioning his family to Zara, afraid she would ask what they said when they heard about her.

Leon would've loved to talk to Nicole about Zara, but Nicole was so stubbornly against the mere idea of Zara that it was like talking to a wall.

'I don't get it, Leon. I thought you'd get over it. It's been months. If you don't think about her, you talk about her. If you don't talk about her, you write to her.'

'I didn't think you'd noticed,' said Leon sarcastically.

'Why? Because I stopped bringing it up? I'm bored, that's why. And honestly, I was kind of waiting for you to get over it and go back to normal. It's been months—'

'I will not "get over it", Nicole. And I hope she won't either.' He sighed. 'I really like her.'

'You like her like her?'

'I do. I more than like her like her. I'm sure you get this feeling too, with Vincent – when you're not with him, you miss him, and you want to spend every waking moment together.'

Nicole hesitated for a moment. 'Of course.'

'Well, that's how it is for me too.'

She patted his hand. 'But I can go see him if I want to. You can't. That's why this doesn't make sense.'

It hurt, because she was right. In a way, at least. Not being able to see Zara was getting to him. The letters just weren't enough anymore. He longed to see her. Day after day, all he thought about was how to get back to Colmar.

That night, he was lying in bed, staring at the ceiling and trying to come up with a plan, as he did most nights. But that night, something felt different. Something was wrong. He started feeling sick. So sick, he tried to get to the doctor's office on the second floor but couldn't get up from bed.

Couldn't even lift his head. He banged as hard as he could on the wall, hoping the boy in the next room would hear. But nobody came. And his face was burning, his eyes so hot and painful he couldn't even open them anymore. He couldn't breathe properly. Couldn't breathe at all.

ZARA

COLMAR

Zara already knew she and Leon had a connection, but it wasn't until one night in mid-February that she realized how strong and deep that connection truly was.

That cold winter night, Zara couldn't sleep. She kept tossing and turning, going in and out of a dream. And in her dream, a woman with long hair, round glasses and a white dress caressed her forehead, then walked away. Zara felt like her whole body was on fire and couldn't keep her eyes open.

'I can't breathe,' she said and held out her hand, trying to make the woman stay.

'I will take care of you. Please relax. I won't leave your side. Just close your eyes.'

The woman placed a mask over her mouth and nose. Zara's head hurt. She looked around from her bed but didn't recognize anything. Unfamiliar noises and sounds.

Everything smelled like bleach and chlorine. She coughed and woke up, drenched in sweat and screaming.

It was still dark out.

Her mother rushed into her room. 'What is it, angel? Did you have a bad dream?'

Zara grabbed her hand so tight she made her mother exclaim in pain.

'It's alright, I'm here. Do you want to tell me about it?'

'I was in a hospital bed I think, and I was sick, very sick and a woman took care of me. But if all felt real, Mama, like it was actually happening. But...'

'But what? Tell me.'

'Although it was real, I knew it wasn't happening to me. I don't know how to explain it. It's as if I experienced it through someone else's eyes.'

Her mother sat on the bed next to Zara and looked at her with a strange, absentminded look. 'I wonder,' she said, almost whispering.

'What is it, Mama?'

'Have you met someone?'

'What do you mean?' asked Zara and gulped.

'Recently? Have you met a boy maybe?'

'How did you...' said Zara, blushing.

'You have,' said her mother.

Zara brought her knees to her chin and hid her face.

'It's alright, angel. Don't be embarrassed. You know you can talk to me about anything.'

So Zara told her. How she'd met him, how they'd been writing to each other. Everything.

'I'm sorry I didn't tell you,' said Zara. 'How did you know?'

'The dreams,' said her mother and smiled. 'They start around the time our paths cross theirs.'

'What do you mean? Whose path?'

Her mother took Zara's hands in hers. 'There's this story – well, story might not be the right word. It's a belief. A belief that's been passed on from generation to generation. I don't know when it all started, but apparently, all the women in our family have experienced them.'

'Experienced what?'

'These dreams. My grandma called them reveries. She started dreaming when she was fifteen, and so did my mother. I, on the other hand, didn't have my first dream until I was in my second year at university. I was pushing a rusty lever up and down, and the same song kept playing over and over, while small yellow lights moved around me in circles. I heard a scream and ran to where it was coming from. A little girl was dangling from a high bar. I knew that if she fell from there, she would die. I jumped to catch her. Then I woke up. And when I did, I knew. It wasn't like any of the other dreams I'd had before. Because in this one, I wasn't dreaming as myself. I was someone else. I saw it through someone else's eyes. Although I didn't know who it was.'

'Just like me,' whispered Zara.

'And just like you, I told my mother. That's how I found out about the reveries.'

'What are they? Nightmares?'

'No, my love. They are the connection. The unbreakable connection.'

Zara stared, confused.

'How can I explain this? Your grandmother believed that

everyone is connected to someone. Everyone. Only most people aren't aware that this connection exists. They go through life not searching for it, not even being open to it, because their minds tell them such a thing is impossible. They get married, have children, have a good, even great life sometimes, not knowing that somewhere out there, there's someone else they were meant to be with. Not their wife or their husband. Someone else. They might have moments when they feel something is missing, or feel lonely despite not being alone, or even question their happiness. But, as it usually happens in life, they soon forget about it, fill the void with something else, and move on. But we are not most people. Once we become aware of the connection, we can't ignore it or forget it. The dreams won't let us.'

'Mama, really. This sounds like one of Grandma's stories,' said Zara, giggling.

Her mother laughed. 'That's what I thought at first too. Your grandmother did have a big imagination. Remember her stories about strigoi and solomonars? Ghosts and wizards?'

Zara chuckled, thinking back to all the fantastic, unbelievable things she had heard from her grandmother when she was a child back in Romania.

'Why did you believe her then?'

'Because I met your father.'

She got up and walked to the window, looking outside at the street covered in darkness.

'A few days after that dream, my friend and I went to the last night of a traveling carnival. A street fair that moved from city to city for the summer. When I got there, I saw in the middle of the attractions an old carousel, and next to it a big, white Ferris wheel. I heard the song from my dream, and I saw the lights. I recognized them. I rushed to the carousel, knowing it was there, somewhere. That big, rusty handle. And it was. It operated the carousel. And I could see the Ferris wheel from there. And the bar where that little girl, whose face I didn't see, was hanging by, in my dream. I couldn't believe it. And then a voice behind me asked if I wanted to go on the carousel. I turned around and—'

'And?'

'It was your father,' she said, her eyes smiling. 'Immediately I realized something. I knew his voice. I had heard it before. Once. A few days before, at school, he passed by me, humming the lyrics of "One night of Love".'

Zara grinned. 'His favorite song.'

'It was after that, yes. I went on that carousel ten times that evening. And by the end of the night, I knew he was the one, and I knew my mother was right. I even asked him if there had been an accident with a little girl a few nights before.'

'And what did he say?'

'He seemed shocked. He said it was an almost accident. He caught the girl in time.'

'Amazing,' said Zara, her eyes wide with wonder. 'Grandma wasn't making it up?'

'As hard as it is to believe, no, she wasn't. The dreams are real. The connection is real and I've always thought of it as a wonderful gift. But it can also be a crippling curse.'

'Why do you say that?'

'Because once you start dreaming about them, you can't stop. You can't let go of the possibility. Even if you can't find them. Even if years pass. You might meet other people,

people you have feelings for, but it's not the same. Because in your heart, there's room for only one. And you'll search for them, even against your will, in every smile, every voice, every person you meet.'

'But you find them, right?'

'Not always. And...' Her mother paused. 'I pray this won't happen to you. But there will be times you wish you could stop the dreams. Times you will want to give back this gift you didn't ask for.'

'Are you making this up, Mamie?' Valerie asks, amused, and leans over to see what I'm reading from. 'This thing about the dreams?'

She reminds me so much of myself when I heard about the dreams for the first time. Same doubtful raise of the eyebrows, same incredulous look, even the same words. This is why I am telling her the story. All the details. So she doesn't make the same mistakes I made. But I can't force her to believe.

She reads for herself the last few lines. She grabs my arm. 'This is just a story, isn't it? It's not real. These dreams are not real. There's no "unbreakable connection".'

'You'll have to make up your own mind about what is real and what is not, honey.'

'Mama, if all this is true, does it mean Leon's life is in danger? In the dream, he seemed sick. What if he needs my help?'

'Nobody can tell you what the dreams mean. The answer

is in your heart. And sometimes dreams are simply...
dreams. Even for us.'

Zara didn't go back to bed. She couldn't. What if something
had happened to him? The next morning, she waited for
his letter. But nothing arrived. That night she wrote to him,
asking him if he was alright. She didn't tell him about the
dream because she didn't want to seem odd, but she couldn't
stand by without doing anything.

ZARA

COLMAR

Three days passed with no news from him. She wanted to go to the baker's wife – the only person she knew in Colmar who had a telephone and wouldn't mind if she used it – and call his school. Something was wrong. Something was really wrong. She could feel it.

On the fifth day, she finally got a letter from Leon.

Dear Zara,

I'm sorry I didn't write sooner. I haven't been well. I am good now though, thanks to a nice lady doctor who took care of me and… actually, thanks to you. I dreamed about you. I had pneumonia, and I scared the doctors with my high fever. They didn't know if I was going to make it and said I was lucky because somehow, I pulled through.

How did you know I was sick? Or maybe you didn't

and just asked me how I was since I haven't written in a few days.

In the dream I had when I was sick... you were here with me. I couldn't see you, but I knew you were there. Right after that, I woke up, and the doctor told me I was out of danger, and I was going to be alright. I know this sounds crazy.

I have been thinking a lot about you, and I want to ask you something. I'd like to try and come back to Colmar, even if it is only for a few hours. I want to see you. What do you think?

Leon

Zara read the letter again and again until she lost count and the words were spinning around in her head. He had been so sick he almost died. Just like in the dream. Was her mother right or was it just a coincidence?

'Did Daddy ever dream about you while you dreamed about him?'

'What do you mean, angel?' asked her mother. They were sitting on a terrace in the square, bundled up in thick blankets and sipping their hot cocoa.

She pulled the letter from her pocket and read it to her mother.

'If he did, he never told me. The truth is I don't know. You see, these dreams don't come with instructions. Just like the connections we have with people don't come with guarantees. Just because you dream of the person you love, it doesn't mean it'll end well. Your great-grandmother spent her life searching for the man she dreamed of and ended up marrying someone else. A good, kind man she cared for, but not the one her heart longed for. She was unhappy and died regretting the love she never had. It consumed her.'

'Do you think Leon's dream means we have a different kind of connection?'

'I wish I had the answers you're looking for, but this is something for you to figure out. It's part of your story. Perhaps it's too soon now for answers.' Her mother smiled. 'What will you do? Are you going to see him?'

'Yes. Although I am scared he might not like me. I'm afraid I will disappoint him.'

For almost three months she had been daydreaming about him but now that he'd mentioned coming back to Colmar, she was nervous. She worried about his reaction.

Zara had never thought of herself as a pretty girl, and the mocking and name-calling of the other kids didn't help either. With her curly red hair, freckles and protruding green eyes, she seemed like an easy target. And it didn't help that she cut her hair short and wore large overalls to hide her skinny legs. The funny thing was, she never considered that she might not like Leon. That was impossible. She liked him, and it didn't matter if he had black eyes or brown, if he was skinny or not, or if he had big ears. She would've liked him even more if he had red hair and big green eyes, so they could be like two twin frogs, leaping away together in the world. She liked him unconditionally. Eyes closed.

'You are a beautiful, smart, special girl. Don't ever think you're not good enough. And if he's who you think he is, he will see all these things in you. He probably already does.'

LEON

VAUD

The moment he got better, even before that, he knew what he was going to do. When he was sick and the doctors were worried he might not make it, his only thought was her. Zara.

'I need your help,' he said to Nicole when he got out of the clinic. 'I have to go to France.'

'Why?' she asked.

'It's pretty obvious, isn't it? I want to see Zara.'

'Obvious but pointless. Even if you manage to get there, you still have to come back to school. You're in for heartbreak, my friend. This whole thing is going nowhere. I mean, it's nice you have a pen pal, as I already told you, but I'd stop at that. Long-distance relationships don't work.'

'How did you get so wise?'

'I have more life experience than you do,' she said, all smug.

'Oh, do tell.'

'It's not like I'm some silly girl, you know. I read books and watch movies; besides, Vincent's sister was in love with a soldier stationed overseas. And that didn't go well.'

He scoffed. 'Will you help me or not?'

'I can't. I'm sorry. If the headmaster catches me…'

Nicole was not one to follow the rules or shy away from a challenge. Leon pushed again.

'Since when are you afraid of the headmaster?'

'Since I got two warnings. You know what that means. I'll be expelled. Then what? I'll be stuck in Paris, in some average school and living with JJ. No way.'

'Is this really why you won't help?'

'What do you mean? Why else wouldn't I?'

'I don't know. You've been against Zara from the beginning. I feel like I can talk about her with Vincent more than I can with you. Don't you find that strange?'

'Why don't you? Go talk to Vincent for all I care. Believe what you want. I just don't want to get mixed up in this. Helping you go there to meet some ghost girl you think you are in love with and getting everyone in trouble for your obsessions. Not doing it.'

'I don't need you to do anything dangerous. Just to find out which senior class is going on that field trip next week, and who already said they're not going so I can take their place.'

She shook her head. 'Not doing it. Stop asking.' Then she gave him a long look. 'If you're that desperate, why don't you ask Vincent? He's a senior.'

He was desperate. He would've done anything to get back to Colmar. But Vincent?

'Let's see how much you're willing to do for this girl,' she said through her teeth.

Leon sighed. 'Vincent. This should go well,' he mumbled.

Later that day, after repeating his speech ten times, he knocked on Vincent's door.

'Do you have five minutes? I want to talk to you,' started Leon.

'Talk then.'

He didn't invite Leon in and stood in the doorway, playing with a pencil.

'I want to ask you for a favor. A big favor.'

Vincent started laughing, as if on cue. 'A favor? Let's hear it.'

'I heard there is a field trip next week and I was wondering if you knew which senior classes are going.'

'I sure do. But what's it to you?'

'I need to be on that trip,' said Leon.

'You do?' asked Vincent with a straight face, although it seemed like he was about to burst into laughter again.

'Yes. It's very important to me, otherwise I wouldn't be here.'

'And why, might I ask, do you need to be on the trip?'

Leon sighed. 'Because I want to go see Zara.'

'Oh,' said Vincent rolling his eyes. 'Zara. The mysterious French girl. She must be something else, for you to be so stuck on her.'

Leon smiled, though he tried not to.

'Come on in, don't just stand there. Always happy to help a friend in love.'

'I'm just trying to find out which classes are going, and which of the boys won't be there, to take someone's place.'

Vincent frowned. 'That's risky business, trouble.'

'Oh, don't you start as well. I've had enough of this from Nicole.'

He studied Leon for a moment. 'Yes, she seems particularly set against this girl of yours. I keep wondering why—' He stopped and stared out the window. 'You know what? I'll help you. My class is going. And one more. There's about fifty of us, and as far as I know, at least four won't be there.'

Leon smiled excitedly. 'So I can go. I can go see her.'

'Calm down. Make sure you wear the dark winter coat and the hat. That's what we were instructed to have on. That way you'll blend in.' Vincent looked him up and down. 'You're tall enough. It should be fine.'

Leon's smile widened even more and now his cheeks hurt. He was so excited he almost hugged Vincent. Almost.

'Come to me in the morning, after we leave. I'll find you an empty train car, so you don't risk anyone recognizing you. You do know we're going to Strasbourg, not Colmar, right?'

Leon nodded. 'The train passes through Colmar on its way there. I'll just get off.'

'You've thought of everything. You really like this girl, don't you?'

'Very much.'

'I'm happy to hear that.'

'You are?'

'You're surprised. Why? Do I seem like such a heartless guy?'

'No, but—'

'Look, Leon, I have nothing against you. I never have. I just don't like to lose. And I don't like to share either, if you know what I mean.'

Leon smiled distractedly. He wasn't really sure he knew what Vincent meant.

He was about to see Zara. Finally. After months of dreaming about it.

'Thank you,' he said, the excitement obvious in his voice. 'I owe you one. A big one. Huge.'

'I'll hold you to it,' said Vincent with a mischievous smile.

ZARA

COLMAR

As time went by, Zara controlled her insecurities and instead focused on the time they would spend together. She was eagerly counting the days and making plans.

'Zara, hurry up, come inside,' her mother said one afternoon, a few days before Leon's return to Colmar. 'I have great news!' she said.

'What happened, Mama?'

'I received a letter inviting me for an interview in Paris. A teaching assistant position.'

'That is amazing news! When are you going?'

'The interview is in two days.'

Zara's smile faded.

'Tuesday? But that's the day before Leon is coming.'

'I know,' her mother said.

'Will we make it back in time?'

'I'll spend the night at your cousin Constance's place then take the 7 a.m. bus; I'll be back around three.'

'*You*'ll be back? Am I not going?'

'There's no point in you missing school and spending sixteen hours on a bus.'

'But we always do everything together,' said Zara sadly.

'Oh, wonderful child,' her mother said and kissed her tenderly on the forehead. 'We are always together, even when we are apart – don't forget that.'

'Are you sure about this, Mama?'

'Absolutely. I have a feeling it is better for you to stay home this time, angel.'

'Her mother sounds like a special person.'

I stop reading.

'She was magic. Pure magic. She was strong and beautiful and smart. She never gave up. Even after her husband died, even when they had nothing to eat – literally nothing but a week-old loaf of bread, she would put on the stove to dry and keep it going longer. She did laundry, mended neighbors' clothes and cleaned other people's houses after she lost her teaching job in Romania. She would've done anything to keep Zara safe. The money she got was barely enough for them to survive from one day to the next. But she always kept her daughter clean and made her go to school.'

'It's sad to imagine such an unhappy childhood.'

'I never said Zara was unhappy. She was not unhappy. There were moments when she was sad for her mother, sad she couldn't help. But most of the time, she had that innocent take on life most children her age have. She would not go hungry; she was loved, taken care of. Her mother told her stories every night at bedtime, magical stories she made up. So what if they couldn't afford books? Or a house of their own? It didn't matter. Somehow, her mother always found a way to make it work. Even after they lost everything in the war, packed all their belongings in a few bags and left the country in the middle of the night, not knowing where they would end up, she still smiled. "It will all work out, angel," she used to say to Zara. "This is not how your story is supposed to end."' I smile. 'She was magic.'

LEON

VAUD

Leon asked around to find out which teacher was in charge of the trip to Strasbourg. He hoped it was his art teacher. As much as he had been upset with him for what happened in Colmar, he was his mentor and JJ's friend, and he would not willingly get Leon into trouble.

But it wasn't him. It was a substitute teacher. All the better. The sub would have no idea who was who. It was all going to work out.

Nicole kept trying to persuade him to change his mind and give up his plan.

'I don't want you to go.'

'Why?'

'I just don't. You don't even know her. Is she worth all of this trouble?'

'Yes,' he said shortly and ended the conversation.

He was getting tired of constantly having to defend his

feelings in front of Nicole. He thought she would give in and support him, but instead, she became colder and colder, barely speaking to him in the days before the trip.

'You will regret this,' she warned him the night before.

'I will regret it more if I don't go.'

The next day, after breakfast, they all gathered in front of the school and walked to the station. The heavy snow and strong gusts of wind made everyone walk with their heads down. All the boys were wearing their long, dark school coats, and had their fur hats on to keep their ears warm. No one noticed Leon didn't belong.

ZARA

COLMAR

Zara barely paid any attention in class that day. When the school bell rang, she grabbed her books and ran home, trying not to think about how nervous she was, but just about finally being face to face with Leon. Finally looking into his eyes and seeing his smile.

She put on the black-and-white wool dress her mother had made for her to wear for Christmas mass – this was a special occasion too – her only pair of winter boots, and the long coat she wore on Sundays before rushing to the Unterlinden to wait for him. She looked at herself in the mirror ten times, arranging her short hair as best she could. She put on a warm hat, changed her mind, then changed her mind again. She put it back on, thinking she would take it off when she saw him. What would she say to him? How would he react when he saw her?

What if he didn't like her? After all, nobody else did.

No, he would. He had to. In the short time they had spent together, she already felt closer to him than anyone else before. And with each letter, and each passing day, she felt she could tell him anything because he would understand. Because he was just like her.

Zara kept checking the clock in the sitting room. Her mother was late. She'd said she would be coming back with the three o'clock bus. Maybe it had gotten delayed, she thought. It had snowed all day and the snow slowed everything, especially on the winding roads close to Colmar.

She couldn't wait any longer. It was fifteen minutes before four o'clock when she left the house. If she made it in time, she planned to hide behind one of the great oaks in front of the museum. Just so she could get a peek.

Four o'clock came and there was no sign of him.

A group of boys walking her way gave her hope, but when they passed and she recognized them from school, her heart sank.

More time passed, and Zara started getting anxious and cold.

He is late, she thought, *but he will be here. He promised.*

She hoped her mother was back already. She'd promised she would cook something special for them that evening. Soup a l'oignon and cassoulet and perhaps some sauerkraut so he could have the best of both French and German cuisines.

The clock tower at Saint Martin's church announced five o'clock.

Zara sat on the sidewalk, looking both ways every few seconds. Listening. Hoping.

Six o'clock.

It was so cold.

Seven.

She pulled the hat lower on her head and tried to stay warm, but she was already shivering. Even her feet were frozen. As much as she tried to think positively, she had a bad feeling. He wasn't coming. Maybe something had happened or maybe he'd never planned to come in the first place, and it had been just something he said. But if her mother was right, and the dreams were real, didn't that mean he was the one? Or was her mother wrong? Countless questions went through her mind.

She felt ridiculous. Foolish. Tears pooled in her eyes.

All for a boy she had not even seen. A boy she would probably never see.

So naïve. To believe in her grandmother's stories. She knew better. There was no fated soulmate. No reverie. The dream meant nothing. Just like meeting her that evening obviously meant nothing to him. If he was the one, he would've been there that day, no matter what.

With her head down, Zara walked back home.

In front of the house, she suddenly had a bad feeling. The lights were off.

She pushed the handle on the gate when she heard the baker's wife behind her.

'I've been looking for you everywhere. There's been an accident, we have to hurry.'

Zara's heart beat out of control. 'What accident?'

'The bus from Paris skidded off an icy road and hit the side of the mountain.'

'Is it Mama? Where is she? Is she alright?'

'I'll take you to the hospital,' said the baker's wife and took her hand.

A thin and pale doctor approached them.

'Are you Zahara Ionesco's family?'

'I am her daughter, yes. How is she, Doctor? Can I see her now, please?'

'I'm really sorry,' he said.

Zara kept thinking it was all a nightmare. 'What do you mean? Why are you sorry?'

'We did everything we could, but unfortunately your mother didn't survive.'

'No, no, this is a mistake,' Zara insisted desperately. 'You're wrong. I want to see her.'

'You should take her back,' he said to the baker's wife.

'No, I don't want to leave. I want to see my mother.'

'Go home and rest and be with your loved ones.'

'I don't have a home. I don't have anyone. Mama is all I have,' she said, sobbing.

ZARA

COLMAR

For days, Zara was inconsolable. She sat in the middle of her bed, looking at photos and crying. Her mother was gone. She was never going to tell her she loved her again, never going to hold her in her arms and make her feel like nothing bad could happen to her. There would be no more Sunday strolls through Colmar, no stopping for hot cocoa and croissants at the small boulangerie in the square, no night-time stories about her magical childhood in Romania, no more theater plays on the radio on rainy evenings. No more singing and dancing in the living room, as the gramophone played old songs. No more of the clothes she made for her, no more Paris without her, no studio overlooking the Eiffel Tower.

She kept seeing her mother's smile and hearing her warm voice as she left the house and the tears kept coming until there were no more left. She was never going to see her again.

Her cousin Constance came over from Paris as soon as the neighbors called her, but Zara didn't want to see anyone, didn't want to leave her room. She was so angry. At herself for not going to Paris with her mother, at Leon since she felt it all happened because of him, at her mother for leaving her. If she had only gone to Paris with her mother, things would be different.

The funeral was small. The priest, a few neighbors, the baker and his wife, Ivan the watchdog and Constance. It was an unusually cold day for early spring in Alsace. Even the sky was crying with freezing tears. Zara, wearing a long black dress Constance had bought her, stood still and silent by the grave. She couldn't believe her mother was gone.

Zara had no idea what would become of her. Where would she live, what would she do?

'Take me to Paris with you,' pleaded Zara to Constance between tears.

'I can't. My husband doesn't like children. I'm sorry. Really.'

'Can I live here then?'

'Here, alone? Of course not. You're only fifteen. I wrote to my mother.'

'Why? Will Aunt Lisa move back here and take care of me?'

'No, silly. You will go live with her. That's if she wants to take you.'

Zara's eyes brimmed with tears. 'Live with her in America? I don't want to leave Colmar.'

'We can't always do what we want,' said Constance, though not unkindly.

The next morning, a woman with short gray hair knocked on their door. The woman was Lisa. Apparently, she'd bought herself a plane ticket immediately after receiving Constance's telegram.

'I loved your mother very much and I'm so sorry this happened,' she said. 'Constance has her own life and I lost my husband years ago. I am alone like you. I would like to take care of you, make sure you have everything you need.'

Zara felt her guard slowly coming down.

'This is what your mother would've wanted. I'm not rich, but I have a good job and my late husband's farm. You will go to school there, learn a new language, make new friends.'

Lisa was a stranger, but she seemed nice and maybe, in time, Zara could learn to trust the delicate brown-eyed lady who smelled of cookies and spring flowers.

Her aunt helped her pack. It wasn't much. Everything fit into a small wooden suitcase that belonged to her mother. A few photos, some clothes, and books. That was her life now.

Before leaving, Zara took one last walk through Colmar. Rue des Têtes, Rue Des Clefs, Rue des Marchands. She passed a street performer playing Edith Piaf's 'Tu es Partout' on his violin. She gave him a coin and, wiping her tears, walked on. She stopped in front of the bakery with the three iron tables in front. She had been there many times with her mother and had wanted to take Leon there too. And now she'd never have the chance.

Head down, dragging her feet, she went back home and

sat on the sidewalk in front of the house. She felt lost, alone, heartbroken.

The walk to the train station was the longest of her life. She was heading into the unknown, leaving everything she loved behind. On the platform, waiting for their Paris-bound train, Zara and Lisa stood in silence. The train to Strasbourg was pulling into the station, and they stepped back to let people out. A wave of busy, hurried men and women dressed in gray, brown and black walked towards the exits, pushing past them.

There was a moment. A fraction of a second when Zara felt a heaviness in her chest. A pressure, cutting her air off. She looked around like she was afraid she was about to miss something. Someone. From the corner of her eye, she saw the back of a man and a boy. The man had perfectly white hair, silver almost, and the boy wore a hat, like the Russian ones. Black, thick. She held her breath. Her heart pounded. Then she couldn't see them anymore. And the moment passed her by. Whatever she had missed was gone. Her eyes filled with tears.

As if sensing her pain, Lisa took her hand. 'Zara, I know how much it hurts right, but—'

'Aunt Lisa, don't call me Zara. It's too painful. It reminds me of Mama and of... It's a silly nickname and I'm not a child anymore.'

'What should I call you then?'

'Call me by my name. Dominique, simply Dominique.'

'Oh, Mamie,' says Valerie, her eyes brimming with tears. 'I'm so sorry. It's you. Zara is you. I didn't know.'

I blink a few times to stop the tears.

I'm still emotional remembering the pain I felt. It never really goes away. You learn to live with it. But it's been over sixty years, and it's still here, in my heart. I suffered after my father died, but I was young and didn't quite understand. My mother's passing crushed me; it changed me. And I still miss her. Every single day.

LEON

COLMAR

Bedroom, classroom, bedroom, greenhouse, bedroom, classroom. That had been Leon's life in the agonizingly long week since the Strasbourg trip.

When Leon had boarded the train for the school trip he'd sat comfortably in an empty car and pulled the curtains to make sure he wouldn't be seen, but before they pulled out, he heard the door behind him and felt a tap on the shoulder. His French teacher, who knew and remembered him much too well after he refused to close an art book during his class, had decided to join the trip at the last minute. Leon's plans were ruined. No more trip. Instead, he was escorted back to the school and straight into the headmaster's office.

The headmaster – known around the campus as obtuse, overly strict, and unforgiving with rule-bending – sat him down and without even giving him a chance to defend himself, thundered, 'For what you've done, I should expel you. But I feel generous today. I will give you another chance. As for your punishment, you will have no privileges for two weeks. No TV, no radio, no mail, no passes for field trips, and definitely no soccer and no skiing.'

Leon stopped listening at 'no passes'.

'A friend is waiting for me in Alsace. Can I at least let her know I'm not coming?'

'You should've thought of that before you lied and sneaked out of school. You are confined to your quarters, your classroom and science laboratory until Easter when you may leave and spend the vacation with your family.'

Who cared about skiing and playing with friends? Why no travel? He had to go back to Colmar. He had to go back to Zara. Why couldn't he at least write to her?

He imagined her waiting for him, sad and confused. It broke his heart.

Leon tried talking to Nicole, asking her for help, but nobody was allowed to come to his room. He sent her a note during class, but she didn't respond. That first night he tried leaving the school, but a teacher was patrolling the hallways. The second night, he tried to sneak out and drop a letter into the mailbox, but one of the teaching assistants saw him and he had to run back to his room. It was hopeless. Leon had no option but to do as he was told.

When he wasn't studying or writing letters to Zara – letters he wouldn't be able to send until his two weeks were up – he went to the greenhouse. First, because he had to and then because he found something there that made him smile. Right outside the greenhouse's entrance, three shrubs of jasmine with hundreds of small white flowers lured him with their divine smell and reminded him of her.

At the end of the first week, Nicole slid a piece of paper under his door. 'I worked my magic, but you owe me big time. Meet me at the greenhouse in an hour.'

Just as he was about to go meet Nicole, the headmaster sent word he wanted to see him in his office. He told him his detention was over but warned him never to do that again.

'I hope you learned your lesson,' he said.

Leon nodded anxiously and rushed out. He had to find his art teacher, beg him to take him back to France. He would call JJ and tell him everything, explain. Or he could call his father. Leon was ready to do anything, just to be able to return to Colmar.

Although he had no idea what Nicole had done to change the headmaster's mind, he was impressed. She had a way with words, he knew that much. And JJ was one of the school's biggest donors.

The moment he entered the greenhouse, he heard her. 'Leon. Where have you been?'

She showed up around the corner and ran to him, hugging him tightly.

'Don't I always save you?' she asked, smiling.

'You do,' he said and kissed her on the cheek. She flushed, looking pleased. He was elated. He didn't have to wait one more week; he could go back to Colmar. 'You did save me and I love you for it,' he said, feeling incredibly thankful.

'I love *you*, you fool. Didn't I say she wasn't worth all the trouble? You should've listened to me.'

A gust of wind blew through the garden, and the jasmine shrubs waved gently in the wind, bringing in their mesmerizing smell. Leon closed his eyes.

Nicole moved in closer and took his hand in hers. 'You

have me. You don't need her or anyone else.' Her face was close to his. Leon pulled back.

'What are you talking about? I'm going back to Colmar as soon as I can. If they let me or not. I *do* need her. I need to see her, to talk to her. This past week has been a nightmare, imagining what she must've felt, waiting for me. I care about her more than I ever thought I could care about someone,' he said, keeping a wary distance from Nicole.

'But you just said—' Nicole didn't get a chance to finish.

'There you are, princess.'

Both Nicole and Leon turned around. Vincent was walking towards them.

'Why am I not surprised to see you with my Nico, trouble?' said Vincent, pulling Nicole to him and kissing her.

Nicole blushed.

'I've been looking everywhere for you.'

She attempted a smile. 'Why?'

'Do I need a reason? I just missed you.'

She looked at Leon, then at Vincent and snuggled in Vincent's arms. 'I missed you too,' she said, while not taking her eyes off Leon.

Leon would've felt awkward if he wasn't preoccupied with his own thoughts.

'I have to go,' he said in a rush. He ran back to school and straight to his mailbox. A postcard from Argentina, from his parents. That was it. No letters from Zara. Not even one.

He thought about sending the letters he'd written, but decided it was better if he explained in person. He had no doubt she would understand and forgive him.

But again, the same problem. How could he go back to Colmar? He couldn't risk it again. He had to play it safe so nothing could go wrong this time. But who could get him there and fast?

'I am desperate,' he said to his art teacher, Mr Pillay, that night. 'And there's no one else I can turn to.'

His teacher already knew Leon had met a girl in Colmar but, until that day, he'd had no idea they kept in touch. Leon told him the whole story.

'I need to go to Colmar to see her. Talk to her. Please!'

Mr Pillay called Leon's parents, but of course they weren't there. The housekeeper confirmed they were 'somewhere in South America'. Thankfully. He knew what his father's reaction would've been. He would've never allowed him to go to Colmar to look for Zara.

The teacher then called his godfather, and JJ, after hearing the story, agreed to let Leon go if Mr Pillay went with him. They were on the first train to Strasbourg the next morning.

When they arrived at the Colmar station, it was busy and even colder than Switzerland. Leon pushed his ushanka hat down on his head and covered his ears, before stepping on the platform and making his way through the crowds.

In the middle of the platform, he stopped for a second.

'What is it?' asked Mr Pillay.

'I'm not sure,' said Leon. 'I don't know.'

He looked around. People were rushing in all directions. Too many people.

'Let's go. We're freezing here,' said his teacher and pushed him gently forward.

Zara was right; it was a small town, and they found the address quickly. The house, a massive two-story with red shutters on a narrow, cobbled street, looked deserted. He rang the doorbell. No response. The shutters were closed, the gate locked. Where was she? He got anxious. Leon spent the next few hours walking the streets of Colmar. Rue des Têtes, Rue Des Clefs, Rue des Marchands. No sign of Zara.

Kids made a snowman in front of a church. A street performer played a French folk song on his violin. A corner bakery put out fresh bread. He wanted to be there with her. The brightly colored timber homes, the wide canals, and narrow alleyways of Colmar made Leon feel he had stepped back in time.

I wish it were possible to go back in time. A few day – that's all I need.

At every step, there was a unique sculpture, an impressive fountain, a monument. All the things he wished Zara had shown him. He saw them but didn't really look at anything. He just wanted to find her. How could he? What was he looking for? Walking towards him was a brunette with brown eyes. On the other side of the street, a blonde with blue eyes. He knew none of them were Zara, but he asked anyway. The girls giggled and ran away.

Leon and his teacher kept coming back to the house, every couple of hours. Late in the evening, they returned to try one more time but the lights were out, and there was no sign of life.

'Try a neighbor,' suggested Mr Pillay.

Leon rang the doorbell at the house next door.

An old woman opened the gate.

'I'm sorry to bother you, I'm looking for Zara Ionesco. She lives at number 24.'

'Ah, the mademoiselle,' she said sadly.

Leon noticed her tone and started to worry even more.

'I tried several times but nobody's answering,' he continued.

'And nobody will, young man. They moved out.'

'When?'

'They left earlier today.'

'Where did they go?'

'I'm not sure, but I heard them saying something about the train to Paris.'

Paris? Of course. He should've thought of that. Where else would she go?

'So she left with her mother to live in Paris?'

'Oh, you didn't hear about what happened then. Poor soul.'

Leon gulped. 'What happened?'

'She died a week ago. Such a loss. She was so young and beautiful.'

'Died? Who died?' The woman's reaction to his earlier question played in his mind. No. Leon clenched his jaw, forcing himself not to break down and cry. His body felt weak and useless. His Zara couldn't be gone.

'Her mother. A bus accident. Such a tragedy.'

'Her mother,' he repeated wondering if he was a horrible person for feeling relieved it wasn't Zara. 'Is Zara alright?'

'Eh, poor girl. As much as she could be, all alone in the world.'

Leon's heart hurt, physically. Just thinking of Zara's suffering made him tear up.

'What happened to her? Who's taking care of her now?'

'I told you. She went to Paris. A relative came and took her away. Or a friend of the family perhaps.'

His Zara was all alone in the world, after having gone through the most horrific experience of her life, and he hadn't been there for her. No wonder there were no letters. Who knew what she must've thought?

'Do you have an address? Do you know where I can find her?'

'I don't know anything,' she said before closing the door. 'They didn't tell me.'

Zara and him, they had talked about many things, things that in those moments seemed important, and they were, but now he realized how little he actually knew about her life. And how little she probably knew about his too. He had felt such a strong, immediate connection with her that all those details seemed trivial and of no significance. He never imagined he would need that information someday. He had no idea if she had any other family outside Colmar. Or if her mother had friends in Paris.

Leon turned to his teacher. 'What do I do now? Where do I search for her? It's a big world out there.'

'If it's meant for you, my boy, this big world will become small, at the right time.'

PART II

'Nothing is impossible
for a willing heart.'
— Jacques Coeur

LEON

14 JUNE 1956

VAUD

'What are you doing? I thought you'd finished all your assignments,' asked Nicole as she sat on the grass next to Leon.

'I'm writing Marc's paper on seventeenth-century Dutch painters.'

'I didn't know you two were friends.'

'We're not,' said Leon, continuing to write.

The truth was, he had no friends left, except for Nicole. The last year had been tough on him. After he returned from Colmar, finding Zara was the only thing he cared about. He isolated himself, stopped going to soccer practice and sailing competitions, and he could hardly be seen in the common areas after school. All he did was sit in his room or alone in the greenhouse, his mind busy coming up with all sorts of scenarios and possibilities.

He used all the address and telephone books he could find. Made dozens of calls and wrote even more letters. There was no Zara Ionesco in Paris. And none of the Ionescos had ever heard of her (or ever answered his letters). He even asked Mr Pillay and JJ to take him to Paris, to the museums – Rodin, Louvre, Orangerie, Marmottan. All the places where he imagined she would go if she lived in Paris. No one had seen or heard of Zara. And when all his attempts at finding her proved to be unsuccessful, he felt like he'd failed her again. Once for not meeting her when he promised, twice for not being there for her when she needed someone the most, and now for not being able to find her.

'If I don't help him, he'll fail the year.'

'Maybe if he hadn't been so busy playing rugby all semester…'

Leon stopped writing and looked up at her. 'His father is picking him up this Friday. That's if he passes and finishes the year.'

'Wait a minute. Marc's father lives in Paris,' said Nicole and looked away. 'You're writing his paper, and in exchange he takes you with him.' She sighed. 'Leon, it's been over a year. You have to stop.'

'One year, two months and twenty-nine days,' he said, smiling sadly. 'Don't you think I know I should stop?'

'Then why don't you?'

He shrugged.

'I miss you,' she said and put her head on his shoulder.

'What do you mean? I'm here all the time. Well, almost all the time.'

'You are, but you aren't.'

She picked up a small white flower and gave it to him.

'I feel like we don't get to spend any time together anymore. We barely talk.'

'We're talking now,' he said and gave her back the flower. He tried to be cheerful and sometimes it worked. But, most of the time, it didn't.

'Who are you taking to the Third-Year Ball?' she asked.

'I don't know. Nobody.'

'Why?'

'You know why. Because it's a couples thing and I don't like anyone that way.'

She scoffed. 'I wonder why.'

He didn't respond.

'Why don't we go together then?'

He tilted his head and stared at her. 'Together? No, that would be weird.'

'I don't think it would. Plus, a bit of dancing and music would do you good.'

'What about Vincent? Isn't he coming back for the ball?'

'I could tell him not to.'

Leon laughed. 'I doubt he would like that. I appreciate what you're trying to do but I don't need a party to cheer me up. I'm fine. You go and have fun.'

'He's coming to see me next week, you know. He wasn't supposed to but says he's missing me,' said Nicole, like she hadn't heard him.

Vincent had graduated the year before and was now studying French Literature at the Sorbonne, but he would come to see Nicole every other weekend. It seemed the headmaster was more inclined to turn a blind eye to rule-bending if it involved the Saint Germains or the D'Angers.

'That's nice,' said Leon absentmindedly. 'Maybe I'll ask him to take me with him to Paris when he returns.'

'Oh, stop it! Really. I'm tired of this. She's gone. Just accept it and move on.'

'Don't start, please. I'm not in the mood to fight with you again.'

'You're never in the mood for anything. All you do is sulk and plan. And search. And sigh. You've become a sad, boring version of the Leon I used to know.'

'You can always walk away, Nicole. I know I'm not the best company. I'm sure you can do better. There must be a party somewhere you can go to.'

He was being mean and, judging by the look in her eyes, he knew it hurt her.

'I'm sorry,' he said.

He understood she was frustrated, but he was frustrated too.

In the year that followed, Leon's efforts to try and find Zara slowly dwindled down until they came to a stop. Not because he had forgotten her or he didn't care about her anymore. But because, by that point, he had tried everything he could think of, and it had gotten him nowhere. It was as if Zara had disappeared off the face of the earth.

Gradually he returned to his group of friends, the ones who still accepted him. He re-joined the soccer team and did his best to not be as 'antisocial' as Nicole accused him of being, though he didn't always succeed. As for his friendship with Nicole, it somehow bounced back after the Zara topic wasn't part of the conversation anymore. It was good to have his best friend back, but it had cost him more than Nicole could ever imagine.

LEON

14 JUNE 1957

VAUD

'Where have you been?' asked Leon when Nicole walked in. She had promised to help him pack, but that was two hours earlier.

'On the phone with JJ, who is ruining my graduation day,' she scoffed and sat on the side of his bed, staring into space, with a grumpy look on her face.

Nicole had never called JJ 'Father'. Never. Not even as a child.

'Sometimes I wonder if he cares about me at all. I don't think he does.'

'What's happened now?'

It was always something. Nicole and JJ couldn't even exchange pleasantries without jumping at each other's throats and it had been that way forever. They didn't seem to see eye to eye on anything.

'I just told him I got into Parsons, and he couldn't care

less. He didn't try to convince me to study art and seemed relieved in a way. But when I told him you were sticking to your NYU plan and a major in business, and not art like he wanted, he lost it.'

'You're making a big deal out of nothing. I'm sure he didn't push you into art because he knows he can't convince you. He and I both know how stubborn you can be,' said Leon and smiled. 'Besides, it's too late now. We're already enrolled,' he said, taking his welcome letter from NYU and waving it in her face.

When he got his acceptance packet from New York University, Leon was thrilled. He was counting the days until they graduated, so he could finally leave the closed walls behind, and head into a free world where he could be who he wanted, do what he wanted. No curfews, no rules, no limitations.

Nicole was the same. After toying with several ideas for her major, she settled on fashion and applied to several schools. Her number one choice was Parsons. And she got in.

She raised an eyebrow. 'Maybe so, but he didn't even try.'

'Would it have made a difference? Could he have changed your mind?'

'Pfff, of course not. All I've been thinking about for the last year is how we'll get out of here, fly to New York and do whatever we want.'

'See? Plus you made it very clear you don't want anything to do with the family business.'

'Either I said it or he would have. I know when I'm not wanted, Leon. JJ is relieved I am not interested in his company because he has his sights set on someone else. All those letters he sent you through the years, those books about art. He's grooming you.'

'Grooming me? What for?'

'I wouldn't be surprised if he offered you the company on a platter one day.'

'I seriously doubt it. Yes, he did send me art books and letters from where he was traveling, but it was just because we kept in touch about the missing Monet and then—'

Leon stopped.

'And then her, right? Why do you keep bringing her up?' she said, all pouty.

'I didn't say anything. You mentioned it.'

'You don't think I know what you were thinking about?'

'Maybe you should be a psychic,' said Leon jokingly, changing the subject. He couldn't go there again.

'I don't need to be a psychic to figure out my father's biggest regret is that I am his child and not you. And your biggest regret is that I'm here with you, and not her.' Once Nicole got something in her head, it was hard to stop her.

'Where's all this crazy talk coming from?'

Leon had tried to help fix JJ and Nicole's broken relationship. But no matter what he said, it never made a difference. She couldn't forgive JJ. Nicole was good at many things. Positive things. But she was also good at holding a grudge. Despite his efforts to patch things up, she would not give the man a chance. JJ had abandoned her. JJ neglected her. JJ chose not to be in her life. What did he expect? That she was going to be the loving daughter who pretended she didn't understand what her father's attitude towards her meant? His coldness, his indifference. He didn't care. He didn't love her. He had never loved her. Leon had heard that speech so many times, he knew it by heart.

'Crazy talk,' he said in a singsong voice, trying to defuse the tense conversation.

'It's not crazy talk and don't you dare minimize it. The very few times my father calls me, mostly to ask me if I need anything, like money, he brings you up. Leon this, Leon that. How talented you are. How good you're doing in school. How lucky I am to have a friend like you.'

Leon laughed. 'Well, the man has a point. You are lucky.'

'Don't get cocky with me. You're the lucky one. Now let's pack your stuff,' she said. 'I can't stay long. It'll take me a couple of hours to get ready.'

Leon laughed. 'It's a high school graduation party, not a royal ball, Cinderella.'

'What do you care? You throw something on and you're ready.'

'Well, yes, obviously. Especially if I'm only going because you're forcing me. So you can't say I didn't go to any of these boring things you seem to like so much. I would've been perfectly happy having an early night, and not feeling queasy and groggy on the train tomorrow morning.'

Nicole and Leon had planned their summer between high school and university in painstaking detail.

'See what a good friend I am?' he said and flicked her arm.

She laughed. 'Early night. You're such an old man.'

'Talking about old, when is your old man coming? Not that I'm dying to see his face, but just so I know.'

'He's not my old man,' she snapped.

'Fine, your young man,' he teased.

'He'll be here,' she said. 'But even if he's late, I'll be with you...'

'Vincent is never late when it comes to spending time with you.'

She smiled absentmindedly.

'Of the three of us, I think he's the most excited about this summer,' said Leon.

'Why?'

'He's going to have you all to himself. Finally. No more three-legged stool. No more "trouble",' he said, pointing to himself.

'I've been thinking about this whole cruise ship thing. I'm not so sure it's the best idea.'

'What are you talking about? You've been dreaming about it for years.'

'Yes, but I thought we'd all go.'

Leon laughed. 'That would be ridiculous. We're not kids anymore. Can you imagine me stuck with you and your boyfriend on a boat? Besides, I'm pretty sure I get seasick, if I remember correctly from my one and only boat ride as a kid.'

Nicole had always wanted to go on a cruise, and to no one's surprise, when Vincent found out, he'd suggested they spend the next few weeks of summer on board the most luxurious American ship, going from New York all the way to Hawaii and the islands.

Now that he thought about it, Nicole had tried to convince Leon to go with them several times. He was going to miss Nicole, that was for sure, but they'd see each other again in New York in a few weeks. Besides, he had plans of his own. He and two of his soccer buddies were going to spend the next six weeks in Europe, touring Spain, France, Germany, Italy and Greece.

'Maybe I could go with you,' she said, almost as if she was thinking it and hadn't realized she'd said it out loud.

'Backpacking through Europe and staying in cheap motels?' He made a funny face. 'I can picture it already. If you don't kill me with your complaints every five minutes, then Vincent will after he finds out I ruined his plans. No, thanks.'

She sighed. 'Are you sure you want to go?'

Leon nodded. 'I want the chance to see all these places before we move across the ocean. Who knows when and if we'll be back?'

Saying that made Leon sad. He hadn't thought about Zara all that day or the day before, and perhaps even the day before that. After all, it had been almost two and a half years since she'd left, and life had slowly followed its course. His time had been filled with school, sports, Nicole, their little dramas and joys, then college admission and recently with getting everything together to graduate and planning for the best summer ever. But now, it had suddenly dawned on him he was moving thousands and thousands of miles away from Colmar. From Paris. From her. If he'd held on to a sliver of hope, that would all be gone when he went back to America.

'Let's hope the answer is never. We have four years in New York, and I can't wait to spend them with you. It's going to be so much fun. We'll have to chat living arrangements,' said Nicole.

'Take it easy, planner. Let's get through tonight first,' he said, smiling.

*

The party started at six and lasted until the morning. Although alcoholic drinks were not officially permitted, everyone brought something. Armagnac, pastis, absinthe, Calvados, Chartreuse. He wasn't much of a drinker, but Nicole seemed to enjoy it.

'He stood you up?' Leon asked Nicole, seeing that Vincent wasn't anywhere in sight and it had been a couple of hours already.

She didn't seem upset about it.

'You're here, I'm here. Let's enjoy ourselves,' she said, all smiles.

A slow song was playing, and everyone paired up, walking together to the dance floor and moving to the rhythm.

Nicole turned to Leon. 'Will you dance with me?' she asked and took his hand.

'Of course,' he said.

Nicole rested her head on his shoulder and moved in closer. Accidentally, Leon stepped on her foot. Then again. When she moved left, he went right.

'Hey, watch it, mister,' she said but didn't seem to be bothered by the fact that they were so bad at dancing together. Then she grabbed his face in her hands, their lips almost touching.

Leon stopped dancing.

'What are you doing?' he asked.

'What do you mean?'

'I—' Was he imagining it, or had she wanted to kiss him? He must have. Nicole loved Vincent. They were just friends.

'Sorry, I – I think I'm just tired.' Nicole's face was bright red.

'I should call it a night. Vincent will be here any moment now; you won't be alone.'

'He's not coming,' she said, her face suddenly serious.

'Why?'

'Because.'

Leon was confused. 'Did you two have a fight or something?'

She shook her head. 'I just told him I didn't feel like going to the party.'

He frowned. 'Why did you lie?'

Nicole shrugged.

'I really don't understand you,' said Leon.

'I really don't understand *you*,' she said, swaying on her feet. She was clearly tipsy, at the very least. She'd had quite a lot to drink that night.

Nicole tried to walk away from him, in what seemed like one of her tantrums, but stumbled and almost fell.

She avoided him for the rest of the night and knowing Vincent wasn't coming, Leon was stuck there, sitting on a chair and watching out for her. Making sure she was alright, while she was busy dancing with random boys and ignoring him. He wondered if all girls were as complicated as Nicole. He knew at least one who wasn't.

When, a few hours later, he got back to his room after carrying Nicole to hers, he took a quick shower and threw himself on the bed, but sleep wouldn't come. He was anxious. Restless. But why? Going back home wasn't scary; it was what he wanted. He closed his eyes again, counting to a thousand, five thousand. But instead of falling asleep, he heard her voice and her beautiful laughter. Zara. He missed her. He still missed her and still thought of her. Packing his bags brought it all back and now he couldn't shake the feeling that he was abandoning her. The memories. The possibility. The hope. Yes, the hope of ever seeing Zara.

He got up and started pacing.

How could he leave? If he went to New York, he'd never find her again.

A loud noise outside his room. Someone pounded on the door.

'Leon, there's an urgent phone call for you. It's your mother.'

DOMINIQUE GARDINER

15 JUNE 1957

NEWPORT, RHODE ISLAND

Two and a half years after she left Colmar—

'Wait a minute. What happened to you in the meantime? You can't just skip years like it's a day. What was your life like? Did you go to art school?' asks Valerie.

She makes me smile. 'Darling, if I tell you everything, we'll never leave this couch. Years can go by, and nothing happens, and then in a day, a minute it can all change.'

She doesn't seem convinced.

'What happened? Well, Aunt Lisa adopted me shortly before my sixteenth birthday as was the law of the country. I had her name now, and she treated me like I was her child, but she wasn't Mama, although I cared for her very much. I remember, right after my adoption, asking her if she wanted me to call her "Mother"; I didn't want to hurt her feelings.

She smiled warmly, as only she knew, and said, "No matter what you call me, I don't ever expect to replace your mother, but I will do my best to make her proud of the way I am raising you. Lisa is just fine, honey. Like we're the best of friends. That's what I hope for us."

'She was truly wonderful: nurturing, patient, kind, and such a hard worker. Between the farm, her job as a nurse and taking care of me, she had no time left for herself. But she never complained. I did though. For quite a while. I complained about everything. I missed Mama, I struggled to learn the language, I couldn't find my place in that new, strange world. Lincoln, the small town where we lived, was not larger than Colmar, yet the people were not as close. They all minded their own business. There was no art museum and no hiding place. I went to a regular high school. Art didn't seem to be part of my life anymore. Just as my mother wasn't. Or Leon.'

Valerie seems deep in thought. 'Did you still think about him?'

'I did my best not to, although it was easier said than done. When I was learning English, and people said I had an adorable accent, it reminded me of him. When the lights went out at school one day, and a boy in my class stumbled on one of the desks dropping his books, I remembered Leon and the night we met. When Lisa took me to New York for the first time to see the Metropolitan Museum, the first thing I thought was that he lived here. And what if he was back for the summer? And what would happen if we were to accidentally meet? Would I even know it was him?'

'What about the dreams?'

'When I left Colmar, the dreams stopped, just like

everything else. It was as if my life stopped. I went to school, the public library, I sometimes walked around Boston, looking at statues and buildings. But it wasn't the same. I had lost something. My passion. Life went on, slowly, quietly, uneventfully. Until the day I graduated from high school,' I say and cover Valerie's bare feet with the blanket.

'What happened that day?'

I wink. 'I had a dream.'

The day before her high school graduation, with no apparent reason, no possible logical explanation, Dominique had a dream.

She was dragging a large brown leather suitcase behind her. The morning sun was in her eyes, and she could hear seagulls wailing. A bright yellow car sped past her. The driver was a man wearing a white suit and dark sunglasses. A piano somewhere in the distance played a melancholic song. On the water nearby, there were boats. The expensive kind, not fishing boats. Yachts. She looked up at the sky. It was so blue and bright, her eyes hurt.

'Mom, what's wrong? What is this all about? Why are we here?' she asked.

'We tried to protect you from this. It's been tough,' she heard a woman's voice say. She couldn't see who was talking, but she knew who it was. Her mother. His mother actually.

She said something else, but Dominique didn't understand or maybe didn't hear.

'I need your help. I don't know what else to do.'

Dominique woke up. It was the middle of the night. She

couldn't have slept for more than a couple of hours. It felt like that dream she had years before. She recognized the strange sensation of seeing things through someone else's eyes. It was a special dream. A reverie. Again, after so long?

That day passed painfully slowly despite the graduation ceremony and all the reasons she had to be happy and excited, because all she did was to think about the dream. It haunted her. She had no idea what it meant or if it even meant anything at all. She didn't recognize the place in her dream.

'Where would we find yachts and fancy cars?' she asked Lisa the next morning.

Her aunt laughed. 'Why? Is that where you want to go to celebrate your graduation?'

Did she want to go there? Why? To continue the fantasy? It wasn't real when she'd had the first dream, and it wasn't real now. Otherwise he would've returned to Colmar. If he was the one, he wouldn't have left her there. And why would she dream again now after all those years?

'Do you know it?' Dominique asked, looking insistently into her aunt's eyes.

'There are many places like this around. It could even be Boston. The harbor perhaps.'

'No, it wasn't Boston. I know Boston.'

'What do you mean it wasn't Boston? What wasn't Boston?'

'Anywhere else?' she asked, ignoring Lisa's question.

'Salem, but not so much the fancy cars. The Hamptons. Or Newport.'

Dominique held her breath. 'Newport. I like the sound of that.'

She didn't know why she'd picked Newport of all places. She just had a feeling about it.

'Is it far? Could we get there today?'

Her aunt thought for a moment. 'Actually, you know what? You've always said you wanted to see the ocean and I could take you to a proper beach. Let's go,' said Lisa.

'Really? We're going now?'

'Yes, but we have to move fast. We don't want to miss the sun.'

Before noon, they arrived at the Kensington bus station. Newport smelled like sea breeze and rain. Seagulls circled orderly above their heads, calling each other. Seagulls. Like in the dream. It all looked familiar. And it was beautiful. Restaurants at every corner, people laughing and relaxing in the sun, a piano playing Italian songs. It wasn't the same song as in her dream. But it was similar. Minutes from the beach, Dominique and Lisa stopped at a crosswalk.

Suddenly, Dominique felt anxious. She looked around, not knowing what she was searching for. Across the street – a man. A young man. He was tall, with dark hair that almost touched his shoulders. With his dark sunglasses, white T-shirt, black leather jacket, and dark pants, he looked like a movie star. She stared, unable to look elsewhere. And although she couldn't really see his face, or see his eyes behind those sunglasses, she was convinced he was staring too. Dominique was sure she had never seen him before, yet her heart was telling her something else.

What if... No, it couldn't be. But what if it was him? Her mother had said her dreams would always be about just one person. *The* person.

The seagulls, the ocean, the boats. She'd seen all of that

in her dream. Through his eyes. And now there he was in front of her. It must be him. Why else would she feel this way about someone she didn't know?

As soon as the light turned green, Lisa started walking, and Dominique followed, not taking her eyes from the boy across the street. He didn't move, standing there like a statue. The sun came out from behind the clouds and Dominique closed her eyes for a split second, blinded by it. When she opened them as if in a dream, she saw someone running in her direction with what seemed like superhuman speed. Before she even had a chance to realize what was happening, she was flying.

LEON

NEWPORT, RHODE ISLAND

L eon had a bad feeling. His mother never called.
'Mom, what is it?'

'Leon,' she said and paused for a moment. 'I need you on the first flight to New York. When you get there, take the bus to Newport. I'll wait for you at the station.'

The bus? She never made him take the bus. Her driver took them everywhere. His mother thought it was humiliating if they were seen on public transportation or, God forbid, walking. Only poor people did those things.

'What is going on?'

'Not over the phone. We'll talk when you get here.'

He sighed. 'I don't want to come back to New York now. I have plans.'

'Leon,' she thundered. 'I need you. I will see you tomorrow.'

Something had happened, Leon thought. Something bad.

It was the middle of the night when he finally arrived in Newport and his mother was waiting for him as she'd said she would.

'Mom, what's wrong? What's this all about? Why are we here?'

She started walking and he followed.

'The summer house is the other way. Where are we going?'

'To your aunt and uncle's house. This is where we live now.'

'What? Why?'

'It's your father. He did some things he shouldn't have.'

'What happened? Is he alright?'

'He's fine, but we're in trouble. Financial trouble.'

'What do you mean? Where is he? Is he in New York?'

'There's no more New York. The bank took our apartment.'

'The bank?'

'We tried to protect you from this. It's been tough.'

'What has? I don't understand.'

'In the last few years, Leonard made some terrible investments and when he lost all his clients' money, he tried to cover up the debt by writing checks in JJ's name.'

'He did what? Stole from JJ? I didn't even know they were in trading together.'

'All of his clients left and JJ offered to help Leonard out. If you ask me, JJ did it to humiliate us. He always wanted to be the bigger man. But now your godfather is furious and will most likely press charges against us to recover his money. How we're supposed to do that, I don't know.'

'Wait a minute, if our NY apartment is gone, what

happened to our art collection? Did you move it here, to our summer house?'

'Is that all you care about? Do you hear what I'm saying? The houses, the cars, the jewelry, they're all gone. The bank accounts are frozen. By the time we filed for bankruptcy, it was too late. The paintings? Why do you think he bought them in the first place? For profit. They were the first to go.'

He tried to wrap his head around the news. His father was a successful businessman, not a thief. And an art lover. He would have never bought the paintings just to profit from them; he would never sacrifice art like it meant nothing.

'That's not true. Dad would never do that.'

'You have no idea what your father would do. You've idealized him, God knows why.'

Leon clenched his fists. 'I don't get it. I can't believe this.'

They stopped in front of a cottage and his mother motioned him to follow.

She unlocked the door quietly and led Leon to one of the bedrooms.

'This is the room your father and I are sharing. You can sleep on the couch tonight.'

He was dumbfounded, looking blankly around the room. His confusion must've been obvious.

'We moved in with your aunt and uncle a few months ago, and they're paying for everything, but I don't know how long it will last. Your father is making it impossible for anyone to live in this house.'

'What do you mean? This doesn't sound like him at all.'

'He's not handling the situation well. He's aggressive, violent. He gambled to try and get the money back. That led to more debt, drinking and God knows what else he's doing when he disappears from home for days,' said his mother, and Leon saw the embarrassment in her eyes.

'Where is Dad? I'll talk to him. We can get him help.'

'I don't know where he is. In a bar somewhere.'

'What? Dad doesn't drink.'

'Oh, Leon,' she said, sounding exasperated. His mother had dark circles under her eyes and a haunted look on her face. She had lost weight and the dress she was wearing looked like a sack on her.

'I need your help. I don't know what else to do.'

'How can I help? I don't know—'

She interrupted him. 'I need you to talk to JJ. I have arranged for the two of you to meet tomorrow at noon. I tried to speak to him myself, but he doesn't want to see me. You're my last hope. Please. Explain the situation and persuade him not to press charges. Convince him to return to Paris. He doesn't need our money; he has enough to last him a lifetime and then some.'

'What makes you think he'll listen to me, Mom?'

She raised an eyebrow and the expression on her face was just like Nicole's when they were talking about JJ. 'You know how much he loves you. You're like a son to him.' Her voice broke. 'He will listen to you, I know it,' she said, her eyes brimming with tears.

'Mom, I'll do it. Please don't cry. We'll fix this and everything will go back to normal.'

She smiled sadly.

The next day, after a very awkward breakfast with his mother, aunt and uncle, he was getting ready to leave and head to the rendezvous point his mother gave him when she stopped him. 'No matter what, don't say a word about this to your father. His ego wouldn't be able to take this.'

'I won't. I promise.'

They parted ways after a quick embrace.

Leon was still in shock as he walked down the street. He couldn't believe what his mother had told him, because it didn't sound at all like the father he knew. Then again, how well did he really know him? In the last few years, they had barely spoken. JJ was much more present in his life than his father had ever been.

'America's Society Capital' was unchanged. Elegant, breathtaking, busy. The city by the sea boasted of rich – very rich – people who were the proud owners of stunning mansions, empty most of the year yet suddenly fashionable after Memorial Day, and of massive yachts with fancy names where late-night parties happened until well into September. Red convertibles invaded the streets and behind the wheels were always the same people. The ladies wearing designer dresses, expensive jewelry, and overly sweet perfume walked hand in hand into exotic restaurants with the gentlemen in white linen pants and perfectly ironed polo shirts. The smells and the fake laughter – that's what he remembered the most from his childhood.

He arrived at the meeting place with JJ wondering how his godfather would react. Leon was embarrassed to be put in such an awkward position. Begging for forgiveness – was that what he had to do? He hoped his mom was right, and JJ cared enough about him to listen. He would pay him back all the money his father lost, as soon as he got a job.

Across the street, a girl with a large blue sun hat and

short beige overalls caught his eye. She was too far for him to see her face, yet he stared, unable to take his eyes off her. Who was she? He wanted to rush across the street. He had to see her. And the light wouldn't turn green already.

Time moved so slow. Seconds were hours. There was just something about the girl across the street. He counted the seconds. Why was it taking so long?

The light finally turned green. He took a deep breath. As she began crossing the street, Leon noticed two things. One was that JJ was walking alongside the girl. And the other was a red car approaching them at an alarming speed. There was no time to think. JJ and the girl were in danger. Acting out of instinct, Leon sprinted towards them.

Everything went dark and quiet until he felt a warm, familiar touch. Someone took his hand, and he felt strangely calm. Then silence again.

DOMINIQUE

15 JUNE 1957

NEWPORT

'Can you hear me?' Lisa kept asking her.

Dominique opened her eyes and tried to move. She remembered a forceful shove, tires braking, and a loud thud. On her right, a group of people formed a circle in the middle of the street.

'Lisa, what happened?'

'A car came out of nowhere,' she said. 'It missed you, thank God, but you were unconscious for a minute. Must've hit your head when you fell. Don't move, alright?'

A car? Yes, there was a car. She had seen it the dream; that dream she just had, through someone else's eyes. It felt like a second, a fraction of a second. The car speeding, running, desperate running, a high-pitched screech, then nothing. Silence and darkness.

'Lisa, I think the car hit someone,' said Dominique.

'What? How do you know?'

'I just know. Please check. Please!'

Dominique saw a tall, thin man dressed in a worn-out brown suit push the other people aside. He looked disheveled, a crazy look in his eyes, and he kept waving his arms chaotically. 'We need a doctor. A doctor! Help! Please help him! What have I done?' he shrieked like a wounded animal.

'Lisa, what's going on?' asked Dominique.

'It looks like you're right,' she said and got up. 'Stay here, please.'

Dominique didn't want to listen and tried to get up, but she was too dizzy. She saw Lisa talking to an older man dressed in white, but she didn't get a good look at him. Had he also gotten hurt? He seemed fine to her. Then she watched as both of them walked to the middle of the road, and Lisa raised her voice. 'I am a nurse, please let me pass.'

A moment later, the old man sprinted across the street and disappeared around the corner.

'We need to call the hospital,' she heard a woman's voice say.

'Someone already went looking for a payphone,' said Lisa. 'Please back off. Give him some space, for God's sake.'

Dominique couldn't just lie there anymore. She got up slowly and made her way past the circle of bystanders to Lisa. A hundred meters or so away she saw an old red car with the driver's door open. There was no one inside.

Dominique's head was throbbing, her legs felt wobbly.

Someone was lying on the ground and it took her a moment to realize it was the young man from across the street. Dark hair covered his face, and when Lisa pushed it aside, Dominique gasped. He looked like he'd been hit in the face with a hammer. All she could see was blood. Everywhere. On his face, his arms, the ground. His eyes were closed, and he wasn't moving. The dream. The image she'd seen minutes earlier. It was him.

'Is he going to be alright?' asked Dominique, close to tears.

The agitated man she'd seen earlier lunged at the boy on the ground, grabbed his shoulders and started shaking him. 'Wake up!' he yelled.

'Get him out of here,' Lisa said, looking around for help, and two men restrained and pushed him back while he kept repeating: 'What have I done? Not him. Not him.'

Lisa did CPR. Again. And again. After ten minutes, she stopped. 'I'm afraid he's gone.'

'No! He's not gone,' cried Dominique. 'He can't be gone.'

'Is he dead?' the scrawny man asked, his eyes crazy and terrifying.

When Lisa nodded grimly, he turned around and ran the other way, screaming like his clothes were on fire. A few seconds later, Dominique heard a car speeding away from them.

The red car was gone.

'What was that all about?' asked someone in the crowd. 'Who was he?'

'He was acting really strange,' a man intervened.

'Poor kid,' said an older woman. 'At least he died a hero. He saved the girl's life. And that old man's.'

Dominique gasped. 'He saved my life?' Suddenly, the shove, the noises, the accident, they all made sense. The boy had run towards her, pushed her out of the way and been hit by the car that would have otherwise killed her. She wondered for a moment if the old man they were talking about was the one she had seen earlier, but she didn't have time now to think about it. Whoever he was, he was fine. The boy wasn't. Lisa's worried expression told her everything she needed to know.

'Please don't let him die,' she begged her aunt. 'Please. Please try again.'

Dominique took his bruised hand gently in hers and whispered in his ear, 'Please, stay with me.'

'There's no use, he's gone,' repeated Lisa, but Dominique wouldn't give up. She couldn't let him die. 'Please stay with me,' she repeated again and again.

The sound of sirens was getting closer and closer. And right before they pulled in, the boy took a breath. Dominique saw his chest moving up and down, faintly at first, then stronger.

She gasped. 'He's alive,' she said quietly. 'He's alive.'

The crowd went silent, and then broke just as suddenly into loud relief. Although he never opened his eyes, Dominique thought he knew she was there. She continued talking to him and caressing his hand until the paramedics asked everyone to step back and Lisa pulled her away.

'You don't look so good. Let's wait for the second ambulance and make sure we get you checked out. A concussion is a serious thing,' said Lisa.

'No, I want to go with him. I don't want to leave him alone.'

'He's not alone. A man went with him; it might've been his father.' As she said this, the ambulance left.

'Where are they taking him?'

'I didn't ask but I assume it'll be the same hospital you're going to,' said Lisa.

The second ambulance arrived a few minutes later and took Dominique to a hospital nearby. After they ran some tests, they decided to keep her under observation for head trauma indicators for the next twenty-four hours.

Later that afternoon, while Lisa dozed off on a chair and nobody else was around, Dominique snuck out of her room and went to the front desk.

'Could you please tell me which room the car accident victim is in?' she asked.

'Which car accident victim?' asked the nurse, patiently.

'A young man with long dark hair. He was wearing a white T-shirt and long black pants.'

'Yes,' said the woman. 'We had someone matching that description. But he was only here for a few minutes. We didn't admit him because we're not equipped to handle such a serious case. He was transferred to another hospital by helicopter.'

'Do you know what his name is? Or where he was transferred?'

'No, we don't have his records. I'm sorry.'

'You don't know anything about him? Anything at all?'

Dominique tried to hold back the tears but to no avail. They were already running down her cheeks, one after another.

The nurse smiled kindly. 'Wait here.' She got up and went to the back of the office.

'Do you know where they took the boy who came in this morning? The car accident victim?' Dominique heard her ask. 'Someone is asking about him.'

A few minutes later, the same nurse returned.

'All I can tell you is that he was in terrible shape and his father, who seemed to be a man of means, offered to pay to send him to New York, to a hospital with a fully equipped trauma center.'

'Are you sure it was New York? And do you know which hospital?'

The nurse shook her head.

'And his name?'

'That's all I can tell you, miss.'

Dominique thanked her and went back to her room.

That night, Dominique fell asleep thinking about the boy, and had a dream. She was in a strange bed, in an unfamiliar place. Everything in the room was bright, and she felt like a skier without goggles on a sunny day – open your eyes, and you will be blinded. How would she know that? She had never even seen the mountains, let alone skied. It wasn't her in the dream. It was him. Again. It was a reverie.

'His heart stopped. We're losing him,' she heard and panicked. She felt a kind of fear she didn't know she was capable of. The kind of fear that instead of paralyzing you, makes you do incredible things like fight a lion with your bare hands, or jump from a cliff into the ocean when you can't swim.

It felt like an end. An end to all things. She couldn't let that happen.

'No,' she screamed, sounding like a wounded animal. And this time it was her voice. Not his.

Dominique heard Lisa calling her name. Once. Twice. She woke up.

'What's wrong?' asked Lisa. 'You were screaming in your sleep.'

'I'm fine,' said Dominique and got up.

'You're not fine. Tell me what's wrong.'

She had never told her about the reveries. 'I had a strange dream.'

'What about?'

'I was in a hospital bed, and I couldn't move.'

'It was just a dream. It's because of what happened. It traumatized you.'

'It's possible. But—'

'What is it?'

Dominique smiled sadly. 'I've had dreams like this before. They started when I met a boy back in Colmar. Leon.'

'I see,' said her aunt. 'And you think this dream has something to do with him?'

'I don't know. Mama believed we are connected to the people we love. That some dreams are more than just dreams. That they're the link to our soulmates. We go through life together, even when we're apart, and sometimes we see things through their eyes.'

Lisa smiled. 'I can't believe Zahara told you about this. Dominique dear, it's nothing but a myth. A story. It's like the people who believe what is meant to be will be, no matter what. Things happen if you make them happen. Just like there is no perfect, one-of-a-kind love. There is love, but you have to work at it and make it happen. It's not written in the stars. Too many women in our family believed in this myth, and too many had their hearts broken.'

'You've never experienced it with your husband?'

'No. I had a few dreams when I was fifteen or so, but I ignored them. I don't believe in them. A few years later I met my husband, we got married and lived a happy life. Dream-free.'

'Was he your soulmate?'

Lisa looked at Dominique curiously. 'Soulmate? There is no such thing, darling. I cared for him deeply if that is what you want to know. And I respected him. He was a good man. The kind of love you're talking about belongs only in books. You sound like your great-grandmother. She believed in this thing with such desperation, it ruined her life. You're a smart, educated young woman. Folktales are for simple people.'

Dominique played with her fingers nervously.

'Wait a minute. Why are you asking me all these things? This dream of yours, don't tell me you believe the boy with long hair is your soulmate. You've never even met him.'

'I didn't say he was my soulmate.'

'Well, you dreamed about his accident, didn't you?'

'I guess.'

'That doesn't mean he is your soulmate,' Lisa said, sounding tired. 'Yesterday was emotionally draining. You saw him get hit by that car, you were hurt too, and then you spent the day in the hospital. Of course you had nightmares; it's how your mind coped with the trauma. You felt responsible and it's natural. I've seen it with patients many times. But that's it. He's not your soulmate any more than the other boy Leon was. You should know this too. Because you can't have two "the ones", at least according to the stories you believe so much in.' She laughed. 'You're young and there will be more young men. Your dreams are just beginning.'

Lisa took Dominique's hand in hers. 'I know you miss your mother and I understand this is your way of keeping the connection with her alive. Believing in the things she did. But it's not healthy to focus on fairy tales. Live your life and enjoy it, because the time you're wasting staring at the ceiling and waiting for your soulmate will never come back.'

'Was Lisa right?' asks Valerie, with a curious expression on her face.

'I didn't know. I thought maybe she was. It's very hard, if not impossible, to believe in things you can't prove. I promised I would put the soulmate story and the dreams behind me, but deep down, I felt a longing for something, for someone. A longing that went beyond any promise. I couldn't explain it, but it was always there. It had been there since that night at the Unterlinden. I felt as if I was in the waiting room of my life. Whenever the door opened, I'd jump to my feet. I was living my life waiting for him, despite myself. I always believed that wherever he was, whatever he was doing, and whoever he was, he would find me, or I would find him. We would find each other, and then everything would finally make sense.'

'And did you find the boy in Newport?' asks Valerie, agitated.

'I called the hospitals in New York but either they wouldn't give me any information or had no patient matching that description.'

'So you never found out who he was or what happened to him?'

I smile.

LEON

22 JUNE 1957

NEW YORK CITY

'What happened? Where am I?' asked Leon. The light blinded him.

'You were in a car accident, but you'll be fine. Try to rest,' his mother said, but the expression on her face said something else. Her eyes were red and she wouldn't look at him when she spoke to him.

Leon's body felt strange, as if it had stopped responding to his commands. 'I can't move. I can't feel my legs.'

'I'll let the doctor know you're awake,' she said and headed for the door.

'Wait,' he pleaded. 'Why is Dad not here?'

She clenched her jaw and took a deep breath. 'I'll go get the doctor,' she said and left quickly.

The room was quiet except for the machines beeping. Leon closed his eyes again and recalled the strange dream he'd had. There had been a girl in the dream, but he couldn't see her face. Behind her was a bright light. He was tired and wanted to leave that place, but the girl grabbed him and wouldn't let him go. She pulled him to her, and her touch felt familiar, warm, and soft. 'Please, stay with me. Stay.'

Her voice was like a song. Like a melody only he heard and understood.

So he didn't leave. He stayed. For her. With her.

Leon heard the door and opened his eyes. JJ stood in the doorway, his head slightly down. His right arm was bandaged and propped against his body, held by a sling. And when he lifted his eyes and looked at Leon, he saw his right cheek was bruised and red.

JJ slowly approached the bed.

'How are you feeling, my boy? You gave us quite a scare last night. The doctors were worried you weren't going to make it. But thank God, you did,' he said in a low, kind voice.

'I can't feel my legs; I can't move them. What's wrong with me? Tell me the truth.'

'The truth,' echoed JJ. 'The truth is you are strong and young, and you will recover. This is the truth. And don't worry. I will not let you fight this fight alone. I will help you with everything I possibly can. We'll beat this. You *will* walk again.'

Leon couldn't respond and tears streamed from his eyes. He was paralyzed. He'd thought as much, but hearing it, said out loud, terrified him.

'What happened? What – what happened to your face? And your arm?'

'Just a scratch, don't you worry about that. You saved my life, that's what happened. And there are not enough words in this world for me to express my gratitude. I will forever be indebted to you, my boy.'

'You don't owe me anything,' said Leon quietly. 'You're family, JJ. You would've done the same for me.'

JJ wiped his tears with the back of his hand. 'In a heartbeat.'

There was a knock on the door. JJ got up and went to see who it was. Leon heard whispers, then saw JJ leaving the room and closing the door behind him.

Someone stood by the door but didn't approach. Someone who was wearing a summer hat. Leon's heart started beating fast. Was it possible? Was it her?

'Zara,' he said, his voice wavering, sounding more like a whisper. 'You're here,' he said a bit louder.

'Of course, I'm here,' he heard, and his heart sunk. 'Where else would I be? I came as soon as I heard.'

Not that he wasn't happy Nicole had come to see him, of course he was, but—

'How are you feeling?' she asked as she pulled a chair and sat next to his bed.

Leon tried to shrug but everything hurt. 'Alright, I guess. All things considered.'

'I was so scared when JJ told me. I knew it was bad news the moment I heard his voice on the phone. I just didn't think, not even for a second, the bad news was about you.'

She looked away for a moment. Nicole wasn't the kind of girl who cried. Actually, Leon couldn't remember a single instance when he'd seen her crying. Not when her mother died, or when she went to her father to hug him at the funeral and he pushed her away, not when she heard Vincent's mother saying all those bad things about her and her father, or when JJ said goodbye to her in a letter from Paris as she was leaving for Switzerland. She was the strongest person he had ever met, at least on the outside. Leon never really knew what was going on in her mind and her heart.

She turned her face to him again and, as expected, she wasn't crying. But she was worried – that much he could tell.

'I'm so sorry, Leon.'

He attempted a smile. Didn't know what to say, really.

'Is what JJ told me true? That you almost died saving his life?'

'You know JJ, always making a big deal out of nothing.'

She jumped from her chair and hugged him tight. Leon grimaced in pain. 'What would I have done without you? Next time, don't be a hero, you hear me? You could've called out for him to get out of the way. You didn't have to throw yourself in front of a speeding car.'

'I don't know if there will be a next time,' he said, his voice trailing off.

'What do you mean?'

'Didn't JJ tell you I might never walk again?'

She raised an eyebrow. 'That's just crazy talk. Of course you'll walk. JJ might not have been much of a father to me, but when it comes to you, he's a bull. He will not stop until you get better.'

'I know he made some mistakes with you, but he loves you. You're his child, not me. He would do the same for you, Nicole, and you know it.'

'Maybe. Maybe he would. Let's hope he'll never have to.'

'Yes, let's hope so.'

'I will let you rest; the doctors allowed me to be in here for five minutes. And only because I lied.'

'You lied?'

She giggled. 'I told them I was your fiancée.' She winked and kissed him on the cheek.

Before she opened the door, Leon called out to her. 'Can you please ask JJ to come back? I need to talk to him.'

'Sure,' she said unenthusiastically.

JJ returned shortly after and approached Leon's bed, looking even more worried than before.

'Nicole said you wanted to see me. Are you in pain? Do you need me to call a nurse?'

'No. It's not that. JJ, I need to ask you…' His voice trailed off. 'Something.'

'Yes, my boy. Anything.'

'The girl. The girl who was there, on the street. Is she…'

JJ smiled warmly and let out a sigh of relief. 'She's safe. You saved her life too, just like you saved mine.'

'She's safe,' he repeated. 'You think I could see her?'

'I wouldn't know where to find her, my boy. I wanted to thank her mother for taking care of you until the ambulance arrived but didn't think to ask for her name. She told me she was a nurse and she sent me to find a telephone booth to call the hospital. I didn't have time to talk to the girl; didn't even get a good look at her. But her mother said she was alright when I asked.'

'Her mother?'

'Yes.'

'A nurse? Then she's not—'

He couldn't continue.

'She's not what?'

'Zara. She's not Zara. I thought – but I was wrong. Zara's mother died and she wasn't a nurse anyway.'

'The girl from Colmar? That was ages ago. Oh, my dear boy.'

'JJ, please, I— Please try to find her.'

JJ stared. 'Alright, please don't work yourself up. I will.'

But he never did. Or if he did, he never told Leon.

ALEXANDER ROBERTS

NEW YORK CITY

Leonard Price Senior died a few hours after causing the accident that almost killed his son. He drove his car off Newport Bridge. 'Guilt,' his wife said. 'Alcohol,' the newspapers wrote. 'Leon, please, listen to me. He was trying to hit me, not you. We think he had been following me for some time. He wasn't thinking straight, and he had no idea we had plans to meet. Your father wouldn't have hurt you intentionally,' JJ said, trying to soften the blow.

'Do not call me that.'

'Call you what, my boy?'

'Leon! I don't want to hear that name ever again.'

'I know you're upset—' tried JJ.

'I am not a child. And no, this will not go away and I will not forgive him, if that's what you were getting ready to say. I don't want his name. I don't want anything from him. My name is Alexander.'

With the same intensity he had loved and admired his father when he was young, he hated him now. For what he had done to him, for not accepting help, for being a coward, for not being who he thought he was. He wanted nothing to do with him.

The media covered the case for weeks. The fraud, the bankruptcy, the drinking, the attempted murder, the suicide. Journalists followed their family day and night, harassing them. His mother wasn't taking things too well either.

'I'm leaving,' she said one afternoon, as she sat by his bedside.

'Going home?' asked Alexander. 'Yes, you should. There's nothing you can do here. The doctors are taking good care of me and JJ refuses to leave anyway.'

'No, I mean, I am leaving the country.'

Alexander didn't expect that and didn't know how to react.

'Like you said, the doctors are doing everything they can, and you're out of danger now. It's just a matter of recovering and whether I am here or not, it doesn't make a difference.'

'No, that's not what I meant.'

'I know,' she said, 'I have to do this, Leon—' She paused. 'Alexander. Just like you are trying to get rid of everything linking you to him, to our old life, I am doing the same. I can't deal with this circus anymore. I can't. I'm exhausted, there's no more money, I'm being watched by journalists all the time, and the people who once looked up to me and envied me for my good fortune have turned their backs on me. Your aunt and uncle are selling their house and moving to London. They have graciously invited me to go with them and I already told them I'd be happy to.'

Alexander took a deep breath and tried not to cry. His mother was leaving him alone again. When he was a child and she didn't oppose him being sent to Europe, Alexander was hurt. It felt like she'd abandoned him. Now she was doing it again, choosing a life without him. How could she leave him like that, in the hospital, not even knowing what would happen to him?

His expression must have betrayed his thoughts, because she got closer to him and took his hand in hers. 'I have no life here. *He* made sure we have no life here anymore. And I want to get as far away as I possibly can. I've never felt more humiliated in my life. You might blame me for running away from it all, but I'm asking you – if you can find it in your heart – to forgive me. To understand.'

'I understand,' he said quietly. Unconvincingly.

'I will of course call you and write to learn news about you and how your treatment is going. I have faith that JJ will do everything he can to help you, or I wouldn't leave you. And, remember, wherever I am, my door will always be open to you, my son. Once I get myself settled in, you can come and stay with me for a while, if you want.'

He smiled sadly.

She got up to leave. 'Oh, before I go, I mustn't forget to tell you I have petitioned to have my name changed back to my maiden name. As long as I am called Catherine Price, I will never be free of this stigma. I suggest you take my name too, if you want to stand a chance at a fresh start. Whether here or somewhere else.'

Alexander agreed and in less than forty-eight hours,

Alexander Leonard Price was no more. Instead, Alexander Roberts lay in a hospital bed in New York, with his godfather by his side, saying one last goodbye to his mother and not knowing if he was ever going to walk again.

Alexander was in the hospital for two months. And during all that time JJ stayed with him. He only left to take a shower and change his clothes and sometimes, following Alexander's repeated requests, he would go home for the night.

Nicole came too, almost every day. She had canceled her cruise with Vincent so she could stay by Alexander's side. She brought him magazines and sweets and entertained him for hours with her hilarious stories about her new friends from New York, and kept talking about the future, making plans for the two of them in New York for the next four years of school.

She even brought Vincent a couple of times, and it surprised Alexander to hear he insisted on coming.

'I'm sorry I ruined your summer,' said Alexander to Vincent on one of those visits.

'It's alright, trouble. You just focus on getting better, then we can all get out of here.'

Alexander smiled. He was making progress, but not as fast as he hoped he would, and the rehabilitation program was excruciatingly painful and difficult.

'There's not much for Nicole to do around here. Why don't you two go at least to Newport if it's too late for the cruise? Spend some time at the summer house.'

'I tried to talk her into it, but there's no reasoning with Nico.'

'You know I'm still here, right?' said Nicole, scrunching up her nose and making a funny face.

'Yeah, well, you are stubborn,' said both Leon and Vincent, agreeing on something for the first time in their lives.

Alexander would've preferred if she had listened to them, because it would've made him feel less guilty about what he was about to talk to her about. All those long hours in the hospital had given him the chance to really think about what he wanted to do. And he'd promised himself that if he ever walked again, he would stop listening to what other people told him he should do, and instead listen to his heart. Because, as he had discovered two months before, life was too short. Too short not to do what you think is right.

He knew his conversation with Nicole needed to happen sooner rather than later, but selfishly kept pushing it back, because he enjoyed her company and was afraid of the outcome. The worst possible scenario was that Nicole would make him choose, but he was hoping it wouldn't get to that. She was his best friend and he didn't want to lose her.

When one day, at the end of a physical therapy session, the doctor who managed his rehabilitation program said, 'It's just a matter of time now. If all goes well, I believe you could take him home as soon as this Friday,' JJ couldn't have been happier. But Alexander knew what that meant. JJ and he had already spoken at length about their plans after his discharge from the hospital. It was time for Alexander to gather the courage and have the difficult conversation with Nicole.

She came to see him that afternoon, but that time she didn't bring any newspapers or candy or anything.

'I just heard,' she said the moment she entered. 'JJ told me. I am shocked he knows how to deliver good news too.'

Alexander smiled thinly.

'You know the first thing that came to mind when he told me?'

Alexander shook his head.

'I was thinking… I know JJ wants to keep an eye on you – because his controlling nature won't let him rest otherwise – but how about you and I talk to him and convince him to let you stay with me? I think I've found just the right place for us and it's got an elevator, so it won't be hard for you to move around. I could take care of you,' she said sounding excited.

'I don't understand. What about Vincent? Isn't he staying with you?'

'He will understand,' she said coldly.

'No man would understand,' Alexander pushed back.

'Ugh, Alexander. Are all men like you?'

He raised an eyebrow in confusion.

'Clueless?'

'I don't follow.'

'You never do and that's always been our problem. I don't want to live with Vincent. I want to live with you,' she said, punctuating each and every word.

Alexander held his breath.

Nicole came back to his bed, took his hands in his and looked into his eyes.

'What I mean, and I think you've known this for a long time—'

He couldn't let her continue, knowing he was about to

do something that would break her heart. He put a finger to her lips and hushed her.

'Before you say anything else, I—'

'Yes?'

'I have something to tell you. And I don't know if prolonging this will make it easier. I am going back to Paris.'

'What do you mean?'

'I am leaving New York. For good.'

Her hands went limp in his. She was obviously in shock.

'Why? I don't understand. We made plans.'

'I know. I know we made plans before all this and I know we said we'd both stay in New York, and I thought that's what I wanted to but a lot has happened and... it's hard to explain but I need to go back.'

She pulled her hands from his.

'Back? Stop saying back. You were never in Paris except for...'

Her nostrils flared. She looked away from him for a few moments and when she did finally look back at him, her eyes seemed watery. 'Does this have anything to do with— No. Right? It can't be. Not after this long.'

He closed his eyes. 'Zara.'

'You're kidding me, right? After everything, after what happened at the graduation, I thought... I mean...' Nicole, who was never without something to say, now seemed speechless. 'Are you sure about this, Alexander? Have you given it enough thought? I think you're making a mistake. There's nothing for you in Paris.'

'I'm sorry. This has nothing to do with us, with our friendship.'

'Our friendship,' she echoed. 'Hah.'

'I mean, we don't have to be in the same place to be friends. Besides, I will visit, and I am sure you will come to visit your father too. And me.'

'Does JJ know?'

Alexander nodded. 'I will stay with him for a while until I figure things out.'

'Of course,' she scoffed. 'He's finally getting the son he always wanted.'

She was hurt. He knew she was hurt and he hated being the cause of it.

'It's the best thing, for everyone. You and Vincent will finally have time for yourselves, and you won't need to take care of a cripple. You're starting school and New York is your happy place – I know it. Your home. It's never been mine. Think about it. This is a good thing.'

'I came back to New York because of you,' she bellowed. 'Not because it's my "happy place". I could've gone anywhere else in the world. I did it for you.' She took a deep breath and seemed to try and calm down. 'It doesn't matter now. You made your choice and there's nothing I can do. So, what's left to say? Have a good flight and a happy life,' she said and, taking her bag, walked to the door.

'Nicole, please, I didn't know. I didn't mean to—'

'You never do,' she said and left.

PART III

'Two hearts in love need no words.' — Marceline Desbordes-Valmore

ALEXANDER

NEW YORK CITY

His mother had been right about JJ. He stopped at nothing to help his godson. When he was released from the hospital, JJ put Alexander on a plane to Paris and moved him into his house where he continued to take care of him. Relentlessly, until Alexander was strong enough to start school and follow his path. And his path always seemed to involve looking for Zara. In every woman he saw, in every museum he walked into. Every voice. Every laugh.

His mother also seemed to be right about one more thing. Her move to London was the best decision for her; at least judging by the letters she sent Alexander. First, his mother's letters came in weekly. In time, they became monthly. And after the phone call letting Alexander know she was getting married again, 'to a wonderful man, so different than your father', the letters were short and far between. They soon got replaced by the occasional postcard, reminding

Alexander of his years at La Rolande. His mother seemed to have everything she wanted. Again. And again, Alexander had no place in her life. But it was easier to accept this time. Perhaps because he wasn't a child anymore. Or because he had been so preoccupied with his own problems since the accident, he didn't have enough time left to think about it. Either way, he wasn't alone. He had JJ and he was all the family Alexander needed.

Three years after the accident and Alexander was finally fully recovered, except for a small twinge in his left leg. Especially when it rained. It slowed him down. He still used the walking stick, just because JJ made him. He was lucky though and he knew it; it could've been much worse. And he still came back to New York for check-ups, with the 'best doctor in the world' as JJ insisted, although that meant he had to fly thousands of miles for it. But if it gave JJ peace of mind, he was willing to do it.

At the corner of East 38 and Third, Alexander and JJ were stuck in traffic, on their way back to JJ's apartment after seeing the doctor. They had just about enough time to pack, have a light dinner, and then drive to the airport. It was time to go back to Paris, to school. The summer was over.

The wind was blowing, and it had started raining. A dense, soaking rain. Alexander raised his eyes from the book he was trying to read and looked out the car's window. It was foggy. He stared at his reflection. The young man looking back had little remaining from the eighteen-year-old self he remembered. Long gone were his James Dean black jeans and long hair, his dark sunglasses and leather bracelets.

Everything was different now. His name was different; his life was different. The next day he was going to be back in Paris; a week later classes would start. His third year at the Sorbonne. He wasn't sure what he would do with his French Literature diploma once he graduated. As long as he stayed as far as possible from business and anything that had to do with his father, he was okay with it.

Alexander wiped the window in a perfect circle, just enough to see the street. On his left, JJ was busy writing down notes for the auction coming up in Paris the next day.

A car honked. A bus stopped and let out people who scurried out of the rain. An older couple on the sidewalk desperately tried to get a taxi. New York, even for five minutes, was dizzying. Paris wasn't quiet either, but it was slower. More relaxed.

Another bus stopped, and more people got off. And for a fraction of a second, just a fraction, he saw someone. A girl in red. Red rubber boots, red trench coat, red umbrella.

'Stop!' Alexander said to the driver.

'What's wrong?' asked JJ. 'You forgot something?'

'I don't know. I—'

The driver pulled over and Alexander got out of the car without a word, leaving his walking stick behind.

'Alexander, your—' started JJ, rolling down the window.

There was no time for all that. 'Stay in the car, please. I'll be right back,' he said and walked away.

He looked left, right. People rushed out of the rain. No girl in red. Only gray everywhere. Had he imagined her? In a way, she reminded him of the girl in Newport. Could they be one and the same? He had to see. He had to know.

And then across the street, he saw a silhouette in red.

If only his leg didn't hold him back. He pushed through, despite the pain, but in a matter of seconds, she disappeared again into the crowd. Alexander continued walking, searching for her. He crossed the street again.

I have to find her, he thought... *I know what I felt. What if it is her? What if it's Zara?*

Seconds turned into minutes. People rushed all around Alexander, out of the rain, to the subway, into buses, coffee shops, office buildings. He saw JJ's car parked on the side of the street, the back window open and JJ staring at him with a confused look on his face.

He dropped his head, feeling defeated and ridiculous.

'Alexander!' he heard behind him, and he couldn't believe it.

Although it had been three years since he had seen her and just as many since he had spoken to her, there was no doubt. It was Nicole. After leaving the hospital that day, she'd simply refused to take his calls and stopped all contact with him. He'd missed her.

He took a deep breath and turned around, not knowing what to expect.

Black suede shoes, a flowy white dress and a white umbrella. So... Nicole. She looked even more beautiful than the last time he'd seen her, like she'd stepped down from a magazine cover.

He smiled. Restrained. Cautious.

Nicole jumped in his arms and pulled him under her gigantic umbrella.

'Millions of people in the city, and I run into you,' she said, all smiles. 'Is this fate or what? What are you doing here? Why didn't you tell me you were in New York?'

If she was just pretending to be happy to see him, she was doing an excellent job.

'I tried. Both JJ and I called you several times in the last month.'

'True, I was a bit busy.'

'In the Hamptons, I heard.'

'Don't – you sound just like JJ,' she said, not trying to mask her disappointment.

He hadn't meant to sound so judgmental. It was her life and she had the right to do whatever she wanted with it. But spending the last three years hearing all about her 'mistakes and bad decisions' from JJ had inevitably influenced his opinion of her.

Alexander laughed, a bit embarrassed. 'I do, don't I?'

She touched his arm. 'It's okay. I forgive you. Anyway, the Hamptons were a bore. I have a feeling JJ's stories are far more exciting and exotic than what truly happens there. He has a flair for the dramatic.'

'He's worried about you,' said Alexander. 'That's all.'

'Ha! He's worried about my name showing up in the press and ruining his reputation – that's what he's worried about,' she said sarcastically. 'It amuses me to see him squirm.'

Alexander was tempted to contradict her, but he didn't. Ever since they were kids, they'd been having this conversation where she accused JJ of not caring and Alexander defended him.

Now, after so many years of watching Nicole and JJ interact – or better said not interact – Alexander had come to the understanding that the truth was somewhere in the middle. JJ did care about his daughter but didn't know how to show it. Didn't know to get close to her, how to build a relationship and gain her affection… except for buying it. After her mother had died, instead of spending time with his daughter, JJ bought Nicole tens of toys and expensive clothes. When she came home for the summer from La Rolande, he paid for extravagant trips that would keep her busy until it was time to go back. Whatever she asked for, he would give her. But the only things he didn't give her were the only two things she truly needed: his affection and time.

And JJ was right too, on the other hand. Nicole did things sometimes just to spite him because she resented him. She did use him and spent his money frivolously, because how else would she make him pay for her suffering? But she also cared about him, although just like her father she had no idea how to show it.

Nicole smiled innocently. 'Anyway, now I'm back, you're here, and the world makes sense again.'

She put her hand on his arm and gazed into his eyes. 'It's wonderful to see you. You look good.'

'You look better,' he said and stopped, afraid it might give Nicole the wrong idea. What was he doing? Was he flirting with her?

'You know what? I had dinner plans, but nothing is more important than catching up with my favorite guy. I'll just cancel them for you. I know a great place where we could go. Just you and me.'

'We actually have to leave tonight.'

'We? As in you and your… girlfriend?'

'Me and JJ,' he said awkwardly.

'Ah, good. You got me worried there for a second. Let me guess, you're going back to Paris.'

Alexander nodded.

'Some things never change. I'll just go ahead and ask then. Did you find her?'

'No,' he said shortly.

'This is a day of great news. I love it,' she said. 'If you can't do dinner, how about we at least grab a drink somewhere? Can you do that much for me?' She stepped in closer. 'I missed you, you know.'

'I missed you too,' he said.

'You did?'

She had a funny little smile in the corner of her mouth. 'How much?'

He leaned down and kissed her on the cheek.

'That little? That's all I get? After three years?' she teased him.

He felt Nicole's warm breath on his face, her sweet perfume in the air.

She looked into his eyes for a moment, then just like it had happened at the high school graduation party, she took his face in her hands. Only that this time, he didn't step back. And she kissed him.

Alexander didn't know how to react. He was surprised but not really shocked. After all, there had been inklings for a long time. She had feelings for him.

'Well, that was worth the wait,' she said and giggled.

Alexander took her in his arms and hugged her tight, trying to buy himself some time. His mind was trying to process everything. And fast. Whatever he did or said, he didn't want to risk hurting her again. How did he truly feel? There was no doubt, the kiss felt good. And Nicole was not only a beautiful woman, but also his oldest friend and one of the most important people in his life, despite their three-year separation. Was it a good idea though?

'What about Vincent?' he asked.

Nicole dismissed it like an afterthought. 'Vincent and I, it was never meant to be. We're not right for each other. Anyway, it's a long story and I don't want to talk about him. I want to talk about us.'

Alexander was quiet again.

Why was he thinking about it so much? What was there to think about? She liked him. There was no doubt about that. It was just that until now he'd refused to admit it to himself because it was too complicated. His heart had always been filled with someone else, and that wouldn't have been fair to any woman he dated.

'Am I making a complete fool out of myself again?' Nicole said, sounding embarrassed.

'No,' he said, not wanting to hurt her again. 'I am probably the fool, not you.'

From the corner of his eye, Alexander saw JJ approaching.

'Father,' she said coldly, before kissing him frugally on the cheek.

'Nicole, what a surprise. Thought you were still in the—'

Alexander interrupted. 'She just got back.'

'I see,' said JJ.

'I've been meaning to call you—' she started but JJ stopped her with a casual gesture.

'It's fine. You're busy,' he said, then turned to Alexander. 'It looks like you two have a lot of catching up to do. I'll just go ahead and pack and I'll see you later. Say, seven o'clock?'

Alexander was tired of thinking. Of waiting. Just tired.

'Yes, I'll see you later, JJ.'

As soon as her father left, Nicole turned to Alexander, 'Where shall we go?'

She was there. She wasn't a dream, a fantasy. Alexander felt ridiculous. A twenty-two-year-old loner, who had never had a proper girlfriend and who, for the last six years, had been waiting. Searching. He was being ridiculous. Maybe Zara had been just a dream. Nicole wrapped her fingers around his. Alexander thought fleetingly about pulling away… but why would he? It was time he moved on.

DOMINIQUE

NEW YORK CITY

Dominique stowed away her small red umbrella and hung the red raincoat Lisa had given her the Christmas before. Dripping water everywhere, she propped her legs on a chair and rested her head on the foggy window.

'This place will not open by itself, you know,' said a deep voice so close to her, she startled and jumped to her feet automatically. The owner. Not the friendliest of people, but not a bad soul either. Just didn't know how to show he was human.

'And clean those windows while you're at it. We don't want people to think this place is abandoned,' he bellowed from behind the counter.

Dominique took a stack of towels and started wiping the glass. Across the street, on the sidewalk, stood a man with a walking stick and his back to her. Dominique felt her knees weaken. Still holding on the towels, she went to the door. Hypnotized.

Turn around; look at me. Turn around, she kept repeating in her head like he could hear her. She walked outside. She didn't care that it was raining, and cold, and she was only wearing a short-sleeve blouse. She took another step towards him. A car honked. And then a woman with a large umbrella covering her face walked up to the man and jumped into his arms. They were a couple. And that woman looked – well, she looked like Dominique never would. Her clothes, her demeanor. Like a princess.

Dominique watched motionlessly as they kissed and walked away together. She stood there, with water dripping on her face and tears running down her cheeks. Her heart crumpled. She felt sad and lonely. And empty.

'What were you doing in New York?' asks Valerie.

'By then I was in my third year at NYU. English Literature.'

'English Literature. Really? How did that happen?'

'When it was time to apply for college, I didn't really know which way to go, but I figured that I would be alright if I followed in my mother's footsteps. It just seemed like the common-sense choice. Besides, books and libraries had always been a part of my life, so, in my young mind, it made sense. And if you're wondering why I was cleaning windows, I got a scholarship and lived on campus, but I worked in that diner, every day after school to make some money. I didn't want to burden Lisa more than I already had.'

Valerie smiles. 'And I'm also wondering about something else.'

'Why New York of all places?'

'Are you a mind reader?'

'No, just old,' I say. 'And yes, a part of me hoped. He'd said he wanted to study business, like his father, and he was from New York. NYU and a few other universities had a business major. All the roads lead there. But it never happened.'

'And now we know why.'

'Now, yes.'

'That day, on the street, did you know it was him? Do you think *he* knew who you were?'

Her eyes are desperate for answers, but some questions are better answered by ourselves. When we're ready.

'I think our hearts knew. But we are rational beings, and it's hard to put away all your fears and doubts and believe in something you can't see. We need proof – that's how we're raised.'

She sits again. I know it's hard to understand and it's frustrating for her. She sees both sides of the story. But I didn't. I only knew my side.

PART IV

'Try to reason
about love and you will lose
your reason.' — Stanislas
Jean de Boufflers

ALEXANDER

5 OCTOBER 1960

PARIS

That evening in New York, Nicole and Alexander went out for one drink, which turned into many more and a three-hour conversation. It was good to see her and spend time together. He knew he had missed her, but only after sitting at that table, across from her, laughing at her crazy stories and adventures, did he realize how much. Nicole had always given color to his life.

'Glitz and glamor,' as she always said.

At one point, she asked him, matter-of-factly, 'What's stopping us now? You're single, I'm single.'

'Well, for one, a few thousand miles,' said Alexander with a laugh.

'Eh, that's nothing,' responded Nicole without even taking a moment to think about it. 'I'll just go with you.'

'You'd do that?' he asked, in disbelief.

'Unless you don't want me to.'

'No, I – of course I would.'

She leaned over and kissed him. Like she meant it.

'Ah, young love,' a woman from a nearby table said. 'Remember when we were like that?'

It was like a whirlwind. One second he was single, searching for a woman in a red coat in rainy New York and feeling his life had turned into a sad, 1940s black and white movie, and the next he was jumping in a yellow cab with flamboyant, beautiful Nicole, rushing to her apartment and helping her pack so she could come with him to France. As his girlfriend.

On their way to Paris and for the first time in forever, JJ didn't seem upset with Nicole. They all sat together, talked and laughed all through the long flight to France. It felt like everything had fallen into place, and like Nicole had said to Alexander just a few hours before, the world made sense again. For all of them.

JJ insisted Nicole stayed with him, just like Alexander, and she didn't fight him on it. On the contrary, she thanked him.

The next night, after JJ's auction was over, he took them both to a restaurant to celebrate winning the painting he had been hunting for half a decade.

'And I have one more reason to celebrate,' he said, visibly emotional.

Both Alexander and Nicole raised their glasses, expectantly.

'I am here with my daughter and my godson, my family and my favorite people in the world, and I couldn't be happier. I didn't think the day when we would all sit together would come anytime soon, and I am beyond thankful.'

When Nicole excused herself and went to the powder room, JJ pulled Alexander close.

'I have always hoped you two—' He cleared his throat. 'You're going to be good for her. Thank you for giving me my daughter back,' he said, his voice shaky.

Alexander smiled and squeezed his arm, trying to suppress the feeling that this was all happening a little too quickly.

It was maybe two days later that he received an unexpected visit.

Standing in front of JJ's door was Vincent.

'Hi,' said Alexander, completely taken by surprise. 'What brings you—'

He didn't get a chance to finish when Vincent's fist connected with his nose. It almost knocked him over.

'What the—'

He put his hand under his nose, which was already pouring with blood. And it hurt really bad.

His first reaction was to punch Vincent back, but he was so shocked, he simply stood there waiting to see what happened next.

'You rat!' said Vincent, his face so red he looked like he was about to burst. 'I could squash you right now. Like the bug that you are!'

Vincent was furious. But, for some reason, Alexander wasn't. He was confused and in pain, but that first instinct to hit Vincent back was now gone, replaced by curiosity.

'Let me know when you're done with the insults, so we can talk. If you tell me what your problem is—'

'What my problem is? What my problem is? Are you mocking me? Do you think you're funny?'

Alexander shrugged. 'I have no idea what this is about. Did I do anything to you? I mean, anything new? Or is this just the culmination of all those years when you passively hated me?'

'I should've given you a proper beating back then. If only I'd known it would come down to this. But you tricked me with your embarrassing story about that girl in France... I really believed you had no intention of taking Nico from me.'

'This is about Nicole?'

'What else do you think this is about? Your pathetic little existence is not worth my attention for anything else. I saw you,' he hissed and his face, which had seemed to go back to a normal color a few seconds before, was now bright red again.

When it seemed like he was about to hit Alexander again, he moved to the side.

'Calm down. You saw me where? Doing what?'

'Don't act dumb with me. I saw you in New York, kissing Nico.'

'So what?' said Alexander, starting to get annoyed. 'You two aren't together anymore.'

Vincent started laughing maniacally. 'Obviously. We're not together now.'

'Huh?'

'Don't pretend like you didn't know. All I got after all these years of being with her was a lousy phone call to tell me she wasn't coming back anymore. That she had come to Paris with you.'

'I don't get it. How—' Then he stopped. 'Wait a minute. You were still together?'

'You're acting dumb again. I don't like it when people lie to my face.'

'Vincent, I didn't know. If this is true, I didn't know. Nicole said—'

'I am not in the mood for more lies. What kind of man are you? What kind of woman would even look at such a man? You're pathetic.'

'Look, Vincent, I'm serious—'

'I should just beat you up and leave you here for dead. The only reason I'm not doing it is because I don't want to go to jail because of you. You're not worth it and obviously she's not worth it either. I am disgusted with you both.'

He turned to leave, then turned back to face Alexander. 'How much fun you must've had, all those years, laughing behind my back. Stupid Vincent, eh? Were you waiting for the perfect moment to strike? You couldn't have done it when we were all kids – no, of course not. It wouldn't have destroyed me enough. Did you two plan this whole thing? How much you must've hated me. But you know what, rat? This will not destroy me. And we'll see who has the last laugh,' he said through his teeth.

Then he shoved Alexander and walked away.

Alexander was shaken up by his encounter with Vincent. Not because he had feared for his life, but because his relationship with Nicole was so new, so fragile. He'd never thought they would start it with a lie. And a lie of those proportions. He decided to take Nicole out for lunch and find out what truly happened, without JJ there to witness it. He asked in three different ways about her breakup with

Vincent but didn't get a straight answer from her. Realizing he wasn't getting anywhere, he had no other choice but to tell her about Vincent's visit.

Her face lost color almost instantly.

'You told me you hit yourself on a door when I asked what happened to your face.'

'I didn't want to cause a scene and involve JJ.' He looked at her. 'Was Vincent telling the truth?'

She shook her head but didn't say anything for quite a while.

'The truth… the truth is he wanted us to get married. We had talked about the future a few times and to be honest, everyone expected us to. Even you, I think. But I knew I couldn't get married to him. The truth is when we met in New York, I was on my way to meet him and end our relationship. I did love him, you see; I did, but I couldn't marry him. I don't even know if I am the marrying type. There was always something that kept me from loving him fully and from seeing myself as his wife. And while it was okay when we were younger, after things got serious, I couldn't go through with it. It just wouldn't have worked out.'

Listening to her talk about Vincent, Alexander wondered if it had been his fault it hadn't worked out between Nicole and Vincent. What if he was to Nicole what Zara was to him? That unfinished business, that childhood love you'd do anything for?

DOMINIQUE

NEW YORK CITY

Months after seeing that man on the street, Dominique still thought about him. She wondered what he looked like. She should've gone to him. At least seen his face. Heard his voice. She had made a mistake. What if it was him? What if the reason she felt the way she felt was because he *was* Leon? What if she never got another chance?

She was just a couple of weeks into the second semester of her third year at university when, one night, she had a dream. A reverie. She recognized the special dreams. She was sitting on a wooden bench, in a large, rather cold room. In front of her was a painting covering an entire wall. A blue, purple, and green painting. She had never seen it before, but the style was familiar.

She woke up troubled by the dream. It was him. He was somewhere, looking at that painting. Or was it all in her imagination? Was she driving herself crazy?

The next night, she had the dream again. Only that this time, it was dark outside and the room was lit by soft yellow lights. The painting. It was so beautiful. A tree. Yes, the green in her dream was a tree. And the blue was water. A tree by the water.

She stared at it, but instead of feeling happy, she felt lonely. Directionless.

She woke up.

The next night, the same thing happened. Dominique knew she couldn't ignore the dreams anymore. She had to find out more about the painting. What if it was at the Met or somewhere close? What if he went there to look at it and she found him there?

Dominique went to the library, not knowing what to look for at first. She had the painting memorized. It was only a few minutes into looking at a catalog of paintings at the Met when she realized why that painting seemed familiar. She recognized the style. It was a Monet. She asked the librarian for help in finding all the museums that had Monet paintings on display, but it proved to be a much harder task than she thought. There were hundreds if not thousands of museums, all around the world.

She looked at New York museums. Nothing. Other American museums. No, it wasn't there. The next logical place for a Monet painting, the one that should've been the first step: France.

Day after day, she looked for it, in all the catalogs and eventually, she found it.

Water-Lilies, Reflection of a Weeping Willow. The Louvre, Paris.

She didn't need to think about what to do next. It was

all clear now. Dominique ran back to the campus and called Lisa.

'Please, don't be mad at me. I know what I'm about to do is hard to understand. But I have to do this.'

She explained to Lisa what had happened. Her aunt didn't encourage her, but she didn't try to stop her either. Over the years, they had had so many conversations about the dreams and her belief that he was somewhere out there, that Lisa knew not to try and convince her.

'Are you dropping out of school?'

'To be honest, I don't belong here. I tried, but it's not for me.'

'Then what is for you?'

'Not sure, but I hope this trip will give me the answers I've been looking for. I've felt so lost for such a long time.'

'All I ever want is for you to be happy, Dominique. If going back to France is what you need, I will support you. Do you need money? How will you pay for your ticket?'

'I have some savings from my paychecks. It's not a lot, but it should get me to Paris. And with a bit of luck I'll have enough for a room somewhere.'

'Out of the question. Go live with Constance. She'd be happy to have company.'

Constance's husband had died a year before. He was found stabbed in a back alley in Montreuil. The police said he owed money to the wrong kind of people. He did owe money, money that Constance had to give back after his death. To banks, to creditors. Their situation was not at all as good as he'd painted it to be. They were drowning in debt.

'Yes, I could do that,' said Dominique, relieved she didn't have to be all alone in Paris.

'What if you can't find him?' asked her aunt.

'I will keep trying until I do,' said Dominique, finally feeling she was fighting for what she wanted. 'I should've done this earlier. Much earlier.'

'You were just a child, honey. Look, do what you think you need to do, and should you decide to come back, I'll be waiting for you, alright?'

Dominique packed that night and camped out in the airport until the next flight to Paris.

She was going to find him. It was meant to be. Just like her mother found her father.

ALEXANDER

1 DECEMBER 1960

PARIS

It was December now and they had been together almost three months.

Nicole was bigger than life, as she had always been. Bubbly, chatty, she occupied the majority of his time. When he wasn't at school, he was with her. And she always had something planned for them. He couldn't complain about getting bored, because every day with her was different.

Nicole made friends easily – she always had – and soon Alexander found himself surrounded by Paris socialites, dragged to brunches and dinners, whisked away to Chamonix for weekends of ski, and Monaco for wild parties. These people, although there was nothing wrong with them, weren't necessarily friends he would've picked for himself. He didn't feel like he belonged in their world. Yes, he'd never lacked for money. But it was different for them. Their lives revolved around money, and they had a fondness for fast cars, expensive clothes, luxury boats and houses.

One evening he was lying on the bed, almost too exhausted to move after one of Nicole's socially active days. She'd taken him to a brunch with her friends, then shopping, then to dinner with other friends. He barely escaped a night out. She lay on the bed next to him, and he turned to her.

'We're so different, do you realize that? You love the attention, the glamor, the fast life. Just like your friends. I don't... not really. Why would you ever want to be with someone like me?'

Nicole smiled. 'Do you remember when we were kids, and we used to lie on my bed like this?'

He nodded.

'And do you remember talking about growing up and what we would do?'

Leon remembered parts of it. It was such a long time ago.

'We used to say it would just be you and me against the world. And we said we'd live in an apartment just like our parents, one with tall windows that overlooked the Empire State Building. And we would get many dogs and cats and—'

He started laughing. 'Dogs and cats,' he repeated as he continued laughing.

'That's not funny,' she said.

'We were seven,' he said, a bit more serious now. 'What did we know about the world?'

'We knew enough,' she replied and kissed him.

So he thought to himself, *I'll try harder. Because she deserves it.* It wasn't her fault he was the way he was.

'Prickly', she teased.

The truth was, it was more than that. Alexander often felt troubled and tormented. And when that happened, and he sensed the sadness coming, he didn't want to be surrounded by people. They made him tired. He preferred to be alone. Sometimes, when he felt that and he couldn't escape, he'd just stop whatever he was doing and leave. He'd go to one of his favorite museums, either the Louvre or Marmottan, sit on a bench in front of a painting and, for some reason, it made him feel better. The silence. The peace. It was comforting. It had happened many times before Nicole came back into his life and it continued to happen now.

He didn't know why he couldn't be happier. His life wasn't bad. He was doing well in school, he loved JJ and spending time with him, he lived in a beautiful house in the middle of Paris, and now he had Nicole; he wasn't even alone anymore. But, still, the sadness came. And the questions. The doubts. Was he doing what he was supposed to be doing? What was missing from his life? It was like a permanent void, a longing for something he couldn't define.

One evening, in late December, when he came back from the Louvre, still sad and convinced nothing could make him feel better, Nicole took him in her arms. And he felt less lonely. When she kissed him and told him she loved him, he said it back. His mind told him it was right. It was a thing that made sense. Their relationship made sense. She was there; she cared for him. And he did care about her immensely. She had always been his 'person'.

DOMINIQUE

19 JANUARY 1961

PARIS

Constance was waiting for Dominique at the airport. She looked much older than her age, had lost a lot of weight and her once beautiful, round face was dried out like a raisin. She kept her hair in a braid down her back, tied with a black bow, and she wore a simple, modest black dress with long sleeves, and a gray coat. At only thirty years old, Constance looked defeated.

They exchanged brief pleasantries then headed to the metro that took them to Constance's house. It was the only thing left to her by her husband that she couldn't sell. Nobody wanted it. It was too run-down. The house was split into two separate, small apartments, on the second and third floor and on the ground floor there was a gloomy-looking coffee shop.

That night, sitting in bed in the studio Constance put her in, Dominique couldn't fall asleep. After tossing and turning for a few hours, she went downstairs to the coffee shop, where she had noticed some books on a shelf in the corner. Anything to occupy her mind. Sitting in the dark, looking out the window, Constance was so absorbed by her solitude she didn't hear Dominique walk in.

'Are you alright?' asked Dominique softly.

'You startled me! How long have you been standing there?'

'Not long. You can't sleep either?'

Constance shook her head. 'I haven't been sleeping for over a year now, not since—' and it sounded as if the thought alone was too painful for her.

Dominique didn't need explanations; she knew what her cousin felt. She'd felt it too, after her mother had died. She still felt it now, although not quite as often.

'How did you find your room? Do you like it?' asked Constance, absentmindedly.

'Yes, it's wonderful,' said Dominique unenthusiastically. 'What's going on with this place? Is it closed?'

She looked around. It seemed abandoned. Old, broken furniture, paint peeling off the walls, only a lightbulb near where the bar should've been, Dominique assumed.

'Unfortunately, yes. It needs repairs and I don't have the money for it. The banks are after me as it is. Oh, how I wish—' she started but stopped, almost looking embarrassed.

'What?'

'When we first got married, my husband and I talked about transforming this place and bringing it back to its old glory days. You know, back in the Forties, before the war, it was a wonderful place where people from all over the world gathered. They drank wine, ate the best Parisian food, listened to music, danced. It was my dream to make it happen again.'

Her dream. Nobody could help Dominique make her dream happen, but she could help her cousin.

'I'll get a job. Two jobs. I don't need much money. We'll put everything aside for the café. And we can talk to the people at these banks. We can explain.'

'Because bankers are so understanding? They don't care. They need their money.'

'Then we'll work harder.'

'Why would you do that? I thought you would be mad at me for not taking you to Paris when Zahara died.'

'It wasn't your fault and it doesn't matter anymore. I want to help. It would make me happy to know I did something good.'

Constance had tears in her eyes.

'Thank you. You don't know how much this means to me.'

Before walking up the stairs, Constance stopped and turned to Dominique like she'd remembered something.

'And maybe we can sell the house too,' said Constance.

'What house?'

'The one in Colmar. The rent we charge is barely enough to cover the house expenses. It's better if I just sell it. It's just another money pit.'

'No!' said Dominique fiercely.

That house was full of her happiest childhood memories – the home she'd shared with her mother. Dominique had always hoped one day she could go back. Maybe to visit. Maybe for good.

'Please, don't sell the house. I'll get six jobs. I'll do whatever it takes. Just please promise you won't sell my home,' she begged, a tear running down her cheek.

'Oh, I'm sorry,' said Constance. 'I didn't know it meant that much to you.' She came over and gave Dominique a big hug. 'I promise. We'll find another way.'

ALEXANDER

COLMAR

Alexander was getting ready to go to the Louvre, when he spotted a letter on the hallway table. It was addressed to Leon Price, at La Rolande, and forwarded to him by Mr Pillay, his former tutor and art teacher.

Dear Mr Leon Price,

It has come to our attention that one of the rare books in our collection, Monet's Impressionism, *was mistakenly assigned to the public space in December 1954, despite having an owner, and was delivered to us for display in the Unterlinden Museum's library.*

Please accept our sincerest apologies for the inconvenience this might have caused you.

The book is in our possession and we would gladly turn it over to you, if presented with acceptable proof of ownership. We apologize for not being able to mail the book but given the limited number of copies and its value, an in-person delivery is the only option we will entertain.

Yours truly,
Ivan Goldman
Unterlinden Museum Curator

He couldn't believe it had been found. Not only that, but it was in Colmar, in their museum. *Their* museum. How wonderful that sounded. The more he thought about it, the more he realized a painful truth. Despite saying he had left Zara in his past, that he hadn't thought about her, that the Colmar episode was just a memory for him, he had been lying to himself. Just the thought of something that had a connection to her made his heart beat like crazy. He wondered if maybe she had something to do with that sadness he couldn't shake, no matter how much he smiled, how good a day was, or how well his relationship with Nicole went. But she couldn't have anything to do with how he felt now, could she? Not after all those years. That was madness.

Yet, mad as it was, he didn't hesitate for a moment to plan his trip to Colmar for the next day and to talk to JJ about it.

He knocked on his door, knowing he was always in his study in the evening.

Alexander told JJ about the letter and the book. 'I'm going to Colmar.'

'Why do I have a feeling this is not just about the book?'

Alexander looked down.

'Maybe it's not.'

'Then what is it?'

'I don't know, JJ. I wish I had an answer. I thought I was over it. Over her, but—'

'Over her – you mean Zara.'

Alexander nodded.

JJ tried to say something, but Alexander didn't give him a chance.

'I know what you're going to say. Please don't. Just let me talk first,' he said, all in one breath.

'I'm listening.'

'I'm still thinking about her six years later. Six years. Not a month. Not six months. Seven years, JJ. Nicole is amazing. She is smart and beautiful and I love her. But what I felt for Zara – what if I never feel like that again for anyone? I guess I'm just looking for answers.'

'Oh, Alexander,' said JJ, smiling. 'It's normal for you to remember her now, because of the book and Colmar. What you and Zara had was lovely, but that's the key here. It was. It passed. Nothing but a fleeting moment. Besides, I didn't want to tell you then because you were infatuated with her, but the truth is you couldn't have been in love with Zara. Not really. That's not how love works. Love takes time and work. You talked to her once and exchanged a few letters. You didn't even see her. It was no more than falling for a character in a book, and God knows, we've all done that at one point in our lives. Love needs to be palpable. You need to be able to explain what it is that makes you love someone. Just like you can explain to me why you love Nicole. That's real.'

'I'm not saying what Nicole and I have is not real. Of course it is. It's just different.'

JJ sighed. 'Alexander, my boy, I'll be honest with you. I

never imagined we'd have this conversation now, after all these years. I was sure that story had ended. Forever.'

'I thought so too,' Alexander said.

'Listen to me. I have more life experience than you do. It is rare that the first person we have feelings for is the one we end up with. Especially if these feelings seem more like an obsession. You need to let her go. Focus on the future.'

'What if you're wrong?'

'What if I'm not and you're throwing away your relationship with Nicole for nothing more than a fantasy? I love you and Nicole both, and you can't ask me to sit around while you're breaking my daughter's heart. She has her flaws, God knows, but she doesn't deserve this. I was so happy to see you and her together. She's better because of you. She's calmer, nicer even. She smiles more. She's back in my life and I don't want to lose her. I know this sounds selfish, but the two of you make a beautiful couple and I believe you'd have a great life together.'

'I know all this,' said Alexander. 'I don't want to throw away my relationship with Nicole. She means so much to me. I wouldn't do anything to hurt her. I'm not doing anything. I'm just going to Colmar to get my book back. That's all.'

JJ nodded, unconvinced.

'Does she know?'

'Not yet. But I will tell her.'

'I normally wouldn't encourage lying, but maybe in this case, you should keep it to yourself. Why put her through all that? If all you're going to do is go there, get your book and come back, no harm done. If something else happens, she will know anyway. You will have to tell her. So, if you really feel you must do this, do it. I'll just tell her I sent you somewhere to recover a painting. Go; get it out of your system. And maybe then you can put it behind you. For good, this time.'

Alexander looked down and closed his eyes for a moment. 'I'm sorry. I realize how all of this must sound to you. I wish it was different. Do you think I want to be this conflicted?'

'Then why do this to yourself?'

'It's hard for me to explain. I'm having a hard time explaining it to myself. I know she's part of my past. But she's a part I can't let go of. No matter how far away I am, how much time passes.'

Alexander hugged his godfather and left.

The next morning, he went straight to the train station, got himself a ticket and by four in the afternoon he was in Colmar.

Inexplicably, he was hopeful. But at the same time, he feared an end. *The* end.

He went straight to the museum, where the curator was waiting for him.

'How did the book end up at the Unterlinden?' asked Alexander.

'It was discovered by the conductor on 1 September 1954, when the train stopped in the Colmar Station and was taken to the Lost and Found office.'

'I see,' said Alexander. Incredible. Of all the places on that route, it had to stop there.

'I assure you, everyone followed protocol,' said the curator, sounding defensive. 'The SNCF waited ninety days for the book to be claimed and only then did they contact us and ask if it was something we were interested in.'

'No, no, I'm sure you did everything by the book,' Alexander said, amused.

'You see, we also took every means of precaution and perfectly preserved it,' said the man, sounding almost proud, and showed Alexander the book. If by preserving, he meant covering it with plain yellow paper, then yes, he had done a marvelous job.

'Everything is in order?' the curator asked, watching Alexander as he inspected it.

Alexander's eyes stopped on the two sets of initials. L.P., then A.P.

'Yes, everything is perfectly fine,' he said.

'Now, let's go through the formalities, and the book will be back with you in no time.'

He recovered *Monet's Impressionism*, after a bit of an adventure because of his name change. But, luckily, he thought of bringing documents along and also offered JJ's number for confirmation. In the end there was no need for the call because the curator accepted his proof of ownership. And now, the book was finally back with him.

Straight from the museum, he went to Rue des Jardins. Finding himself in front of her house again, all the old feelings came rushing back as if they'd never left.

He rubbed his hands together and ambled to the front gate.

The house didn't look abandoned, although the mailbox was full – a few days' worth at least. But the lawn was cared for, there were flowers in the garden. He saw a curtain moving, and his heart started beating like crazy. Was it Zara? Had she come back?

Alexander rang the doorbell until an old woman came down the steps.

'I'm sorry to bother you, I'm looking for Zara.'

'Who?' asked the old woman, looking curiously at him.

'Zara Ionesco.'

'They all moved out, young man, years ago.'

'And they never came back?'

'Would you come back from Paris to live here?'

'I would,' he murmured to himself. 'Do you by any chance know what happens to their mail?'

The woman shrugged. 'If it's house related, I open it so I can pay the bills with the money we get from rent. The rest, I put in the study. Nobody seems to be using that room anyway. Too many old books, too much dust.'

'I see. Could I come back later to leave something for her?'

'I just told you—' she started but Alexander didn't let her finish.

'I understand. I would still feel better if I left it with you. Maybe she will come back someday.'

The woman shook her head sadly. 'I doubt it.'

'I'll return shortly,' said Alexander.

He walked back to the museum and with a strange little smile on his face he sat on a bench in the yard, took out a pen, opened the book and started writing. He felt the inside of his coat pocket, got out a small notepad, and wrote some more. When he was done, he put the note inside the book and stayed there, looking at the museum. Somehow, someday...

When he felt strong enough to say goodbye to their magical place, he went to a nearby store, bought a large envelope, put the book inside, sealed it and went back to Zara's house.

The old woman unwillingly took the package.

Alexander had hoped there would be a chance, but deep down he'd known she wasn't going to be in Colmar. If only one day she would come back, find his package and then she would know. She would understand. He'd always hated the thought that she left thinking he didn't care about her. It broke his heart, when all he wanted was to see her, when all he felt was for her. If only she knew.

DOMINIQUE

PARIS

The next morning, Dominique grabbed the paper, looking for jobs.

She went to several interviews. Secretary, archiver, baker, seamstress, librarian.

It was a long day, and as the sun set, she found herself walking towards the Louvre. Where she'd wanted to go all day long. The reason she'd come to Paris in the first place.

Going from room to room, she finally found it. The dimly lit hallway, in the west corner of the museum. Three paintings on the walls. One of them, the willow Monet.

In front of it, the bench from her dream.

She was there, where *he* had been so many times. Her dreams told her. Dominique sat, where he sat, looking at the painting and waiting. An hour. Two. It was getting late.

She got up to leave when she heard footsteps. Her heart pounded.

Someone was coming her way.

Dominique walked to the painting across from the Monet, pretending to look at it.

The footsteps stopped. A man showed up in the archway and Dominique held her breath.

A tall man with dark hair. Dark hair, like the boy in Newport. What a curious thought.

'Oh, hello,' he said in a gentle voice. 'I didn't know anyone else was in here.'

'Hello,' she answered, hearing her voice like it was someone else's.

She took a better look at him. He had something noble about his manners and way of speaking. And he was handsome. He was a bit older than her, olive-skinned with big, round, kind eyes. He wore thick-framed eyeglasses and an impeccable black suit that gave him a smart, chic look.

Dominique blushed, realizing that she was studying him.

'Are you alone? Waiting for someone?'

She smiled. 'I'm—'

'I'm sorry. I didn't mean to pry.'

'Don't apologize,' she said, looking into his eyes and hoping to see or feel the certainty. Was it him? Her mother said she would just know. But how could she be sure?

'Are *you* waiting for someone?' she asked.

'For you.' He laughed, not taking his eyes from her. 'No, I work here. My family owns one of the Louvre wings. We're big into arts. Our house is—'

She interrupted him. 'Filled with paintings.'

'Yes,' he said and smiled. 'And sculptures, drawings. How did you know?'

Her heart thumped. It looked like it was him. What was

she expecting to feel? For the rest of the world around to cease to exist? To see fireworks? Hear music?

'This might sound strange,' she said, pausing to look for the right words, 'but did you go to school in Switzerland?'

He tilted his head and looked at her intensely.

'I did. Yes,' he said apprehensively.

'Do you remember a trip to France? Colmar? A field trip to the town library and—'

'When our teacher almost called the police? That was quite an adventure,' he said, laughing.

Dominique tried not to cry.

'How do you know all this?' he asked. 'Did we meet when I was in school? We did, didn't we? And I don't remember. That's why you were looking at me like that.'

'Leon, it's me,' she said, her eyes brimming with tears.

He opened his mouth to say something, but no words came out. He looked like he had seen a ghost, which was probably how Dominique looked too.

'You don't remember? The museum in Colmar,' she said, her voice cracking.

His eyes grew big. 'Oh my God, Zara! You're Zara.'

She didn't even try to stop the tears from running down her face now. She was happy. She had found him. Finally, she had found him. What more certainty was there? It was him. After all those years...

'You're beautiful,' he said. 'I didn't think you would be this beautiful.'

Dominique blushed. 'You are very handsome too.'

He smiled. 'I know we just— I mean, is it too forward of me to ask you to accompany me for dinner? To talk? I'd love to, if you want.'

He seemed unsure, all of a sudden. And nervous.

'I would love that,' she said without hesitation.

They walked to a nearby restaurant, where he got them a table in the back of the dining area, after chatting for a moment with the hostess.

'We'll have more privacy here,' he said.

Dominique smiled as he took her coat and pulled her chair.

It was surreal.

'Zara,' he said and from the way he said it, it was clear he felt the same way. 'I can't believe it's you. It's so… incredible, isn't it?'

'It is,' she said smiling. 'You know, nobody has called me Zara since Colmar.'

'Isn't that your name?' he asked.

'It was a nickname. My mother used to call me that. Her name was Zahara, and since everyone kept saying how much we looked alike, she started calling me Zara. You know, like a mini version of her name.'

'That's nice,' he said. 'I always assumed it was your name. Then what is your name?'

'Dominique,' she said. 'Dominique Gardiner.'

He smiled. 'Dominique. I like it.'

He played with his water glass for a moment, like he wanted to say something but didn't know how to.

'You know my name is not Leon either, right?'

'It's not?'

He chuckled. 'What kind of name is that? No, just a nickname. Don't even remember where I got it from. Maybe because, as a kid I was always brave; like a lion. That was such a long time ago. I'm still brave, though. I can prove it to you,' he said and grabbing a fork from the table, got up like he was waiting for an imaginary enemy.

'No need to, I believe you,' said Dominique.

She was about to ask, but he probably already knew what she was thinking.

'My name? Vincent. Vincent Saint Germain.'

With an ample gesture of his arm, he bowed to Dominique, then took her hand in his and kissed it gently. 'Enchanté, mademoiselle.'

Her cheeks were on fire, and she knew she had blushed again. There was something about Vincent, something over the top, almost theatrical. He didn't seem to care if people were staring or that he made a fool of himself. He was charming and amusing, just different than what she imagined he would be. Leon from the museum was a bit more restrained. No, not restrained. He was just different. But she was undoubtedly different too. Wasn't she?

By the end of the appetizers they had covered the first years of their lives. By the end of the first course, they had almost reached present day. He was asking most of the questions, with a curiosity that surpassed even Dominique's. What did she do after she left Colmar, where did she go, how did she end up in Paris?

As she was telling him about her life in America with Lisa, Dominique hesitated for a second before asking him.

'Were you in Newport four years ago?'

'I don't think so, no. Why?'

'No, you'll think I'm crazy,' she said, embarrassed.

'I won't. I promise. Tell me.'

And she told him. About the boy across the street, the accident. How she had thought it was him. He'd had black hair, just like him, but she hadn't been able to make out his features because of how badly he had been injured. And how she'd looked for him, but to no avail.

He listened to her without saying a word. After he finished his glass of wine and poured another, he smiled and assured her that while he didn't think she was crazy or anything like that, it hadn't been him.

'What about a year ago in New York?

'I was in New York, yes. Why? What happened there? Don't tell me it was another accident, because that wasn't me either.'

'There was this woman. And you were kissing her. I mean, I don't know if it was you. I thought it was. Or I felt as if it was, to put it better, but again, I couldn't really see your face.'

'What did she look like?' he asked, deep in thought.

'Blonde, tall, very elegant. Like a model.' She felt a tinge of jealousy just remembering that moment.

His eyes fixed on her. 'In front of the Empire State Building?'

Dominique gulped and nodded.

'You were there too?' he said, almost to himself. It sounded like disbelief, more than anything else.

'So it was you!' said Dominique, not knowing if she was glad he'd confirmed it. 'Who was she?'

His eyes avoided hers for a second. 'Nicole,' he said in a low voice.

'Who is she? Is she your—'

He gave a wry laugh. 'Was. It's ancient history. She's

destroying someone else's life now. Not that I feel sorry for the guy. He deserves it.'

Something in his eyes made Dominique uncomfortable. His anger – almost hate – towards that man and woman she knew nothing of made her wonder what they had done to deserve it. It must've been something really bad, because the Leon she knew wasn't the type of person who hated someone for petty things.

'I'm sorry, that came out wrong. Now you must think I'm this hateful, vindictive person, when in fact, I'm not.'

'I didn't think that,' she said kindly.

Dominique was relieved, but again, just the idea that he had been with someone else, and she'd stood there and watched them kiss made her heart break a little. Although, what did she expect? That he was going to wait for her all his life? Just because she had?

They shared dessert and had one more glass of wine.

'Did you find it?' she asked, all of a sudden.

'Find what?'

'The painting. The Monet.'

'The Monet. No. I have plenty of other Monets now. My parents own quite a few.'

It was strange seeing him brush it off so quickly, when it had been his biggest dream, but a lot had happened in the last seven years. He wasn't a kid anymore.

It was late when they finally called it a night.

Vincent took her home and behaved like a perfect gentleman.

Before they said goodnight, he took her hands in his and looking her straight in the eye, asked, 'Are you disappointed?'

'Disappointed? In what?'

'In me? Am I different to what you expected?'

All through their romantic dinner, through their flowing conversation, the laughter and the stories, she felt something was different. But she was so caught up in the moment, that she didn't stop to think about it. She didn't want to. When he asked, in a way, it confirmed what she had been feeling. It was different than what she thought. Not that *he* was different – though maybe he was – but what she felt or what she thought she would feel was different. But she didn't tell him. She couldn't tell him. It would've broken his heart.

Here she was, standing in front of this man she had dreamed of for so long, and instead of being out-of-this-world happy, she was questioning everything.

'I could never be disappointed in you, Leon,' she said.

'Vincent,' he corrected her gently.

'Vincent.'

'I wondered when Grandpa Vincent would show up. I was getting a bit worried there. I knew your meeting had to be something special,' says Valerie with a dreamy look on her face. 'And he was so handsome when he was young. I saw the photos.'

'Yes, he was,' I say. 'And very elegant and charming. But out of my league, as you young people say. Way out of my league.'

Valerie chuckles. 'Nobody is out of your league, Mamie.'

PART V

'One always returns
to one's first love.' —
Charles-Guillaume Étienne

DOMINIQUE

1 MARCH 1961

PARIS

The day after they met, Vincent waited in front of her house with a big bouquet of red roses. Standing in the middle of the street, honking the horn again and again and again on his perfectly white sports car until she came out, he seemed like the embodiment of Prince Charming in her mother's fairy tales. He was dressed the part, he looked the part, and even the way he wouldn't take his eyes off her was like something out of a book.

Dominique rushed out. 'Everyone is staring at you,' she said in a hushed voice.

'Let them,' said Vincent, with a laugh. He always seemed so comfortable in his own skin. He handed her the bouquet, and she felt the light touch of his fingers against hers.

'They suit you.'

'Thank you, they're beautiful,' she said, her cheeks aflame.

He then went around the car and opened the door for her. 'Are you ready?'

'Where are we going?' she asked as she sat on the passenger seat next to him.

'It's a surprise,' he said and smiled.

After a short drive, Vincent told Dominique they were about to arrive and asked her to close her eyes. She did. A couple of minutes later, the car slowed and came to a stop.

'Can I open them now?'

'Not yet,' he said.

She heard him leaving the car, then taking something from the trunk. 'I'll be right back.'

A minute passed. Two. Dominique desperately wanted to peek but managed to keep her eyes closed despite the temptation.

'Alright,' she heard Vincent say. She heard the sound of her door opening and then she felt his hand taking hers.

He helped her out of the car.

'Voila,' he said. 'You can open your eyes now.'

'Wow,' was all she could say, standing in front of a beautiful castle. 'Where are we?'

'Château de Vincennes. And it's all ours for the next few hours. I thought you would like to have lunch here. I brought some things,' he said with a large smile and showed her the picnic basket and a blanket.

'Is that for us?'

'Yes,' he said. 'But I didn't know what you wanted to eat, so I packed a bit of everything.'

Not letting go of her hand, he led her through a narrow path, across the castle's grounds, and onto a private clearing.

It was like a small park. Not far from them, under a gazebo, a group of musicians were playing classical music.

He sat the basket down and laid the blanket. They say next to each other, admiring the castle and listening to the music.

'This is—' she started but stopped, looking for the right words. 'Amazing. You do know how to impress a girl,' said Dominique and laughed quietly.

'You like it? Is it a good surprise?'

'Like it? I love it. Thank you... for bringing me here and putting all this together. I've never been to a château before. Never even seen one up close.'

'I'm happy you're happy,' he said, taking her hand in his and kissing it gently.

It was ten days after their first date, and just as many outings, when one evening, as they were sitting on the beach at Les Calanques de Cassis near Marseille, admiring the sunset, Vincent wrapped his arms around her, pulled her close to him and kissed her. Their first kiss was passionate. She had been waiting for it for years, dreaming of it. Dreaming of that moment. Yet, after it happened, instead of silencing all her doubts and questions, their first intimate moment fueled them. The kiss was great, and Vincent was an incredible man, there was no doubt about it, but still something kept her from giving her heart to him, unconditionally. Something she didn't know how to explain.

'You are a fascinating woman, Dominique,' he said, looking at her intently, and kissed her again. 'I can't get enough of you. I didn't think I would feel this way so soon.'

Although it didn't feel soon at all for Dominique, she loved hearing that. She had feared he would perhaps feel the same doubts she was feeling or decide that grown-up Dominique was not as interesting as young Zara and end their relationship. But he didn't seem to have any doubts at all. About her, or about them as a couple.

'Where have you been all my life?' he asked jokingly one day as they kissed.

Dominique just smiled. Her first instinct was to say, 'looking for you', but she couldn't say it. Why, she didn't know.

They started seeing each other all the time. That Sunday, he took her to Comédie-Française and then to a fancy dinner. It wasn't even a month since their first date when he introduced her to his family. Then to his friends. Gifts followed. And the first weekend with his parents at Chamonix, in their chalet in the mountains.

Vincent made it easy for Dominique to fall for him. What was there not to love about him? He was every girl's dream – educated, handsome, intelligent, attentive. He made her feel like she was the only woman in the world, the only person who mattered to him. He opened the door for her, pulled out her chair at dinner, gave her his jacket when she was chilly. He listened to her carefully, even when she was making small talk, and took her seriously. And he never seemed to be tired of hearing about her interests and passions. It made Dominique feel special. Cared for. Loved.

She was happy with Vincent. When they were together, she smiled more, she felt surer of herself. He gave her that confidence, that support she needed.

Being with him, holding his hand, kissing him, hearing

him say, 'I love you. You are everything I ever wanted,' felt so good. It didn't make her heart race like she imagined it would when she was a child, but it felt amazing. She didn't need to feel butterflies in her stomach every time he kissed her to know she loved him. To know he loved her too and would do anything for her.

When sometimes at night she would sit in bed, staring at the ceiling, and her thoughts would trail off, she'd stop them. What was there to think about? They were meant to be, weren't they? The dreams said so. Her mother said so. Dominique had no idea what her mother meant by 'you will know', other than what she was feeling. And that was enough. She knew he was good for her, they had a great time together, and she could see herself with him. When he talked about their future together, she could picture it. Their children, their perfect life. That was all that mattered, right?

When Vincent heard Dominique was looking for a job, at first he was against it.

'You know, you shouldn't be working at all,' he said, looking concerned. 'I am wealthy enough that you will never have to worry about anything for the rest of your life.'

Dominique smiled. 'I like to work. It makes me feel useful. Besides, Constance needs my help. It's not just about me. It's my family.'

'I could give her the money,' he insisted.

'I appreciate that, I really do, but this is something I truly want to do for her.'

'Very well then,' he said, sounding unconvinced.

Dominique knew he wanted her to be happy, so he wasn't going to fight her too much on it. 'I'll keep an eye out for a nice, clean, easy job.'

'I don't mind getting my hands dirty or working hard,' said Dominique.

'But I mind,' he said, gently pulling her into an embrace. 'Let me take care of you.'

DOMINIQUE

9 DECEMBER 1961

PARIS

'I have just the right thing for you. You love books and art and I think I found the perfect place,' said Vincent one evening when they were driving to his parents' house for dinner. 'I know the owner of the biggest bookstore in Paris: Galignani's.'

'I've heard of it. Do you think I should try and apply for a job there? I don't have much experience but—'

'I have already talked to him and recommended you for a position. In the beginning it's going to be bookstore assistant, but with your knowledge of art and talent, I am sure you will do great there.'

Dominique leaned over and kissed him on the cheek, excited. 'Thank you. You don't know how much this means to me.'

'I do,' he said with a smile. 'And I'm happy I could help. And one more thing.'

'What more could it be? You've done enough already,' she said, not trying to hide her gratitude.

'I have also talked to a friend of the family. He's a banker in the 8th arrondissement and he will review Constance's existing loans to try and find some solutions. He's the best in his field. You can rest assured that if anyone can help her, it's him.'

'You are a wonderful man, Vincent Saint Germain. I am a lucky girl,' she said, smiling through tears.

'You know as well as I do that I am the lucky one,' he said and caressed her hand lovingly.

Dominique was happy with her job at Galignani's. Surrounded by art books, she taught herself everything there was to know about painters, Impressionism and Monet. Always Monet. The job paid well, it wasn't a hard job, and she didn't have to work long hours. On the contrary, it left her plenty of time to spend with Vincent and also to help Constance, who had slowly started to clean up the old café. The bank agreed to extend the loan and even gave her additional funds – clearly all thanks to Vincent's intervention. And with the money from Zara's job and Constance's waitressing, there was hope now. It wouldn't be easy or fast but if they kept at it, one day it would happen.

One morning at Galignani's, Dominique finished arranging the books and stepped back to admire them. Perfect. She moved on to the next shelf. *What is going on here? Constable can't sit next to Turner. They will kill each other. Monet and Manet, no, no, no. Who put them together?*

She went downstairs to the storage room to bring back more books and albums when she heard the bell, a sign someone had come into the bookstore.

'Can you please locate order number 812 in Monday's delivery?' the owner asked her through the intercom.

'Right away,' said Dominique and went to the 'hold' shelf.

She found the book, wrapped in brown paper. 'Order 812 – prepaid,' it said on the hand-written label. *Discourses on Architecture* by Viollet-le-Duc.

Dominique smiled. It was the first time someone had bought that book since she took the job. She grabbed it and was on her way up when she met the owner's daughter on the stairs.

'Do you have it?'

Dominique stared. 'What?'

'The book my father asked for.'

'Yes, it's right here,' said Dominique showing her the brown package.

'I'll take it,' she said and pulled the book out of Dominique's hands.

'It's alright, I'm sure you have better things to do,' insisted Dominique.

'I said I'll take it,' said the owner's daughter and grabbed it from her.

Dominique went back downstairs, feeling disappointed. She wondered what'd gotten into her. She wanted to see the person who ordered that book. Not a lot of people were passionate about Viollet-le-Duc.

A couple of minutes later, the owner's voice came even louder through the intercom.

'Come up, will you? The customer is also asking about *Monet's Impressionism*.'

Really? The same person? First, Viollet-le-Duc, now *Monet's Impressionism*.

She ran up the stairs, almost tumbling and falling.

'Too late,' said the owner and made a gesture towards the door. 'He was in a rush.'

Without thinking, she rushed outside, looking for a man holding the brown paper package under his arm. No sign of him. Something about that moment gave Dominique pause. The coincidence of it. The pairing of the two books. The feeling she had inside. Of loss. Like she'd just missed something.

ALEXANDER

PARIS

Back from Colmar, Alexander was struggling more than ever. He didn't know if it was his trip to Colmar, or the letter he'd written to Zara, but something in him was screaming. What was he doing? His life didn't look at all how he'd imagined. And the Sorbonne wasn't turning out to be what he had hoped for either. Or he wasn't the same anymore. In the last year, he had felt more and more detached, less motivated, less sure of himself and of what he wanted to do with his life. He'd thought he wanted to teach literature, write a book, or be a book critic but his heart wasn't in it.

Lately, that nagging feeling of not belonging and of living someone else's life kept him up at night. And now, it was acute. Suffocating. It had gotten so bad he had considered dropping out of school, even though he was so close to getting his diploma.

One winter day, a few weeks into his last year at the Sorbonne, Alexander made up his mind to not finish the semester. He would quit school and take some time to think things over, decide what he wanted to do next. He packed his things with the rush known only by someone who had made a hard decision and was trying to carry it through before they changed their mind.

As he stuffed his bags with clothes, books, and photos he stumbled onto a small wooden box that had been sitting underneath some old papers on his bookshelf for the last few years. His heart raced. The mere sight of it brought back such strong memories and feelings.

Alexander pulled the curtains to the side to allow more light into his room and carefully opened the box. In it, yellowed by the passing of years, were letters, postcards, notes, newspaper clippings. Some letters were his own, never sent. Among them, the twenty-eight letters he wrote while in detention at La Rolande. He didn't have the strength to open them. The others, though, those he knew by heart; he had read them many times after he had received them and even more after she disappeared. They were all from Zara.

Alexander opened one letter, then another and another, and the more he read, the more his smile widened.

Everything he needed to figure out was right there in front of him. Clear as day. Alexander held the letters close to his heart and whispered, 'Thank you, Zara. Thank you,' as he unpacked his bags after weeks of being in limbo.

In her letters, besides Bartholdi, Zara kept mentioning Viollet-le-Duc – the diocesan architect of Paris, famous for his creative restorations of buildings throughout France.

Why hadn't he thought of this before? Of course. Art

restoration. Art. Hadn't that been his real dream all along? Finding lost paintings? He didn't do it for his father. He did it because it made him happy and Zara knew it. She'd known it from the beginning.

And he could do so much more than just being a painting detective. He could save lost paintings from oblivion.

Alexander immediately called JJ and told him.

'Ecole des Beaux-Arts,' said JJ, without hesitation. 'You could easily transfer and make up for credits. This is perfect, Alexander. You've made me so happy.'

He was happy too. For the first time in a very long time.

Making an impact on the world, ensuring the next generations got a chance to marvel at the fantastic creations of days past. That was something that made him feel excited about the possibilities. Making an impact by preserving centuries of history, by salvaging priceless and unique works of art.

He wrote down 'restoration', grabbed a jacket, and ran down the stairs. Went to the school library and found the name of the book he was looking for, *Discourses on Architecture* written by Viollet-le-Duc, but they didn't have it there. A colleague suggested he ordered it from Galignani's.

'Please locate order 812,' the bookseller said while holding a button on the desk.

'Right away,' a woman's voice answered.

Alexander's head snapped back. Something in her voice gave him pause. He had a strange feeling in his stomach. For some reason he couldn't take his eyes off the side door.

A young woman with long brown hair and bright, inquiring eyes walked through the door seconds later.

'This is for you, Monsieur,' she said and gave Alexander the Viollet-le-Duc book.

Alexander took it and hesitated for a moment. 'T-thank you,' he stuttered.

Was it the same woman whose voice he'd heard earlier? He couldn't tell. It could've been the same but distorted by the intercom. Although standing in front of her now, looking into her eyes, he didn't feel anything. And when she gave him the book and their hands accidentally touched, still he felt nothing.

'Your name wouldn't be Zara by any chance, would it?'

It wasn't the first time he'd asked a woman that. He knew it wasn't her, yet...

She seemed confused. 'No, Monsieur. My name is Florence. Can I help you with anything else?'

'Do you have a catalog of art books?' asked Alexander.

'Are you interested in something in particular?'

'Monet. I want to know if you have *Monet's Impressionism.*'

'I can help you look for it,' said Florence, but the owner interrupted them.

'Our bookstore assistant is quite the Monet expert. Let me call her.'

'Ah, Father,' said the young woman, rolling her eyes.

While he waited, Alexander thought he saw a copy of *Monet's Impressionism* and grabbed it with trembling hands. Alas, his mind was playing tricks on him. It was just a random book. What did he expect? That Zara had sold the book to a bookstore? Why was he still looking for it?

He'd found his copy, given it to her, and gotten his closure. No, he had to stop. Enough was enough.

The man pressed the intercom button. 'Can you come up, please? The customer is asking about *Monet's Impressionism*.'

He was ridiculous: asking random women if they were Zara, seeing the book everywhere. He had to stop.

'No need, sorry to have bothered you. Thank you for the book, but I have to go,' he said, and left.

Alexander hesitated for a second in front of the door, without knowing why, his hand still on the handle. Then he let go and walked away.

DOMINIQUE

PARIS

It had been a year since Dominique moved to Paris. She loved Vincent, her job, her small studio overlooking the Eiffel Tower, and Constance and her dedication to Le Petit Coin café. She had a good life and she was happy, so why was she still having those dreams? Those reveries? She thought they would stop once she found Vincent, but they didn't. She dreamed of museums, the Louvre, and of walking along the Seine. Of late nights sitting on a terrace and looking at the sky. Of paintings and sometimes faraway places. Why did she dream of Vincent in Milan when she had just said goodnight to him in Paris? The dreams didn't make any sense anymore and all they did was to confuse her and make her overthink everything, all the time.

How she wished her mother was there to advise her, to explain to her how it all worked. To comfort her and tell her it was normal, that they were perhaps just regular dreams.

Dominique tried talking to Constance about it, but she acted like she had no idea what the dreams were and quickly ended the conversation.

So she called Lisa.

'You know me and these dreams. I'm not much of a believer. I've always thought there's an explanation for everything. Maybe you dream of Milan because you want to go visit, and of museums because you love them so much.'

Although not much help with the dreams, Lisa did give Dominique something to think about.

For a while now, she'd had this lingering feeling that something was missing from her life.

Almost like a sense of purpose. She enjoyed the bookstore and wandering the Parisian museums and looking at paintings, but sometimes when she noticed other people, mostly tourists doing the same thing, she felt small. Like she wasn't leading the life she was supposed to. What if there was more to it than arranging books? She was proud to help people and see their joy when they got a book they had been looking for, but she needed more. Perhaps she could do something with her art knowledge. But what? There was no obvious choice she could make.

One night, she had a dream. She was walking on a street close to the Louvre, and she could see its massive gates in the corner of her eye. Then she stopped in front of a boy who was handing out fliers and took one. The writing wasn't clear; all she was able to read was 'January and June'. 'This has your name all over it,' she heard before she woke up.

The next day, Dominique kept thinking about the dream and in the evening, after work, she went to the Louvre.

She walked around, until she thought she found the exact spot from her dream. But there was no boy there with a stack of papers in his hand. Disappointed, she went back to her room at the Louvre. The secret room with the Monet. Vincent wasn't there. He had left that morning for Milan, to review some paintings.

She sat on the bench for quite a while. When she got up to leave, she spotted something under the bench. A piece of paper. She picked it up.

Ecole de Louvre

*Become an Art Curator at the world's largest
art museum*

*Imagine yourself responsible for the biggest
Impressionism collection in the world*

Classes start in January and June

She stared at it.

Art curator? Impressionism?

Dominique was elated. It was all so obvious. So simple. Why hadn't she thought of it before? Among other things, art curators did restorations like Viollet-le-Duc. And she would work on Impressionists.

Maybe Lisa was right and there was an explanation for all her dreams. Just like she was right that Dominique loved museums. Whether she'd had the dream because subconsciously she wished to do something with her life that involved museums, or she had the dream for some other reason… Either way, it had led her to the answer she had been looking for.

Dominique rushed home.

'Constance, where are you? I have news, big news!'

'What's going on? Did we win the lottery?' asked Constance.

'Better than that. I know what I'm going to do.'

'Do with what?'

'My life.'

Constance laughed. 'I thought you already knew. You'll marry Vincent, you'll have beautiful children, a big house, and everything will be perfect.'

'No, I mean what I'm going to do with *my* life.'

'Isn't that your life?'

'We're all meant to do something in this world. I think you are meant to restore this café and become the most beloved chef in the whole of Paris. France, even.'

Constance smirked.

'And I am meant to become the best art expert in France. Why not?'

'And how are you going to do that?'

'I'm going to Ecole de Louvre.'

'They have a school at the museum?'

'The best art school in the country. In Europe. In the world.'

'I thought that was Ecole des Beaux-Arts,' said Constance.

'Not if you want to be a curator.'

'And you want to be a curator?' she asked, somewhat amused.

Dominique nodded excitedly. 'I will study museology and art history, and yes, it will take me quite a few years, but this is it for me. This is what I want to do. I want to learn all there is to know about art, and there's no better place for it. And guess what? Classes start in a few days.'

'Dominique dear, where did this come from? This new idea of yours? Don't tell me. One of your dreams?'

Dominique smiled innocently.

Constance sighed. 'When will you understand dreams are dangerous? They only lead to disappointment.'

'Are you speaking from experience?' Dominique snapped.

Constance looked away.

'Wait a minute. Did you have these dreams too?'

'I don't want to talk about it.'

'Constance,' pushed Dominique.

'I said I don't want to talk about it.'

'I should've known. Lisa had them too when she was young, but she chose to ignore them. Of course you had them as well.'

Constance made a dismissive gesture with her hand. 'Even if I did, I *chose* not to listen to them. Just like my mother. Not everyone can be like you and live in a fantasy. Here on Earth, the rest of us struggle with petty things like surviving, having money for food, looking out for our family.'

'That's not fair. You and Lisa are all the family I have, and I do my best to help. And I will not stop, just because I go to school.'

Constance's face fell. 'I'm sorry, that was mean. You are helping a lot and I wouldn't be here if it wasn't for your support. The café would be just a dream.' She got up to leave then stopped. 'You know, we're not just cousins.'

'What do you mean?'

'My mother adopted you. We're – we're like sisters, aren't we? And sisters are supposed to stick by each other,' she said and hugged Dominique. 'If this is really what you want, go for it. Whether it came from a dream or not.'

DOMINIQUE

9 DECEMBER 1962

PARIS

B ecoming an art curator was no easy feat. Four years of studying and internships at various museums in Paris just to get the degree, then eighteen months of full-time apprenticeship at art institutions in Île-de-France through the Institut du Patrimoine. Those were six years of her life she would dedicate to studying and there were no guarantees she would get a curator position when she was done. There were only a handful of spots every year and over two hundred art students fighting for them. More knowledgeable art students. Better prepared. With years of art classes behind them, and wealthy and influential families who supported them.

But that didn't stop Dominique. She threw herself into her passion, with all her energy, and when she wasn't working or helping Constance, she studied and read as much as she could. She was going to make it. No matter what it took.

In October, at the end of the second semester at Ecole de Louvre, she was in the top three in her class. Because of her excellent results, she was given a choice between the Louvre and Marmottan for a three-month museum internship, and managed to surprise everyone when she didn't go for the obvious. Marmottan meant more to her than ten Louvres, but how could anyone understand?

One morning, on her way to the mezzanine of the museum for her daily archiving tasks, she noticed a door that usually stayed locked was now slightly open. She hesitantly went in.

The walls were covered in paintings, sketches and drawings, all nicely framed.

'They are lovely, aren't they?' she heard and turned to see an older man behind her.

'I'm sorry. I...' she said apologetically.

'No need, young lady. I don't mind company.' He looked at her for a moment. 'Have we met before?'

'No, I don't think so,' said Dominique.

The man nodded, then walked around the room, hands behind his back, looking at the paintings. He stopped in front of a pile of unframed artworks and browsed them.

Dominique approached him. 'This is the Fontainebleau Forest, isn't it?'

'It is indeed; you have a good eye,' he said, sounding a bit surprised.

'It is not signed. I wonder who the artist is,' said Dominique, mostly to herself.

'Any guesses?'

Dominique carefully checked out the paintings on the

walls. Then went back and forth between them and the small unsigned canvas a couple of times.

'It's a Cezanne,' she said, sounding like she'd had a revelation.

'Is it?'

'I believe so. Although it looks like a painting from his early years because of the heavy brushstrokes and thickly layered paint on the canvas. See how the texture of the composition is visible to the naked eye? The only thing that doesn't match is that early in his career he was mostly doing studio work, not landscapes. Apart from that, it all lines up: the dark shades, the violent nature of the view and angle. It is a Cezanne,' she said all in one breath.

She smiled, embarrassed, and felt foolish for jumping in and showing off like a schoolgirl.

'You do know your art, young lady,' he said.

'Dominique. My name is Dominique,' she said, smiling.

'I will surely remember that name.'

The museum's curator showed up in the doorway. 'JJ, I've been looking everywhere for you. There's someone upstairs who is dying to meet you.'

The old man took a small notepad from his shirt pocket and wrote something on it.

'If you're ever looking for a job as an art dealer, come see me,' he said and left the room.

The note said:

AngeD'art
Rue de l'Exposition no. 8, Paris

She had heard that name before. AngeD'art. The man

who was running the company, Jean Jacques D'Angers, was a legend. Jean Jacques. The curator had called him JJ. It must've been him. Even Vincent's mother, Margaux Saint Germain, spoke highly of him, and she was rarely impressed by anyone. He was to art people what the Louvre was to museums. The top of the top. But Dominique had no plans to become an art dealer. She wanted to be a curator. There was no place for her at AngeD'Art. She wasn't in it for the money. Yet, she couldn't help feeling proud she'd made such a good impression on a man like him and the meeting gave her confidence.

As soon as she finished archiving, she went to the curator and asked him for the Cezanne nobody wanted to touch.

'I know I'm just an intern, but I'm asking for a chance to prove what I can do.'

He said no. The next week she asked again. And again. Until he finally said yes.

All because of Monsieur D'Angers, she thought. *I hope I get to thank him one day.*

ALEXANDER

9 DECEMBER 1962

NEW YORK

When JJ offered him an initial one-year contract in the New York office, after he graduated from Ecole des Beaux-Arts, Alexander felt he had no other option but to accept.

Alexander knew he had a long way to go to make his dreams come true. For now, he was caught between what his godfather wanted for him and what he wanted for himself. JJ kept pushing him towards continuing his career with AngeD'Art and even though he wouldn't admit it, he was training Alexander so he could one day take over the business. Alexander didn't want to disappoint his godfather, but he wanted to stay true to his dream as well. He imagined dedicating his life to restoration like Viollet-le-Duc did, which ultimately meant he wasn't about to be JJ's successor. Alexander knew this was a delicate matter and he kept postponing having *that* conversation.

JJ was the second generation to preside over AngeD'Art, and he had worked hard to get to where he was. When he was young, he established his reputation as a scholar and art historian when he became involved in authenticating the works of dominant French, English and Spanish artists. He took over the management of the New York and Paris branches in 1935, the year his father died. Over time, JJ added galleries in Santorini, Tokyo and Milan. Under his leadership, the company became one of the most recognized and respected in Europe and North America, but without a proper successor, it would all go to waste. JJ wanted to make sure it ended up in good hands, and his mind was made up on Alexander.

Alexander shadowed JJ for the first six months, then, as time went by, he took on more and more responsibilities. They went to numerous auctions around the world and without realizing, Alexander started becoming what JJ had wanted all along.

As the end of his year in New York drew close, Alexander got ready for his first solo art transaction. Monet: *Waterloo Bridge, London*. It was a raving success.

'If you continue like this, the Paris office will soon be yours. I've been looking for someone to manage it for years,' said JJ with a big grin on his face.

Going back to Paris. Yes, he definitely wanted that. He missed France. As much as he liked New York, there was something about Paris that pulled him back in.

On Alexander's birthday, Nicole called and asked for a favor: 'Please go pick up the painting JJ had delivered at the

Metrier Gallery in SoHo. It's urgent; he needs it tonight for the auction.'

He was surprised JJ hadn't been in touch himself and even more surprised she cared about the company's business. Maybe it was a sign she was willing to give it a shot. He would've loved to work with her. She was smart and even as uninterested as she was, she proved to have a keen eye for valuable works of art. As if it was in her blood.

Alexander rushed to the gallery.

'Surpriiiise!' he heard from all corners of the massive room. The place was filled with work colleagues, Nicole's friends, artists – over a hundred people. Nicole jumped into his arms and kissed him as everybody sang 'Happy Birthday'.

'I have something for you. Wait here.'

She rushed to the corner of the room and from behind a curtain she picked up a large, flat box. 'Happy Birthday,' she said.

He tore open the paper. It was a Joaquin Sorolla. A painting titled *Fifth Avenue, New York*.

'I thought it was only fitting that you have a New York painting of your own, to remind you of our first kiss,' she said.

'Nicole, you shouldn't have. This must've cost a fortune.'

'Who cares?' she said giggling. 'Do you like it?'

'Of course,' he said.

He did like it and he was moved by her generosity, and he didn't let it show that he felt a bit troubled, all of a sudden; unknowingly, she had reminded him of what he was actually doing that day on the street. In the rain. Before his first kiss with Nicole.

That whole evening, that over-the-top extravaganza, though not what Alexander would've chosen for himself, touched him. This beautiful woman, who could've had any man she wanted, had chosen him. She wasn't running from him, she wasn't enigmatic, she wasn't hiding somewhere in the corner of the world, far from him. She wasn't some childhood fantasy. She was Nicole. And she was his. And it seemed like she was the best it was ever going to get for him. Perhaps it was time he started thinking about their future together.

PART VI

'We love truly only when we love without reason.'
— Anatole France

DOMINIQUE

PARIS

First Annual Fundraiser and Charity Ball
Wednesday, 9 December 1963
Château Saint Germain, Île de France
Starts at 18:00, Attire black tie
RSVP

Château Saint Germain was about sixty kilometers south of Paris in the middle of the Fontainebleau Forest. It took Vincent, Dominique and Margaux over an hour to get there, but still they made it before anyone else.

The moment she stepped out of the car, Dominique's jaw dropped. The hundred-acre park surrounded by water was like something out of a fairy tale. In the Saint Germain family since the thirteenth century, it was a castle in the true sense and it was epic, inside and out. From the oak furniture, priceless paintings, large marble stairs, chandeliers and ballrooms for hundreds of people to the Roman sculptures, romantic fountains and perfectly trimmed trees. For Dominique it was magic. For Vincent and his family, it was just one of the few dozen properties they owned around the world. Nothing special.

When Margaux told her about her project, back in the autumn, Dominique asked why she wasn't joining the Louvre initiative. They were already doing an annual charity event. But Margaux was determined. She wanted to help French struggling artists, not just raise money for museums. She would try and sell their artworks to wealthy, influential people in her circle.

Her circle was not so keen to open their checkbooks for donations yet again though, so soon after the Louvre. And when her assistant suddenly quit, less than three months before the event, and moved to London, Margaux had asked for Dominique's help. She'd gladly accepted although almost nothing had been done and at the same time, she had to help Constance finish restoring the café, and her exams were coming up at school.

The two of them spent countless evenings thinking of a plan. Sometimes Vincent would join as well, when he wasn't busy with the other family businesses. They sent letters all around Europe. They curated the list of paintings for weeks, made catalogs and brochures, made countless phone calls and Vincent even took several trips to Italy, Spain and Greece to try and convince people to come. There were some RSVPs, but not enough to make a difference and there was no way knowing if they had succeeded or not, but to go through with the night.

'You look beautiful tonight,' said Vincent, looking at her admiringly.

'Thank you,' she said. 'You don't look too bad either.'

He laughed and kissed her.

'I love you,' he said.

'I love you too,' she answered, and when he took her in his arms to kiss her again, she jokingly pushed him inside. 'You have to go. We have a schedule here.'

At six o'clock, a dozen people came. A few minutes later, more. And more. And more. Dominique and Margaux greeted the guests at the entrance, while Vincent waited for them inside, showed them around, told them how the night would unfold, and offered them drinks.

Within an hour, there must have been almost three hundred people inside, so they had to open two more rooms to accommodate all the guests.

'Already more donations than the Louvre got all night, and we've barely begun. We did it, Dominique, we did it,' said Margaux, visibly pleased and excited.

'We sure did,' said Dominique, smiling. She was proud of what they had accomplished.

She grabbed a glass of champagne and went on another tour of the room. There were still people they hadn't talked to, and Vincent couldn't do it all by himself.

Dominique took a step and stopped like something held her in place. Had someone called her name? She turned and looked around. Faces she recognized, others she didn't. But nobody seemed to pay particular attention to her. Another step. That presence; it was overwhelming. A pressure in her chest like something was taking her breath away.

She found herself searching, without knowing what for. She was about to turn around when a large group in front of her broke out into two smaller groups.

In the middle of them, a man. Staring at her.

When their eyes met, it was as if a void ate everyone else. They were the only two people there and nothing and nobody else mattered.

There was something familiar about his presence, something that wasn't possible, really, as if she had been longing for him, missing him, without even knowing it. Why was he looking at her like that? Why couldn't she turn her eyes away from him? What was this feeling she had? It wasn't nervousness, she wasn't scared, yet her heart beat out of her chest. Who was he?

A head above everyone else, he had spiky-looking hair, was a bit scruffy, and had a lopsided smile, almost like a smirk. He seemed oblivious to everything around him, like it didn't interest him in the least: the company, the food, the glass of wine in his hand, the conversation. People moved around, left and right. He stood still like a statue. Looking at her.

Then a couple stopped in front of Dominique. 'Beautiful evening, isn't it?' the man said.

Dominique slapped a big smile on her face and nodded, all the while trying to peek behind them. When they finally moved away, he was gone.

Out of nowhere, almost like magic, he appeared in front of her.

Up close, he took her breath away. Those eyes. They were almond-shaped, and the color was like the sea. No, like evening clouds. Sapphire. Spellbinding. Hypnotic.

They both stared but neither of them said anything for what seemed like an eternity.

He took yet another step towards her and not letting go of her gaze, whispered in her ear, 'I've never seen anything more beautiful in my life.'

He smelled like summer rain and cinnamon.

Dominique gulped. Her breathing accelerated. 'Excuse me?'

He smiled and pointed at a painting on the wall by the door.

'Who said contemporary artists are not as talented as the masters? How much do you think it will go for?'

His voice was bewitching. Not too deep, not too high. Serious somehow. But not too serious. Perfect.

'That one is not for sale and it's not contemporary either. It's *Bocca Baciata* by Rossetti. Over a hundred years old.'

He smirked or maybe it was just his way of smiling. She didn't know.

'Is it now?' he asked.

Silence again. Staring into each other's eyes.

It should have been awkward, but it wasn't. It was tense. Just being there with him felt forbidden somehow. Dangerous.

'Are you here to bid on paintings?' she said.

With a certainty she had never experienced before, he took her hands in his.

What was he doing? Who did he think he was? She didn't even know him. And there were people around. She pulled her hands and backed off, but he didn't seem bothered.

Dominique didn't want to admit it even to herself. But his touch felt so right. Like it wasn't the first time their fingers had come together. No, it was like she knew him. She knew his face, his voice, his perfume. Those amazing eyes. Yet she didn't. She was sure she had never seen this man before.

What was going on with her?

Her body was reacting to him in a way she couldn't explain. Like it recognized him.

He leaned down. Their faces were close now, so close that Dominique felt they were one, not two people anymore. Their bodies almost touched.

His lips. So close to hers. His breath on her cheek.

'I think I know why I'm here,' he whispered in her ear.

She looked into his eyes. *I think I know why I'm here too,* she wanted to say but couldn't. *I'm here because of you.*

'There you are,' she heard behind her and recognized the voice. It was one of Margaux's friends. He backed off.

Dominique turned. 'Madame Laurent,' she said, feeling ashamed. Like she had been under a spell.

'Look at you, Mamie. Even now you're blushing. And they say people in the old days didn't know how to have fun,' chuckles Valerie and winks.

'I had never done anything like that ever before.'

'Yes, yes. It's called lust,' she says and grins.

'It wasn't that. It was beyond physical attraction. I lost control of myself and it both scared and fascinated me. If he'd asked me to run away with him that very moment, I would've. Without hesitation.'

'Naughty Mamie,' teases Valerie. 'Read on. I want to know what happened next.'

'I've been looking everywhere for you, darling. What a marvelous night, isn't it? Oh, I'm sorry, did I interrupt?' asked Madame Laurent, and Dominique turned back to the man, but he was gone.

The woman took her arm as they walked towards Margaux. 'Who was that fine gentleman?'

'I don't know,' Dominique murmured.

She was telling the truth. She didn't know. And yet... she did. She knew something. She felt something, although she didn't understand what. A certainty. Peace. Home. A memory.

'Well, as long as his pockets are wide, he's welcome,' she said and winked.

'Vincent!' exclaimed Dominique. How long had he been standing there? Had he seen what happened?

'I was about to come looking for you. We just got a major donation,' he said, taking her in his arms and showing her a check.

She looked at it blankly.

'Aren't you happy?'

'Oh, no. I am. Of course I am. That's wonderful.'

Suddenly his expression changed.

'Everything alright?' asked Dominique, turning to see what he was looking at.

A woman was coming towards them. A doll-like face, light blue eyes, long blonde hair, and a sparkling golden dress with a deep cut that showed off her long legs. She was the kind of beautiful that made both men and women turn their heads. There was something familiar about her; about the way she handled herself, the way she walked.

The woman ignored Dominique, came straight at Vincent, and threw her arms around his neck. 'Vincent, dear,' she said in a flirtatious tone.

He took a step back. 'What are you doing here?'

She grinned. 'Aren't you going to introduce me?' she demanded.

Vincent grabbed Nicole's arm, turned to Dominique and said, 'I won't be long.'

'What was that all about?' Dominique asked Margaux, watching them walk away. 'Who is she?'

'Nicole? She's trouble, that's who she is. I don't like her around Vincent.'

'That is Nicole? His ex-girlfriend Nicole?'

Margaux smiled. 'It wasn't serious, don't worry. She wasn't good for him.'

'She's beautiful,' said Dominique.

'Beautiful but troubled.'

'I'm sure she's not all that bad. Vincent dated her, after all.'

'Everyone makes mistakes,' said Margaux.

Suddenly, Dominique found herself wondering what would happen if things didn't work out between her and Vincent. Especially after what had happened that night. Would Margaux tell the family and their friends the same thing? 'Who? Dominique? A troubled woman. Just another mistake he made.'

'I need to get some air,' Dominique said to Margaux, trying to sound casual.

'Of course, dear. You're feeling alright, I hope. Don't let Nicole bother you. She's nothing but a distraction. You're all he has eyes for. I raised a smart man.'

Dominique wasn't as preoccupied with Vincent and Nicole as might've been expected because her mind was somewhere else. With someone else. Him. Who was he? Why did she feel they were there to meet each other? How was that even possible when Vincent was the man she'd dreamed of ever since she was a teenager? Her mother told her there could be only one. What was happening to her?

That man, whoever he was, in just a few minutes, seconds even, had made her feel things she didn't know she was capable of feeling. Things she'd never felt for Vincent.

Dominique stood on the terrace, watching the snow fall on the perfectly trimmed trees, and a shiver went through her body. It wasn't just the cold, no, it was more than that.

Suddenly she knew why she'd pulled her hands from his. Why she'd backed off when he came too close to her. Not because of Vincent. Not because of Margaux. Because she was afraid. Afraid of her own reactions. Of what she would do had he tried to hold her hand again. Had he tried to kiss her.

The truth was, before that evening, she'd thought what she had with Vincent was the best it was ever going to get. That the love she felt for him was everything her heart was capable of. But now, she questioned everything.

Yes, with Vincent, there were no butterflies in her stomach or weak knees. There was no longing. But there were other things. Important, big things. She had a future with Vincent and it looked secure, even perfect. Just like him.

Yet, that night, everything she thought she wanted didn't seem to matter anymore, all because of that man. That man who could've been a random stranger off the street. She would've given it all up for a chance to look into his eyes, for a minute with him. For an embrace. A kiss.

ALEXANDER

PARIS

After taking over the Paris office in the spring, Alexander's life became even busier. In the last nine months, he'd had enough of art charities to last him a lifetime. JJ took him everywhere. To auctions, negotiations, gallery openings, charities, even estate sales. They had traveled the world twice over and JJ had no intention of stopping or even slowing down. It kept Alexander away from Nicole, and neither of them liked it. They missed each other and tried to talk on the phone every few days. But she was lonely and was getting a bit tired of it all, despite being kept busy by her countless friends. He was tired too, of planes and hotels and always being on the move. But he was looking forward to the next trip, because it would be an extended one – two or three months – and it was New York and Nicole was coming with him.

When he received the invitation from Margaux Saint

Germain, he wanted to decline. He had just gotten back from Milan and was exhausted. Besides, who was to say Vincent wouldn't be there? Of all the people he was looking forward to seeing again, Vincent was probably at the very bottom of his list.

But JJ, who had his own agenda involving a Degas and a reclusive and stubborn owner, insisted. Alexander was to convince the man to consider selling it.

'I wish I could go, but my meetings are probably going to run late in the evening, too late for me to make it in time. Please go and try to seal this deal.'

Nicole had insisted too.

'We can't miss it. Everyone will be there. It'll be our last social in Paris before we leave.'

'We're only going away for three months. Not forever.'

'Maybe, maybe not. So, are we going? Are we? Pleeeease,' she'd said in a catlike voice.

And now the two of them were standing, hand in hand, in front of the castle.

She always looked amazing, but that night Nicole had taken it to the next level.

'I'm going to have to guard you tonight,' said Alexander jokingly. He wasn't the jealous type, he'd realized since the two of them started dating. She turned heads wherever they went, and he felt proud, rather than anything else. Proud to be with such a beautiful woman.

'You'd better,' she teased him. 'Who knows what might happen?' She kissed him. 'I love you. Now I have to go mingle, and you have to schmooze that collector guy.'

'I love you too,' he said.

The moment he entered Château Saint Germain,

Alexander, with a restless certainty, knew something was about to happen. Something was about to change.

He tracked down the Degas art collector and was talking to him when he saw her. He tried to look away, but he couldn't help himself.

Then she disappeared from view, and he thought that was the end of it.

In front of him, a large group were discussing the merits of charity and how if those artists couldn't afford to make a living out of their paintings, they should get a day job like everyone else, and not beg for money. Alexander almost intervened, but the group dispersed before he got a chance to.

And when it did, behind them, he saw her. Again. And this time, he didn't look away. He couldn't. She was calling to him, like a siren, like a dream.

She was stunning, bewitching. A beautiful girl, but not in a forced, artificial way. She wasn't trying too hard. She just was. With curly red hair down to her shoulders, she looked like a flower in a pale yellow dress that complemented her luminous green eyes. There was something about her, something that drew him in like magic.

Their eyes met, and a warm feeling came over him.

She was otherworldly. Standing in front of him, not looking down, not looking away. Just standing there and staring at him. Like she was there on purpose. Like she was there for him.

It was bizarre how in a way she reminded him of Zara, although there was no reason for that. He didn't even know what Zara looked like. And it had been ten years. Why would he think of Zara now? She also made him think of that day in Newport. Of that girl with the sun hat. The girl whose life he'd saved and who'd saved his life in return. It was like this red-haired beauty, whose name he didn't even know, was the embodiment of all the girls who made up his heart and soul.

Alexander didn't hear what people were saying. He didn't feel time passing.

All he wanted to do was look at her, hear her voice, hold her hand. Kiss her. Yes, kiss her. It was beyond him. He couldn't control it.

He didn't remember walking to her, or what he said or how they ended up holding hands. But he remembered what he felt. So vividly, so strongly. When he looked into her eyes, he felt happier than ever before. Surer than ever. All that after spending a few minutes with a woman he knew nothing about.

But then, she was pulled away, and it was a rude awakening from the dream. Letting go of her was painful, physically painful and the reality of it hit him. What was he doing? Nicole was somewhere in that room. It wasn't right. Whatever he thought he felt wasn't even possible. He didn't know this woman. He couldn't possibly have these feelings for her.

Alexander backed off and lost himself in the crowd.

He found Nicole surrounded by a large group of people – some that he recognized from their outings. She was, as always, the center of attention. He took her arm like he was looking for shelter from himself. Nicole wrapped her arms around his neck, but when she tried to kiss him, he turned his face and kissed her on the cheek.

'What's wrong?' she asked.

'Nothing. I think I'm just tired.'

He hoped being by her side would help. That it would make him feel better and forget what had just happened. But it didn't. With each passing minute, he felt more anxious and more uncomfortable. He didn't care about the marriage of Princess Anna – whoever she was – nor the upcoming plays on Broadway, the latest gossip on Monsieur Creteil, the new yacht someone had bought or whatever else the people around him talked about.

'Let's just go,' he said.

'Can we stay a bit longer? I'm hoping they'll bring something to eat. I'm starving.'

He forced a smile and mumbled to himself, 'It's a bad idea.'

A couple took Nicole aside, and Alexander walked away. He didn't want to look for her, he just wanted to close his eyes, go outside, get into his car and leave. But he did look for her. She wasn't anywhere. It was as if she had been a figment of his imagination. A dream.

He walked outside, wondering if he could stay there. Nicole was ready to leave, but with each passing moment, the strength that had got him outside and away from her faded away.

Was he making a mistake? Just like he had made a mistake leaving Zara in the museum, alone, that evening?

If he was making a mistake, there would be a sign, he thought.

He turned around, went back to the entrance and stood there waiting.

If you feel the same way, if you feel something, anything, if this is not a dream, come outside. Please, come outside, he said to himself more like a prayer than a thought.

On the balcony, just a few feet away from him, he heard a noise and then saw a silhouette.

For a moment he couldn't believe it was really happening. Slowly, almost afraid, he walked towards the terrace.

She was standing with her arms on the railing, looking out in the courtyard. As if she was searching for something. Could it be that she was looking for him?

DOMINIQUE

PARIS

Dominique heard a noise and turned around. He was standing there, looking at her, and it should probably have surprised her, but it didn't. She held his gaze. Purposefully. There was something about this man that attracted Dominique like a sunflower turning toward the sun.

Two strangers staring at each other. Why did she feel he wasn't a stranger? Why did she feel she knew him better than she knew herself?

Her hands trembled, and she hid them behind her back. *I should say something*, she thought when she noticed someone behind him, by the terrace door.

'Alexander, there you are.' The voice sounded familiar.

Alexander. His name was Alexander.

'Dominique, it's so nice to see you again,' he said with a smile. 'It's been far too long.'

She smiled back. It was Jean Jacques D'Angers. 'It's nice to see you too.'

Dominique was surprised he remembered her.

'Do you two know each other?'

Neither Dominique nor Alexander said a word.

'She's the girl I told you I met at the Marmottan,' said Jean Jacques D'Angers.

'Is she?' said Alexander, holding her gaze.

Dominique couldn't help comparing him to a painting she had seen at Musée d'Orsay. It changed, depending on the lighting in the museum and who stood in front of it. Different people saw different things in it. Beautiful things. Surreal things.

'Monsieur Matthieu told me all about your work at the Marmottan,' said Jean Jacques D'Angers to Dominique, then turning to Alexander. 'She should show you what she did with the Cezanne from the blue room. Nobody thought it could be saved. Until she worked her magic.'

Dominique blushed. 'You're too kind, Monsieur D'Angers.'

'Oh, please, call me JJ. Monsieur makes me feel old.' He chuckled.

'How serendipitous you two should meet. Maybe you can convince her to join us, Alexander. I tried once, but alas, unsuccessfully. She would make a fine art dealer. Fine, indeed.'

JJ looked at her. Then at him. 'But let's leave that for another time, shall we? It's late and we have an early flight tomorrow morning. We should get going, get some sleep,' he said, his mouth twisted in a slight grimace.

'Of course,' said Dominique, her face on fire.

'Actually, JJ, I'd like to stay a bit longer,' said Alexander, not taking his eyes from her.

'Are you sure?'

'Yes. We'll see you at the airport in the morning.'

'Very well then. Have a lovely evening,' he said, and went down the stairs to his car.

His words. His certitude. Her heart. Maybe it didn't make any sense, and it was wrong, and against all the rules and the dreams and what her mother had said about there being only one for each of us. But she couldn't help herself. She was drawn to him in a way she had never felt before. Or maybe she had once. A long time ago.

ALEXANDER

PARIS

'You knew that painting wasn't for sale,' she said.

'But everything else I said was true. I have never seen anything more beautiful in my life.' He smiled. 'Your name is Dominique?' he said quietly.

She wasn't Zara. He knew that now. But no matter what her name was, no matter who she was, she was bewitching. Intoxicating.

She nodded. 'And you are Alexander,' she said, almost echoing his thoughts.

He didn't say anything. Didn't know what to say.

They were both quiet for a minute. From time to time he would look at her and she would smile, almost embarrassed.

'JJ talks a lot about you,' he finally said. 'He's very impressed with your work.'

She played with her fingers. 'He's too nice.'

'JJ is not generous with compliments. If he says you're good, you must be the best.'

Her cheeks turned red. She was adorable when she blushed. There was a humility and a simplicity about her that was refreshing. 'What got you into restoration? There's not a lot of money in it.'

'It's not all about the money,' she said, almost snappily.

'Oh, no, I'm sorry, I didn't mean – I meant it in an admiring way. I wish I could do it too. Always been fascinated with restorations.'

'What's stopping you?'

He smiled.

'So what do you do if you're not doing restorations?'

'I'm an art dealer for AngeD'Art.'

'That's nice,' she said.

Did she think it was nice? He couldn't tell.

'You know JJ's company is the biggest in Europe and the third in the world. An art dealer position would be well… what am I saying – extremely well compensated.'

'I know.'

'Yet you're not interested. Why?'

'Have you ever had a dream?'

He gazed into her eyes. *If you only knew,* he thought.

'Is this your dream? This art charity?'

'Part of it, yes.'

'Then I won't even try to convince you to join AngeD'Art. Dreams trump money.'

She smiled.

'I admire you for not selling yourself, not selling out your dreams,' he said. 'And for sticking to your guns. I hope I get to do it one day too,' he said.

'What?'

'Follow my heart. If I pursued art restoration, I wouldn't be able to work for JJ as an art dealer anymore. You see, it's complicated with him and the company. He has big plans for me, and I don't want to disappoint, so my dream will have to wait for a while. But one day I will gather the courage to do what I dream, otherwise—'

'You will regret it for the rest of your life.'

'I will regret it for the rest of my life.'

They both fell quiet again, looking into each other's eyes.

DOMINIQUE

9 DECEMBER 1963, 9 P.M.

PARIS

She heard voices, and instinctively moved to the side and away from Alexander.

'There you are,' said Vincent. 'I've been looking everywhere for you.'

Dominique gulped. His arrival was like a wake-up call.

'Oh, sorry,' she said feeling embarrassed. 'Did something happen?'

She didn't know what to say.

He took her hand and pulled her to him. 'Yes. Something happened,' he said with a serious face.

She stared.

'I missed you.'

Dominique smiled but it probably looked more like a pained grimace. He leaned down to kiss her and she offered her cheek.

Vincent finally looked in Alexander's direction.

'How are you? Long time,' he said to Alexander.

'Vincent,' replied Alexander, equally cold.

'What's all this? A happy gathering?' she heard a woman's voice. 'What did I miss?'

It was Nicole. With a condescending smile, she made her way to Alexander and latched on to his arm. 'I see everyone has met my wonderful future husband.'

Dominique held her breath. Nicole was now dating Alexander? Vincent's ex-girlfriend Nicole? Could the night get any worse?

Alexander smiled awkwardly. 'Well, we're not there yet,' he said, glancing at Dominique. Were they, or weren't they? Maybe he was Nicole's boyfriend, just like she was Vincent's girlfriend. Just as bad. Engaged or not, the situation couldn't be more awkward. She wanted the ground to crack open and eat her.

'But we will be soon, love,' she said, like it was a given. 'I am starving and there's nothing good here,' whined Nicole in a childlike voice.

She turned to Dominique. 'No offense but the catering is lacking.'

Dominique opened her mouth to say something, but no words came out.

'Why don't we all go grab some dinner? It's not too late. We'll be back in Paris by ten and there are plenty of cafés still open. Café de Flore for instance,' said Nicole.

'I'm kind of tired,' said Vincent, giving her a rather pointed look.

Alexander said nothing.

Dominique said nothing.

'What's wrong with you? You're acting like old people. Let's go. This party is so over.'

Alexander looked at Dominique and smiled. A small, almost apologetic smile.

Dinner or no dinner, it was already a disaster.

And she could buy herself some time. With him.

What a bad person she was. Thinking of him even then. Vincent was next to her and the only thing she was preoccupied with was how to squeeze in five more minutes with Alexander although he was clearly taken. They both were.

'Let's go,' insisted Nicole. 'I hope you boys didn't drink so you can drive.'

'I'm fine,' mumbled Alexander. Vincent nodded.

Alexander and Nicole went to Alexander's car and Vincent and Dominique to Vincent's.

'We'll see you there,' said Nicole.

'Is everything alright?' asked Vincent on the way back to Paris.

'Of course.'

'Are you excited about dinner?'

'Of course,' she said absentmindedly.

'Did you see that Siberian tiger on the side of the road?'

'Of course.'

Vincent stopped talking.

A couple of seconds later, Dominique turned to him. 'I'm sorry. You were saying?'

'Are you sure you're alright? You seem distracted.'

'I'm just tired, I guess.'

They got to Café de Flore before Alexander and Nicole.

'Monsieur Saint Germain, what a pleasure. Let me take you to your table,' said the hostess, walking up to Vincent.

'You have a table here?' asked Dominique.

'I used to have dinner at this restaurant every week back when—'

The maître d' came to their table and bowed slightly before Vincent. 'We're honored to serve you tonight, Monsieur Saint Germain.'

Vincent nodded absentmindedly. 'Can you bring us a bottle of '43 Veuve Clicquot Ponsardin?'

'Right away, Monsieur Saint Germain.'

Nicole and Alexander joined just as the waiter brought the bottle and the glasses.

'Champagne, how nice of you,' said Nicole, sounding painfully fake. 'My favorite.'

'What made you choose this place?' asked Vincent, looking at Nicole.

She raised an eyebrow. 'It's nice. I – I missed it.'

Dominique wondered what was going on between them. Above all, though, what was she doing on that double date, sitting across from a man she couldn't even look at without blushing?

'Tell me, Vincent, how did you two meet?' asked Nicole.

Vincent stared at her, clenching his jaw.

'We bumped into each other at the Louvre and we've been together ever since.'

'That's nice,' said Nicole, showing her perfect white teeth.

Barely above whisper level, Dominique asked, 'What about you?'

'Did you say something?' asked Nicole.

'I was asking how you and Alexander met.'

'Us? Oh, that's such a lovely story, isn't it, love?' she said and looked at Alexander. 'We grew up together actually. We're childhood sweethearts.'

Alexander stared into space.

Dominique noticed Vincent and Nicole were giving each other these occasionally aggressive, occasionally strange looks over the table.

'What is it that you do exactly, Alexander?' asked Vincent.

'I am an art dealer for AngeD'Art.'

'Don't be modest, love. You are not just an art dealer,' intervened Nicole. She looked at Vincent defiantly. 'He's one of the best art dealers in Europe.'

'I'm sure that's not true, Nicole,' said Alexander, slightly embarrassed.

'So you're like a sales agent for paintings?' pushed Vincent.

Alexander forced himself to smile. 'In layman's terms, yes.'

'What about your restoration plans? Tell him about that,' blurted out Dominique.

Vincent and Nicole gave her deadly looks, but Alexander smiled at her, the kind of smile that made her feel she could do no wrong. Even if she had said something inappropriate, even if she'd put him on the spot, it was alright.

'I am interested in art restoration as well and I'm seriously considering it as a career. There are so many valuable paintings just sitting around in museum basements, in someone's attic or hanging in a hallway or kitchen next to the stove where they cook fried eggs. Most people don't know they are destroying works of art. Almost always they don't even understand their value. I could salvage them and have them restored. Even if I don't end up selling them, they could be shown in museums for everyone to admire.'

Vincent coughed suggestively. Dominique looked at him and he motioned her with his head as if to say, 'This is too serious and boring for a dinner conversation.' The truth was, for a minute there, she had forgotten he was even at the table. Or Nicole. It was just Alexander and her.

'My mother has paintings all over the place. Gauguin, Modigliani, Klimt, Picasso. I distinctly remember some are dangerously close to the kitchen. Or was it the bathroom? I don't know,' said Vincent and laughed. 'Alexander, you should stop by and take a look. Save them.'

Dominique and Alexander looked at each other and completely ignored him.

'Dominique,' said Vincent louder.

She turned to him like she'd been hit by lightning. 'Sorry, did you say something?'

The waiter interrupted. 'Are you ready to order now?'

Nicole answered first. 'I'd like the coq au vin.'

'Steak and frites for me,' said Dominique.

'Same for me,' said Alexander as soon as she finished ordering.

The waiter looked at him. 'Coq au vin or steak, monsieur?'

Alexander smiled wide. 'Steak, please.'

'Then I'll have the coq au vin,' said Vincent.

The air was charged with tension and even the waiter felt it. Dominique saw it in his face.

ALEXANDER

PARIS

Dominique was every bit as fantastic as he thought she would be. He was so mesmerized by her and so fascinated by their conversation that he started thinking about ways to get Nicole and Vincent out of the picture, without being too obvious.

He felt what he'd always dreamed he would feel. Those feelings and those tingling butterflies, that amazement when someone else was talking. The more time he spent with Dominique, the more he realized what he had been missing.

The night was almost over but he didn't want it to end. What if they never saw each other again? He couldn't let that happen.

When the dinner was over, they all walked outside. It smelled like... was it possible? Yes, it smelled like jasmine. 'I'll have to leave my car and send the driver to pick it up. We'll get taxis,' said Vincent.

'I've had very little to drink,' said Alexander. 'I can drive.'

'No, it's fine. We'll get a taxi,' insisted Vincent.

Ten minutes later, no luck.

'You won't find a taxi at this hour,' said Alexander to Vincent. 'I can take everyone home, no problem.'

Vincent either didn't realize what he'd agreed to, or he felt cornered into agreeing.

'Who's first?' asked Alexander, trying to sound casual. He knew very well who was first.

Vincent. He lived in Saint-Germain-des-Prés, the most expensive area in Paris. Of course. Next, JJ's house where he and Nicole lived.

'Where are you going?' asked Nicole when he dropped her off.

'I have to take Dominique home as well,' he said.

She was quiet for a moment. 'Don't stay long,' she finally said and walked into the house.

'Where do you live, Dominique?' Alexander asked when they were left alone in the car.

'Rue Amélie, in the seventh, near Champ de Mars. But you shouldn't go to all this trouble for me. It's not far from here; I could walk. It's such a beautiful night and I love Paris when it snows.'

They had made it to the end of his street when he stopped the car. 'Do you want to walk?'

'Sure. That's fine,' she said and opened the door. 'Thank you. Have a great evening.'

He smiled, got out of the car and followed her.

'Where are you going? Your house is the other way,' she asked, visibly confused.

'Aren't we walking?'

'We?'

'If that's alright with you.'

She nodded, and he hoped he didn't make her uncomfortable. That was the last thing he wanted.

DOMINIQUE

9 DECEMBER 1963, 11 P.M.

PARIS

When they got out of the car, it was so hushed, except for the snow crunching under their feet. The moon was perfectly round, like a brie wheel. Dominique felt Alexander's gaze on her and it made her both comfortable and nervous.

Now that they were alone, she could tell him anything, but she was tongue-tied. *I don't want this night to end,* she thought. *If it ends, it will all go back to how it was. A world you're not part of. What I feel now with you, I'm afraid I will never feel again. If this is love, I've been missing it all my life.*

No, she couldn't say that. It was all too crazy and irresponsible. She caught him gazing at her again and, afraid he'd guessed what she was thinking, she looked away.

'Tell me about yourself. About your job as an art curator,' he said sounding nervous.

'Intern art curator. I have a few years until I finish school. What do you want to know?'

'Everything. What is your favorite painting from the collection you help manage?'

'There are so many. I recently finished restoring one that's close to my heart. It is a lily pond painting by Monet.'

He took a deep breath.

'Monet?'

'Yes, he's my favorite.'

'I liked him too, a long time ago,' said Alexander.

'What happened?'

'Too many things. Painful things.'

'All I know is that once you discover Monet, you can't help but love him,' she said.

They continued walking. A window closing broke the silence.

'I'd love to stop by the Marmottan sometime. Maybe you can help me rediscover Monet,' he said.

They were getting close to her apartment building. She wasn't ready.

'It's just around the corner,' Dominique said.

'Oh, so soon?' he said, sounding just like she felt. She wanted more time. She wanted to stop him from leaving; she wanted him to stop her from leaving.

It was wrong. But how could something be wrong when it felt so right?

ALEXANDER

PARIS

Walking next to her, talking to her, listening to her beautiful voice, and looking into her eyes. It was perfection as he'd never dared to dream before. He didn't feel the cold or how tired he was, and he wasn't thinking about the consequences. It was just them that night and he would've done anything to keep it going.

Alexander wanted to get to know her, to be part of her world, even if it was for just a short while. Even if the next day she said it was a bad idea, that she had someone else, he had someone else. Tonight, there was no one else. There was nothing else in their perfect little world except the snowflakes that danced around and sat quietly on her face, the tree branches that bowed as they passed, and the lights that flickered to let them know they were taken care of. Guided.

How many times in life can you feel the same thing? He

was feeling now the exact same way he'd felt ten years before for Zara. And if he didn't know her name was different, he could've sworn Dominique was Zara. Because his heart was telling him such love could only happen once.

Dominique stopped next to a tree, took her gloves off and picked up a flower someone had probably thrown away. A small, almost lifeless white rose. 'I'm going to save it,' she said. 'I will take it home and care for it.'

He smiled.

She did the same with a book, so wet you couldn't see the printed words anymore.

She hid it under her coat and walked on like nothing had happened.

'I love books,' she said. 'I've always loved books. They're like a magic gateway to, well, to everywhere. To all the places we'll never go to, to all the people we'll never meet.'

'I studied literature in college before art,' he said.

'Then you must know what I'm talking about. What made you change your mind?'

'About what?'

'Art?'

'I think it's because you can only ignore your heart for so long before it takes over.'

She stopped and, for a moment, he thought she would say something, but she didn't.

When their hands accidentally touched, a lightning bolt shot through his body. He wanted to feel that again. But not by accident. On purpose. Would he offend her though? Would she run away if he tried holding her hand? What if she thought he did that all the time and he was that kind of man? After all, she didn't know him. Oh, but he wanted her to know him. All of him. The good, the bad, the scary, the embarrassing, the funny and the painful. He wanted to tell her about his father, about his past. Yet, when she asked about his family, he avoided the subject. It was too soon. He worried she wouldn't like him anymore if she found out about his broken family. About what his father had done, and how his mother didn't care about him.

Time went by too quickly. They walked some more, talking and enjoying each other's company. With her, he felt something he couldn't define at first, but the familiarity of her presence was what he had experienced as a boy in Alsace. The same intensity, passion, and heartbreak when he thought about saying goodbye. No, he didn't want to say goodbye.

DOMINIQUE

9 DECEMBER 1963, 11.30 P.M.

PARIS

'We're here,' she said when she saw the coffee shop downstairs.

'Already?' said Alexander, the regret poignant in his tone.

A car stopped at the curb, in front of them. It was one of Vincent's Rolls-Royces.

'Vincent,' she said, her voice shaking. 'Is everything alright? What are you doing here?'

'I shouldn't have left you alone,' he said, looking intently into her eyes.

Then he turned to Alexander. 'I didn't realize you live in this neighborhood too.'

His tone gave Dominique chills.

Alexander raised his eyebrows and looked straight at Vincent but didn't say anything.

Vincent turned back to Dominique. 'I wanted to make

sure you got home alright. Let me take you upstairs,' Vincent said and took her arm, almost a little too tightly.

Just as Vincent opened the door, Dominique turned around. She didn't know what unknown, invisible force made her do it. She turned to see if Alexander was still there, to see him one more time. He was walking in the opposite direction and turned at the same time. Their eyes met, yet again. That moment. That look. Was that when she knew her life would never be the same again?

DOMINIQUE

11 MARCH 1964

PARIS

At the beginning of spring, on a Wednesday, she was supposed to meet Vincent after her weekly shift at Le Petit Coin to have dinner with him and his family. Dominique had struggled in the last three months. As much as she tried to forget about that night, about Alexander, she couldn't let go. It worried her and made her feel guilty that Vincent might suspect something was different about her, so she tried extra hard, calling him out of the blue, just to hear his voice, buying him small presents, suggesting they go away somewhere for a weekend, or two, thinking the more time they spent together, the easier it would be for her to forget about Alexander. To forget about that impossible dream. Because it was just that. She was ridiculous and childish to still think about him.

She and Constance had just reopened Le Petit Coin a couple of weeks before, and it was still a bit hectic. They had been working on it for over a year – painting, remodeling, bringing in new furniture and doing final touch-ups – but they had finally made it. The charming little restaurant with a pleasant terrace for dining in the warmer months was unrecognizable. They did their best to restore the interior as closely as possible to the ambiance and feel of its golden days with red leather booths, a zinc bar, and soft candlelight plus a single bar-like small table next to the window for people-watching – which immediately became Dominique's favorite spot.

Constance reworked the menu as well and hired two more people. On the first day, they had no customers. Same on the second day. And the third. On the fourth, a young couple came in and had coffee. The next day, a group of people had lunch. By the end of the week, you couldn't find a table at rush hour. Word got around that the café had the best food, music, and ambiance in the area. Masses of people trickled in, and they never stopped coming.

That Wednesday, Dominique was running late for lunch at the café, before her afternoon shift. The deal with Constance was for her to work there one day a week after school, and then to help out with planning, buying supplies, and reservations when she had time during the week. Dominique walked in, went straight to the kitchen and got herself a plate while trying not to step on Constance's toes. She threw together her usual ham and cheese brioche topped with a fried egg and béchamel sauce. A glass of sparkling water with mint syrup and she was all set. But her favorite spot was taken. A man was sitting with his back to her, looking out the window.

She didn't need to see his face. She didn't need to hear

his voice. It was him. Alexander. How and why he was there she didn't know. Just like she didn't know what to do. She took a step back and tripped on a chair that fell to the ground. By the time she picked it up, he was standing next to her. Smiling.

'We keep seeing each other.'

'Seems so,' she said, smiling back. She'd tried so hard to forget about him and now, here he was, in front of her.

'What are you doing here?' she asked.

'I was just in the neighborhood and noticed this place. Looked inviting from the outside.'

'And from the inside?'

He stared into her eyes. 'It looks… beautiful.'

Her heart beat so fast she felt it in her throat. 'You know you were sitting in my chair?' she asked with a serious face.

'I was? I'm sorry, I didn't know,' he said, quite apologetic.

'It's okay,' she continued in the same serious tone. 'You can have it today. But just so you know, it's the best seat in the house.'

'Is it?'

'What do you see?' she asked, looking out. Anything to stop staring into his eyes.

He looked out the window, squinted, took a few moments and looked again from left to right and back again, as he probably thought she was looking at something specific.

He turned to Dominique. 'People? Cars? Buildings?'

'What about that little girl carrying the sleigh behind her? She is probably going up the hill to play with her friends and catch the last snow of the year. And the nice little old man who left the flower shop with a bouquet of red roses? I bet it's his wedding anniversary. A big one – forty or fifty,' she said, smiling. 'And that couple, holding hands and laughing.'

'I get it. This is the best seat in the house,' he said, and his whole face lit up with his smile. If he was handsome when he was serious, when he smiled, he was drop-dead gorgeous.

From there on, the conversation rolled out naturally. They talked about anything and everything. About nothings and big things. From songs to dreams, and books to fears. Time flew by, her lunch hour was almost up, and he had to go back to work as well.

'I'm glad you stopped by,' she said, walking him to the door.

'Me too. I enjoyed our people-watching. We should do it again sometime.'

'I am here every Wednesday,' she said and winked.

'Then maybe next Wednesday?'

Seeing him, talking to him. Amazing and terrifying at the same time.

Did she know it was wrong to see him again? She didn't even think about that. Or maybe she did. For a second. But she pushed the thought away. 'I'd like that. I'd like that very much.'

ALEXANDER

PARIS

He'd lied. He'd lied through his teeth. He didn't just happen to be in the neighborhood.

For three months, he had lived in complete limbo. It was a perpetual battle between his heart and his mind; between his feeling for Nicole, their relationship, his obligations, conscience and his impossible, intoxicating feelings for Dominique.

When he went to see her at the café, Alexander didn't tell her how many sleepless nights he'd spent wondering what he should do. How he'd asked JJ about her, hoping he wouldn't suspect anything. How those three months in New York he did everything humanly possible to get her out of his heart. He took Nicole out for dates, he spent so much time with her, thinking, hoping she could make him forget. He didn't tell Dominique how ever since his return the previous week, he'd been following her from school and how he watched her through the café's window until a customer saw him, and he had to leave.

That Wednesday when he walked in, he had no idea what would happen. He thought she might not come and that perhaps it was for the best. Or that she would come but push him away or tell him she wasn't interested in talking to him. Or that she would come but he would immediately know she wasn't as amazing as he'd imagined she was and their connection was only in his mind. After all, who falls in love like that?

But she smiled and talked to him. And again, those feelings came back. Their connection was real. *She* was real and more incredible than even that first night. But as their time together came to an end, his conscience also started nagging him. He knew what their situation was. He knew who she was dating. What could he offer her? Nothing. Besides, he was with Nicole. And he loved Nicole, didn't he? What was he doing there then, with another woman?

Alexander prepared himself to say goodbye. But when their hour was over, he couldn't. Seeing her again, spending time with her again even if it was for just one hour. Even if he had to wait a whole week. That's what he wanted more than anything. No, he couldn't say goodbye to Dominique.

DOMINIQUE

22 APRIL 1964

PARIS

The next Wednesday, Dominique rushed back to the café after school, so excited to see him again, not wanting to miss a single minute of their precious hour. All the way to Le Petit Coin she wondered. What if he didn't show up? What if he'd changed his mind?

But just a few minutes after she arrived, he passed in front of the window, waving; a big smile on his face.

'I'm so glad you're here,' she said. 'I want you to try something.'

'Oh, I thought you were just happy to see me.'

She smiled. 'Sit down,' she said and went behind the bar. 'I'll be there in a few minutes.'

'What are you making there? The suspense is killing me,' he joked.

She came back with a small tray with two cups of coffee.

'What do you think?' she said, looking intently at his reactions as he took the first sip.

'Oh, wow, this is so good. What kind of coffee is it?'

'Cinnamon coffee. My own recipe.'

'Cinnamon is my favorite spice,' he said.

'Mine too!'

She looked at him for a moment. 'Pick a number. Any number between one and one hundred.'

He raised an eyebrow, seeming more amused than confused.

'Seventy-seven.'

'Seventy-eight. I won. So you have to go to the bar and pick up that plate with the biscuits.'

He started laughing. 'Sure. This seems like a perfectly fair game.'

She laughed too.

Alexander came back the next Wednesday. And the next. And the next. Wednesday became the most beautiful day of the week. She could barely sleep on Tuesday nights, and on Wednesday mornings, she'd wake up before the sunrise. When she'd see him coming, her whole world would light up.

They didn't do anything special. They would grab their coffee and macarons, stare out the window, laugh, talk, and enjoy each other's company. There were moments when they sat side by side in complete silence. It was never awkward; it just felt right.

*

'I brought you something,' he said sometime at the end April, a few weeks into their perfect Wednesdays.

From his coat's pocket he took out a small piece of paper and after unfolding it, he put it in front of her.

It was a small drawing of a young woman with flowy red hair and haunting green eyes, playing the harp.

'Who is she?'

'The model was Alexa Wilding.' He smiled. 'This became a painting called *La Ghirlandata*, almost a hundred years ago.'

Dominique studied it carefully.

'Thank you for showing it to me. It's exquisite,' she said, giving it back to him.

'It's yours,' he said.

She opened her mouth to say something, but barely managed a faint, 'Thank you.'

'You don't like it,' he said and sounded insecure all of a sudden. 'You think it's silly?'

'No, don't say that. I love it. She's so beautiful. I just didn't expect—'

'I immediately thought of you when I saw it. There's something in her eyes—'

Dominique blushed.

'I wish I could've brought you the original painting, but all I could smuggle out of my godfather's collection was this early sketch. You know this is a Ro—'

'Rosetti,' she interrupted excitedly.

'Because the first time we talked, it was about a Rosetti, I thought…'

Dominique was speechless and so moved, she was afraid it would show just how much. She would've kissed him.

At least hugged him. Instead, she just touched his hand for a fraction of a second, then pulled her hand back. They smiled at each other. No need for words.

Alexander was such a beautiful person inside and out, and the more she got to know him, the more she liked him. He was funny but serious, profound but not dull, sophisticated but not overcomplicated. Even after all that time, she still found him enigmatic and intriguing, like a book you read again and again because you know you'll discover a new meaning every time.

Around him, she felt both comfortable and nervous. It wasn't bad nervous, it was good nervous, but it made her slightly clumsy and occasionally awkward. She had to constantly remind herself not to stare at him or 'accidentally' touch his hand. Just like she had to remind herself not to talk about some things. Like Nicole and Vincent. For Dominique, it was her way of protecting herself from her conscience perhaps. From reality. Like an ostrich hiding its head in the sand. If she didn't talk about Vincent, it was as if, for those sixty minutes, he wasn't part of the equation.

The past was another subject they didn't talk about. She'd tried to ask Alexander questions about his childhood, his parents, but all she got from him was that his father had been JJ's best friend and had died when Alexander was young, and that his mother lived in London, but they didn't really keep in touch. He was obviously scarred by whatever had happened to him, and she didn't want to make him relive painful experiences. From that moment on, they never talked about the past; sometimes they would talk about the future, but mostly they lived in the present. Hour to hour, week to week. And that one hour together was an escape from everything and everyone. It was their safe space where bad things didn't happen. Where they were happy.

'Where would you go if you could? And you can pick any place, any country, no matter how far,' she asked one day.

'I wouldn't go anywhere. I think I'm exactly where I'm supposed to be,' he said with a smile.

When they stopped talking to take a sip of coffee or look out the window, the tension was so palpable you could almost see the sparks fly.

It was clear for everyone who had eyes to see. It was clear enough for Constance.

'What are you doing, Dominique?' she asked her after Alexander left one Wednesday.

'What do you mean what am I doing?'

Constance frowned. 'You know very well what I mean. With this man.'

'Nothing. Just talking.'

'It doesn't seem like just talking to me. Can you imagine what Vincent would feel if he saw you?'

'We're just friends, Constance.'

Her cousin shook her head.

She was lying to herself and now to other people too. They were not friends. She loved him. She wanted to be with him and not just on Wednesdays. Not just for one hour. She wanted more. She wanted to explore Paris with him, hold his hand, and feel his breath on her face. To feel his hand in hers. To kiss him. She wanted to lie on the grass and look at the stars together. Oh, she wanted to dance with him. She imagined his arms wrapped around her. She remembered the song that was playing the night they met and blushed, feeling embarrassed, even ashamed. Because she knew it was a forbidden dream.

It wasn't just about them. There were two other people involved. And no matter how hard she tried, her conscience nagged at her. Incessantly. How much longer could she keep it up? How much longer until both worlds would crash into each other like a freight train, destroying everything in its path? She knew she was headed for disaster. But she couldn't give him up.

ALEXANDER

PARIS

With each passing week, he was falling deeper and deeper in love with Dominique. His life, the life that he knew before meeting her was turned completely upside down. He had never felt happier than in those short, precious moments with her. For an hour, he didn't feel that sadness; he didn't have those thoughts that he didn't belong, that he didn't know what he was doing with his life. They were all gone. His life was perfect for that one short hour. And then agony for the rest of the week. When he wasn't with her, she was all he could think of. The days in between seemed to crawl and sometimes he missed her so much he couldn't breathe.

Those days in between were also becoming harder and harder to navigate. As much as he tried to pretend nothing was different, he couldn't do everything as he used to. Especially when it came to Nicole. For one, he avoided sleeping in the same bed as Nicole, although they still lived in the same house. In JJ's house. And to do that without having to lie to Nicole or make her feel rejected, he chose to travel for four or five days a week, making sure though he was always back on Tuesday night or Wednesday morning. When he came back, he was either too tired and fell asleep almost immediately or sometimes he'd nap in the office while he was working.

Even if that didn't raise suspicion – although he feared it did – his mood was harder to control. And Nicole, who knew him so well, sensed the change in behavior.

'I wish you would stop traveling so much,' she kept saying to him, every time he packed for another trip. 'You're always so tired because you work so much. There's no time left for anything else.'

'It's my job,' he said. 'And, as you know, a big part of my life. You knew that from the beginning.'

'I thought I was a big part of your life,' she said.

He sighed.

It wasn't right that he was lying to her. And it wasn't fair that he was pushing her away and making her feel like she was in the wrong. He knew that. And it ate him inside. But she kept saying it and saying it until she forced him to react like that. It wasn't the first time Alexander felt she was purposefully pushing his buttons, trying to annoy him and to cause a fight.

It had all started sometime at the beginning of the year, while they were still in New York and he wasn't yet seeing Dominique. Back then, he was trying so hard to focus just on Nicole and not to think about Dominique at all. Not that he succeeded, but he tried. He agreed to go with Nicole to all her events, no matter how long or tedious they were, he spent hours with her in stores while she tried on countless clothes, he took her out to romantic dinners and was extra affectionate with her. He gave her everything he thought she wanted from him, and everything he thought would help him forget about Dominique. But it seemed that the more he tried, the more she became irritable and moody.

JJ saw the change in him too. It wasn't surprising, since they were spending so much time together.

'Alexander, what is wrong, my boy? You haven't been yourself lately.'

'Nothing, I'm fine,' he said to JJ one evening as they were driving back from Giverny after failing to buy an early-days Monet. It hadn't been a good day for JJ either. He hated to lose.

'You can tell me. Whatever it is.'

He did want to talk to someone; he was afraid he would otherwise explode. But he couldn't admit everything to JJ. It would hurt him and that was the last thing he wanted.

'I'm just worried about a friend, that's all.'

'Hmm, a friend. Tell me about him,' said JJ. 'Maybe I can help.'

'Not much to tell. He's in love with a girl, and he's convinced she's the one for him.'

'Well, that's beautiful,' said JJ. 'What worries you?'

'You see, she's with someone. And he has someone too.'

'That's not good,' said JJ, looking out the car's window.

'He asked me if it's wrong if he sees her. As friends, you know? You think it's wrong?'

'Of course it's wrong. They can't be friends if he's in love with her. They shouldn't see each other again.'

ALEXANDER

30 JUNE 1964

PARIS

'Why do you love art so much?' he asked when, one day, as she was talking about a painting restoration she was working on, her eyes sparkled, and she couldn't stop smiling.

'There is art in everything we do. Even in this cup of coffee,' she said and chuckled. 'See how perfect it is? How exquisite?'

She continued talking about her painting. He was mesmerized. He could have listened to her talk about the clouds and the sky forever and ever and it wouldn't have bored him. Her passion, energy and optimism were contagious, and she kept surprising him in every possible way. He had never met anybody like her. Or better said, he hadn't met anyone like her in a very long time.

In what felt like a minute, summer started with its long days and warm, starry nights. They had been seeing each other for almost four months. It was incredible how fast time had flown by. Every single Wednesday, no matter what they had to do or where they had to be, they'd make it back in time for their one hour of pure happiness. He organized his work around it, his trips, his whole life. But he knew he couldn't do it forever.

On the last Tuesday of June, JJ told Alexander they had to go to Milan for a few days. The Degas they had been trying to buy for over a year, the one that had been off the market for decades, was finally available, and they had both been invited to the closed-door auction. And they had to leave that very night. Alexander tried to get out of it but JJ wouldn't have it. Not this time.

That meant he was going to miss their Wednesday for the first time. Alexander had to see her, even if it was for a minute; he had to tell her he was leaving. What would she think if he didn't show up?

That afternoon he went to the café. When he passed in front of the window, he had a bad feeling, and the moment he entered the café and saw the look on Dominique's face he got his confirmation. Something was not right.

The place was packed, even more so than usual, but it only took Alexander a moment to see why Dominique was giving him that blank stare. Vincent was at the bar. Alexander knew the two options he had were both bad. Turn around and leave, thus admitting in front of himself and Dominique they were doing something wrong, or stay and possibly jeopardize her relationship, embarrass her and himself and blatantly lie to someone's face.

He stopped. What should he do?

Vincent got up from the bar, walked over to Dominique,

kissed her and made his way to the door. Alexander instinctively stepped to the side to avoid a face-to-face encounter.

Vincent went to his car, sat behind the wheel and kept looking at the café and Alexander knew what that meant. He was waiting for her.

Moments later, Dominique came over. 'Alexander, what are you doing here? We always see each other on Wednesdays,' she said.

She sounded scared. Guilty. Even slightly annoyed.

She was right. They had a deal – one hour on Wednesdays and nothing more. When that one hour was over, she would go back to her life, her real life. And he would too.

'I wanted to see you. To talk to you.'

'I can't. Vincent is taking me out for dinner. I couldn't say no,' she said awkwardly.

Why would she say no? Vincent was her boyfriend. As for the two of them, they were, by all accounts, just friends. No need for explanations. He shouldn't have come. He should've called or sent her a note.

'Let's talk tomorrow,' she said swiftly. 'Our usual time?'

'I'm going to Italy with JJ for a few days, and I won't be back until Monday. That's why I came now. To tell you. I thought—'

'I understand. Then I will talk to you next week,' she said and, waving, she was gone.

He had been fortunate until that day, never having to watch them together. Even if his imagination had tormented him, it was not nearly as bad as seeing Vincent kissing her, holding her hand, whispering in her ear. Watching her leave with him was unbearable and he had never felt worse in his life. That almost meeting was enough to seed even more doubt into Alexander's tormented soul. What if the reason they were only meeting on Wednesdays and she had never suggested or encouraged anything more was because she didn't feel as strongly about him as she did about Vincent? What if she loved Vincent, truly loved him? And what if he was, selfishly, getting in the way of her happiness?

Alexander turned to leave, but someone was blocking his way.

'Constance,' he said, surprised. He knew her, had seen her every week for months now, but they never talked except for the occasional hello and goodbye.

'Alexander,' she said, 'I was wondering if you and I could talk for a few minutes.'

He didn't expect that.

'Of course,' he said and followed her to a booth in the back.

'We should have privacy here,' she said.

She looked at him for a few moments like she was sizing him up.

'I will get right to it.'

'Please do.'

'You and Dominique have been spending a lot of time together,' she started.

He forced himself to smile. Where was she going with this?

'She told me you are seeing someone. Is that true?'

He clenched his jaw. 'Yes.'

'I don't know what your intentions are. Just because Dominique says you are friends, it doesn't mean I necessarily believe her. I wasn't born yesterday.'

'We are friends,' he said.

'You are not a very good liar. You two have that in common.'

'Excuse me?'

'I'll be as blunt as I need to be. I want you to stop seeing her.'

He raised an eyebrow. 'Why?'

'Well, for one because you know as well as I do this is wrong. And it's affecting her; she's struggling, because she's just not that kind of woman.'

'I know what kind of woman she is,' said Alexander. He didn't need anyone pointing fingers. He felt awful as it was, especially after what just happened with Vincent. He wasn't that kind of man either. But what he felt for her made him forget everything. Made him silence his mind, and only listen to his heart. He would've never offended Dominique by suggesting something inappropriate, but he couldn't stay away from her either.

'If that's not a good enough reason, Vincent just asked for my blessing.'

'What?' he asked, unable to hide his shock. 'Blessing? What for?'

'He is going to ask her to marry him, at the big party on her birthday.'

The floor ran from under him.

'But that's only a week away,' he said in a lost, scared voice.

'Exactly. You need to let her go. Give her a chance to be happy. He will make her happy and give her everything she ever wanted. She was perfectly content before you showed up and she can be again. But for that, you have to allow her to find herself. It's just not healthy; whatever it is that's going on between you two needs to stop.'

DOMINIQUE

1 JULY 1964

PARIS

When she saw Alexander walking into the café, knowing Vincent was there, the guilt paralyzed her. She felt like such a bad person. A liar. A cheat. And then seeing the look on Alexander's face crushed her. He was hurt. It was so obvious. How had she ended up in such a horrible situation?

What about Nicole? Nicole loved him, just like Vincent loved her. It would destroy both of them.

What about the dreams? What about all those years of searching and wishing she would find him? She *had* found him. What more did she want? Vincent was the one, wasn't he? And she was now about to throw it all away for a feeling she couldn't even explain to herself. What was it that she felt for Alexander after all? An infatuation, physical attraction? But no matter how hard she tried to convince herself, she knew better. It was so much more. So much, that she couldn't breathe without him.

How had she let things get so far? What was she going to do?

At the restaurant that evening, all through dinner, Vincent barely spoke. From time to time it seemed like he wanted to say something but ended up just looking at her with an incredibly sad look on his face. Sad and almost disappointed. He must've realized something was wrong. And it wasn't just about that day; it was the last three months.

Just a few weeks before, he'd come to her school after classes, excited about a trip he had planned for them to Saint Tropez.

'It's going to be wonderful. It's not full tourist season and we'll have the place almost to ourselves. We can leave on Friday and come back the next Thursday. A week of paradise,' he said.

'I can't,' she said in a panicked tone. 'I can't go.'

'Why? You only have two classes next week; that's what you said.'

'Constance needs me here on Wednesdays. I can't miss Wednesdays.'

'I'm sure she'll understand. It's just this one time.'

'I can't, Vincent. I'm sorry.'

Back then she saw the same look in his eyes as now. But she chose to ignore it. Just like she chose not to think too much about the fact that she had stopped kissing him so much, almost not at all, that she found excuses not to see him, that after their dates she was tired all the time and wanted to go home and sleep.

She had tried to act normal, but she couldn't. And Vincent didn't deserve that. He had done nothing wrong. No, she couldn't do it anymore; she couldn't go through what she'd gone through the other day: sneaking around, hiding like a thief, lying. Who was that woman? It couldn't have been her; she had principles and morals. She and Alexander had both made promises to other people. They should've just stayed away from each other. She'd known it was going to end up in heartbreak.

The next day was a Wednesday. With dark circles under her eyes from a sleepless night and hours of crying, Dominique made all possible efforts to conceal her pain. But no matter what she did, she couldn't help but experience a deep sense of loss as she walked to the café from school, knowing Alexander wouldn't be there. *The happiest day of the week*, she thought. *I can't do this anymore. It's excruciating and it's just not right. No more.*

When she walked in and he was waiting at their table, Dominique's heart jumped for joy and ached at the same time.

'Alexander,' she said, not hiding her surprise. 'I thought you were in Italy.'

'I told JJ I had something to do for lunch and that I'd take the afternoon train. I wanted to see you. First of all, to apologize for yesterday. I didn't mean—'

She stopped him. 'You did nothing wrong.'

'Then why did it feel wrong?' he asked.

Dominique looked down. 'We can't do this anymore.'

'We can't do this anymore,' Alexander said.

It was the only time she wished he didn't have the same thoughts she did. But he did.

She couldn't believe she'd said it, but there was no other way. He wasn't going to leave Nicole or he would've done it already. And she couldn't ask him to leave her. What right did she have? But still, seeing him now in front of her, she didn't know how she would go through with it. How could she wake up the next morning knowing she would never see him again? How could she let him go?

But he was never hers, was he? The past few months had been nothing but a dream. The most amazing dream. But also the most painful. After they'd first met, she thought not seeing him was the worst thing that could happen. But now, after they'd spent all that time together, being so close to him – and yet so painfully far – had proved to be a hundred times harder. She'd felt like a ghost, dragging herself from place to place, counting the days to each hour of happiness.

Oh, but how desperately she wanted the fantasy to continue. How desperately she wanted to ask him to choose her. Dominique knew she was letting her mind lead, she was following the rules, and doing what everyone expected her to. After all, in the last months, she'd gone with her heart and look where that got her. Nowhere. To heartbreak.

Hearing the same thing from him hurt her. Deep down, she'd hoped against hope he would stop her. That he'd say, 'No, we can't do this. It's crazy. We are made for each other. I love you.' But he'd agreed with her. He wanted it to be over. They had gone too far.

'So this is it,' he said with a blank expression on his face. Like he was empty inside.

'I guess so.'

On the spur of the moment, she walked over to him, put her arms around his neck, and hugged him. Like a woman who was saying goodbye to the only man she'd ever loved.

Knowing she couldn't watch him walk away, she turned and walked out of the café, not looking back. Afraid that if she did, she was going to run back to him and ask him to forget everything she'd said. Of course she wanted to see him. Next Wednesday, and the next. Every Wednesday until the end of days. But it was too late. She walked on, head down, crying.

'Why didn't you tell him? Why didn't you tell him how you felt?' asks Valerie.

I close my eyes for a moment.

'When was a good time to say goodbye? The more we were together, the harder it got for me to be without him. I thought I was doing the right thing. I wanted to be what everyone expected me to be. A principled woman, a righteous woman. Constance would stop giving me ugly looks; Vincent would stop looking at me that way and I would stop feeling so miserable. The world would go back to normal. The truth is, as I walked out, I knew I'd made a mistake. The biggest mistake of my life.'

ALEXANDER

PARIS

'Whatever it is, it looks bad,' said JJ when they were coming back from Milan.

Alexander wiped his tears before JJ got a chance to see his face. He couldn't remember the last time he had cried. But now, he couldn't help himself. He'd lost her. How could he have lost her when he loved her more than anything? When he couldn't breathe if she wasn't around? When she was all he thought of? He didn't know if he believed in soulmates, but if there was such a thing, she was his. She was part of him. How could he live without a part of him?

'It's nothing. I'm just tired, I guess.'

JJ patted his hand. 'Is it your friend again? What happened to him?'

'He listened to my advice,' said Alexander bitterly.

'Well, that's good.'

'It's not good because he lost her. And now he's lost too.'

He shouldn't talk to JJ about this. His godfather was a smart man. What would he say if he knew the friend was him?

'What happened?'

Alexander played with his fingers.

'Nothing. That's the problem. He wasn't man enough to do what he felt. He was a coward and chose the easy way out and he set her free. He let her walk away. But the problem is… she walked away with his heart. And two days from now, he will lose her forever. And he doesn't know how he will live knowing he let go of the one who was meant for him.'

'Does he love her that much?'

Alexander nodded, unable to speak.

JJ peered into the distance and didn't say anything for a few minutes.

'Then you haven't been such a good friend and you should apologize for your bad advice and tell him this: true love comes once in a lifetime and that is if you're lucky. If you're like most people, you will love, but not the kind of love that makes you feel invincible, that makes you both the happiest and the most miserable person in the world, the love for another human being that is bigger than the love for yourself. The one who makes you feel you can beat any odds, can defeat any monsters and overcome any obstacles… that love will not go away in time; it will grow stronger. If you choose to ignore it, it will eat you alive. Such love cannot be hidden forever, just as you cannot pretend there is love where there isn't,' he said pensively.

'If he truly loves her and she truly loves him, but they are both in relationships, they will not only end up hurting themselves and destroying their lives but also ruining the lives of those two other people as well.'

JJ sighed. 'If I had a one in a billion chance of being with my Demetria again, I would take it in a heartbeat, and I would fight for it against all judgments, against my family, against the world if they would dare to go between me and my love. You'd better go and find your friend before it's too late.'

Alexander knew what he needed to do. What he should've done months ago.

'You're back,' Nicole said when she saw him standing in front of her door.

He smiled thinly. 'Can I come in?'

'Do you need to ask? How was Germany?'

'Italy.'

'Oh, yes, Italy. How was it?'

'It was alright. We got the painting.'

'JJ must be ecstatic.'

'He is.'

'You need to stop traveling so much. I barely see you anymore.'

Here it came. That was how it always started. He would say it's his job, she would get upset and they'd end up fighting.

This time he didn't blame his job.

'Do you want a glass of wine?' she said and smiled as only Nicole knew how.

He shook his head. 'We need to talk.'

'You sound so serious. What is it?'

'It's about us. Our relationship. It's not working out,' he said, after thinking about it for a few moments. There was no easy way to do it.

Her smile disappeared. 'What do you mean?'

'I'm not happy, you're not happy and it's been like this for months.'

She seemed surprised. Almost shocked.

'Is this about the fights we had? I was just nervous, you know. You're always away and I felt lonely. It will be much better once we get married,' she added in a sweet, subdued voice.

'There isn't going to be a wedding and it's not the fights. I'm sorry, Nicole. I just can't marry you.'

'Stop saying these things, Alexander. You're confused and you're hurting me.'

She was mad and rightfully so. He'd let things go too far. He was afraid of taking chances. He didn't want to lose JJ. And, as strange as it sounded, he didn't want to lose Nicole either. He cared about her and he didn't want to hurt her. But he'd ended up making a huge mess of everything.

'I'm not confused,' he pushed back.

'If it's not the fights, then why? Tell me why. I'll be better. I'll do whatever you want me to do. I'll fix whatever is broken.'

'There's nothing we can fix.' He breathed in deeply. 'Nicole, you're a big part of my life, my oldest and dearest friend. We've been through a lot together, and I care about you so much, but I don't... I don't love you that way.'

'If you didn't love me then why were we together in the

first place?' Her voice was loud now. 'Because JJ wanted us together? Because you felt sorry for me? Because you were lonely?'

'Because we made sense. Because we knew each other inside out. And I never said I didn't love you. I did, and still do, and I thought – I hoped – I could learn to love you more, love you the way you love me. I tried, but you can't choose who you love. Your heart does that for you.'

That seemed to hurt her even more.

'You tried? Am I so unlovable you had to force yourself to feel something for me? Am I ugly? Do you think I'm ugly? Or not smart enough or—?'

She was in tears.

'I didn't mean—' Bad choice of words. He realized that now. 'I'm sorry,' he said, afraid he was being cruel. He didn't want to be cruel. She had done nothing to him. And he wasn't lying. He did love her. Just not enough. Not as much as he loved Dominique. They had a bond, a connection he didn't share with Nicole. It wasn't anyone's fault.

'You're beautiful, and smart. You know that. You're not unlovable. It's not your fault. You did nothing wrong. It's me.'

She grabbed Alexander's arms and looked in his eyes pleadingly. 'I thought we would always be together. Don't do this. We can try harder. We were happy together, weren't we? We can be again. Please, tell me you'll try again. You'll try harder. I'll try harder.'

'I can't tell you that. It would be a lie.'

What he was telling her now was also a lie. He was lying by omission. And by not telling her there was someone else, he encouraged her to hold on to him, to their relationship. To continue hoping. It wasn't fair to her and it was dishonest.

'Nicole, I'm in love with someone else,' he said. 'I tried to fight my feelings; I tried to stay away. But it's stronger than me. I can't fight it anymore.'

She covered her ears and started making loud nonsense noises.

'I know you heard me,' he said. But she didn't stop.

'I should go,' he said. Then walking up to her, he took her hands off her ears. 'I'm sorry, Nicole. I truly am. I never meant to hurt you.'

He was going for the door, when he heard a swoosh and a magazine landed next to him.

'Stop saying you're sorry. I don't want your sorry. I want you to take it all back. Let's pretend you didn't say that and I will never mention it ever again. Look, it never happened,' she said with a strange, almost manic look in her eyes.

'I can't. Nicole, please, don't make this harder than it already is. It's over.'

In the span of a few seconds, her complexion changed. She turned pale, almost white.

'This whole thing is making me sick,' she said and ran to the bathroom, locking herself in. He could hear her retching.

'Are you alright?' he asked through the door.

'Go away,' she yelled.

'I want to help you,' he tried.

'I don't need your help. I don't need anybody's help.'

'Nicole, please.'

'Get out. Now!'

He felt terrible for leaving her like that, but he knew there was no way she would talk to him. She was capable of locking herself in the bathroom until the next morning. He would try and talk to her in a few days, to make sure she was alright. And then, maybe in time, she would see it was for the best to go their separate ways. They didn't belong together. Never had.

He opened the door and walked out. Although it broke his heart to know he had hurt Nicole, he couldn't help but feel relieved as well. It was over. He was free. Finally free to follow his heart.

DOMINIQUE

7 JULY 1964

PARIS

The next Tuesday night, after all the customers left, Constance went home to take a shower and Dominique stayed behind to lock up the place.

She was turning twenty-five the next day, and Margaux had planned a grandiose gathering of over a hundred people, at one of the fanciest restaurants in Paris, overlooking Champ de Mars and Tour Eiffel. Dominique didn't want to go. She didn't feel like partying or celebrating but crying and hiding in the corner of her room.

Before going upstairs, she decided to walk for a few minutes to clear her head. It had just stopped raining. The air was warm, soothing, and the summer wind was blowing just enough to make the trees whisper. It was a perfect summer night but amidst all of that beauty, Dominique felt so sad and empty. She missed Alexander so much it hurt.

Why had she let him go? She should've stopped him. What would she do without him?

Every time she was alone, her thoughts inevitably flew to him. Imagining new conversations, remembering old ones. Sometimes she thought she heard his voice.

'It's a beautiful night. Do you mind if I walk with you for a few minutes?' she heard, and it wasn't her imagination this time.

'Alexander,' she said, and her voice caught in her throat.

They strolled side by side for a while, not saying a word. The moon was barely showing under the clouds. Being outside the coffee shop together reminded her of the first night they met and she felt so many emotions at the same time. Excitement, nervousness, confusion. What was he doing there?

Dominique's knees trembled when Alexander took her hand and helped her jump over a puddle. He let go of her hand and she didn't know if she was relieved or sad about it.

He stopped and took her hands in his. 'Tomorrow is your birthday,' he said. 'And I had to see you. I don't know if it's too late. I hope it's not. I tried to stay away; believe me, I tried. To set you free and let you be happy with him. But I can't. I can't, for the life of me. My mind was telling me it was the right thing to do, but my heart is saying something else.'

He spoke so fast Dominique could barely follow him. He looked nervous and she could feel his hands trembling in hers.

'Alexander?' she said, almost like a question.

'I'm not making any sense, am I?' he said with a sigh.

'The truth is, from the first second I saw you, I knew it. I knew what I felt. Even before that. Like we were meant for each other, like we've known each other—'

'Forever.'

'Forever.'

They both said it at the same time.

He took a deep breath and she could see he was emotional.

From a window, somewhere, Edith Piaf's 'Sous le Ciel de Paris' started playing.

They both stood in the middle of the street, looking at each other, not saying a word.

She closed her eyes, listening to the lyrics.

'Dance with me?' he asked.

Dominique opened her eyes; he was standing in front of her motionless, like he had roots as old as the trees around them.

When their eyes locked, she knew her head was saying *no* but her heart was saying *yes*. How could it be wrong if it felt so right? How could he not be the one? *Shut up, mind. Shut up, dreams. You are all wrong.*

He took her hand and just like that, she was in his arms. She thought it would be awkward, but their arms seemed to have been made to hold one another.

They danced, and their faces were dangerously close. Just like at the ball. Dominique's heart was beating out of her chest.

All those feelings she kept trying to ignore invaded her whole being.

They were dancing as if it wasn't the first time they had danced together. They fit in each other's arms like the last two pieces of a puzzle. Their bodies were slightly touching, and it was as if the lights, the music, the universe were all pushing them in the same direction. Towards each other. Alexander leaned down, and their faces got closer, so close that Dominique felt like they were one person.

There was so much tension in the air and so much anticipation. He leaned down a bit more and kissed her on the cheek before taking her face in his hands and gently kissing her on the lips. A soft, sweet kiss.

He pulled back, and she felt his warm breath on her face. Dominique knew she didn't want the moment to end. It felt right. No, not just right. Perfect. She instinctively reached for him and pulled him back to her, surprising herself. She lifted herself up on her toes. Her hand clasped the back of his neck and her lips pressed against his. He returned the kiss, deeper, more passionately than before. She reciprocated, and she stopped keeping score. What started off as a gentle brush of lips turned into a passionate, mind-blowing, heart-exploding kiss. The world stopped – all the sounds, the smells, the wind. Time itself stopped. She felt in that kiss unspoken words, passion, longing and most of all she felt love.

Dominique stepped back and took another look at him, trying to make sense of what had just happened. It was all confusing and powerful.

'Is this really happening?' she asked, her voice cracking.

'It is. And I've known it ever since I saw you. Before that. I know how this sounds and how it makes me look, but I want you to know that you are the one for me. Only you. Always.'

Could it be possible? Could she be that happy?

'I don't want this night to end, and I don't want you to

go back to your life without me. I don't want a life without you in it.'

'Kiss me,' she said with a courage she never thought she was capable of.

He listened. Then he kissed her again. And again. Everything was spinning.

'I don't want to spend another minute without you. I don't want an hour on Wednesday. I don't know how I managed for so long. I don't remember what I did before tonight. I think… I think all I've done was wait for this. For this moment. For you.'

She grabbed his hand and he followed. A few minutes later they were upstairs, in her studio. The windows were open, and the wind blew the curtains to the sides.

He took her in his arms and pulled her close to him. Tight. As if he was afraid he would lose her. He caressed her hair, her face. Then he kissed her forehead, her cheeks, her neck, her lips. He was taking his time at first. Until his lips met hers. Then he must've forgotten about time. And patience. Because his lips were savage, passionate.

Dominique was out of breath.

Alexander stepped back and looked at her.

'Ever since I saw you, I've dreamed of this and I never thought it would happen. I – I want to remember it,' he said.

She stood there for a moment, her breathing agitated, her chest moving up and down with anticipation. She pulled him back to her, her fingers drawing the contours of his face, and finally resting on his lips. How many times she'd imagined his beautiful lips. How many times.

She kissed him again. And again. His hands explored her, her shoulders, the small of her back. She melted into him and in that moment, it was perfect. And beautiful. And meant to be.

The Eiffel Tower was looking at them, quietly, dimly lit. A silent witness to the moment they had both been waiting for... dreaming of. A witness to their love.

'I had never spent the night with a man before,' I say and fear I am blushing. Even now, after fifty-five years.

'What about Grandpa Vincent?' asks Valerie.

'No, we never...'

I'm thinking of how I can explain this, without sounding too old-fashioned.

'I wanted the first time to be with the man I was going to spend the rest of my life with. I had decided that a long time ago when I was a teenager. Although the dreams told me it was Vincent, I always felt something was off. I think something in my heart was telling me what my mind didn't want to hear. So I waited.'

'And that night you felt Alexander was the one for you,' says Valerie and I wonder if she's beginning to understand.

ALEXANDER

PARIS

When he woke up next to Dominique, Alexander knew beyond a shadow of a doubt that was where he was meant to be. In her arms. Forever. He watched her sleep, for the longest time, and he couldn't get enough of looking at her.

'Good morning,' she whispered, slowly opening her eyes.

He covered her mouth with his. 'Good morning, birthday girl.'

It was so simple, yet so perfect. She was perfect.

They had breakfast in each other's arms.

'I've never been happier,' he said before kissing her.

'I want to spend today with you.'

He chuckled. 'I want to spend tomorrow with you. And the day after. And the day—'

She ruffled his hair. 'You know what I mean. I want to spend my birthday with you. Just you.'

'Are you sure?' he asked.

'Of course I'm sure. Why?'

He sighed. 'Constance told me about the party.'

'Oh, the party.' She slapped her forehead. 'I will take care of it. I have to talk to Vincent and make things right. End it. I should've done it long ago.'

He smiled widely. It was really happening.

She stared at him for a moment and he knew what she was thinking.

'I broke up with Nicole.'

'Good.' Then she blushed. 'Well, not good. I'm sorry for her, but—' She took him in her arms. 'I'm so happy, Alexander.'

He wanted to tell her he loved her. So much. He'd wanted to say it the night before, millions of times. He'd wanted to say it for months. But he had a plan. For once, he wanted to make everything perfect. The way she deserved.

He pictured himself sitting with her at their table, drinking their coffees and laughing like they had been doing every Wednesday. Then he would drop on one knee, open the jewelry box, take her hand into his, and looking into her eyes, he would tell her, 'I don't remember ever being more certain of anything than when I think of you, of us. Please forgive me for taking such a long time to say it, to admit it to the whole world. To myself. The past few months have been the best and the worst of my life. The best because I met you, and I understood what real love is. The worst because of all the minutes, hours and days I've had to spend away from you. But not anymore. I won't waste another second. I love you and I want to say it a thousand times, and when you get tired of hearing it, I will say it again... for the rest of our lives.

'I felt so lost for so long and now I understand why. I had been looking for you, in every woman I saw, in every smile. I feel that's what I've been doing all my life. The truth is, the first time I saw you in that ballroom I kept looking at you and all the time I thought: I know you, we've met before, I don't know if in this life, or maybe in my dreams, but we have, haven't we? Let's make this the first Wednesday of the rest of our lives. Will you marry me? Will you make me the happiest man in the world?'

'What are you thinking of?' she asked.

He grinned. 'That I have to go soon. I need to do something. Something important.'

'What?'

'I can't tell you yet. You'll have to wait until tonight to find out.'

'Is it a gift for my birthday? Because if it is, I don't want presents. I have everything I want,' she said and caressed his face.

Alexander winked. 'I hope you will want this one,' he said.

'Ah, the suspense,' she joked. 'Well, I have to go to school anyway, and over to Margaux and Vincent and then we'll be free. Finally, free.'

He kissed her again. 'If you could go anywhere for your birthday, where would you go?'

He'd never felt the need for grand gestures with anyone before and until that day thought he wasn't much of a romantic. But for her, he would've done anything.

She thought for a moment. 'Anywhere, as long as I'm with you.' She giggled.

'Hmm,' he said. 'What is your absolute favorite thing in Paris then?'

She started to say something, but he stopped her. 'And don't say being with me.'

They both laughed.

'There's this bistro, Barbelle. I've never been but I heard it's like a slice of heaven. It has the most amazing early-blooming Asiatic lilies that attract hundreds of butterflies, especially in the summer. But it's impossible to get a table. They have a six-month waitlist. Maybe more.'

'Alright,' he said, content. 'I have to go now. I'll call you later, at the café, to tell you where we're meeting tonight.'

She smiled. 'I'll be waiting.'

He took her in his arms and kissed her for what seemed like an eternity. It was so hard to leave, but he knew it was the last goodbye. The next time they were together, he would propose, and then they would never have to be apart again.

Later in the afternoon, he came home from the jewelry store, walking on clouds. He had spent hours looking for the perfect ring. And he'd found it. He couldn't wait for their life together to start. He could see it. All of it. And it was beautiful.

Alexander had to call in three different favors to get a table at Barbelle that night. He was just about to dial Le Petit Coin's number to tell Dominique he would pick her up in an hour for a 'little surprise' when the doorbell rang.

'Nicole,' he said, unable to hide his surprise.

'Going somewhere?' she asked. He was dressed in a nice black suit. Alexander instinctively touched the pocket of his vest for the small jewelry box. It was there, close to his heart. He exhaled, relieved.

'Yes, as a matter of fact, I am.'

'Can we talk? Just for a few minutes,' she said, standing awkwardly in the doorway.

He let her in.

She took a few hesitant steps and stopped in the middle of his living room.

'Do you want to sit down?' he asked.

She nodded and sat on the sofa, while Alexander pulled up a chair.

'I'm actually glad you stopped by,' he started. 'I wanted to call you later today and check up on you. I felt really bad about how things ended between us. And I – I wanted to tell you how much I care about you and how I wish I could change all of that and turn back the time, so I wouldn't hurt you. I never meant to hurt you, Nicole. You are and will always be an important part of my life. And I hope one day you will forgive me. I understand it might take time.'

She took a deep breath.

'I don't know if it was a good idea to come here,' she said sadly.

'You can always talk to me, no matter what,' he said, but that seemed to make her even more sad.

'I barely slept last night, wondering what I should do,' she started.

'Do about what?'

'Yesterday, after you left, I felt very sick and decided to call a doctor.'

Alexander got up. 'Is there something wrong? Are you ill or something?'

'I'm not ill. But I have been feeling sick quite a lot lately.'

'I don't understand.'

'Alexander...' She stopped for a moment before continuing. 'I'm pregnant.'

His whole world crashed. Crashed and burned. Everything collapsed in an instant. Everything he wanted, everything he dreamed of... gone.

'Pregnant?'

She nodded.

He was trying his best to remain calm, but his hands were shaking.

'Are you sure? How? I don't understand. We haven't, I mean, it's been three months since we—'

'Yes. Exactly. I'm three months' pregnant,' she said and held her head in her hands.

Alexander got up and paced the room, rubbing his hands. A sudden chill ran through him.

'What – what are you going to do?'

'I don't know. I really don't know. I didn't even know if I was going to tell you, until I got into the taxi that dropped me here. It's all so overwhelming.'

She wasn't looking at him.

He had to think. Had to calm down and think.

'You know what made me come here after all?'

Alexander stared at her, stunned, speechless. He could barely hear the words coming out of her mouth.

'You. I'm here because of you.' She looked down. 'Because I know how much you suffered when your father was not there for you. I remembered you saying that you would never abandon your child like that and make them feel unwanted, and how when you would have a child, you would be the father you always dreamed of having. And I realized, I don't want to take this away from you. Because I love you and I know what an amazing father you would make.'

When she finally lifted her eyes and looked at him, tears were running down her cheeks.

Alexander gasped. In the shock of it all, the news that had turned his world upside down, seeing Nicole cry was not something he ever thought he would see. Ever.

Instinctively, he walked over and took her in his arms. What had he done? What had he done?

'I'm sorry if I made a mistake coming here. I know you don't love me,' she said between sobs, 'and I know what this must be doing to you.'

He tried not to cry. He had to be strong.

They stayed embracing for a while, neither of them saying anything.

'Nicole,' he finally said, lifting her chin and looking in her eyes. 'You did the right thing by coming here and telling me. And I know it couldn't have been easy. But it's my child and, yes, I will do the right thing as well. I will marry you,' he said.

He didn't love her. Looking in her eyes now he felt a mix of tenderness and pity and a sense of duty. But not love. Not that kind of love. But there was no other way, and he knew it.

Nicole started sobbing now, her body shaking in his arms. 'You will? Are you sure?'

He took a deep breath. Sure? No, he wasn't sure. But he

couldn't allow himself to think about it too much. It was the right thing to do.

'I am sure,' he said and caressed her hair. 'And I think we should go to New York, just like you wanted. We shouldn't stay here. It's better this way.'

'Really?' she asked, wiping her tears.

He nodded.

He asked her to give him a few hours to sort out his business, then they would meet up the next morning to discuss travel plans.

'We should tell JJ together,' he said. 'Tomorrow.'

She agreed. They hugged on her way out.

Nicole took his hands in hers and held them tight. 'I do love you very much, Alexander. This is going to be a new beginning for us. And we'll be so happy. You'll see,' she said.

As soon as she left, he fell on the sofa and held his head in his hands, rocking back and forth. He wanted to cry, to scream, to yell.

Alexander didn't know how long he stayed there, feeling his life ending, wondering if it wouldn't have been better if he ended it himself. What was the point of living if he couldn't be with the woman he loved? What was the point of anything? The only thing stopping him was the baby, that innocent soul who wasn't guilty of the way it came into the world.

No, he couldn't be like his father. He'd sworn to himself he was never going to be like Leonard. He had to do it, for the child. He'd made the right choice. The most difficult decision he had ever made. But there was no other way.

ALEXANDER

PARIS

He walked out of his apartment ten times, and ten times he went back in.

How could he possibly face Dominique? How could he tell her the truth? But how could he not? Maybe he could just call her. No, that would be such a cowardly thing to do. Dominique didn't deserve to be treated like that. But, as it was, she didn't deserve any of what was happening. Either way, no matter what he was going to do, whether he ran to New York like a coward or faced her, he would break her heart. He would do the one thing he promised himself he was never going to do – hurt her.

No. He had to go and tell her. He owed her that much. He owed their love that much.

He took his time getting to her studio. Didn't drive, didn't take a taxi or a bus, but instead walked, trying to postpone the inevitable. The unimaginable heartbreak he was about to cause her. To cause himself. As if, until he told her, it wasn't really true. It wasn't yet true. They were still the happy couple who had kissed that morning, and he was still the same man who went shopping for an engagement ring. But they weren't, and Alexander knew it.

The sun was setting when he finally arrived in front of her building.

The light was on in the studio, and for a few minutes, he just stood there, in the middle of the street, watching her window. Hoping to catch a glimpse of her. Of the Dominique who had sparkles in her eyes not tears.

He took a few deep breaths, gathering the little courage he had, and picked up a few pebbles off the road. He didn't want to ring and let Constance know he was there. Just as he was about to throw the first pebble, the curtain moved, and a silhouette appeared in the window.

'Dominique,' he whispered. 'Oh my God. What have I done?'

She opened the window wide. 'Alexander! Thank God, you're here. Come on up.'

A few seconds later, she buzzed him in.

Every step of the staircase took him closer to the end. Closer to her, but further from her than he had ever been.

She was waiting for him at the top of the stairs and when his foot touched that last step, she jumped in his arms and kissed him. 'I was so worried. Where have you been? I thought something had happened.'

He stood there, transfixed, unable to move, like had had turned into stone.

She pulled him into the studio and closed the door behind them.

'Do you like my dress? I bought it just for you. For tonight.'

She did a pretend pirouette. She was so beautiful. So perfect. His Dominique.

He tried to swallow but couldn't. Tried to breathe but couldn't.

'Is everything alright? What's wrong? Why are you not saying anything?'

'Dominique,' he started but couldn't continue.

He took her in his arms and hid his head in the folds of her dress, afraid she might see his tears. He couldn't cry. He couldn't break down. He had to be strong. For her. He held her so tight, he was afraid she couldn't breathe anymore.

Alexander let go.

'You're scaring me,' she said. 'What's wrong? Please, tell me. You know you can tell me anything.'

'I do have something – something to tell you,' he said and taking her hand, he led her to the small window seat.

'We can't...' His breathing was so agitated he could barely speak. 'We can't see each other anymore.'

He couldn't even look at her, afraid he was going to break down.

Was it too late to take it all back? Maybe there was another solution. Maybe he could just take care of the child, provide for him or her, but not actually be there every day. And then what? He'd be like his father. Like JJ. As much as he loved his godfather, and as much as he took his side in front of Nicole, the truth is he had always judged him for not being there for his daughter, for leaving her with just a nanny, a stranger, to take care of her. And look what that had done to JJ and to Nicole. It had broken both of them, in ways that could not be fixed. No, he couldn't make the same mistakes.

'What do you mean?' Her tone was a mix of confusion and disbelief.

'We just can't be together. I...' He was trying not to cry.

'Alexander, I don't understand. Are you making a joke? Because it's not really funny.'

There was still doubt in her tone. And hope. Hope that it was a joke. He could hear it in the inflexions of her voice.

'Nicole is pregnant,' he said and got up. He couldn't look at her.

Silence. Perfect silence. Not a gasp, not a sound.

'I see,' she said eventually.

'I have to do the right thing. I have to marry her. For the baby.'

Silence again.

'Of course.'

He heard her take a deep breath, a shaky deep breath and he knew she was crying. Alexander couldn't turn to face her. He couldn't look at her, imagining her pain and knowing he was the cause.

'I'm sorry,' he said, his head low. 'I'm so sorry, Dominique.'

'It's alright. You have to do the right thing.'

He finally turned to her. Dominique's face was expressionless. Pale. She stared into space, almost like he wasn't even there.

'Please, please forgive me. Please don't hate me,' he said. Almost begged.

'I don't hate you.'

She got up and walked over to the door.

'I think you should go. It's not appropriate for you to be here, at this hour, when—'

Dominique opened the door and stepped aside.

He grabbed her arm. 'This is breaking my heart. Let's not say goodbye like this. I'm begging you. Don't you understand? I—'

She stared him down. An ice-cold look in her eyes. 'Don't you dare say it. Just don't. Not now.' She yanked her arm out of his hold.

Dominique was changed. Cold. Distant. She was acting like a stranger. Like there had never been anything between them. Like she hated him. No. Worse. Like he meant nothing to her. She wasn't his Dominique anymore. And he deserved it all. But how much it hurt.

He reached out his hand to touch hers, but she avoided his touch.

With his head down, tears pooling in his eyes, Alexander walked out the door.

He couldn't bring himself to say goodbye, so he didn't. He just left.

He'd come so close, so close to having it all. And now he had lost it. He had lost everything. Her. His dreams. Her love.

He wiped his tears and went down the stairs.

His life was over. He had hurt the person he loved most in the world. He'd hurt her in the worst possible way, and he didn't know how he was going to live with that. How he was going to live with that image of her, looking at him like he meant nothing, like they had meant nothing.

DOMINIQUE

PARIS

Dominique stood there for a few moments, her head pressed against the door, her hand still on the handle. Her breathing accelerated. So many emotions invaded her senses.

First, revolt and rage. Why did she get that glimpse into absolute happiness, for it to be taken away in a heartbeat? Why did she have to meet him? Why did she have to fall in love with him? Why? So she could suffer like that? How could she have been so wrong about him? About them?

Then, a panic. Had she been wrong? What was she doing?

And in the end, a moment of clarity. Dominique opened the door and ran down the stairs in her bare feet, jumping three, four steps at a time. As fast as she could. Like her life depended on it. What if it was too late? What if he had already left?

She reached the front door and jumped into the street. Desperate.

He was still there. Standing in the middle of street, looking up at the sky as if he was waiting. For a miracle maybe.

'Alexander!' she called out to him, his name rolling off her lips like a desperate cry for help. Like a gasp for air.

His gaze met hers.

Dominique didn't know if she ran towards him, or if he ran towards her or if, perhaps, they met in the middle. All she knew was that her arms were now around his neck, her feet off the ground like she was flying, as his lips pressed on hers. He kissed her again, so passionately, so intensely she felt they were going to melt into one being and no one would ever be able to tell them apart, no one could ever separate them again. She kissed him with the fervor and desperation of those last moments together. Of that goodbye she knew was coming.

'I'm sorry,' she said and wouldn't let him go. Feeling him next to her, feeling his heart beat next to hers, the warmth of his body. Knowing it was the last time. It was almost too much for her to bear.

'I am the one who should be sorry. You did nothing wrong. I alone did this to us.'

'I shouldn't have reacted like that. I was shocked. And selfish.' She caught her breath. 'I didn't want us to say goodbye like that. I didn't want that to be the last image I have of you and me. I couldn't live with it.'

She felt tears coming, but she forced herself to be strong. She had to be strong. For him.

He caressed her face so lovingly and so gently, her heart, already ripped to pieces, broke a bit more. 'I don't want to say goodbye to you at all. I don't want to be without you. Oh, how I wish—' he whispered.

She took his hands in his. 'I know. I wish that too. But it's not possible. We both know it. And it hurts and it's unfair, but you are doing the right thing, and we'll have that as our comfort. Your child will have a father, a wonderful father.'

Alexander didn't seem so confident. 'You *are* going to be wonderful,' she said.

She didn't want to make things worse, but words poured out of her, straight from the heart. Unfiltered. Raw. 'I'm sorry I will not get to see it. I'm sorry I didn't tell you sooner how I felt. I'm sorry I wasted so much of our precious little time. Maybe things would've turned out differently. I wish I could do it all over. I wish…'

She stopped for a moment. 'But just like all our other wishes, it's not possible. We just have to be strong. And say goodbye.'

She couldn't believe she was saying that. She couldn't believe it was truly over. And in a few minutes, maybe a few seconds, he would leave, and she was never going to see him again.

'I can't,' he said, his voice so weak she barely heard him. 'Goodbye sounds like forever. And I cannot handle forever not being with you. Let me at least have that hope. If there's no goodbye, there is still that chance that someday…' He had tears in his eyes.

She put a finger to his lips. 'That wouldn't be right. If you continue to hope, you will never be fully invested in your real life, your life with your wife and child. You will be there with them, but not truly there with them.'

He closed his eyes for a moment. They both knew she was right.

Alexander took her in his arms and they stayed like that for a while, neither of them saying a word.

Dominique didn't want to be the one who said it first, but she had to be strong. There was no other way. Seeing him in pain like that, it hurt her more than her own suffering.

She slowly let go and pulled back.

'Goodbye, Alexander,' she said and gulped. My God, he was right. How final that sounded. How devastating.

He looked in her eyes for a few more moments. 'I want to remember,' he said.

She took a step back. He took a step back. They were still holding hands.

One more step. Their hands barely touched.

One more. They let go.

She headed towards home; he walked the opposite direction.

A second. Two. Three.

Dominique turned. To see him one more time. Even as he was walking away.

But Alexander wasn't walking away. Not yet.

He had turned too, facing her, and now they were staring in each other's eyes, from across the street, like they had done that day, many months ago. Before it all started.

He smiled, put his hand on his heart, then raised it up in the air and mouthed, 'Goodbye.'

He had finally said it.

She placed her trembling hand on her heart too. Then she turned and rushed inside, afraid she wouldn't be able to control her emotions for much longer. That she'd run after him and beg him not to leave. Beg him to choose her.

Behind the closed door, Dominique broke down; she fell to her knees, her head in her hands, and started to cry. Quietly at first, then sobbing.

It was over. He was gone.

DOMINIQUE

PARIS

Not even two hours after she had said goodbye to Alexander, someone rang the downstairs buzzer.

In all the chaos of that long, heartbreaking day, Dominique hadn't had a chance to call Vincent and tell him she wasn't going to show up for her own birthday party and now it was too late. Margaux had sent a car to pick her up and the driver was waiting in front of the house.

Dominique didn't have time or energy to change out of her dress, so she pulled her hair up in a ponytail, put a little makeup on, just enough to hide the evidence of her tears, grabbed her shoes and went downstairs.

Neither Vincent nor Margaux had done anything to hurt her. She would go, stay for a little while, then say she wasn't feeling well and make it an early night. Then, when she and Vincent had a moment alone, Dominique would tell him the truth. The truth she should've told him a long time ago.

Dominique was in tears just thinking about it. She had waited too long to admit the truth to everyone, even herself. She didn't love Vincent; she loved Alexander. Even though he had just left her broken-hearted. Even though he was about to marry another woman. And now Dominique was the one who was about to break the heart of someone who loved her. She would end her relationship with Vincent, because she had to do the right thing. She loved another man more. She had kissed another man. She'd spent the night with another man and because of that alone there was no future for her and Vincent anymore. Her conscience wouldn't let her.

When she showed up at the restaurant, Vincent didn't give her a chance to have the serious conversation she wanted to have and the night went by in a flash. He seemed giddy, almost manic, hugging her and going for kisses that Dominique successfully deflected.

'I've missed you,' he said, holding her hand. 'So much.'

Dominique looked away, feeling suffocated, trapped, guilty.

Vincent grabbed a champagne flute from one of the waiter's trays and lifted it towards the center of the room and like magic, everyone stopped talking. They all turned to him, quietly.

'Dear friends and family,' he said. 'Dominique and I wanted to thank you all for being here with us, on such a special occasion.' He turned to her. 'I know you're going to open your presents tomorrow, but you won't find any from me in there. Because my gift to you is here,' he said and put his hand on his heart.

'These last two years have been the greatest of my life,

and the reason for my happiness is standing in front of you all tonight,' he said and gestured towards Dominique. 'They say when you find something good, don't let go, and I don't plan to. Therefore, I wonder what she thinks about spending two more years with me... and all the years after.'

Dominique felt the walls closing in on her.

Vincent kneeled in front of her, an open jewelry box in his hand. 'Will you marry me, Dominique Gardiner?'

There was a moment she was tempted. Tempted to say yes. Maybe she could learn to love Vincent like she loved Alexander. She hesitated. But only for a moment.

'Can we go somewhere to talk?' she whispered in Vincent's ear. It must've been her tone or the look in her eyes, because his face drained of color.

She pulled him aside and he followed. Behind them murmurs, whispers.

In the hallway, Vincent stood in front of her, wordless.

For the longest time she had believed Vincent was what she needed. He had all the qualities one looked for in a husband. But none of it mattered when she met Alexander. Love was not something you ticked off a list. Love was the list itself, the ultimate goal.

'I can't marry you, Vincent. I'm so sorry. So very sorry.'

What followed was a sight Dominique never thought she would witness. Vincent cried, and seeing him unravel in front of her made her already broken heart shatter even more.

'Please, don't cry,' she pleaded. 'It's not you. You didn't do anything wrong. You deserve the best in the world. You deserve a woman who will love you more than anything, more than anyone.'

He wiped his tears. 'I thought that woman was you,' he said roughly.

She gulped. 'I thought so too, but – I love someone else,' she said, barely audible.

'Someone else,' he repeated. 'Why does this always happen to me? Why? I'm never enough. It's never me, it's always someone else.' He clenched his jaw. 'Very well then. I get it. I will – I will go. Goodbye, Dominique.'

'I'm sorry. I'm really sorry,' she said, but he didn't hear her. He had already left.

With mixed feelings of sadness and a strange relief, Dominique watched Vincent leave. It was the end of a relationship that had been important to her. It was probably also the end of a friendship – and that was the most painful part. But she had finally done the right thing. Even if it was too late.

ALEXANDER

NEW YORK

He didn't know who or what gave him the strength to not break down and cry in front of Dominique that evening in Paris. It had taken every ounce of self-control to walk away. He walked away, knowing that although he did the right thing, the responsible thing, he'd broken her heart and at the same time, he'd broken his, in a way that no heart should ever be broken.

He was never going to love anyone else. There was no room in his soul for anyone but Dominique. She was part of him. And knowing she loved him too brought him solace and comfort, in a selfish kind of way. Made him feel his life had been worth living. He'd met her, he loved her, she loved him. And for a while, a short while, he was the happiest man in the world. He would now live through those memories. Nobody could take those away from him.

Could he have done things differently? Yes. And if he

could go back in time, if he had another chance, he would know not to hesitate, to tell her what he felt the first moment he felt it. Then, maybe he could've prevented what happened.

Alexander had to learn to live with the pain, the void, and the longing. He had to learn to live without her. He had been so close to happiness, and once again, lost it. Perhaps it wasn't meant for him. Perhaps love, that kind of love, was not in his destiny.

In New York, Alexander took his role as a future father seriously. He and Nicole moved into her Manhattan penthouse, close to AngeD'Art so he could be just a few minutes away if she wanted something. And she did. All the time. She needed attention constantly, and he never complained. He arranged the baby's room, helped her get everything they needed for the child. Nicole decided to delay the wedding until after the baby was born because she wanted to look perfect on her big day.

It had been five months since he left Paris and his heart ached more than ever. Five long, excruciating months of being away from Dominique. *Just the beginning,* he thought. *You will never see her again. Get used to the idea.*

He was so broken sometimes, he couldn't pull himself together. Couldn't do his job, couldn't even hold a conversation or look at a family with a baby without feeling completely destitute.

JJ came to New York to spend the last few weeks with them, before the baby was born, and help with whatever they needed. It should've made Alexander feel better, but not even JJ could pull him out of the abyss.

Things would've continued that way, had it not been for one fateful afternoon in early December, just a couple of

328

weeks before Nicole's due date. Alexander had been useless at work and a distraction to everyone else, so JJ sent him home early.

Alexander let himself into the apartment he shared with Nicole. She was in the bedroom, with the door closed.

'I told you to stop calling. I won't change my mind,' he heard her say.

A long pause.

'I don't want to risk him finding out.'

She was already raising her voice.

'So what? You can't prove it and I will never admit it. It's your word against mine. Who do you think he'll believe?'

Alexander moved to the bedroom door.

'Raise it together? Is this a joke? I don't care if it's yours. You will never be the father.'

Alexander stopped, frozen in shock.

'No, you cannot see the baby. No!'

He heard something being thrown around the room.

'You can hire all the attorneys you want.' She paused. 'No. No. Stop saying it's your baby. It's *my* baby. My baby, you hear? You have no right.' She sounded hysterical.

Alexander opened the door to the bedroom and just stared, completely dumbfounded.

Nicole was lying in bed. When she saw him, she slammed the receiver down.

'Wh-what are you doing home so early? These salespeople,' she said trying to sound casual. 'They keep bothering me.'

He opened his mouth, but no sound came out. He couldn't breathe and the walls seemed to get closer and closer as if they were about to squash him.

It wasn't his baby? What was going on? He was so mad and confused, and frustrated. He wanted to grab Nicole and shake her and yell at her. How could she do this? How could she lie to him, and for how long? How long had she known this?

He'd left everything behind. He'd left the woman he loved because he was trying to do the right thing. And what for? For a lie?

Nicole knew about Dominique; she knew what she'd made him give up. What kind of person does that? What kind of woman was she? He'd known her all his life, and he knew she loved him, but he'd never imagined she would stoop so low.

The phone rang and rang but Nicole didn't move. Alexander walked over to answer it, but she jumped in front of him with a mad look on her face and pulled the cable out.

'Who was on the phone?' he asked, his anger barely contained.

'Nobody, I told you.'

'The nobody who fathered your child,' he said through his teeth, trying to control his rage. 'You know what? I don't even care who he is. That's your problem.'

Her face fell.

'What are you talking about?' She followed him from room to room, as he picked up his clothes, books, work papers and threw them into suitcases.

'Stop packing! Why are you packing?' she yelled.

He didn't bother answering.

Nicole suddenly started sobbing and threw herself on the floor.

'I did all this for nothing. Look at me; I'm fat as a whale. And what for? You couldn't have just married me?'

'Oh my God, Nicole, what kind of person are you? You got pregnant on purpose with another man's child and then you trick me into marrying you?'

'What was I supposed to do?'

'What's happened to you, Nicole? Why would you ever want to marry me like this?'

'Because I love you. I've always loved you. Ever since we were kids. I would do anything for you. I was desperate.' She looked at him, eyes pleading. 'Please, don't go. We can work this out. I know I can make you happy. Let's start over.'

'You're not making any sense. And no, I don't want to start anything over. I've made enough mistakes. I'm leaving now,' he said firmly.

Her tone changed again. This time it was so aggressive it was almost menacing. 'Curse you, Alexander. I curse you. You don't deserve anything good. For what you've done to me, you will not have a moment's peace. You think you can abandon me and go back to her and live happily ever after? Never! You will never have what you want!'

She sobbed hysterically as he closed his suitcase.

'You know what? I'm happy it's not your child. Do you hear me? I'm happy. Ecstatic. You wouldn't have been a good father. Or husband. I don't need you. Go! Go back to her. Isn't that what you hoped I would say? Go. I hope you both rot in hell.'

'I feel sorry for you,' he said, and without looking back, stormed out of the apartment.

Before going to the airport, Alexander went to JJ's hotel and told him everything.

JJ was saddened and mortified, but not shocked. 'I should've known she would do something terrible one day. I just never thought it would be this bad. I'm sorry, my boy.'

'What are you sorry for, JJ? You did nothing wrong.'

'I met with Dominique after you left. I was saying something about Nicole, and the baby and I immediately knew. I saw it in her eyes. I think I knew before, but I chose not to. What an old fool I am. I should've figured it out the first time you asked me about her. And one Wednesday I stopped by the café to talk to her and saw the two of you. I knew. You were both so happy. That is what love looks like. I recognized it. That is what I felt for Demetria, God rest her soul. I'm sorry, my boy, I'm sorry if I'm to blame in any way for what is happening now. I so desperately hoped it would work out between you and Nicole – but it was a selfish hope. I knew you would be what she needed; you would be good for her. But I never stopped to think about what was good for you. And who was right for you. I want you to know that I regret it terribly. I should've supported you. But I'm doing it now. And I promise you, I always will. No matter what.'

It meant so much to Alexander to hear JJ understood what he'd gone through and recognized the love they shared. But, what good did it do now? He had lost her.

'It's too late, JJ. She's probably engaged, if not even married to Vincent by now.'

JJ smiled. 'She's not. Vincent proposed the day you left, but she said no.'

'How do you know? Are you sure, JJ?'

'We became quite close after you left. I stop by the café often and we talk. The last few months have been tough on her and she's been in a lot of pain. The same pain I've seen in your eyes. You tried to hide it, but I know you.'

Alexander hugged him. He felt like jumping up and down and hugging everyone.

'It will not be easy, and it might take a while, but if this is what you want, if she is who you want, you will find a way. True love always finds a way.'

Dominique probably wouldn't forgive him right away. But he wasn't going to give up. Never again. And one day he would hold her in his arms, kiss her and finally tell that he had always loved her. And always would.

PART VII

'It is love, not reason,
that is stronger than death.'
— Thomas Mann

DOMINIQUE

9 DECEMBER 1964

PARIS

Diving through the air, plunging to her death, Dominique's life didn't flash before her eyes. She didn't have any last thoughts or wishes. Only one goal, vivid and irrational like an obsession – to survive. She had never experienced such a horrid sensation before. A sinking feeling in her stomach as her body accelerated. The desperate cries of people around her filling the thin air.

A deafening thud muffled the cries, the lights went off and a blast of freezing water took Dominique's breath away, knocking her unconscious. There was ice everywhere. When she came around, she felt a thousand knives going through her arms and legs as she struggled to stay afloat. Her body was deadweight, pulling her to the bottom of a freezing, black, deep hole.

'I cannot die, not now, please, not now.'

Dominique opened her eyes and instinctively gasped for

air. Her heart raced and she ran her hands over the sheets. No water, there was no water; and the familiar sight of the Eiffel Tower through her bedroom's window calmed her down. She was okay. She was safe.

It wasn't her in the dream. It was him. One of her reveries. But this one was unlike any she'd ever had. Her hands trembled. Her whole body was trembling. She was in a complete state of panic. Never had a reverie been so dark, so final.

She stretched out an arm, grabbed the phone from her nightstand and dialed Vincent's number.

He picked up after the third ring, his voice sleepy.

Dominique listened to him saying 'hello' a few times, then hung up.

They hadn't spoken in almost six months and she couldn't just say, 'I called you at six in the morning because I had a dream that you were dying.' And a good thing that she didn't because he was just fine.

So that wasn't a reverie. It was just a dream. Just like maybe all the other ones before it, for so many years, had been just that. Dreams.

That's when she saw it. The blinking light on her answering machine. There was a message from a few hours earlier.

Dominique hesitated before pushing the button.

'Dominique, are you there? Please pick up.' The voice on the machine paused for a moment. 'I'm at the airport. I'm coming back tonight.' He sighed. 'Nicole and I are done. She lied to me. It's not my baby, Dominique, it's not mine. I left—'

A garbled voice spoke over the PA. The last call for a Paris-bound flight.

'I know I hurt you. I know you might not want to talk to me ever again and I'm so sorry for everything. And I know I should tell you this in person, but I couldn't wait anymore. I don't want to wait anymore.' He stopped for a moment. 'You are the one. It's always been you. I'm sorry it took me so long to say it. I love you! Only you. Always. Don't give up on me. I'm coming back.'

Tears ran down her cheeks. Alexander was coming back to her. Her prayers were answered. Her biggest wish was coming true.

The realization hit with flooding horror.

The reverie.

Dominique ran down the stairs. She opened the door to the café. There was no line. No one sitting, no one eating. A group of people stood around the television and the only sound was the voice on the news. She felt sick.

'We're interrupting our broadcast for a special news report,' the anchor said. 'At approximately 0500 hours local time the Trans-Oceanic Airways Flight 651 from New York to Paris crashed in the English Channel, 100 kilometers off Le Havre. The aircraft was carrying 255 passengers and 8 crew members. Search and rescue teams have been deployed to Le Havre but at this time it is unclear if there are any survivors. The cause of the tragedy has not yet been confirmed. This could be one of the deadliest commercial aircraft accidents in France's history. We will report back with details as soon as they become available.'

Dominique stood there, incapable of thinking or feeling anything.

And then it all went quiet. And dark.

DOMINIQUE

11 DECEMBER 1964

PARIS

It was still quiet when she woke up, but it wasn't dark anymore. Bright artificial lights blinded her, and it took Dominique a couple of minutes to open her eyes.

The plane from New York to Paris crashed... crashed, kept echoing in her mind, like a thought from another life.

Constance, who was by her side, told her she'd collapsed in the café and she had to call the ambulance. When the doctors asked her what had happened, she'd told them Dominique had not been eating properly lately so perhaps she fainted. She hadn't done anything properly since Alexander left. Barely slept, barely ate, sat in her room for hours. She'd cut all ties with Vincent after she rejected his proposal and the only people she allowed in her life were Constance and occasionally JJ. Mostly because he insisted on checking up on her and taking her for a walk now and then. No, she wasn't well. She hadn't been well in months.

'She will be fine if she gets some rest and drinks plenty of fluids,' the doctors assured Constance initially. A few hours later though, they decided to keep her under observation a bit longer after Dominique told a nurse she didn't have a reason to live anymore. Constance said that for those two days, when asked by the doctors, Dominique couldn't tell them who she was or what she was doing there, but she kept begging them to stop the nightmare. Not surprisingly, they came back with a diagnosis: post-traumatic stress disorder. Cause of trauma: unknown.

Nightmare? Yes, she remembered the nightmare. That and walking into the café, barefoot and still wearing her nightgown, hearing that man on TV and feeling her world come to an end. Everything else was blank.

Constance took her home as soon as the doctors allowed her to.

'Where is he? Tell me the truth,' she kept asking Constance. 'Are there any survivors?'

'Why don't you try and get some rest?' she said. 'We'll talk about it later when you're feeling better.'

'I can't wait. I know he was on that plane. I need to know what happened to him. Is he alright? Where is he?'

'Vincent was on the plane?'

Dominique shook her head. 'Alexander. Alexander was on that plane.'

She tried not to cry again. 'I had a dream about him last night. A reverie. I saw the plane crash. I didn't know what it was, but I saw it. Something has happened to him; he might be hurt, and he needs me. I have to go to him.'

'This is all because of a dream? The same dreams who told you Leon was the one? The same dreams who told you

Vincent was the one? And the boy from Newport? And the man from New York? How many "the ones" are there for you? Listen to yourself. You don't know what you want, my dear. You're using these dreams as a crutch. Why would he even be flying to Paris? Isn't his wife supposed to give birth right about now? See? You're wrong. And you've been wrong before. Your dreams are just that. Dreams. Not some special gift. They're a curse if you ask me—'

'You don't understand, Constance,' said Dominique, exhausted. 'I think I was wrong and Mama was wrong too. But not about the dreams. About the connection. There is more than one. You can love more than one person. Do you know how I know this? Because I love him. I love him, like I never loved Vincent. Maybe not all connections are created equal and only one is unbreakable. This is the one. *He* is the one. Nothing else matters. Nobody else matters.'

'Dominique, you're rambling. Whenever something happens, the dreams are to blame. I know you've been through a lot, but, please, try and be rational about this. This reverie fantasy has to stop. It's been going on for too long. Enough, please, before it's too late. Just stop.'

She sounded quite angry.

Dominique tried to calm herself. 'I'm sorry, I didn't mean to upset you. I'll stop. I'll do whatever you want me to do. Just tell me he's alright. I don't want anyone to understand me. I just want to know he's alive.'

'I don't know if he's alive, alright? I don't know. I'm sorry. There are survivors, I heard on the news, but I don't know who they are or how many. I haven't left your side for two days.'

'Do you mind leaving me alone for a while? I'm tired. Maybe I can get some sleep.'

Constance tucked Dominique in and promised to come back in a few hours to check up on her and bring her something to eat.

The moment she closed the door, Dominique jumped out of bed. She didn't have a TV in her studio, but she did have a radio. She turned it on and searched until she found news about the accident. They repeated the address of the hospital where they had taken the victims.

She kept hitting play, rewind, play on her answering machine and the more she listened, the more she convinced herself that couldn't have been the end. No, their story couldn't end like that. No, it must've been a mistake.

He was alive. He had to be alive. Her love would keep him alive. No matter what her mother said. She was wrong before; she could be wrong now too. What if he could hear her in the dreams? What if she could make him stay? Anything was possible.

There was no time to lose. She had to find him.

DOMINIQUE

12 DECEMBER 1964

LE HAVRE

The Medical Center Alain Quesnay in Le Havre. That's where they took the victims of the crash. It was 200 kilometers from Paris. No time for packing, every minute mattered.

From the train station, she went straight to the hospital's front desk.

'Alexander Roberts,' she blurted out. 'Is his name on the list?'

A nurse looked through a long list of names.

She knew what he'd told her in the message, she knew what she dreamed, but she still held on to the hope that maybe he had taken a different flight.

'Please wait, and someone will be with you soon.'

'What does that mean? Can I see him? Can you please tell me where he is? At least tell me he is fine. Please, please tell me he is alive,' she said her eyes brimming with tears.

The nurse repeated like a robot, 'Please wait, and someone will be with you soon.'

Dominique heard raised voices coming from the stairs, then saw nurses running around agitated, a doctor talking to a guard and gesticulating, a whole lot of people and a flurry of frenzied activity.

She couldn't hear what they were talking about, at first.

The doctor went into one of the rooms and returned with a file, which she showed to the guard. She spoke fast and her voice was high-pitched, agitated, but as loud as she was, there was too much noise in the waiting room for Dominique to properly hear more than bits and pieces.

'...Violent. We restrained him. I don't know how it happened.'

The guard said something back.

'"I need to get out of here. I shouldn't be here." Over and over and wouldn't stop. Be on the lookout,' the doctor said as the guard walked away in Dominique's direction.

'What's happening?' she asked him when he passed her.

'A patient disappeared. They think he ran away during the night.' He scoffed. 'That's the last thing I needed today.'

Dominique continued waiting. It was a while. Every time she asked at the front desk, she was told a doctor would be with her soon. What was going on? Where was Alexander?

'Mademoiselle Gardiner?' Dominique immediately recognized the high pitch. It was the doctor who was talking to the police earlier. Her name tag read 'Dr Thomas'.

'Yes,' said Dominique tentatively.

'You are looking for information on one of the victims of the accident?'

Dominique got up. 'Yes. Alexander Roberts.'

'I'm sorry I kept you waiting. We had a situation here. Are you family?'

'No. Not yet. I mean—' Dominique took a deep breath. 'Where is he? Can I see him?'

'I'm sorry,' she said, and, at that moment, Dominique had a sensation of déjà vu.

A hospital in Colmar. Ten years before. The same feeling. The same panic. It couldn't be happening again.

She grabbed the doctor's arm, feeling dizzy. 'What are you sorry about?'

'I'm afraid he didn't make it. There was nothing we could do. He died on impact.'

'No, no, you're wrong, you're wrong,' Dominique kept repeating. He wasn't dead. She didn't feel he was dead. She'd asked him to stay with her. And he would've never left her. She'd saved him. If the dreams were good for anything, then they should be good for that. She didn't care if they were wrong about everything else. She didn't care if she broke all the rules, if she went against fate and what was predestined. She loved him too much for him to die. The doctor was mistaken.

'I want to see him. Please, let me see him.'

The doctor seemed to avoid looking at her. 'The family already identified him.' She patted her hand. 'And I'm afraid there's not much to see.'

'What do you mean?'

'Most of the victims have suffered massive injuries and they're beyond recognition. It would be better for you to remember him as he was.'

'This must be a mistake. It must be.'

'I'm so very sorry, mademoiselle, it is a terrible tragedy. I understand.'

'Dominique,' she heard and turned.

JJ was standing behind her. When she saw him, she burst into tears.

'Please tell me it's not true. Please tell me he's not dead.'

He took her in his arms and held her for a long time. Dominique couldn't stop crying.

'You shouldn't be here,' he said. An incredible sadness in his voice.

His eyes were red. He had been crying too and he looked completely destroyed.

She knew what that meant but couldn't accept it.

'No,' she wailed. 'No!'

'I'm sorry. I'm so sorry. Let me take you back to Paris. You're not well.'

Dominique fell to the floor and couldn't stop crying.

'I want to see him. Why won't they let me see him?'

He squeezed her hand. 'I did. Trust me, you don't want to. It's better if you remember him as he was.'

'I don't care what he looks like. I want to see him. I want to be with him.'

'Dominique,' he said firmer now. 'I am going back to Paris and I'm taking you with me.' Lifting her from the floor, he held her by the shoulders and led her to his car.

She had no energy left to fight him, to break loose. The pain, the incredible pain of losing Alexander numbed her.

For hours, in the car, she didn't say anything. What was there left to say?

Nothing made sense anymore. Nothing, and the tears wouldn't stop.

JJ struggled too. 'He told me everything before – before.' He couldn't continue. 'I know how much he loved you and I'm so sorry. I know how it feels. Now that he's gone—'

'I don't want to hear it, JJ. I can't. Please. Just don't.'

She couldn't accept that he was gone. It was all a big mistake. This wasn't how their story was supposed to end.

DOMINIQUE

17 DECEMBER 1964

PARIS

Back in Paris, Dominique couldn't let go. She didn't sleep, didn't eat, stopped going to school, to work. She stayed in the coffee shop, at their table, waiting for him to come back. He was coming back. He'd promised.

Hearing JJ talking about the funeral was like a nightmare.

'I convinced his mother to let him rest here. He always said Paris was home,' he said.

'I don't want to talk about this, JJ,' said Dominique.

'I know you don't. Nobody does, believe me. Especially me.'

'I just can't sit here and listen to you talk about him as if he's gone.'

'He is gone,' JJ said sadly. 'The sooner you accept it, the better it's going to be for you. Trust me, I've been through this before.'

She did trust him, but not with this.

'You are coming to the funeral though, right?'

Dominique shook her head. 'I can't.'

She left the room and went outside. She couldn't hear any more of it. She just couldn't. He wasn't gone. In her mind, in her heart, he wasn't gone. Why would she go to the funeral?

But the next morning, Dominique found herself taking the bus to the Père-Lachaise Cemetery, although she still felt they were making a mistake, and whoever they were burying, it wasn't Alexander. But if she wasn't going, JJ would be hurt. And he was hurting enough already.

When she arrived, it was snowing. The wind blew hard, whipping her face and making her eyes tear up. The cemetery was full of people and she realized other victims of the crash were being buried on the same day. Everywhere she looked, there were new tombstones; all with the same date of death – '9 December 1964'. It was heartbreaking. Dominique pushed on, trying not to break down and cry, when she saw an older woman who looked painfully familiar. Dominique walked towards her.

'Are you Mrs Roberts? Alexander's mother?'

The woman dried her tears with a handkerchief.

'Are you a friend of Alexander's?' she asked and took Dominique's hand in hers. Her fingers were cold and bony.

'My name is Dominique Gardiner.'

The woman's face changed abruptly. She let go of Dominique's hand like it burned her.

Then, behind her, she saw Nicole. Dressed in all black, her long blonde hair tucked away in a black pillbox hat, her face covered by a short black veil, she was dabbing her eyes every few seconds with a handkerchief.

Nicole saw her too. With a swift move, she lunged at Dominique, grabbing her by the collars of her coat. 'How dare you show your face here? You took Alexander away from me. You confused him, bewitched him and made him forget all about his family, and the promises he made,' she said, looking at Dominique with pure, unadulterated hatred. 'Abandoning me, after he promised we would get married and have a family, giving up the life he was supposed to lead. And for what? A simpleton without a penny to her name? What could he possibly see in you? I don't know what you did and how you did it, but I know it was you.'

'No, please, you have to listen to me. I—'

'You killed him! What was it? You couldn't have him so nobody could?'

She was hysterical and everyone was looking at them.

'I loved him more than you ever did. I gave him everything. I waited for him for years to finally get his life in order, so we could be together. And you ruined everything. You took it all away from me,' sobbed Nicole.

Alexander's mother took Nicole by the shoulders, trying to calm her down, but Nicole wouldn't have it. She wrestled out of the woman's embrace, but JJ showed up and took her aside.

Dominique was shaken.

'Nicole is right. You are to blame for all this. You have some nerve coming here after everything you've done,' said Mrs Roberts.

'Mrs Roberts, I loved Alexander with all my heart, and I will always love him. I never tricked him into anything. Nicole is wrong,' said Dominique, trying to reason with her.

Alexander's mother broke down crying. 'I don't want to

talk to you anymore. I don't want to see you again. Ever. You don't deserve to be here. Leave. I don't want Nicole to suffer more than she already has. Don't you dare say how much you loved him. I want her to think of Alexander as her fiancé, not the doormat you turned him into.'

JJ stepped between them, and turning to Dominique, he said, 'I think you should go.'

Dominique's eyes swam with tears. People shook their heads and stared at her with looks of disgust. She ran away, her head down, and didn't stop until she reached the gate of the cemetery. She wanted to go as far away as possible from that place. But then she stopped.

Where would I go? Where would I go without you? What would I do? If I am wrong, and they're right, you are dead. You are being buried now, and I didn't even say goodbye. I didn't get a chance to tell you all the things I wanted to tell you. How can I leave you here alone?

She turned around. She couldn't attend the funeral, but nobody could keep her away from him. So she waited. She waited in the cold until the sun set and everyone was gone. And then she went to his grave, dropped on her knees, and between tears, she told him. She told him how much she loved him and how there was no reason for her to be without him. And she told him she was never going to leave him. She was never going to stop waiting for him.

Valerie wipes away her tears with the back of her hand, hoping, perhaps, that I won't notice.

Maybe it is too much for her. It is a lot for me too, to relive all this. I don't say anything and close the book.

Valerie stares at me, confused. 'What? This is it? This can't be how your story ends.'

I smile. 'My mother used to say that all the time. This is not how your story ends.'

'Tell me this is not how it ends,' she says, almost begging me.

'No, this is not how it ends. I just thought we'd take a break. Cookies and cocoa are not exactly dinner. Let me make you something to eat.'

'No,' she says, with a fierce look on her face that reminds me of myself. Many years ago.

Before I can say anything, she runs to the kitchen, and comes back with the fruit basket.

'I'm eating, look,' she says and takes a big bite out of an apple.

I chuckle. She really is like me.

'Please, go on. I want to know what happens next.'

PART VIII

'Come back. Even as a shadow, even as a dream.'
— Euripides

DOMINIQUE

PARIS

Lisa retired, sold everything in Massachusetts and came to Paris to live with 'her girls'.

Dominique knew the real reason she came, despite Lisa's protests that she did it because she needed a change. She was worried. Constance was worried too.

'Dominique, you need to eat something. You look like a ghost,' said Constance. Lisa nodded approvingly.

Dominique sat at their table by the window, with a plate of macarons and two cups of cinnamon coffee in front of her. One for her and one for him.

'I'm not hungry.'

'Don't care if you're hungry or not. You have to eat to live.'

Dominique took an apple from the kitchen and bit into it. 'Happy now?'

She grabbed her keys and headed for the door.

'Where are you going?' asked Lisa.

'You know where I'm going.'

'It's been over six months. You have to move on with your life,' said Constance.

'I don't want to move on. Don't you understand? You can't move on from love. I still dream of him, Constance. I dream of him trying to talk to me. I can't hear what he's saying but I feel like I'm getting closer. If I could just hear the words, I would know what to do.'

'Don't tell me you still believe he's alive.'

'I never stopped believing. And I never will. Never.'

'It's the grave you took me to, earlier today, isn't it? Why did you keep going back? Why torture yourself?'

'It was the only constant in my life. The only link, if you like, to him. Ironically, in a way, because I refused to believe he was dead. Yet there I was, every single day. I stayed there for hours, talking to him, telling him what I was doing, although it wasn't much. I tried to go back to school, to continue the life I had before, but I couldn't. My dreams, my plans, they made no sense without him. Lisa and Constance tried to help, and so did JJ, but I couldn't pick up the pieces. Nothing made sense anymore; everything was pointless. My hopes of becoming a curator all turned to ash. I isolated myself from everything and everyone.

'The pain would not go away. Worse, it grew stronger. What I felt for Alexander didn't die the day of the accident, nor did it become smaller or less intense. It became more profound, more mature. It became forever. As time passed, I knew there was never going to be another man for me. My heart was full, and there was no room for anything or anyone else.'

DOMINIQUE

PARIS

'Dominique, you have to let me help you,' said JJ.

'I'm fine, JJ. Please stop worrying.'

'You're not fine. Alexander's been gone for over a year. You're a young, beautiful, smart girl. You can't keep this up forever. Do you want to wait tables at Le Petit Coin all your life?'

'I have to make a living.'

'Do you think this is what he would've wanted your life to look like? You know how much he loved you. And when you love someone, you want them to be happy.'

'I loved him too. I still love him. Even more now. And I am happy because he's here,' she said and pointed to her heart.

'I know,' he said sadly. 'It's not easy. But such is life. Tragedies happen. And the ones who are left behind have to bear the cross of living on without the ones they loved most. But still, they do it. Slowly they learn how.'

'I don't want to learn to live without him. Because I don't feel that I am without him. He's everywhere. In everything I do. He's at the coffee shop, here, at the museum. I hear his voice in the whispers of the trees. I see his face when the sun shines.'

They always cornered her. JJ, Constance, Lisa.

'Did Constance put you up to this?' she said.

'Nobody put me up to anything. I'm worried about you, that's all. You dropped out of school, you gave up everything you loved, everything you dreamed of.'

'You don't understand. It's quite the opposite. I didn't give up on the one thing I loved. On the one thing I wanted most of all. I'm fighting for it. The only way I know how.' Her voice softened. 'I'm sorry, JJ. I don't mean to hurt you. But I can't give up on him.'

He was hurt. She knew her attitude hurt him.

After the crash, he had spent so much time with her, always inviting her to AngeD'Art or coming over to the coffee shop. He seemed lonely, feeble and aged, not by days or months but years. Sometimes he would tell her she was all he had left, and it made her sad, but it also made her feel guilty. Like she owed him something. She knew his relationship with Nicole had never been good. Dominique felt terrible for JJ, and she understood why he spent so much time with her, thinking he was helping, wanting to be useful. Because Alexander was gone and Nicole didn't want him in her life, he took Dominique under his wing. She understood but she felt suffocated. She wanted to be left alone. Alone with Alexander.

★

'JJ called earlier,' said Constance sounding serious when Dominique came back from the cemetery, as usual. 'He asked if you could stop by his office. He sounded bad. Maybe he's sick.'

Afraid something had happened to him, Dominique rushed to AngeD'Art.

JJ hadn't been doing well lately. His relationship with Nicole had deteriorated even further, especially after the baby was born. She refused to tell anyone who the father of the child was and didn't allow JJ to be in their life either. They fought a lot. Ugly fights, JJ said. About her lifestyle, her choices as a parent, the men she dated – and there were many – the money she spent. A few months after giving birth, she had been seen at a lavish party in New York. Then she was spotted drunk at another party, in the arms of a known playboy. The tabloids were filled with news about her. The socialite heiress gone wild. The widow on the loose. The bad mother.

Dominique found JJ sitting at his desk, head in his hands, staring blankly out the window, a pile of newspapers spread on the floor. Although JJ avoided talking about it, she knew how much it must hurt him to see his daughter the subject of tabloids. From new conquests to scandals, offensive language, exorbitant parties and drunk driving, she had done it all lately.

'What's wrong, JJ? Is it Nicole?'

'I'm sorry to drag you into this, but I don't have anyone else.'

She took his hand in hers, reassuring him it was alright and she understood.

'I've tried to come up with excuses for her behavior ever since Anne was born, but all this mess has taken its toll on me too.'

'I know. Maybe she just needs time. It could be her way of coping with Alexander's—'

She couldn't say it. Couldn't say 'death'. Disappearance?

'Time to do what? To spend more money? To date more men? I've had enough. I will cut off her financing. Today. That's it. I've had too many years of this – this humiliation, this ingratitude. I am ashamed to say she's my daughter,' he said in a shaky voice.

Dominique's first reaction was to agree with JJ, but something stopped her. At one point, Alexander had loved Nicole. And Anne, that innocent child, was not to blame for any of it.

'If you cut her off what would she do? She doesn't know any other life. She'll be lost. Before you make such radical decisions, try to fix what's broken. Talk to her. Reason with her. She's your daughter.'

'I don't think this can be fixed. Nicole has been living off the family money for years, using our name and embarrassing me. The only time she seemed to be doing better was when she was with Alexander. But before that and after it's just been a nightmare. She's never had a job, never wanted to do anything.'

His face turning red, he got up, pacing around. 'I had a brutal conversation with her. She asked for money. Lots of money. She wants to move to Monaco to live with some man she met at a party. To buy a house and buy him a business too. Yet another man and another investment.

When I asked what would happen to Anne, she said she'd send her to a boarding preschool in England as soon as she turns three, as that is the minimum age for admittance.'

He was in tears. 'She doesn't care about the baby. I don't think she ever wanted her.'

'I don't think that's true, JJ. I'm sure she cares about Anne.'

'You're too good to believe it, that's why. But I know better. She keeps telling me how the baby reminds her of the life she could've had with Alexander and how painful it is to be around her. What kind of mother says that?'

Dominique didn't want to argue, but what Nicole said did explain her behavior after the plane crash, didn't it? Dominique knew that Nicole cared about Alexander, loved him – yes, in her own selfish way, but she did love him – and had pictured her life with him. Nicole had told her that at the funeral. Yes, she had been angry and aggressive, but behind all that, Dominique could see Nicole was hurting. She had lost Alexander just like Dominique and, despite everything, they had that in common.

'Everyone deals differently with pain, JJ.'

He scoffed. 'You didn't run around with random men just to show how much you're suffering, did you?'

JJ had gotten himself too worked up, Dominique realized, so whatever she said now wouldn't help.

'All that matters is that Anne is taken care of and safe,' she eventually said.

'That's what I'm worried about,' he grunted. 'That she can't be safe with Nicole.'

DOMINIQUE

PARIS

JJ agreed to give Nicole the money she wanted but only if she left Anne in Paris, with the nanny, to live in JJ's house. The child would be better off. Nicole agreed without hesitation.

Anne and her nanny came to live with JJ the next week.

Dominique found herself visiting more often and although, initially, she kept her distance from the baby, she was drawn to her and enjoyed being in the child's company. Dominique couldn't help but smile every time she saw her. Anne was a beautiful child, and so good. You barely knew she was there. She didn't cry, didn't fuss, and stayed where her nanny put her for hours at an end, playing with her dolls, talking to them, dressing them up.

'May I?' asked Dominique one day, when Anne was struggling to dress up a big porcelain doll with blonde hair just like hers.

The child looked up with her sweet, round, blue eyes and gave her a big smile, then handed the doll over.

'She must like you,' said the nanny. 'She never gives Camille to anyone.' The woman winked. 'She's her favorite.'

Dominique helped Anne dress up Camille and then sat next to her, watching her as she played. The girl did seem to take a liking to her, and every time she saw Dominique open the door, she jumped up, all smiles, and handed her the doll. It was a sign she wanted to play with her. And Dominique was more than happy to oblige. Although she knew Anne wasn't Alexander's child and she had never been Nicole's biggest fan, she felt bad for the baby, and protective, almost responsible, in a way she had never experienced before. At a time when grief was the emotion most familiar to her, there was something soothing in knowing she could bring a smile to Anne's face. Something truly fulfilling.

As for Nicole, she called once a month, and the conversations were shorter than five minutes. Was the baby okay? Could she have more money? In July, she called to ask for even more money; she had bought a yacht and was planning a big party. This time, she didn't ask about Anne.

The next time there was a phone call from Monaco, it didn't come from her. A police officer was on the phone.

Nicole had been involved in a boating accident. It all happened so fast, she died before the Coast Guard reached her.

The news that the socialite heiress had lost her life traveled the world fast. The investigation concluded that she had tripped and fallen overboard while she was intoxicated. The rest of the party had been in no better shape and by the time they'd noticed she had disappeared, it was too late. They never recovered her body.

A month after the funeral, JJ had to make a decision regarding Anne. With her mother gone, he had to legalize the child's situation.

'I am thinking of finding a nice foster family for Anne. They can adopt her, and she would have a proper mother and a proper father,' he said to Dominique one day.

'What? You want her to be raised by strangers?' asked Dominique, frustrated. 'You said you want to get custody.'

'I thought about it, but look at me, Dominique. I am old; I can't raise a child on my own. Besides, she needs a mother. Just like Nicole did,' said JJ and his eyes filled with tears.

Dominique gazed over at him. He looked tired and old all of a sudden.

JJ grimaced. 'My poor little girl. My poor Nicole. How did I let you down so badly?'

Dominique put her hand over his, comforting him silently.

'No, truly. What do I know about taking care of a girl? I wasn't capable of raising my own child. I did such a poor job and wasn't there for her when she needed me.'

'You did raise Nicole all on your own. And you did the best that you could. Just like you are doing now. But you're not alone anymore,' she said with a smile.

'What are you saying?'

'I can take care of Anne,' said Dominique, not knowing where it came from.

'You would do that?'

'Yes. If you get custody, I will assume full responsibility and take care of her.'

He quietly lit his pipe and sat there for a moment, looking at her. 'You, of all people, would raise Nicole's child?'

'Anne is your granddaughter, and she has been through enough. I could offer her what she never had. Love and care. I don't have anything else and getting to know her has been the one comfort in my life,' said Dominique, smiling.

'Before you make any final decision, I need to tell you something,' said JJ.

'What is it?'

'Anne is not Alexander's child.'

'I know. Alexander called me before boarding his plane in New York.' She looked away. Two years and she still couldn't talk about that night without crying.

'You know? And you still want to take care of her?'

She didn't hesitate. 'Of course.'

'You are truly a bright soul, my dear.' He sighed. 'Alright then. But on one condition.'

Dominique looked at him, wondering what that could be.

'That you move out of that studio of yours and into this huge house I have all to myself.'

She agreed. For almost two years she'd had no purpose in life, no reason to go on except for going back to Alexander's grave every day to talk to him. But Anne needed her. And she needed Anne. And maybe JJ needed her too.

DOMINIQUE

PARIS

Dominique's life completely changed after she moved in with JJ and Anne. Her priorities shifted. Anne came first, everything else second. She surprised herself at how quickly she became attached to the little blonde angel who looked exactly like her mother. She even surprised herself at how she looked at things now. Waiting tables and giving up her dream career was not what she wanted to teach Anne. She wanted to raise her to believe in herself, to believe she could do anything she put her mind to. And to never ever give up on what she really wanted.

Not long after, Dominique went back to school and reprised her internship.

She went to Alexander's grave and told him she wasn't abandoning him; she would still come back, every day, but later in the day. She had to do this for the baby.

JJ was still in the process of getting custody of Anne, but

things were going well. Or at leas she thought they were going well.

One morning, when she was preparing breakfast for Anne before going to work, the doorbell rang. JJ had just left a few minutes before.

'Did you forget your ke— Vincent!'

He was the last person she expected to see. It had been three years since they broke off their engagement and Vincent left France. She'd had no idea he had returned nor what he was doing standing on her doorstep now.

He seemed changed. Subdued almost.

'It's good to see you,' she said and she meant it.

He smiled thinly.

'It's good to see you too. I know I'm showing up out of the blue. I'm sorry, I should've called first, but I was wondering if we could talk.'

'Don't apologize, it's alright. Come in. How have you been? How did you know where to find me?'

'I can't stay long,' he said, sounding serious. Grave. 'I have a meeting with my lawyers in an hour at La Defense.'

'That sounds serious,' she said, smiling.

'It is. I'm going to petition to get custody of Anne.'

Dominique froze.

'What do you mean?'

He clenched his jaw. Yes, Vincent was changed. He didn't smile anymore. He didn't seem as comfortable in his own skin as he used to, and you could feel it right away.

'I didn't want you to find out like this,' he said. 'But I also didn't want you to hear this from JJ or from the press.'

'I don't understand.'

'Anne is my daughter.'

370

Dominique took a step back. 'Your daughter?'

He nodded.

'That means that you and Nicole—' she said, her mind reeling.

'I'm sorry,' he said and, judging by his expression, he was. 'I never meant to hurt you, Dominique. That was never ever my intention.' He clenched his fists. 'I knew I shouldn't have gone to that charity thing. I knew it was a mistake. I should've kept you away. I should've stayed away. If only… then things would be so different now,' he said with a pained look in his eyes.

'Is that when it started? At the ball?'

He nodded, looking embarrassed.

'Wow,' she said. 'All that time. Why didn't you tell me, Vincent? If you loved her, why didn't you tell me? I would've understood. Things would've been so different. All our lives would've been so different. Alexander—'

She stopped. She was just about to blame Vincent for Alexander's death, but she couldn't bring herself to do it. He looked so defeated as it was and so lonely and remorseful.

'I don't know what I felt. I was very confused. Nicole and me, we were together for many years and it ended so abruptly, I guess it was never truly over. Maybe. I'm not sure. Even after all this time I'm not sure. But one thing is certain. It was wrong. We were wrong and we never meant for any of this to happen. It just—'

'—happened,' said Dominique, trying to process everything.

'I'm so sorry. We really messed up, didn't we? All of us.'

His eyes shone. 'If we had only been brave enough, perhaps now Alexander and Nicole would still be alive.'

Dominique had tears in her eyes. He was right. If only…

'You know what's ironic? I loved Nicole; I am not going to lie about it. But I loved you more. I only realized that when I lost you. I could've married Nicole after Alexander…'

He looked away for a moment.

'I could've. She would've said yes if I asked. I think. But I never asked. Never. Because the only woman I ever wanted to marry was you. With Nicole, it was this unfinished business, this childhood fixation. There was a lot of history. But I didn't discover what true love was until I met you.'

Dominique gave him a long, level look.

'I know it's hard, if not impossible, for you to believe that. And maybe you never will. But I promise you, it's true. What would I gain by saying this now? I know you will never give me a second chance.'

It sounded so final and he seemed so resigned. That wasn't the Vincent she remembered. But as much as he inspired pity, as much as she had no right, she couldn't help but be furious with him.

'I'd like you to leave,' said Dominique.

Vincent got up. 'This doesn't change the fact that I'll petition for Anne's custody. Please understand. She is my child. She is not a mistake and I will never let her feel that way. She needs to be with her father.'

'Do whatever you have to do, Vincent,' she said coldly.

For six months, they were in and out of the courtroom.

JJ hired lawyers, an army of them. So did Vincent. The two most powerful families in France fought over the fate of an innocent three-year-old. Things were said, secrets

372

were revealed, the media was overjoyed and time and time again, Dominique feared JJ would give Anne up to avoid the scandal. But he didn't.

What Vincent didn't know, and what ultimately led to him losing the trial, was that Nicole had never put his name on the birth certificate. He had no proof he was indeed the father. When Vincent's lawyers asked the judge to accept a modern paternity test that had just been introduced, their proposal was denied, on the basis that the science behind these experimental tests was yet to be proven. The only evidence the court accepted was a blood test, and although it showed that the baby's blood type and Vincent's were compatible, it didn't prove, with certainty, Anne was indeed Vincent's, and ultimately the judge ruled the results as 'inconclusive'.

Vincent claimed he had been kept away from his child by Nicole, who never let him see Anne, and now JJ was doing the same. He tried everything. More months passed.

Finally, the verdict came in. Full custody would be given to JJ. Vincent didn't even get visitation rights, and he wasn't acknowledged as Anne's father. It was over.

Vincent was crushed, holding his head in his hands in the courtroom, unable to move or react. Looking at him, Dominique realized, with a pang, that she was sorry for him.

DOMINIQUE

24 DECEMBER 1967

PARIS

Finding out Anne was Vincent's daughter had been a shock for Dominique. But in no way did it change what she felt about the child she had now come to consider her own. She took care of her and loved her unconditionally. It made Dominique smile how, although she wasn't her flesh and blood, Anne seemed to be so much like her. She felt lucky. Despite everything, despite the pain, the sorrow, the loneliness, she was lucky to have Anne in her life. That made her realize how unhappy Vincent must feel. Whatever mistakes he'd made, he was paying for them tenfold. If he had loved Nicole, he'd lost her, just like she'd lost Alexander. Then he'd lost his child. And, if he was telling the truth and he'd loved Dominique, then he'd lost her too.

The Sunday before Christmas, Dominique and Anne went to a farmer's market to buy a fresh baguette and Anne's favorite apple tart, when Dominique saw Vincent crossing the street. He walked with his head down and didn't notice them. Dominique wanted to walk on and avoid running into him but Anne wouldn't budge and stared with a curious expression on her face in Vincent's direction. Dominique pulled her away.

That night, Dominique couldn't stop thinking about Vincent, and Anne's reaction when she saw him. Did she have the right to keep father and daughter apart?

The next day, at breakfast, Dominique pulled up a chair and sat next to JJ.

'I know that face,' said JJ, with a smile lifting the corner of his mouth. 'You want to talk about something. Please, just don't tell me you're moving away somewhere. Anything but that.'

'I saw Vincent yesterday,' she said.

JJ nodded casually.

'He looked bad. Not bad...' She stopped. 'Sad mostly and lonely.'

JJ wasn't smiling anymore.

'I know you won Anne in court and I'm not trying to make things complicated, but I think we should consider giving Vincent a chance to meet her, at least. What do you think?'

She was convinced JJ wasn't going to take it well.

'I think you are a good, kind woman, that's what I think,' he said, deep in thought.

'You know, I used to resent Vincent when Nicole lived in New York and spent time with him. I always thought he was behind all her messes. I should've known better,' said JJ.

He came back to the table.

'Now, I feel sorry for him. It's not his fault we ended up in this situation. He was caught in it, like the rest of us.'

'Does this mean you'll let him come visit Anne?'

JJ smiled. 'If you're alright with it, I am as well.'

Christmas Eve came, the first one as an extended family. When Vincent arrived, he could barely hold it together. He was sweating and fidgeting at the thought of finally holding his child in his arms. He was terrified his daughter would cry when she saw him or even run away, he admitted to Dominique. But Anne did what she never did with anybody else. The moment she saw him, she ran to him, jumped in his arms and wouldn't let go.

With Anne in his arms, in between tears, Vincent looked at Dominique and mouthed a thank you.

She nodded.

A bit later that night, he took her aside.

'You don't know how much this means to me. It's everything,' he said.

'I would never try to keep you away from your child. No matter what happened between us and what the court has decided. I want you to know that.'

'Nicole didn't want me in Anne's life. Some part of her still wanted to pretend, even just to herself, that Anne was Alexander's baby, I guess. She just wouldn't listen to reason. I've been away from my baby for so long. Too long. I hope it's not too late,' he said, still emotional.

'It's never too late,' she said kindly.

He stretched out his hand to touch her arm, but immediately pulled it back.

'I don't deserve your kindness.'

She then did what he didn't dare. She laid her hand on his arm in a comforting way, neither of them saying anything, only smiling at Anne who was playing in the next room.

DOMINIQUE

PARIS

As time passed, Vincent and Anne's relationship grew so deep it was as if they hadn't been apart at all. He spent more and more time with her and Dominique, and even with JJ.

'Your daughter is gorgeous. Look at those eyes,' a woman said as she and her husband passed by Dominique, Anne and Vincent playing with a ball in Jardins des Tuileries.

'Thank you,' said both Dominique and Vincent and continued passing the ball to Anne, who ran after it and giggled every time it escaped her.

'What a lovely family,' the woman continued. 'Just lovely,' she said, looking at them so admiringly Dominique almost felt embarrassed.

It wasn't the only time it happened. To everyone who saw them together, Vincent and Dominique seemed like the happy parents of a beautiful young girl. It was a strange dynamic. While the two of them were not romantically involved, they acted as a couple, raising Anne, spending weekends together, going on vacations.

'No wonder everyone thinks we're married,' said Dominique to Constance one day. She didn't know if Vincent had relationships, and he never flashed any women in front of her or Anne. If he dated, he did it discreetly.

As for Dominique, she was too busy caring for Anne and finishing her training at Institut du Patrimoine to consider any of the men who had asked her out. Besides, she loved Alexander and was convinced that going on dates would betray that love.

All she wanted now was to finish her training and follow her dreams in the real art world. She sent in her application for curatorship to all the possible museums in Paris and waited. Weeks passed, graduation day was almost there, but she didn't get any offers. *I should've heard something by now, gotten at least one offer,* thought Dominique, seriously worried. December 1st was the last day of school. She passed the last exam and was going to graduate in a few days. But still no sign. This had been her dream for so long, she'd never thought it wouldn't work out.

On the day of her graduation, after four months of waiting, an envelope arrived. She was invited to interview at the Marmottan, of all museums, for the position of associate curator in charge of painting restoration.

DOMINIQUE

PARIS

It was now almost two years since Dominique and Vincent had been raising Anne together.

A couple of weeks before Christmas, JJ called Dominique and Vincent to his office.

'Please, sit down, and stop looking so worried. The reason I asked you here today is to tell you something you already know,' he said with a smile. 'I'm not young anymore and my health is deteriorating. For these reasons I want to make sure I deal with all the important things while I still can.'

Dominique wanted to contradict him. *You are not that old, and you are healthier than any of us,* she wanted to say but she bit her tongue.

'First on my list is making sure Anne will be well taken care of after I'm gone. There's a decision that needs to be made,' he said. Seeing Dominique's and Vincent's surprised reactions, he explained. 'You two have been taking care of her better than I could've ever hoped for and have given her love, a real home, and a family. But when I am gone you will not have the legal right to keep her. I don't know if you realize this.'

Dominique had never considered the legal implications. The thought of losing Anne had never crossed her mind. But JJ was right. On paper, neither Dominique nor Vincent were anybody to Anne. She would be taken away from them if something happened.

'Isn't there something we can do, JJ? Anne belongs with us,' said Dominique and looked over at Vincent, who nodded approvingly.

'I've discussed this with my lawyer, and he advised we should begin the adoption procedure without delay.'

Dominique wondered what the rush was about. Was JJ not well? He didn't look sick.

'This is what he told me,' said JJ. 'I will spare you the legal terms. If both of you want to adopt Anne, you need to be married, and two years after your wedding date you can request adoption – the two-year wait time requirement is waived if both of you are aged twenty-eight years old or older at the date of the request. Which is your case, thankfully,' said JJ before continuing. 'The other option is for only one of you to adopt Anne. Either you, Dominique,' he said, looking at her, 'or you, Vincent,' he concluded, his eyes now fixated on Vincent.

Dominique tried to wrap her head around what he had just read. She couldn't give up Anne, and she couldn't take her away from her father. That left her with only one option. Getting married to Vincent.

'I told you it would be an important decision.'

Dominique left JJ's feeling dazed and confused and she was sure Vincent felt the same.

As soon as they found themselves alone, Vincent asked in a low voice, 'We're not even considering option two, are we?' He seemed lost for words.

'I think we shouldn't rush it.'

'But you heard JJ; we need to make a decision.'

'What I need is to clear my head. I'll go get some fresh air,' said Dominique and left.

She walked for hours, with no direction or purpose. When she returned home, Vincent was in the living room with Anne. They didn't talk about it then, and both acted as if nothing had happened. As soon as they put her to bed, Vincent poured them two glasses of wine, before sitting comfortably on the sofa.

'I've been thinking about it and I have an idea. Anne's vacation from kindergarten begins in a couple of days, I don't have to go back to the university for three weeks, and your new job starts in January, so how about you and I spend some time together?'

She didn't know what to say. Time alone? They hadn't done that in over five years.

'My parents plan to go to New York for the holidays. We can send Anne with them and we'll them join for New Year's. I think it would do her good to be away from Paris for a while and you know my parents adore her.'

He was right. Anne loved her grandparents and they loved her. The only thing that worried Dominique was the prospect of spending all that time alone with Vincent.

DOMINIQUE

Issy-les-Moulineaux

The night after Margaux took Anne to New York, Vincent invited Dominique out to dinner to one of their favorite places in Issy-les-Moulineaux.

He ordered champagne, at which point Dominique got a bit fidgety. Something in the air made her uncomfortable.

'I have been doing a lot of thinking after our talk with JJ,' said Vincent.

'Me too,' she admitted.

'I still love you. I never stopped, despite what happened. Watching you take care of Anne and seeing what a great mother you are has only made me love you more. You are the kindest and warmest person I have ever met. You and I both know, I'm sure, that according to almost all standards the three of us have been a family for the past couple of years, a happy one. I can't imagine my life without you in it, or without Anne, and I think we have a great thing going,' he said. 'I want us to get married. For Anne, for us, for our family.'

Dominique wasn't ready for such a declaration. She hadn't realized he still loved her, not in that way anyhow. She didn't speak for a couple of minutes, sipping her champagne, trying to buy some time while thinking about how she should phrase what she wanted to say.

'Our time together has been good, you're right, and you and I make a good team. We're doing a great job raising Anne together. And I do care about you, Vincent, and in a way, I do love you—' She stopped and looked into his eyes knowing what she was about to say would hurt him. 'But I don't love you like you want me to. I'm not in love with you. I'm sorry, I—'

He interrupted her. 'I don't expect you to love me the way I love you. I think there is still someone else in your heart, Dominique, even after all this time. I am aware of it, and I'm not lying to myself. But to hear that you love me too, in your own way, is more than I could have hoped for. For now, it's enough that I love you. And who knows what might happen in time?'

He took out a small jewelry box from his pocket and placed it carefully in front of her. 'I don't want an answer right now. I would be happy if you would wear the ring as a sign that you're thinking about it.'

She looked at him, unable to speak, moved – almost to tears – by his speech and love for her. Dominique put the ring on her finger, and he got up and kissed her on the cheek, then raised his glass and, with a big smile on his face, toasted to 'Anything can happen.'

DOMINIQUE

PARIS

Dominique couldn't sleep. What was she going to do? How could she decide?

She put on a warm jacket, winter boots and rushed to the metro station. It wasn't too late. She could still catch a train to Père-Lachaise.

It was dark, and the wind was picking up. They announced a blizzard on the radio.

When she arrived, it was almost midnight and there was no one else in the cemetery.

She blew the snow off the stone, gently, carefully just like she had that morning.

'I feel so lonely. So tired. What am I going to do? I don't know how to go on without you. I don't want to go on without you. It's been five years. Today. I did what everyone wanted me to do. I went back out there. I went back to school; I did it for Anne. I know she's not your child, but to me, she's mine and I would do anything for her. But this? What am I going to do now? How could I possibly marry Vincent? I still I love you. I've never stopped loving you. I can't shake this feeling that if I marry him, I would be betraying you, forgetting you. I feel you're out there, somewhere. I don't believe you're gone. Am I losing my mind? Everyone seems to think so.'

She sat in the snow.

'Can you hear me? Please, please, if you can hear me. If you're out there, somewhere, please help me. Help me understand why I've been feeling this way since that day. Why I can't move on. I know you tried to tell me something. Why can't I understand it?'

She forced herself to remember the reverie. The dream she had when she woke up in the hospital, after the plane crash. She had tried so many times, but maybe never with so much desperation as that night. She was at a crossroads and if she couldn't remember then, it would be too late. She'd be losing him forever and she couldn't do that.

Dominique closed her eyes and lay down in the snow. It was so cold. But it was also peaceful and quiet. So quiet. Slowly, she stopped being cold. She stopped shivering.

The dream. The reverie. It was coming back to her.

And in her dream, she opened her eyes. No, it wasn't her. It was him. *He* opened his eyes. He was lying in a bed. A hospital bed. He couldn't move and couldn't speak. There were nurses and doctors around and they kept asking what his name was, but he couldn't tell them. Why not? What was wrong with him? His head hurt so much and he just wanted to get out of there but couldn't move. He needed to leave; he knew he had to be somewhere else but didn't know where. And he panicked, not only because he didn't know how sick he was but also because he felt lost in that world. He was angry and started screaming for them to let go. Why were they holding him? They needed to let him go.

'I need to get out of here; I shouldn't be here. I need to get out. I shouldn't be here.'

Suddenly, something grabbed Dominique, and she was floating. A bright light shone in her eyes. Noises. Loud noises.

'Does she have a pulse?'

'Weak. Temperature is twenty-eight degrees. Breathing is shallow. We're losing her.'

Silence. Peace.

'Dominique? It's me. Dominique, can you hear me?'

She recognized JJ's voice.

'Can you open your eyes?'

She did. Slowly. Her eyelids were heavy as rocks.

'Thank God. You gave me such a scare. Don't ever do that again, you hear me?'

Her throat hurt. She could barely speak.

'I was right, JJ. I was right. I saw him. I saw him in my dream.'

'Please relax now. You need your rest. Whatever it is, we'll talk about it later.'

A doctor walked in and checked a monitor next to her bed, asked a few basic questions and seemed satisfied.

'You have severe hypothermia. If Monsieur D'Angers hadn't found you when he did, you would've died. You shouldn't have been out there in that blizzard. You're very lucky.'

She felt lucky. On that hospital bed, hooked to machines, she felt lucky.

She was the luckiest woman in the world because she knew something nobody else did.

Alexander was alive.

She'd seen it with her own eyes. She'd seen it in her dream.

DOMINIQUE

11 DECEMBER 1969

PARIS

JJ came to pick Dominique up from the hospital, to drive her home. They both sat in the back seat of his car, as JJ's driver pulled up the screen between them.

'I didn't tell Vincent what happened. I said you had to go to Colmar for a couple of days. Family matter. He doesn't need to know. It'll just stay between us,' he said.

Dominique stared out the window.

'JJ, I have wanted to tell you something for two days now.'

'I don't know if I want to hear it.'

'It's about Alexander.'

'I had a feeling.'

'You know I always said that I don't believe he died in the plane crash, that I had this feeling he was somewhere out there—'

389

'Not this again, Dominique. I don't have the strength for it anymore,' growled JJ.

'Please listen to me. I had a dream when I was at the cemetery. I've had it many times in the last five years, but only now have I remembered it fully and understood it. Alexander didn't die in the crash. All these years when I kept saying he wasn't dead, all these years,' she said, with tears in her eyes.

'What dream? Why are you doing this? Is it because of what we discussed? About you and Vincent? You can just say you don't want to marry him; there's no need for all this.'

'Please believe me. I know you think I'm in denial and I'm mourning. But I am telling you, now, more than ever, I know I am right.'

He looked exasperated. 'Be reasonable. What do you think happened?'

'I don't exactly know what happened. In my dream, he seemed scared. He seemed disoriented. Maybe he just—'

'What? He just got up and left the crash site? You know as well as I do that's not possible.'

'No, not the crash site. I think he made it to the hospital and when he was a bit better and he could move, he—'

'Dominique, please. For my sake, stop. You bringing this all up again is tearing me apart. I loved that boy like my own son. I buried him five years ago. I mourned for him.' JJ sighed. 'I lost my wife. I know how hard it is to accept it, how life doesn't seem to make sense anymore. I buried myself in my work, because that was the only way I knew how to cope. You keep imagining he's still alive somewhere. That is your way to cope. But just like it didn't help me, and it cost me my relationship with Nicole, this isn't helping you either. You're a smart woman, but you've allowed yourself to believe in this fantasy for far too long and you're forcing all of us to go along with it.'

'I'm not crazy, JJ. He is somewhere out there. I can feel it.'

'I've known Alexander all his life. I know the kind of man he was. He wouldn't have just left the hospital and not reached out to us. Why would he? He loved us. He loved you, more than anything. If he could, he would've come back to you even if he had to walk all the way from Le Havre to Paris. Do you see how irrational you're being?'

'I don't know why he left the hospital or why he didn't come back. I don't know. But what I do know is that when I got to the hospital after the crash, everyone was searching for a patient who had just disappeared in the middle of the night from their bed. A man. A man who had survived the plane crash. It has to be him, JJ. It has to be.'

'It has to be? Why? Because you had a dream? I have all sorts of dreams; none of them ever come true.'

'They're not like my dreams,' she said.

As close as they were, she had never told JJ about the dreams. He was a very rational, practical man who didn't believe in such things. Besides, she wouldn't have known how to explain her dreams about 'the one' to him, when she was still trying to understand why she dreamed about two 'ones'. Leon and Alexander. JJ surely wouldn't have taken her seriously and the dreams were such a big part of who she was, she didn't want to expose herself to those kinds of conversations. Nobody but the women in her family knew about them. Nobody but them could understand.

'Why can't you just let it go? Let him go? What do you want from me, Dominique?' asked JJ in an exasperated tone.

'I want you to believe me. I want you to support me.'

'Support you in doing what?' he asked. 'We buried Alexander. If a man did disappear, it wasn't him. Do you understand?'

'You don't know if the man you buried is Alexander,' she pushed back. 'There's no proof. Did you ask for proof? Why didn't you let me see him? Why didn't anyone let me see him? Because it wasn't him.'

'Oh, Dominique,' he said sadly. 'There is proof. Listen to me,' he tried but she wouldn't have it. Enough with everyone fighting her on this. She knew what she felt.

'I'm going to look for him. What if he needs us? Something must've stopped him from getting in touch. Something really serious, really bad.'

'This is madness. You know I would do anything for you, but not this. This scenario is all too convenient because it is what you wish for. The reality is harsh, my dear. He is gone; he has been gone for five years. You have Vincent who loves you; you have Anne. You should be happy. Marry this man, have this beautiful family both of you have built. Enjoy them; enjoy life. Let go of the past that's been eating you inside for so long. Let go of your fantasies. He is gone, and he is not coming back,' said JJ.

'I will not give up on him. If there's even the smallest chance I am right, I will go to the end of the world and back for him. Until I have exhausted all possibilities.'

When Vincent came home later that day, Dominique's bags were packed.

'I need to go away. It'll be a few days, maybe more. I don't know,' she said.

'Where are you going?' he said, as he sat on the sofa, his hands on his knees. He seemed tired. A bit defeated. Like he already knew the answer to that question.

'There's new evidence showing Alexander didn't lose his life in that crash. I need to find out; I need to go there and make sure. You understand, don't you?'

'I don't know if you can ask me to understand. I will not stop you, if that's what you are worried about. But I can't really understand or accept either. You're chasing a ghost. You've been chasing a ghost for years and it's been weighing heavily on me. On us. Our family. You are here, but you're never truly, fully here.'

It wasn't the first time he had heard from her over the years that she thought Alexander was alive. And, in a way, she had hoped Vincent somehow learned to accept the idea as one of her oddities. But, hearing the pain in his voice, she realized how hard it must've been for him to keep hearing she loved another man, even though he was there, next to her, and the other man was nowhere, dead by all accounts.

'You can't fight ghosts, Dominique. I've tried for many years but I've failed miserably.'

'Vincent, I'm sorry, I don't mean to hurt you. It's just—'

He stopped her. 'Look. I will not stand in the way of what you believe. Not because I don't want to, but because I realize that if I do, I risk losing you for good.'

He held his head in his hands, quiet for a few moments.

He sighed. 'If you want to get it out of your system, go! Go, find out what you need to find and end this already. But

I want you to promise that when you come back, we put this behind us and if you do decide to give us a chance, it'll be a real chance. I can't compete with ghosts, but I am here, and I love you and Anne, and I will do everything I can to make you happy.'

'I know you will, and I love you too,' she said, then suddenly it dawned on her. If she loved him, then why was she leaving him to go chase an illusion? The answer was as simple as it was a heartbreaking realization. Because she loved the illusion more. Because she had never let Alexander go. Because maybe some 'ones' are more than others.

Vincent smiled sadly, almost as if he'd heard her thoughts.

'Who knows? This trip and the time apart might be good for us. Maybe then we'll finally be able to start our life together,' he said sadly.

Dominique hugged him, grabbed her bags and left, not knowing what awaited her once she stepped outside of her home.

'Grandpa Vincent's always loved you, hasn't he? Even when you didn't love him back?'

'He was a patient man. He did everything he could to make up for his mistakes and, through the years, through all my searches, he never stopped being kind and loving. And I loved him too. I wasn't lying when I said it. I just didn't love him like he deserved to be loved.'

DOMINIQUE

12 DECEMBER 1969

LE HAVRE

Dominique took the night train and arrived in Le Havre early in the morning. It pained her to be there again; in that place that brought back incredibly distressing memories of a dark and confusing time when all she had loved was taken away from her in an instant.

She went straight to the hospital and asked to see Dr Thomas, the doctor she had talked to after the plane crash.

Minutes later, she came over to talk to Dominique.

'We met five years ago,' said Dominique.

'I'm sorry,' the doctor said. 'I don't remember. How can I help you?'

'I wanted to ask you a few questions about a former patient, one of the survivors of Sainte-Adresse,' said Dominique, allowing herself to feel hopeful again.

'That was a long time ago, but I'll do my best. Which patient?' she asked.

'A man in his twenties. Dark hair, tall. I believe he ran away from the hospital a few days after the plane crash.'

'Oh, I remember, yes. Are you family or a journalist? We've had several reporters come by in the last few days. With the fifth anniversary and all.'

'Journalist.' Last time when she said she wasn't family, everyone refused to talk to her. So she had to lie.

'I didn't know his story made the papers.'

Dominique didn't respond. 'What happened to him? Did you find him?'

She was trying to make it all sound like professional curiosity, asking questions as she imagined a journalist would, but she was having a hard time restraining her nervous energy.

'We looked everywhere in the hospital and searched the grounds. And I know that a few phone calls were made to inquire about him, but we didn't find him.'

'What about the police? Didn't they get involved?'

'The police? No. Not then anyway.'

'What do you mean not then?'

'A few weeks later, a gendarme discovered the body of a man who died of hypothermia a couple of kilometers away, on the side of the road. We all thought it was the missing patient and many of us felt guilty for not searching for him more. But the police identified the man as a local homeless person, and the case closed on that one.'

Dominique breathed, relieved. It wasn't him. There was still hope.

'Is there any way he could've survived, in your opinion?' asked Dominique.

'It's hard to say. Not likely, I am afraid.' She looked pensive. 'I mean, he was hurt, with no papers, no money, on foot in the middle of winter. The odds were stacked up against him.'

'If you knew all this, why didn't you search for him? How could you just leave Alexander out there like an unwanted dog?'

'We had a lot to deal with those days. Our hospital was over capacity. As much as we felt bad about his situation, a lot of other patients needed us. And, after all, he left of his own accord. Even if we would've found him, we had no right to forcibly keep him here—'

The doctor stopped talking suddenly. 'Alexander? That was his name?'

'*Is*, not was. Is his name. Alexander Roberts, yes.'

Dominique was furious and frustrated. What kind of doctors left a patient wandering out in the cold in his condition?

'Alexander Roberts,' the doctor repeated, then without any explanation went to the front desk, opened a drawer and started going through files.

Dominique was confused.

'Aha. I knew I had seen that name before. Alexander Roberts. You must be mistaken, mademoiselle. Alexander Roberts is not the man who ran from the hospital; that would be impossible, because Alexander Roberts died on impact in the crash.'

Oh, how much it hurt to hear those words again. But

they weren't anything new. They said he died; she said he didn't. And just like always in the last five years, she went on her rant. She knew it by heart.

'You have no proof that the man you identified as Alexander Roberts was indeed him. I was told his body was—'

She tried to be strong.

'His body was beyond recognition. Nobody could actually identify him. That man could've been anyone. Any other man you mixed up on the passenger list. There were quite a few unaccounted for. I don't need to hear this again. I know it all too well. You have no proof.'

'That's incorrect. There was an investigation done, I can assure you. It's him, mademoiselle. It says here, in the file: he matched the physical description we got from the police – approximate age, height, hair color.' She flipped a page. 'And we found his passport and other papers in the jacket he was wearing.'

'This must be a mistake,' Dominique said, feeling faint. 'You're wrong.'

The doctor took out a few papers from the folder. 'We have copies of his documents,' she said and showed them to Dominique. Copies of his passport, his business card from AngeD'Art, a photo of his wallet.

Dominique was shaking. She had tears in her eyes.

'He's gone,' whispered Dominique. 'The dream didn't mean anything. None of the dreams meant anything. It's all a lie. It's all—' She stopped, unable to breathe. 'They were all right and I was wrong. How could I have been so wrong?'

'Mademoiselle,' said the doctor, concerned.

Dominique took one look at her, then darted out of the hospital, running until her legs failed her, until the physical pain was greater than the mental anguish and she couldn't cry anymore.

'It wasn't him. So he died after all,' says Valerie and her voice is so sad, it breaks my heart all over.

'So many people had told me that Alexander was dead, yet I persisted in my belief they were wrong. That time, though, I'd reached the end of the road. Yes, a man had survived, just as I thought, but it wasn't my Alexander. It was just a random man. I had nothing else to go on. Was it time? Time to put an end to the suffering I had caused myself and the people around me? How many times did I lose Alexander over the years? How many times did I have my heart broken into millions of pieces? How many nights did I cry myself to sleep? I didn't regret trying, I was right to believe, but it was time to stop. I remember walking down the street, looking back at the house and feeling a huge part of my life, the most important part, was ending. A part I'd wished, hoped and prayed would last forever. It was over and I had to accept that it doesn't always end with happily ever after. I had to break my promise and "give up on us" to save what was left of my life. But Alexander had broken his promise too... He was not coming back to me.'

Valerie is in tears. I pat her hand and she attempts a smile.

PART IX

'There is no disguise which can hide love for long where it exists or simulate it where it does not.' — François de La Rochefoucauld

ANTHONY PELTZ

CAMBRIDGE

'Cheers all for tuning in on 106.7 this fine day. It's Sunday, ten past six – time to look back at the week in history,' said a chirpy voice on the radio.

'How are you feeling?' asked Mary.

'Confident. If all else fails, I'll use my charm,' said Anthony, and smiled, knowing that wasn't what she meant. She worried about him, especially around the holidays, although he'd stopped mentioning the dreams a while back and did his best to pretend everything was fine.

Anthony watched Mary move around the kitchen, getting everything ready with the precision of a Swiss clock. He smiled.

'What would I do without you?' he asked and winked.

'You'd be just fine,' she said returning the smile. 'You know you would.'

Mary had been the one constant in Anthony's life ever

since he moved to Cambridge five years ago and he wasn't exaggerating when he said he'd be lost without her. She was his assistant, his friend, his mother, his confidante, the shoulder he cried on. Mary cooked for him, cleaned his house, helped him with his work, did his shopping, washed his laundry, and when he felt lonely or tired, she stood by his side, comforting him.

In her late sixties, but with the energy of a twenty-year-old, she was a war widow who, just like Anthony, had had to reinvent herself and build a new life from nothing. She had helped him in too many ways to count because she knew it had been hard for him all those years, but she didn't know *how* hard. Anthony tried to shelter her from the darkest corners of his mind, from the thoughts that still kept him up at night and tormented him.

He often wondered if she knew he was a ghost of a man. That, despite all her efforts, and his efforts, he was hollow inside? That he still dreamed the same dream, after all those years? That he smiled because he had to, not because he felt it? That he had a thousand unanswered questions and he would've given up his life for the answers? Did she know he believed there was someone out there who his heart belonged to, forever? He just didn't know who that person was. Just like he didn't know who *he* was.

From the outside looking in, it seemed Anthony had everything. A good life, an excellent financial situation, and a fantastic career. The director of The Louvre had called him 'the most promising art restorer in recent history' in an interview for *Le Monde* the previous year, and the world's most prominent museums had been after him ever since. Because of it, Anthony had too much unwanted attention, and he'd had to build a character for himself. Solitary, difficult, private.

'In more recent history only tragic anniversaries, I'm afraid. Starting with the 1950 PanAm Flight 214 struck by lightning near Maryland, killing 81. Two years later, the heavy smog over London killed at least 4,000 people,' said the voice on the radio. 'And in 1964, on 9 December, Trans-Oceanic Airways Flight 651 from New York to Paris crashed in the English Channel, near Le Havre, killing 165. The deadliest accident in France's history.'

'Why do they always have to remind people of tragedies?' said Mary and turned off the radio. 'Aren't there enough bad things happening right now in the world? We have to relive the old ones too?'

She didn't like to hear news about accidents and deaths, as her life had been sad enough.

Anthony stopped short. 'Le Havre, 9 December, 1964,' he murmured to himself.

It was probably nothing. Why would that date mean anything to him?

'I have to go; I'll be back in three days,' said Anthony.

Mary gave him a worried look.

'I'll be fine,' said Anthony. 'I knew this day would come. Can't hide forever,' he said attempting a smile.

The truth was that Paris terrified him and Mary knew it. What exactly made him feel that way, he couldn't say; there was something about Paris that when even mentioned made Anthony uncomfortable and nervous. So nervous, his hands would sweat, and his mouth would go dry.

ANTHONY

PARIS

Anthony took the train from Cambridge to London and from there to Paris. As he crossed the border, the pit of his stomach felt queasy and he was a bit lightheaded.

Maybe this wasn't such a good idea after all, he thought.

He arrived at Gare du Nord as the sun was rising, and millions of thoughts ran through his mind. It was the first time he'd visited the capital, yet some places seemed familiar. Smells, noises, overwhelming sensations. The city seemed busy. He hated crowds and had become quite reserved, somewhat antisocial in the last years. He could spend days and days working on paintings, without feeling the need to see or talk to anyone. Sometimes he forgot he needed to eat or sleep. It was just him and the art.

In front of the Louvre, he wanted to turn back and run.

Wherever. Anywhere. Just skip the meeting with the board; he decided against it because too much was at stake and he had worked too hard to give up now.

The Louvre board members received him like he was a VIP, but he didn't feel like smiling and shaking hands. Not that day. He was restless. There was something in the air, and something in his heart ached. They approved the funding, the headquarters, and officially appointed Anthony as the lead of the European Art Restoration organization. What'd he worked for so hard, what he'd hoped for, had just happened and he couldn't even celebrate.

'We will see you tomorrow afternoon, Monsieur Peltz,' said one of the members. 'By then, we will have finalized the list of candidates for the fifteen spots and I'm sure you're going to be pleased with the quality of the art specialists we're presenting you with.'

The best he could do was to force a smile. When they asked if he wanted to stay for drinks after, he excused himself. He couldn't wait to leave. It was as if what had just happened wasn't his biggest dream come true.

On his way out, Anthony noticed a plate announcing a temporary Monet exhibition. Instead of heading for the exit, he followed the signs until he reached an open, light-colored gallery where one massive painting dominated the room. *Reflections on the Water-Lily Pond*, c. 1919, 200 × 1,276 cm, oil on canvas, Restored at Musée Marmottan by D.S.G.

It took his breath away. What was it about this painting? Did it mean something to him?

But it wasn't just that beautiful painting that gave him that strange sensation and he knew it. It was this city and this day, it was a name and a touch he sometimes thought he felt, the sound of a voice, a haunting feeling and an obsessive dream. A dream he'd done his best to ignore so he could move on with his life. But that dream was overpowering him now.

There was a woman in his dream. She was surrounded by light and color. Like a painting. Like a perfect painting. He knew her voice, but he couldn't see her. She was always there with him. Every night. Every single night of the last nine years. Sometimes, she would talk to him, although he didn't always understand what she said. Other times she seemed lonely and cried. There were moments when she was happy, and he was happy too. The dream would always end the same way. 'Don't go. Stay with me,' she would whisper. Every single time.

ANTHONY

PARIS

'Mister Peltz,' he heard a man's voice and recognized one of the members of the board. 'I see you've discovered our latest restoration.' He beamed with pride.

Anthony turned to look at what the man was pointing to. It was the Monet.

'Yes, I-I...' he stuttered. Had to control himself. 'I did. It's a flawless restoration. Beautiful work.'

'It is, isn't it? Since you're here, you should meet our newest art curator. She's responsible for it.'

All of a sudden, not far from where he was, he heard voices and laughter. A man. A woman. Another man. Laughter again.

'Don't go anywhere. Stay here, I'll be right back,' he heard the woman say, then footsteps and the sound of a door closing.

Anthony's heart beat out of his chest. That voice. He

knew that voice. He knew it better than his own. 'Don't go. Stay with me.' Was it possible? Was it the same voice? The voice from his dreams. Was it her?

Anthony took a step back, and for a fraction of a second he contemplated hiding or turning around or just rushing out of there. Was he ready? Was he truly ready to see her? To find out the truth about himself?

He'd never felt more nervous or scared. Not even nine years ago when he didn't know if he was going to get caught and end up in jail or if he was going to make it alive to the next week. That was a different kind of scared. It was physical. It was about survival. This time it was about so much more and it took over all his senses.

Two men dressed in light beige suits came into the gallery. One of them was holding a camera and a flash, the other was writing something in a notepad. They were talking loudly among themselves and he recognized their voices from earlier.

'Journalists from *Le Monde*,' whispered the man. 'They're here to take her photograph for an article. We're so proud,' he added.

Footsteps on the hallway, coming their way. Anthony gulped.

'That must be Dominique,' said Monsieur Brainly with a big smile. 'I'll introduce you.'

'Dominique? Her name is Dominique?' he asked, his voice barely above a whisper.

He felt weak, a deaf pain in his right leg, a throbbing pain in his temples.

The room was spinning, and Anthony leaned against the wall, trying to calm his nerves and his shaking hands.

'She's going to be so excited to meet you,' said the board member, but Anthony barely heard him.

'Excuse me, I – I have to go,' he said and ran in the opposite direction. He ran as fast as he could and didn't stop until he was outside, in front of the museum.

He felt like he was about to be sick. The world around him was still spinning. Images. Sounds. Monet. 'Don't go. Stay with me.' A flash of light. Pressure in his chest. The throbbing pain in his head.

He felt his body falling to the ground, like a dead weight, and he knew it was happening but there was nothing he could do to control it, to stop it.

In that moment, Anthony's life flashed before his eyes. But not the life he knew.

'Don't go. Stay with me. Alexander, come back to me.'

'Dominique?' he asked not knowing where that came from. 'Dominique!' he yelled.

He didn't have any last thoughts or wishes. Only one goal, vivid and irrational like an obsession – to survive. That feeling, that horrid sensation. It was painfully familiar. A sinking feeling in his stomach as his body hit the hard surface. Voices crying for help. What was happening? Who were all those people? A deafening thud muffled the cries, and a blast of snow and ice took his breath away, knocking him unconscious. Water. Ice-cold water everywhere. He felt a thousand knives going through his arms and legs as he struggled for air. Fighting to stay afloat, his body was dead weight, pulling him to the bottom of a freezing, deep, black hole. 'I can't die, not now. Please, not now. I need to get out of here.'

'Mate, hey, mate, you alright?'

Anthony opened his eyes and instinctively gasped for air. He looked around. There was no water. No people crying for help. Only two curious tourists who stared at him and whispered something to each other.

Tears ran down his cheeks.

'Are you okay, mate?' he heard the man repeat in a thick Australian accent. 'Need me to call someone?'

He couldn't speak.

'Maybe we should stop a gendarme,' said the woman who was with him.

'I know you, we've met before. I don't know if in this life, or maybe in my dreams, but we have, haven't we?' He kept repeating the words, as tears ran down his face.

'You ill, mate?' the man repeated. 'Let me help you up.'

He heard the words but couldn't process them. Nine years after his life ceased to exist, he understood who the ghost was, and how Anthony had come to exist. He remembered everything. Himself. Her. The memories started coming back when he went to Paris, but he couldn't accept it. He couldn't believe it was true. But now, there was no denying it. And he couldn't stop shaking and crying. Her face was vivid in his mind. Her touch. Dominique. His love. His only love.

ANTHONY

12 DECEMBER 1973

PARIS

What he did for the rest of the day, where he went, who he talked to, how he eventually got back to the station, boarded the train and made his way back home... he couldn't remember. It was all a haze. When he arrived home, it was past midnight and Mary was asleep. The house was quiet. He went to his study, poured himself a glass of scotch and fell into his chair.

Mary found him there the next morning.

'Anthony,' she said, and shook him a bit. 'Where have you been? I've been worried sick. You were supposed to come back early yesterday.'

'I'm fine, Mary, don't worry.'

'But I do worry. Thank God you're alright. How did it go? How was Paris?'

He lifted his head and looked at her for a moment, then put his head back on the desk.

'That bad? I knew you shouldn't have gone,' she said in a motherly way.

'Oh, Mary,' he said. 'I—'

'What's wrong? What happened?'

He put his hand on hers. 'I can't talk about it right now. Please, don't feel sad. I just – it's just so much.'

She smiled as she did every time when Anthony retreated into his own world. She knew when to give him space; she had learned in all the years they had lived under the same roof.

'It's alright,' she said kindly. 'You will tell me when you're ready.'

She then pulled back the curtains and opened the windows to let the air in.

'It's stuffy in here. I'll make you breakfast; you must be starving.'

'I'm not hungry. Actually, I need to go, take care of something, but I'll be back soon.'

He went straight to the public library and asked to see newspapers from December 1964. He searched for articles about the plane crash. Seeing his name on the list of victims was heartbreaking and shocking. *Why would they think I was dead?* he kept wondering. Then he realized. It must've been the coat. *How ironic,* thought Anthony. There had been a man onboard who was shivering and unwell. He had given that man his coat without a second thought. His coat. With his passport and wallet.

They thought he was dead. Nobody had looked for him because they thought he was dead. His heart broke imagining what Dominique must have gone through, what JJ would have gone through. They'd buried him. They'd mourned for him. How would they react to finding out after almost a decade he was alive?

When he returned home, he paced around in his study for hours.

'How about dinner?' asked Mary.

He looked out the window, absentmindedly. 'I need to go back.'

'Go back where?'

'Paris.'

'But you were just there.'

He sighed. 'I shouldn't have come home and bothered you. I should've just stayed there, but I didn't know what to do. I didn't know where to go.'

'You can't bother me. This is your home,' she said. 'Why don't you take a few days to rest, and then you can go to Paris again? It will still be there.'

'I don't want to rest. I need to go back.'

She didn't push him any longer. When Anthony's mind was set on something, Mary knew not to interfere.

He took a bath, changed, and Mary helped him pack fresh clothes in his suitcase.

'I have to be back at the Louvre tomorrow,' he said.

It was both a truth and a lie. He did have a meeting but not for another two days. That wasn't the real reason why he was going to Paris. He was going back because *she* was there.

'This is the name of the hotel, and the phone number. If you need anything, call me,' he said, writing it down for her.

He took the night train again to Paris.

Although he had been there just the other day, it was as if that had never happened.

It wasn't him who had gone to the Louvre. It was Anthony. But who was Anthony and who was Alexander? Where did one stop and the other begin?

He experienced everything now as if he hadn't been back in Paris for nine years. It was all so new, so raw, so beautiful. Full of memories and feelings.

When he saw the Eiffel Tower in the distance, his heart sank. Le Petit Coin was so close. All he needed to do was take a right turn instead of going straight. He hesitated. He could still do it. Next right. Next right. Then what? He had been gone for so long. A lot could have happened in nine years.

He kept walking and walking, for what seemed like forever. It got dark and cold, and he kept walking. He was afraid that if he stopped, he would do something impulsive. He would make a mistake.

Anthony couldn't think. Couldn't focus. Not even as he finally decided to call it a night and arrived in front of the hotel that evening and went up to his room. It got even worse there. When he pulled the curtains, the tower's beam lit up his room and blinded him. He was so close to what he wanted more than anything. To the person he wanted more than anything. Yet, so far. So painfully far.

For the rest of the night, he sat on the floor, in the middle of the room, drinking from a bottle of red wine and thinking. Putting together all the pieces of the puzzle of the last few years.

His oldest memory was waking up in a hospital. Trying to move but realizing he was tied to a bed. Feeling scared. Setting himself free. Snatching a patient's clothes and shoes from one of the rooms and sneaking out the back door.

Panicking. What had he done to be restrained like that? Was he a criminal? Had he hurt someone? It had seemed so easy, so natural for him to steal that man's things. Was he a dangerous thief?

Then he remembered stumbling out of the hospital, wearing those shoes two sizes too large, walking with difficulty, and pushing himself until he couldn't move anymore. He remembered falling in the snow, convinced that was the end.

The next image that came to him was waking on the side of the road. It was dark and he was cold, so cold he could barely move, and his teeth were chattering violently. Where was he? What year was it? Who was he? What had happened to him?

A truck stopped a few meters in front of him and a man came out and after taking some boxes from the back, went into a store.

Desperate, confused, and afraid he was going to die if he stayed there in the snow for much longer, he propped himself up and with the last ounce of strength, climbed into the back of the truck.

Anthony took another gulp of wine and closed his eyes for a moment.

His last thought before he'd passed out in that truck was that he couldn't die. Because he had to be somewhere. Someone was waiting for him somewhere. Where and who, he didn't know. But that was what kept him going. What gave him strength. What made him not give up.

He woke up when a strong light flashed in his eyes. There were voices. A man. A woman. He couldn't understand what they were saying, he didn't know what was happening, only that someone grabbed him and it felt like he was floating above the ground.

'Mr Peltz,' he heard a voice and at first, he didn't react. Whoever was talking was not addressing him.

'Mr Peltz. Anthony,' the voice insisted. A woman's voice.

He opened his eyes.

'Good, good,' she said. 'Well, hello. Welcome back,' said the woman who was dressed as a nurse. She smiled kindly at him.

Why was she calling him Mr Peltz? Was that his name? He still couldn't remember anything that happened before he'd run out of that hospital. Where was he?

He looked around and to his horror, he realized he was in a hospital.

'Where am I?' he asked, his voice low and shaky.

'You're in Southampton, Mr Peltz. In the hospital. You have been involved in some kind of accident. But you're going to be alright,' she said, and his confidence calmed him.

Southampton? Was that where the first hospital had been as well? No, it couldn't have been. They had spoken French in that other place. They spoke English here.

'How – how did I end up here?'

'I was about to ask you the same thing, but it might be too soon for you to remember. A delivery driver from London found you in the back of his truck after he got off the steamboat here, in Southampton. He called the ambulance and here you are. That's all we know.'

He remembered the truck. That part was clear. Or at least as clear as anything could've been in his mind at that point.

'How long have I been here?'

'Almost two weeks,' said the nurse. 'You've slept quite a lot and it helped, because your injuries have healed just beautifully,' she said satisfied. 'Your name is Anthony Peltz, is that correct?'

'My name?' What was he to say? Yes? No? Why did they think his name was Peltz?

'We found your passport in your coat pocket, but everything was soaking wet; you were probably covered in snow and it had melted in the truck. Unfortunately, the ink is all smudged. We thought it said Anthony Peltz but couldn't be sure.'

In his coat? He didn't have a coat.

Oh, the coat. The one he'd stolen from the other hospital.

He froze. What about the picture?

'Can I please get my wallet? There's something in there I need to check.'

'Of course,' she said smiling.

She handed him a transparent plastic bag.

'I'm sorry your passport is destroyed. You will have to get a new one when you go back to Cambridge.'

He nodded. 'It's alright.'

'I will give you some space,' she said, 'and I'll be back with your lunch.'

'Thank you,' he muttered.

With trembling hands, he opened the bag and took out the wallet and the passport.

He slowly flipped the first page. The nurse was right;

it was ruined. The black and white photo completely destroyed; the name barely legible. It could've been Peltz or Reltz or Deltz. The first name was Anthony though. And the date of birth was gone too. And yes, there was a home address but apart from number 122 and the name of the city, Cambridge, everything else was gone.

It was as good a name as any other. What was he to do? Say he took someone's wallet? And admit he was most likely a criminal, not just a petty thief? Why else would they have tied him to the bed like that, unless he had done something truly vile?

Everyone needs a name, he thought. It was better if he went along with it.

The man he stole it off was in the contagious ward of the hospital. Tuberculosis, it said on the door. The new Anthony hoped the old Anthony would make it and walk out of there alive, and his only bother would be to replace his documents. He apologized to him in his mind.

The nurse returned with a tray of food.

Before leaving, she stopped in the doorway.

'Is there anyone you would like us to call to let them know you are alright? Parents? Wife? We looked up Peltz in the phone book but couldn't find anyone.'

A lump rose in his throat. Did he have someone? A wife perhaps? He looked at his left hand. No wedding band. No trace there had ever been a wedding band there.

'No. Nobody. I don't have anyone.'

Anthony gulped down the rest of the wine. He got up, stumbling, and grabbing a second bottle from the small refrigerator. It was white wine this time, but he didn't care. 'Good hotel,' he mumbled. 'Two bottles. They must've known I'd need it.'

He opened it and sat back on the carpet, with his back resting on the side of the bed.

His thoughts went back to Anthony. To his life. The last nine years.

He remembered leaving the hospital with only the fifteen pennies he had found in the wallet, no idea where to go, what to do or how he was going to survive. All he knew was that he had to, no matter what it took.

He stopped at the first inn he saw, close to the hospital, and inquired about the price of a room; he couldn't afford it. He kept walking and checking inns and hostels, motels but they were all too expensive. So he slept under Northam Bridge the first night. And the second. He used his money to buy bread and stay alive.

A week or so later, he was walking the streets of Southampton, when he saw the Southampton City Art Gallery, and immediately his thoughts went to the dreams he'd been having ever since the accident. He dreamed of pictures that looked like drawings or paintings. Random colors almost mashed together. Purple, green, yellow. Had he been an artist?

He hesitantly walked in, expecting to be thrown away by a guard. But he wasn't. Although people looked at him funny, and most of them avoided him, no doubt because he hadn't taken a shower in a week and his clothes were dirty, nobody bothered him. He stayed there for hours, just staring at paintings. Had he been an artist? Did he know anything about art at all? Maybe he had worked in a museum, just like that one.

The next day he returned. And the next. And the next.

In the evening, on his way back to the bridge, he'd pass the town library. And on one of those days, he got an idea. He went in, and searched for books about art. If it had been a part of his life, perhaps reading about it would jog his memory. He looked for the colors in his dreams, for patterns, for something familiar.

It had now been a few weeks since he was homeless. At night it was cold and scary and lonely. But during the day, he had things to do that kept his mind busy. He started using public bathrooms to clean himself up. He offered to sweep the sidewalk in front of stores and got some change for it, enough to buy himself bread. He drank water from fountains, and even got a clean change of clothes from a clothing shop after he helped them carry their heavy boxes inside. The rest of his time, he spent it in the museum and the library.

The weather was nicer now and he swapped the bridge for a park bench. A few weeks later, his daily trips to the library proved to be his salvation. Joseph, the librarian, who was also passionate about art, seemed to take a liking to him. He would help him pick out books, explained art concepts, and sometimes he would even sit with him. He was a nice man.

'I don't know much about your situation,' he said to Anthony one day, 'but I like your determination. And you seem to love books. How would you feel about working here? It's only a few hours a day and it doesn't pay much, but it's something. We also have a room, here, above the library. It's small and outdated, but if you want it, it's yours. It comes with the job.'

Anthony teared up.

He found out, months later, there was no job available at the library and no room that came with the job. Joseph paid him out of his own money and gave him the room he was supposed to use to deposit books.

Anthony's life improved considerably. He had a clean place to live, a job, and he was doing something that seemed to have a link to his old self. Although he didn't know what that was. But he kept going. Kept reading and learning, hoping it would help bring back his memories.

But then there were the nightmares. It was dark, he was falling from somewhere high, and he was cold. He called out a name over and over and someone grabbed him. In that chaos, amid noises he couldn't understand, a whisper. 'Stay with me. Don't go.' He stopped panicking. Whatever was happening, he wasn't alone. He didn't follow the strange noises and he stayed. He would wake up covered in sweat, crying, screaming and unable to remember the name he was calling desperately.

Tormented by these dreams, he sometimes found it hard to carry on during the day. It all seemed so hopeless. His mind vacant of any memories, his life like an empty shell. But he had to keep going. He had to do whatever he could to try and remember.

Although he now had less free time, he still went back to the museum. He liked to get lost among paintings for hours – until the museums closed – then the next day, he would scour the library shelves for books about them and read everything he could get his hands on. There was something familiar, comforting about being surrounded by art, by all that beauty, all those colors.

A few months later he was visiting the Southampton City Art Gallery when he saw an ad for an open night guard position, and he immediately applied.

Now he had money to pay for a rented room, but when he told Joseph he wasn't going to abuse his hospitality any longer and get his own place, the old man stopped him.

'There's no bother, Anthony. You can stay here for as long as you need. But if I were you, I'd use my money on something else.'

'On what?'

'I think you should try to figure out more of what you're meant to do.'

'What do you mean?'

'Art. It's something that you're not only interested in but also something you seem to be very good at. It's like a talent and it would be a shame to waste your talents. Have you thought about doing some classes? Maybe getting a diploma? Then you can aim for a slightly more creative job than that of a night guard. I think you could do so much better for yourself.'

After thinking about it quite a bit, Anthony listened to Joseph and that fall he enrolled in evening school to study art history, while still keeping his library job during the day and the museum job during the night.

It was on a cold winter night, when a transport arrived at the City Art Gallery, that everything turned around for him. Paintings, some by known artists, some by less known. And among them, three deteriorated artworks, almost beyond recognition. The curator decided they couldn't invest the time, the money or resources into restoring them and asked that they be removed and disposed of. 'There is no value in them,' he insisted.

But Anthony, instead of destroying them, took them home.

And from there on, he did everything he could to salvage them using his own money, working extra shifts at the museum, asking local artists for help with colors and materials.

He taught himself how to do it, asked his teachers for advice, read tens of books, looked at hundreds of paintings. Progress was slow, because he was still learning and because the money wasn't enough and he had to wait for each paycheck to buy materials; besides, he could only work on the paintings at night. Four years later, a few months after graduating school with honors, he finally completed the three restorations.

And when he finished them and notified the museum he had salvaged the artworks – which were now evaluated at two million pounds – his luck finally changed.

Word got around about the up-and-coming art expert. In a few months, he got multiple job offers. One, a very well-paid art dealer position with one of the biggest art groups in England and the other, a barely paid art restorer at the Fitzwilliam Museum in Cambridge. He took the restoration job without hesitation.

He said goodbye to Joseph and promised to visit; he kept his promise, year after year.

Anthony got up and looked out the window. There were lights everywhere. Sparkly, colorful, dizzying lights. Paris was once his home; now it felt foreign. Just like he felt in his own life. His life...

His life in Cambridge felt like a completely different story, not just a different chapter.

It didn't take long for the Fitzwilliam Museum to become as famous as its new art restorer, but the more attention he got, the more Anthony withdrew. He didn't need people looking into his background; he didn't want to be asked questions he couldn't answer. He was sure he had done something terrible in the past, and he was afraid that someone would recognize him. Museums all over the world wanted to work with him, collectors approached him, journalists started calling about interviews. His apartment in downtown Cambridge was too easy to access by everyone and anyone. So Anthony bought himself a house in an exclusive part of Cambridge, on Latham Road. His new property, on a tree-lined, no-through street, had a beautifully landscaped south-facing garden, bordered by tall pine trees, and over two acres of land. Enough, Anthony thought, to maintain his privacy. He also had to hire someone to handle all these calls and requests he was getting.

Without mentioning his name, he placed an ad in the newspaper for an assistant. He had an ulterior motive for this too. He was lonely. Successful and busy, but lonely. He missed having someone around. In Southampton he had Joseph, but here it was just him.

Qualified men and women of all ages came to interview. And one unqualified woman. She had been a nanny, a cook, and a live-in maid for years; a woman who had no family, just like him.

'Would you consider a live-in job?' he asked after meeting her the first time.

She smiled. 'Will I get to cook?'

'If you want to.'

'And who will do the shopping?'

'Who would you like to do the shopping?' he asked.

'Me, of course,' she said. 'How about cleaning the house? Who will do that?'

He shrugged. 'Both of us, I don't know.'

'Fine. I'll take the job,' she said.

Hiring Mary proved to be the best decision Anthony had made.

Time passed. He had a good life now. Stable, albeit predictable, but that wasn't a bad thing and he thought less and less about his old life. The one he couldn't remember.

He was right to let go back then. For almost a decade, he didn't remember anything, and it would've driven him mad to think about it all the time. He didn't remember who he had been before, where he was from. Nothing. Until that day. Nine years later.

Nine years. He'd had no idea who he was, and now everything had come back to him like in a dream. Like watching a movie. All at once. What his real name was, what he had left behind, what he had lost.

The sun was almost up, and he had no more wine.

He didn't want to cry. He tried not to.

ANTHONY

PARIS

Anthony finished at the Louvre late in the evening. They had given him 250 candidates for the fifteen open positions. He had his work cut out for him.

The night before, he'd made a big decision; he just didn't know if he was strong enough to follow through. When he checked out of the hotel, got into his car and drove towards the seventh arrondissement, in the proximity of the Eiffel Tower, he still didn't know.

He was scared and doubted himself, but he couldn't leave. Not without seeing her.

But it had been so long. How would she react? Would she recognize him? He looked in the car's mirror. The man staring back at him didn't look at all like the Alexander who had boarded the plane nine years before. He had a scar across his face, a long bushy beard to cover it and long hair in a ponytail. Would she care? Did she still love him?

Of course, she did, just as he still loved her. So much more. Impossible to measure or quantify. He had loved her even when he couldn't remember her. His soul hadn't forgotten.

Anthony tried to come up with a plan – what to do, what to say. He stopped a couple of streets away, went into a brasserie and stayed there until it got dark, but he still couldn't make up his mind. One thing was certain: he couldn't wait anymore; he was already nine years late.

Anthony left the brasserie. What if Constance had sold the place? What if Dominique had moved? No, she loved Paris. Where would she go? He kept asking himself questions and answering. His stomach felt like a huge pit, his mouth dry, and despite the cold weather his hands sweated. Walking slowly to the café, out of instinct almost, he stopped across the street. The small coffee shop was still there, still open, and the colored Christmas lights made it look nice and happy. The place was crowded, and he had to take a few more steps until he could see perfectly inside. The people in the café couldn't see him because the street was pitch black. Good. That made him feel less nervous.

He didn't know what he would do. His head was telling him it had been too long. People changed. Her life might be completely different now. With someone else in it. But his heart... his heart told him never to give up. That he was too close now to turn around. If he could at least see Dominique for a minute. If he could tell her how sorry he was, how he'd never meant to hurt her, how much he loved her. That he'd never forgotten her. Somehow, it would all work out.

One more step and at the table where they usually sat,

the face of an angel looked in his direction. 'Dominique, Dominique!' he shouted, but she didn't hear him. She was so beautiful, just as he remembered her. It was like time had stopped for her, thought Anthony and touched the window with his hand. Ever so gently. Almost as if he was afraid.

'I will remember this forever as the moment when I was brought back to life,' he said, in a whisper. As he went to the door, a little girl jumped into Dominique's arms. A step behind her, Vincent leaned down and kissed Dominique. Vincent kissed Dominique. Anthony stopped breathing, looking at them. They wore matching wedding bands and they looked happy together. 'She is married. Dominique is married,' he said in disbelief.

And they had a daughter together. She was about eight or nine and she looked like Vincent. So Dominique hadn't waited for him. Not at all. JJ must've been wrong about her not getting engaged to Vincent. She obviously had, and they'd soon had a child.

With every moment spent looking at them, his heart ripped into pieces. Tiny pieces that couldn't be glued back together. Dominique got up, startling Anthony. She turned to speak with Constance and that's when he saw it. She was pregnant. He felt like crying and screaming at the same time, breaking everything around him, running from it all. He felt like going back in time and forgetting it all again, forgetting her. He had lost Dominique for such a long time and in the last few days he thought he'd found her, only to lose her again, this time forever.

Why had he got his memory back? To go through all this suffering? And what was he supposed to do now? Go back to his life as if nothing had happened? He never should have come.

Anthony sat on the curb, picturing Dominique by his side, eating their macarons and drinking their cinnamon coffee, laughing, holding hands. Imagining she would feel he was there, and she would come running out, take him in her arms and tell him she loved him. Tell him that what he'd just seen was nothing more than a nightmare. Tell him she hadn't forgotten about him. She had never given up on them.

He tried to imagine what their life would've been if it hadn't been for that stupid, horrendous accident that ruined his dreams. As he was sitting there, in the cold winter night, shivering and fighting his tears, he realized that it was all too late. *He* was too late.

Dominique had moved on; she had built a new life for herself, a family of her own.

He couldn't even blame her. He had been dead to her for a long time and it was better if he stayed that way. Alexander Roberts ceased to exist nine years ago when a plane crashed at Sainte-Adresse. 'There had been survivors. Anthony Peltz made it,' he said to himself, 'but Alexander didn't. How could he, when his reason to live no longer existed? He stopped existing when she forgot about him.'

He got up and looked at her, knowing it was likely the last time, and mouthed, 'Only you. Always.' And then he walked away.

DOMINIQUE SAINT GERMAIN

PARIS

Apart from JJ's stroke three years before, which had left him with a right-side paralysis and in a wheelchair, Dominique's life had been peaceful and quiet, predictable even, especially after she married Vincent. But she didn't complain. He was a good husband and a caring father to Anne. They attended social events where she wore expensive clothes and jewelry and met important people. They had everything one could want, and Dominique was envied by many for her 'luck'.

This was especially true when, in early November, as they were celebrating their fourth anniversary with family and friends, Dominique and Vincent announced they were expecting a baby. Anne, who was eight years old and had been begging them for a little sister or brother for years, was on top of the world. She had started making plans of her own; how she would take care of the baby, what they would do together. Vincent was smiling from ear to ear as he shook everyone's hand, and Dominique let everyone touch her belly and smiled graciously. She was happy too; of course she was. A baby was a blessing and she was going to give her child all the love and care in the world, just like her mother had given her.

There was a small part of nostalgia in the back of her mind, or the reminiscence of the what-if in her heart. A baby marked yet another milestone in her life, totally different to the life she had dreamed about. But she couldn't allow herself to think about that. Not anymore. It wouldn't have been fair to anybody: her baby, Anne, her husband. Whatever she once dreamed of was long gone. The dreams were long gone. She could barely remember the last time she had had one. Not in years.

The news kept on coming and the excitement in Dominique's life didn't seem to have an end. A couple of weeks later, she received the most coveted job in the art world of France, perhaps even Europe – curator at the Louvre. After so many years of hard work, she had finally got it.

Even her last project at the Marmottan got picked up by the Louvre – a Monet Lily painting she worked on for months to restore. Coincidentally or not it was the same painting on the cover of *Monet's Impressionism*. The book that changed her life many years ago. The Louvre board gave her a special gallery for a temporary exhibition. And recently, they'd nominated her for one of the spots on a newly created elite restoration group.

Now it really looked like any woman who knew her, or

knew of her, had reasons to be envious. It did seem like she had it all – the loving husband, the perfect daughter, the baby on the way, the successful career. And she did, didn't she?

The whole family planned to meet at Le Petit Coin to celebrate Dominique's latest success and to have the pre-Christmas dinner, as they did every year. Lisa, Dominique, Vincent and Anne arrived first and waited for JJ.

Dominique's heart always shrank when she sat at that table. Their table. 'Best view in town.' She heard the words as if only days had passed, not years. A lifetime ago.

'I told you not to put up so many Christmas lights,' she said jokingly to Constance. 'The entire street is in complete darkness. Did you blow the fuses in the neighborhood? You'll get sued if a clumsy Parisian breaks a leg on the ice.'

'You know I like to dress up the place. They should come in and have fun, not stay outside in the dark,' Constance said and laughed.

They all sat at the table in the corner, bringing more chairs and squeezing in to fit everyone. It was a lovely holiday dinner, prepared by their very own 'world-famous chef de cuisine', as Vincent called Constance.

But during dinner, there was a moment. A fleeting moment when Dominique felt compelled to turn and look at the window behind them. Only a moment.

'You didn't know he was there, did you? But why? I thought you always felt his presence.'

'It had been so long since I stopped believing, since the

dreams went away, and I got good at pretending there was no unbreakable bond. I had been living an ordinary life for four years. A comfortable, no-surprises, ordinary life. I loved Vincent in my own way, and we had a good thing going. It wasn't what I had dreamed of, but dreams, I convinced myself, were just that. Dreams.'

I close my eyes for a moment. 'When we look back, whether it's something we did five minutes or sixty years ago, we all think we know what we should've done. When we look at others making wrong decisions, we shake our heads and say, "I would never. I'm better than that." We all want to believe we're special or extraordinary in some way. But the reality is, for most of us at least, what makes us truly extraordinary is the love we have for someone, the connection we have with them. If we deny that connection, if we reject that love, we're ordinary people. Who make ordinary people mistakes. Who have ordinary people faults and who fail to recognize extraordinary, like most ordinary people do.'

'Mamie, you're anything but ordinary.'

'Yet, that evening, and in the last four years I was painfully ordinary. As soon as I stopped listening to my heart, as soon as I denied the very connection that made me extraordinary, I was.' I smile. 'But you know what?'

Valerie stares curiously.

'That fleeting moment was all it took to bring it all back. And that night I had a dream, for the first time in four years. I felt the connection again. Because that evening, in the coffee shop, although I didn't want to listen to my heart, I did. I just didn't know it yet.'

'What did you dream about?'

In my dream, I was in the coffee shop, at the table, just like I had been that evening. I held my breath.

'Did you hear that?' I asked Constance.

'What?' she asked distractedly.

'I thought I heard something.'

Then Anne came back to the table with Vincent and jumped into my arms. Just as it happened.

'Are you alright?' asked Vincent.

'Yes, I'm fine.'

'That is a dazzling dress. Let me see you, dear,' said Lisa and I did a pretend pirouette. A few minutes later JJ was wheeled in by his live-in nurse and everyone sat at a table, eating Constance's amazing holiday specials. In my dream, everything was happening exactly like it had a few hours before. Well, not exactly. They all enjoyed themselves. Except for me. I felt the need to be alone. Pregnancy moods, I told Vincent and Constance.

I didn't know what made me feel so sad, but it wasn't the hormones. I walked to the window and stood there, looking out, although I couldn't see anything past my reflection.

I touched the window and instead of a frozen glass I felt a warm – in a way familiar –touch. My heartbeat accelerated; my body shivered. 'This can't be,' I whispered.

I ran outside. It was cold and pitch black.

I sat on the curb and tried to calm my beating heart. I thought I was losing my mind. There was nothing there. Just darkness, shadows and freezing wind.

And then a silhouette appeared right next to the café's window.

'Only you. Always,' I heard.

'Only you. Always,' I echoed, fighting back the tears.

Then I woke up.

PART X

'Nothing is real
but dreams and love.'
— Anna de Noailles

ANTHONY

CAMBRIDGE

He tried to convince himself nothing had changed. Anthony had built himself a full life, and who was he to ruin all that?

It had been weeks since the board had approved the plan and given him the money; he needed to show them they weren't making a mistake by trusting him.

No more running after impossible dreams, Alexander, Anthony, whatever your name is, he said to himself. *It's time to live in the real world. Make the best of what you have.*

The first step was to recruit the best specialists. The core team would have fifteen members and Anthony looked over the list he received from the Louvre that had over 250 candidates. People from all over the world: sculptors, painters, auctioneers, scholars, young, old. How would he choose? The organization's headquarters was at the Louvre, as requested by the board, and that was fine with him, but one thing he couldn't do was to accept their offer for a permanent office there. 'I will be traveling so much I will not need it. Besides, I still have my restoration workstation at the Fitzwilliam Museum in Cambridge, and it's only fifteen minutes from where I live. Makes more sense.'

The board didn't insist. Thankfully. He couldn't very well show up at the Louvre one day and risk running into her and Cambridge seemed far enough. Safe enough.

Anthony sat at his desk with the list in front of him, along with piles of résumés and portfolios. Aaron Johnson. Diane Wills. Francis Gerber. Flora Garcia. Dominique Saint Germain. L.B. Brown.

He stopped. Dominique. His Dominique. No, not his. Vincent's Dominique.

He read her résumé twenty times. Of course, she had to be the perfect candidate. Associate curator at the Louvre, leading restoration projects at The Marmottan. Specialized in Impressionism, an expert in Claude Monet. Dominique Saint Germain. Those initials. D.S.G. It was she who had restored that Monet painting at the Louvre, the Lilies mural. That's why he'd felt what he felt. *How strange our souls are,* he thought.

'I can't do this,' he said and moved her résumé and portfolio to the rejection pile. Then his hand went back and hovered over the envelope. 'No. I shouldn't. Being that close to her, the pain would be unbearable.'

A few candidates later… 'But is it correct to dismiss her because I can't control my feelings? From what I see she is the most deserving to be on the interview list.'

He groaned. 'Think of what you're saying, Anthony.

Interview her face to face. Is this how you want Dominique to find out you're alive? And what for? You will undoubtedly ruin her life and you have no right to do that. You have 249 other people to choose from.' Anthony stopped. He had been talking to himself out loud while his intern stood in the doorway looking at him.

'Is everything alright?' asked the young man.

'Yes. Fine. I have decided not to interview the candidates. Please let our contact at the Louvre know. I will send them a test and will hire the ones who pass.'

The boy left.

'Now what? What is the test? You are getting yourself in trouble. You just can't stay away from her, can you?' he said out loud, noticing too late the boy was there again.

Embarrassed, Anthony laughed.

'When should I say you will be sending out the tests?'

'Tomorrow.'

'And when should they send them back by?'

'I don't know. Give them a week. Say, 18 January?'

He spent the rest of the day and night writing and erasing. The test was either too hard, too easy, too close to Dominique's skillset, or too far from it. Finally, he settled on one.

'Only a handful will pass, at best, and then I will get a new set of candidates and that's that,' he said to himself, sealing the envelope before he could change his mind.

A few days later, he started receiving envelopes. Did he go through all of them three times looking for Dominique's? Probably more than that. Her name wasn't there. On the

443

day of the deadline, he had fourteen candidates who had passed the test. Dominique's envelope was nowhere to be found. Only one spot left on the team and she hadn't sent in her answers.

On that last day, five more envelopes came in the mail. No, No, No, No... Yes.

The last one had all the correct answers. No name on the test. He checked the back of the envelope. Sender: Dominique Saint Germain.

DOMINIQUE

22 FEBRUARY 1974

PARIS

After the holidays Dominique went back to the Louvre and to her new challenge: the nomination to be part of the European Restoration Initiative – a team of hand-picked, highly skilled art specialists, led by a restoration master and professor at Cambridge University.

It all sounded amazing and she was excited to start preparing her application for the role until she found out who the team lead was. Anthony Peltz. He was widely regarded as one of the most influential and powerful art historians and restorers in Europe. That was the good news. The problem was his reputation. He was quite the character in the art world: a recluse, difficult, demanding, and always unsatisfied. At one point, she considered withdrawing her name from the list, but on the last day, she decided, for some unknown reason, to give it a chance. She completed the test and sent it to the Louvre, per the instructions received. 'All correspondence should be addressed to The Louvre Museum, European Restoration Initiative, Mr Anthony Peltz.'

Much to her surprise, on 21 January, she got the acceptance letter and the contract she needed to sign. Should she? Shouldn't she? Why put herself through that? But why miss the opportunity? Days went by and Dominique couldn't decide. She went about handling her regular curator responsibilities, doing her best to pretend the turning point in her career wasn't dangling in front of her eyes.

More than three weeks after she received the contract – which she had yet to sign – word came that the first batch of salvaged art from a rundown mansion in Surrey was to be sent by Anthony Peltz to one of the art specialists. Nobody knew which one of the fifteen would be the lucky one. In that batch, there was a Le Havre painting by Monet. Dominique took that as a sign she needed to grow up, get over her insecurities and accept the challenge given to her.

The Louvre Museum
European Restoration Initiative
To Mr Anthony Peltz

Mr Peltz,

I want to start off by apologizing for not being able to confirm my involvement in the European Restoration Initiative sooner, due to some pressing matters at Le Louvre.

I am aware it has been a while since I received the proposal to join the team, but if there is a spot left and the offer is still valid, I would like to offer my services from here on.

Respectfully,

Dominique Saint Germain

The Louvre Museum

European Restoration Initiative

To Mrs Dominique Saint Germain

Dear Mrs Saint Germain,

I have only heard wonderful things about your work and could use someone with your skills and talents on the team. Your profound knowledge of Impressionist art is something we have been looking for and are currently missing from our organization's know-how.

Please rest assured of my deepest gratitude for your offer, which I accept with pleasure.

Yours truly,

Anthony Peltz

Dear Mr Peltz,

Thank you for the second chance. I will not disappoint you. I was informed one of the art pieces you have recovered is a Le Havre by Monet, and I want to express my enthusiasm and willingness to take on the lead with the dedicated team that will restore it.

Please allow me to be the one responsible for bringing it back to life.

Respectfully,

Dominique Saint Germain

Dear Mrs Saint Germain,

It would be my pleasure to appoint you in charge of the Monet.

I have made all the arrangements and the painting is scheduled to arrive at the Louvre at 2 p.m. on 22 February. Your presence for the reception of the painting is vital, as it can only be released to the person indicated in the international transit papers. If for any reason you cannot carry out this task, do let me know at once. Don't forget that once it arrives, it will be your responsibility. Please examine it and send me your recommended restorations. I trust the Monet will be in good hands, Mrs Saint Germain.

Yours truly,
Anthony Peltz

He was giving her the Monet. That was beyond her most optimistic scenarios. All she had to do was show up at the delivery.

On 22 February, Dominique was coming back from AngeD'Art's public relations experts, where she negotiated a royal coverage for the incoming Monet. She was running late so she picked up her pace. Once on Rue de Rivoli there was no point in rushing; she was only a couple of minutes from the Louvre. But she couldn't miss the second chance to make a first good impression. Besides, if she wasn't there, the painting could not be received. She kept walking fast. Meters from the entrance to the museum, Dominique felt a sharp pain in her abdomen. Then another so strong, she let out a short scream.

ANTHONY

CAMBRIDGE

A week went by. Two. Almost three and he hadn't heard from her. No explanation for not being at the Louvre to receive the Monet. Thankfully, he was able to stop the painting, at the last minute, from being sent back to Surrey. Monet was safe. But what about Dominique? Was she safe? What had happened? Where was she?

The Dominique he knew loved Monet more than... more than many of the things in her life, and she wouldn't have – willingly – abandoned the painting.

Nobody at the Louvre was helpful. Not the board of directors, not her colleagues, despite his multiple attempts to contact them and get an update on Dominique. Finally, one of them told Anthony she had been on leave since 22 February.

On leave? Since 22 February? The day she was supposed

to get the Monet. Something happened, he thought. Ghost or not, I can't sit around, do nothing and not know what happened to the woman I love.

But Anthony knew he couldn't just go to Le Petit Coin or her house to look for her and risk being recognized. He had to find another way into the café.

A young painter selling his sketches on Seine's Rive Gauche became his way back into Le Petit Coin.

'All you need to do is go across the street into that coffee shop and see if she's there, if she seems okay, whatever you can find out. She's hard to miss – a beautiful young woman, with long red hair, big green eyes. Here, take this,' he said and pulled out of his wallet a folded piece of paper. The photo he had ripped from *Le Monde* a couple of months ago. It showed Dominique standing in front of the Monet painting at the Louvre, and next to her, in a wheelchair, JJ. It was hard for him to look at that photo. Not only because Dominique was in it, but because JJ was too. He seemed so old, so frail in that wheelchair and it broke his heart to see his godfather like that. It broke his heart that JJ thought he was dead, that he had mourned for him. *At least he has Nicole and Dominique,* he thought.

'Monsieur?' said the young artist, bringing Anthony back to reality.

'Yes. Here is the photo. Only that she's pregnant now. Visibly pregnant,' said Anthony passing him a one-hundred franc bill.

A few minutes later the street artist returned. 'She was there, monsieur, and she seemed alright but upset about something. It looked like she had been crying and her mother or her friend consoled her,' he said. 'But I almost came back to tell you I didn't find her,' he said.

'What do you mean?' asked Anthony.

'The woman in the café is not pregnant. I looked twice. No baby belly, monsieur.'

DOMINIQUE

25 MARCH 1974

PARIS

Seeing Vincent's sad face and watching Anne trying to hold back her tears was just as heartbreaking for Dominique as the miscarriage itself.

It had all happened so fast. The pain had been so unbearable, she couldn't take another step. She asked a passerby for help and they phoned the hospital. She was rushed to the emergency room, and all the way there all she could do was to hope and pray the baby was okay. But when the bleeding started, she knew the baby wasn't fine. And the doctors confirmed the devastating news. The baby hadn't been 'fine' for a while, she was told; his heart had stopped beating weeks ago.

'You could've died too,' said the doctor, trying to comfort her. He went on to explain that she'd already had blood poisoning and she risked serious conditions, some irreversible if she had waited longer.

Vincent, who had been by her side through it all, comforted her and assured her everything would be alright.

But Dominique didn't want to hear all that. She didn't want to hear anything from anyone. It wasn't going to be alright. Her baby had died and she was mourning the son she never got a chance to hold, the hopes and dreams she had for him, for all of them together. And she felt guilty. She hadn't been able to protect her baby.

Dominique didn't get up from bed for days.

'Maman, I made you breakfast,' said Anne one morning. It had been days since she had left her room.

Dominique was just about to tell her daughter she didn't want anything, when she saw the look in her eyes. Sadness, worry, pain. All so visible on the face of her eight-year-old daughter, who was mourning the loss of her unborn brother as well. It wasn't just her who had suffered a loss. They all had.

'Thank you, my angel,' she said, forcing herself to get up. 'I'll eat, but on one condition.'

'Anything,' said Anne.

'That you eat with me.'

Anne smiled and sat in bed next to her mother.

'Dada is so worried about you,' she said.

'I know, honey, I'm sorry. I haven't been feeling very well lately.'

'Because of the baby.'

Dominique nodded.

'But you're not upset with Dada?'

'Of course not. He did nothing wrong.'

'Are you upset with me then?'

'Oh, honey,' she said and hugged her daughter tight.

'Why would I be upset with you? You're the most wonderful daughter.'

'In the whole world?' asked Anne, smiling.

'In the whole universe,' she said.

'I love you, Maman,' said Anne, tears pooling in her eyes.

'I love you too, honey.'

Later that day she finally left her room. It wasn't easy and it took Dominique weeks to fully recover, not only physically but also mentally. But she knew she had to do it. By the end of March, she decided it was time to go back to work. Even if she wasn't fully ready to face the world, she had to get dressed, leave the house and force herself back into her old life. She owed that to her family and herself.

Everyone had been supportive and caring, but all she wanted was to be treated like before, and for everybody to stop looking at her with pity and let her go back to normal and to her job.

'That's if I still have a job,' she said, thinking about the European Restoration Initiative.

On her desk at the Louvre: a pile of letters, cards, and a few bouquets of flowers. *Enough,* she thought, and wanted to throw them all away but stopped right before tossing the correspondence in the trash, when she saw an envelope from Anthony Peltz.

Dear Mrs Saint Germain,

I was told you would be coming back to work at the end of March and I wanted to let you know the Monet has been waiting in storage for your return. I have attached all the details.

Please keep me posted on the progress you're making.

Thankfully, we have secured a new round of funding, so I will be traveling for the next three, maybe four months to try and find other artworks in need of our help.

But do continue to address all letters for me to the Louvre Museum and they will forward them along. Rest assured, I will always find time to read your notes and write back.

Yours truly,
Anthony Peltz

Dominique was moved. Moved and intrigued by his message and although she suspected her colleagues had mentioned her health issues to him, they denied it. Why was he nice to her? Anyone else would've reassigned the Monet long ago. Fourteen other people would've given anything for a chance to work on it.

She was thankful, though, for having that unexpected break and didn't want to risk questioning it too much. Not knowing how to thank him properly, she decided the best way was to do her job to the best of her abilities.

DOMINIQUE

CAMBRIDGE

Dominique worked hard with her team to revive the Monet and over the last few weeks had received a couple more paintings from Anthony Peltz, shipped from Germany and Italy, precious artwork that somehow survived World War II, hidden in attics and basements.

She did her best not to break her promise to Anthony Peltz and kept him up to date with the progress of the restorations.

Her letters to him were initially simple, short notes. Sparse, once every couple of weeks. Then they became more frequent as he wrote back with questions and suggestions, sometimes challenging her decisions, other times praising her good judgment. The more he replied, the more she wrote back. *He is a man I could have long conversations with*, she thought.

Luckily, she was trained in having interminable

conversations, especially about art. She chuckled thinking of all the late evenings when she and Anne would sit by the fire sipping hot cocoa and talking about Renoir, Degas, Pissarro, and Monet. Always Monet.

Anne inherited the love for art from her grandfather perhaps, along with a passion for all things beautiful, and that inexplicable weakness for Monet. When she was a little girl, instead of playing with dolls and staying busy with tea parties and dress-ups, Anne taught herself how to paint from Dominique's books and albums. When she learned how to read, there was no stopping her. She was a sponge for all things art.

One Friday in May, after coming home from school, Anne pulled Dominique away and told her, in the most secretive way possible, 'You have to take me to London.'

'What's in London?' asked Dominique amused. 'Don't tell me. An art exhibition.'

'A once-in-a-lifetime art exhibition, Maman,' she said enthusiastically.

Dominique chuckled.

'Never-before-displayed Monet paintings, from a private collection. Only for the weekend.'

'What weekend?' Surely, she couldn't mean that weekend. It was already Friday night.

'Tomorrow and Sunday. Can we go? Maman, please, can we go? This is the only thing I want. Look, don't get me anything for my birthday.'

'Your birthday is in December. By then you'll find other things,' she said, smiling.

'I promise, nothing else, please,' Anne whined. Anne always remembered she was a child when she wanted something desperately.

Dominique's first reaction was to say no. Too last minute, too complicated, too far. Then her daughter's words echoed in her mind along with memories of herself as a little girl. 'This is the only thing I want.' She gave in. If it was in her power to make Anne happy, to make her dreams come true, she always did. People might've judged her and thought that was bad parenting, but Anne grew up happy, respectful and not too spoiled.

They planned to be on the first flight to London the next morning and come back that same night because JJ wasn't well, and Dominique didn't want to leave him alone for too long.

What Anne 'forgot' to mention was that the museum was not in London; it was a hundred kilometers north, in Cambridge. When they finally arrived, the Fitzwilliam Museum was already flooded by a sea of visitors, all in a hurry to get inside for different exhibitions, so it took them a while to find the end of the line for the Monet art gallery. It looked like a solid two-hour wait.

Dominique hadn't anticipated that many people being interested in a collection of paintings, but she'd obviously misjudged a Saturday morning in England.

Anne was anxious so Dominique asked the ticket lady if her daughter could go in and wait inside until she could buy the tickets; especially since the event was free for children under the age of twelve. The woman said it didn't make a difference to her if it was fine with her mother to leave the child unattended. Dominique trusted her daughter more than she trusted most adults. She kissed her and sent her in.

An hour and a half later, Dominique finally got in, and immediately realized how difficult it would be to find Anne since the place was swarming with people.

She made her way through the crowd and must've been halfway through the immense hall when she stopped short, looking around, almost in disbelief. She knew this place. She had dreamed about it the night before. Paintings were being hung on the walls in her dream, but it was the same place, she was certain. And there was a man. Who was he? What was he doing? It was such a short dream. She couldn't remember. Ever since she'd started having the dreams again, they were shorter, not like before. They were few and far apart, most of them confusing. Voices and faces she couldn't remember. And sadness. There was a lot of sadness.

Dominique started walking again, looking for Anne when suddenly she found herself unable to breathe. On the other side of the hall, her eyes singled out one person. A man. Actually, a man's back because he faced the opposite way. There was something about him. His height, posture, something reminded her – no, it wasn't possible, but it reminded her of Alexander.

Her heart raced to the point of having actual palpitations.

Dominique breathed in and out a few times and closed her eyes for a second, thinking the illusion would go away but when she opened them, that man was still standing there.

They say you see the people you love in every person you meet – it's only natural. Dominique tried to calm herself.

It's not him. She knew that, but still, her heart told her something else. She stood there, among all those people pushing her to make way, but she didn't budge. She couldn't move and risk losing that illusion.

For a few seconds, she forgot about the rules of humankind, about living and death, about what was possible and not and just looked at the back of a man her heart told her was the love of her life. A few seconds were more than she'd had in almost ten years.

'You didn't hear me calling you?' She heard the voice like she was in a dream.

Anne stood next to her with a big smile on her pretty face.

'Best day ever. Thank you, Maman, I love you.' She jumped into her mother's arms.

When Dominique finally turned around, the man was gone. Had he been there in the first place or had she imagined it? Wished it? Dreamed it? Her mind was a trickster. It knew how much her heart desired it to be true, how much her soul longed for him.

He is gone. He has been gone for a long time, Dominique. You were fine. For almost five years you were fine. You let go. Didn't you? Dominique now wondered if she ever had. Given up on him. On their love. Even when she said she didn't believe, when she forced herself to move on, there was always a part of her that hoped against hope. Her soul longed for the missing piece. And it seemed it was more powerful than ever. That longing. That feeling of living someone else's life, smiling someone else's smiles and saying someone else's words. She had never really given up, had she?

'So close. You were so close to finding him. What did you do? Did you look for him?'

'I looked for him everywhere, but he was nowhere to be found. He disappeared, and I thought it was all a dream or wishful thinking. I didn't know for sure. And if it was him, then why didn't he come to me?' I ask and wink.

'You're tricking me, aren't you? You saw each other outside, right? He came to you.'

'I'm afraid not,' I say and see the disappointment in her eyes.

ANTHONY

PARIS

Weeks after the Monet exhibition in Cambridge, Anthony still thought of that day and the mix of emotions that took his senses by storm. Excitement, longing, love, panic.

He didn't know what caused that acute feeling of fear. That she wouldn't understand why he hadn't told her the truth and she would hate him for it. That her love for him had long been gone. That she had forgotten him. That it had never been real.

Or that after five seconds with her, he would get the confirmation his new life was a complete sham and a lie. That it meant nothing without her in it and he couldn't continue doing the right thing and not telling Dominique he was alive.

He saw her the moment she walked in. He shouldn't have lingered and risked being seen.

Wasn't that what you wanted? Why are you running away now? You were the one who dreamed of seeing her, being close to her. Is this close enough for you? Is it? What did you think would happen? You should've kept your distance. This was inevitable the moment you secretly made your way into her life again. Inevitable. Stupid man, Anthony scolded himself as he went up the stairs to his office on the second floor of the Fitzwilliam Museum.

He felt alone. He felt like a fraud. What was the right thing to do; did he have any options? He was caught in a vicious circle.

Since the exhibition, his letters to Dominique were replaced by short notes. But she seemed to become more persistent the more he withdrew. Was he making a mistake, yet again, by trying to distance himself from her?

Dominique's letters slowly became more than just about the paintings. She dropped a thing here and there about her life, the museum, her adventures in Paris, and he slowly got caught in it. How could he not? He was starving for anything Dominique. The smallest of details.

One day, in early June, he received a short note from her letting him know she was taking a couple of weeks off to spend time with a family member who was gravely ill.

For some reason, he immediately thought of JJ and, doing his best not to arouse suspicion, he asked for details.

It was indeed JJ. He had suffered a hemorrhagic stroke a few years back and a second one a few weeks before. He had been recovering slowly but his muscles were extremely weak, and he had difficulty walking. So weak, he needed a wheelchair. Which Anthony already knew from the photo. But it was worse than he imagined.

JJ's speech was slurred to the point of being hardly comprehensible and oftentimes he showed signs of mental confusion. He'd also developed glaucoma in both eyes and that made life much harder for him.

Dominique told him that JJ missed his art, he missed being useful, and spending time in his library, reading his books and going to auctions all over the world. He talked about his wife more and more, the friends he had lost decades before, his childhood adventures.

Dominique couldn't give him back the life or the people he had lost but at least she could make sure he would know how much he was loved and how many people cared about him.

'I want him to spend his birthday with his family,' she wrote to Anthony, 'and although the doctors say JJ is confused most of the time and won't appreciate the effort, I think they are wrong. JJ knows – I know he does. I will sign his release papers on Friday, after they finish all the tests they need to run. I don't want to make him stay in the hospital a minute more than necessary.'

There was love and suffering in her words. So many things he didn't know about Dominique. She called JJ her mentor and the father she never had. *When did that happen?* wondered Anthony. *It's not only the physical time I missed. It's a big part of her life, a part I should've been in.*

The news about JJ brought tears to Anthony's eyes. He loved JJ. He had been like a father to him too, even before his father had died. He was always the one man he could count on, his support system, the voice of reason. Even when JJ was wrong, he did it all out of love.

Anthony put the letter down. She was taking him home

the next day. He still had time. What harm could that do now? He hadn't wanted to risk seeing his godfather before, because he was terrified JJ, with all his good intentions, would have told Dominique he was alive. But now... he had to go. He couldn't live with himself if he didn't. He would go and see him, just for a few minutes, thought Anthony, and without wasting time, got in his car. He drove without stopping and seven hours later he arrived, as the sun was setting.

He went straight to the hospital and after, convincing the nurses he was JJ's nephew who had come all the way from England to see his ailing uncle, Anthony slowly opened the door and stepped in, hesitatingly.

JJ looked even smaller than in the photo, and he had aged not by ten years but by twenty or more. His face was shriveled, and he'd lost weight. Even in his sleep, his mouth twisted in pain.

Seeing that powerful, strong man reduced to a sack of bones, his brilliant mind emptied and wondering idly, crushed Anthony. Losing his father as a young man had been painful but also abrupt and unexpected. Watching JJ suffer was torture.

He approached the bed and heard JJ's irregular breathing. The moment he touched his hand, JJ opened his eyes wide and fixated on Anthony. Anthony was startled for a moment although he knew his godfather couldn't see him.

'You came. I was hoping you would. I almost lost hope,' JJ said, weakly.

Anthony froze. What did he mean by that?

'Where have you been? What took you so long?'

'I'm here now,' said Anthony in a calming tone.

'They said you were dead but—' A tear rolled down his cheek.

'It's alright, don't think about that now.'

His presence was upsetting JJ. He shouldn't have come. He'd made things worse; what a selfish thing to do.

'Please forgive me. Will you forgive me? Say you do.' JJ sounded frantic.

'There's nothing to forgive, nothing,' said Anthony and caressed his cold forehead.

'I should've done more. And then they told me you were dead. For years I felt responsible,' he said, making a visible effort to speak.

'It's not your fault. Nothing is your fault. It just happened; it was an accident.'

Was he talking about him? Did he know who he was? Dominique said in one of her letters that JJ had been reminiscing about Leonard quite a lot recently. Maybe he thought he was Leonard. After all, JJ's mind was not what it used to be.

'An accident.' The corners of his mouth turned up in a tiny smile. 'So many accidents. My poor girl. An accident too. I mourned for her, I mourned for her. I was such a bad father.'

Anthony didn't know what he meant. 'Who, JJ?'

'My poor Nicole. Such a shame, a young, beautiful life lost. So many accidents,' he repeated.

'Nicole is dead?' asked Anthony in a raised voice, unable to hide his shock.

'Dead. Dead,' he repeated.

Was JJ lucid or was he delusional? In all the emotional rollercoaster of getting his memories back, it hadn't crossed Anthony's mind to look up Nicole. He'd just assumed she was somewhere, happily married to someone, away from JJ and his world.

She was dead. His best friend. No matter what happened at the end between them, no matter how they parted ways, he had never stopped caring about her.

A tear ran down Anthony's cheek, while JJ sobbed quietly. He took JJ's hand in his and comforted him.

'I don't want to forget. I have forgotten so much,' JJ said.

He wanted to show something to Anthony but couldn't and ended up doing a jerky movement of his whole body.

'Can you open that drawer there? There's a book in it. Take it, it's yours.'

He seemed to try to remember something.

'In it is everything you need, everything you've been searching for all this time,' he said to Anthony, who thought these were the ramblings of an old man who was no longer in touch with reality.

He took the book. It was a copy of *Monet's Impressionism*. How ironic, Anthony thought. He'd left his copy at Zara's house, many years before, hoping that she would eventually find it and understand what it all meant. What *she* meant to him. And she would come looking for him. How many times he dreamed that, somehow, the book would bring them together.

'I trust you will know how to find what you are looking for. Even if you don't know you're looking for it.'

Anthony opened it, to see what was on the first page. He knew it couldn't be the same copy, but for some reason, he still wanted to check.

No. It wasn't the same. But it did say something on the inner cover. 'From JJ to A.P.'

'Not now,' said JJ as if he saw him.

Anthony immediately closed the book.

'Wait until after I'm gone. It shouldn't be long now.'

'Don't talk like that,' said Anthony, trying to believe what he said.

'It's alright. It's time. I'm tired,' JJ said.

Anthony kissed his godfather's forehead as JJ seemed to fall back asleep.

The tiny old man smiled, the kind of smile people have when they say goodbye.

DOMINIQUE

13 JUNE 1974

PARIS

Dominique kept her promise and made JJ's birthday celebration one to remember. The biggest reward had been the joy in JJ's tired eyes. Being able to do one last thing for the man who had been by her side all those years, who'd helped and supported her, given her a sense of family and a home, made her happy. She couldn't repay him for all the good things he'd done for her, but she could show him how much he was loved. They all got him presents and Constance cooked his favorite dishes.

JJ's last days were peaceful and warm, filled with love and laughter.

They lost him on the stormy night of 13 June 1974. He died quietly in his bed, surrounded by the people who loved him and cared for him until the last moment.

Although Dominique had known what was coming, it

was still a hard, sad time and both she and Vincent did their best to shelter their daughter from it.

But JJ had been in Anne's life from the start, and the void left by his departure could not easily be filled. She wanted to hear stories about Grandpère, from his youth, stories he told Dominique on many evenings by the fire or outside in the garden. About his time in Switzerland, at the boarding school of La Rolande – a coincidence which quite shocked Dominique – his trips around the world, the time when he had met his wife, his career in the art world. More and more, Anne seemed interested and quite fascinated with La Rolande and kept asking her parents why she was not going to the same school as Grandpère.

A couple of days before he died, JJ called Dominique into his room and said he wanted to talk to her. Dominique smiled, remembering days long gone when she and JJ would lock themselves in his office and plan to conquer the world.

'I have something for you,' JJ said and asked Dominique to bring an envelope from his desk. 'I cannot give you what you wish for the most, but I wanted to make sure I at least give you a comfortable life,' he said and smiled absently.

'I don't know what to say. Thank you! Do you want me to open it now?'

'Wait until I am gone. It shouldn't be long now.'

'Don't talk like that,' said Dominique, upset.

'You sound just like Leonard.'

'Who?'

'Leonard. He came to see me,' said JJ, and Dominique sat on the side of his bed.

'Who's Leonard? I've never heard you talking about him,' she said.

'But you did, a long time ago. Leonard, Alexander's father.'

Alexander's father? The only thing she knew was that he had been JJ's best friend and he died when Alexander was a teenager. But neither Alexander nor JJ ever gave her details about what happened to him. She didn't even know his name until then.

'I was sure he wasn't dead.'

'Who?'

Dominique knew right away JJ was having one of his episodes when he couldn't distinguish reality from fiction. She smiled like she always did when he went down that path.

JJ ignored her. 'I didn't want to tell you, but I knew. Deep down, I believed it, but I didn't want to say anything. He said he isn't upset and he forgave me. He said it was just an accident,' said JJ in one breath.

'That's good,' said Dominique, hoping that would be the end of it.

'I gave him something as well. Something I've been holding on to for a long time. It was his to begin with; I just returned it. For him and his boy. That child deserves the best in this world. How much I loved him,' said JJ and sighed.

Hearing JJ talk about Alexander, and seeing how much JJ still loved him after all those years, made her feel less lonely in a way. She and JJ were so alike; it was as if their hearts were made from the same mold. Two hearts still beating for Alexander.

'I'm so glad you sent him to me. I don't know how else I would've found him,' he said.

'I didn't send anyone. Where did you meet this man?' she asked, wondering if she encouraged his delusions.

'I don't remember. I don't know.' He sounded frustrated.

Dominique sighed. She didn't mean to cause him pain. She'd thought it was better to play along than to ignore him, but she was obviously mistaken.

'I know. In the hospital. You told him I was there, didn't you?' said JJ all of a sudden.

'In the hospital?'

'Yes, that's it,' said JJ. 'He came to see me in the hospital, right before you brought me home. What have I been trying to tell you? You're not listening to me, young lady,' he said and smiled.

Dominique didn't tell anyone. The only other person who knew JJ had been in the hospital, except for their family and close friends, was her boss, Anthony Peltz.

ANTHONY

CAMBRIDGE

When he returned from Paris, Anthony went home and as usual, when he was distraught, straight to his study.

Mary knocked on the door.

'Come in,' he said and quickly wiped the tears with the back of his hand.

'I thought you could use this,' she said and brought him a tray with tea and some biscuits.

'Thank you, Mary.'

She sat on a chair across from the desk, looking at him.

She usually didn't linger, especially if he seemed preoccupied. Unless he wanted to talk, and then they would both drink their tea and eat their biscuits. And talk. And talk. They hadn't done that much lately.

'I saw the address of the hospital in Paris,' she said. 'On

your notepad there. I didn't mean to spy, it's just that I've been worried about you lately.'

He smiled sadly.

'I just found out someone I cared for deeply has died. And because that wasn't enough, someone equally dear to me is gravely ill and he's probably going to die as well, soon. I went to say goodbye.'

She nodded. 'Someone from your old life?'

Anthony lifted his eyes and looked at her. 'My old life?'

'The one when you weren't Anthony Peltz,' she said. There was no anger or betrayal in her tone. It was simply a statement.

'How did you—'

'I didn't. Until now,' she said. 'But I always suspected, I guess.'

'Why didn't you say something?'

'I thought you would tell me when you were ready.'

'That I was a fraud?' he said sadly.

'I never thought you were a fraud. It didn't take me long to figure out there was something in your past... something that you either didn't want to remember or couldn't. And those nightmares you kept having, they just confirmed it. You are anything but a fraud. You are the most honest person I know.'

'You know I stole someone's wallet once?'

'I'm sure that if you did that, it was because you didn't have any other options.'

'Oh, Mary,' said Anthony, broken-hearted.

He wrung his hands, not knowing where to start.

Mary poured herself some tea and pulled the chair next to him.

'Why don't you start,' she said, as if she could hear his thoughts, 'by telling me what your name is.'

He took a deep breath. 'My name is – was – Alexander Roberts.'

He then told her what happened.

Mary listened, and from time to time, he saw her looking away for a few moments, then wiping her cheek with the back of her hand.

When he was done, Mary was sniffling quietly, and her eyes were puffy and red.

'Poor, poor man,' she said and the pain in her eyes hurt him even more. 'What are you going to do? Are you going to get her back?'

'I can't do that to her, Mary. She's married; she has a daughter. A family of her own.'

'But you love her.'

'And that's why I have to let her go. *Because* I love her. And I want her to be happy.'

She sniffled again.

'I'm so sorry, Alexander, for everything you've been through. My heart is breaking for you.'

'Anthony,' he said. 'I am Anthony. I haven't been Alexander in ten years. And I will never be Alexander again. That life is gone. It's gone and I can never get it back. Just like I can never get Dominique back. She's moved on with her life, as she should. I am but a memory.'

The phone rang. He was needed at the Fitzwilliam.

'I want you to be happy,' said Mary as he was on his way out. 'You deserve to be happy.'

'Happy...' repeated Anthony lost in thought. 'I don't think happy is in the cards for me,' he said and, after hugging her and assuring her he would be alright, Anthony left.

He was barely in front of the house, when she caught up with him.

'Don't give up. You love her unconditionally. You loved her even when you didn't remember her. You love her and she loves you. That is so rare, Anthony. Fight for that love.'

He smiled as he walked away. 'Yes, she *loved* me. Loved, not loves. Goodbye, Mary. I will see you later.'

DOMINIQUE

15 JULY 1974

PARIS

A month after JJ's passing, Dominique finally opened the envelope he had given her. In it was his testament. Anne would inherit AngeD'Art when she was of age. Until then it was to be managed by an appointed administrator. Dominique inherited JJ's priceless collections of paintings, drawings and sketches, the mansion in Paris and a lump sum she could've used to buy a private island of her own easily. The rest of the money went to an art organization based out of Milan and to an unnamed account at a private bank in Switzerland.

He kept his promise and made sure they were well taken care of and beyond. So he was still somewhat lucid when they had that strange conversation before he died. There might be some truth to his story and for some reason, her thoughts kept going back to Anthony Peltz.

Dominique wondered why she felt the need to talk to

that man, to share with him details she wouldn't share with anyone else. He never told her anything about his life despite multiple attempts to get him to open up, to make him come to the Louvre at least once, to meet him. She got the sense he was never in one place very long, with all the travel to find artwork that needed their help. Yet somehow he was always there, somewhere, answering her letters without delay. Never giving her too much or too little. Just enough to keep her on her toes.

Why am I thinking about him now? Obviously, Anthony is not the mysterious visitor JJ talked about. That is, if there was such a person and it wasn't a figment of JJ's imagination.

And again, her thoughts went back to him, even when she tried to stop them. And it wasn't just then. It was a lot lately. Something in their conversations, in the way she imagined him from his letters, something was familiar, soothing but at the same time heartbreaking and unsettling. He was intriguing and interesting, fascinating sometimes and he reminded her of a time long gone, and of feelings she thought had been buried.

All of that from a man she had never met. He could've been forty-five or seventy-five, bound to a wheelchair or a professional runner, married with six children or a confirmed bachelor. Yet, in her imagination, he wasn't any of those things. He was something else. He was someone else.

Although she did her best to pretend nothing was happening, Dominique felt guilty most of the time and could barely look her husband in the eye. It wasn't that she did anything, no, at least she had that peace of mind, but she knew what she felt. She 'saw' Alexander in Anthony. That was the truth. His spirit, his passion, his heart. There were moments when she read Anthony's letters and she could swear she even recognized words and expressions.

Dominique realized how that would sound to any normal person out there. How that would sound to Vincent. Ridiculous. Pathetic. Desperate.

If he only knew, after all those years, that she still thought of Alexander, she still loved him – probably much more than she ever did – she still dreamed about him, she still talked to him when she was alone, telling him how she was and how much she missed him.

If he only knew how in the last months, every time she received a letter from Anthony, she felt she had received a letter from Alexander. Even though she didn't really think it was possible Anthony was Alexander, she was consumed by the 'what-if'.

Vincent must've felt something was different about Dominique because he kept pestering her with questions until she decided enough was enough. Her husband had the right to know and she needed to tell him, in a selfish sort of confession.

So she did. She told him she had been exchanging letters with a man she believed, somehow, had Alexander's soul or spirit. Simpler yet, with a man who was similar to Alexander.

He reacted badly. Which was to be expected.

'I thought we were done with this nonsense. It's been ten years, for God's sake. What will it take for you to just get over him? Do you think I'm stupid? Or blind? Don't you think I know how many times you've gone to bed crying because of him? How you turn your head on the street after men who look like him? Don't you think I know why you agreed to marry me?'

'We both knew, going into this marriage, we had pasts that were most likely going to stick around,' said Dominique, trying to calm him down.

'Stick around, yes. But this is not sticking around. This is meddling and interfering and taking over our lives. Your heart is closed, Dominique. It has been closed for a decade. You only ever had room for one person and since he's been gone you've been desperately trying to get him back, no matter what the cost, no matter in what shape or form. We were doomed from day one.'

'Don't say that, Vincent. You know how much I care for you.'

'Care? If I hear that word one more time, I'm going to be sick. Tell me you love me if you want to convince me. Tell me you love me more than you love him.'

Dominique's eyes filled with tears. She couldn't tell him that.

'Tell me the biggest dream of your life is not to see him walking through that door right this second. Tell me that if he walked in, you wouldn't leave me behind like a used carpet.'

Dominique raised her eyes and looked at him, desperately looking for the right words.

'I would never do that, Vincent. We are married; I made a vow to you. No matter what you think I wish or dream—'

That last remark seemed to infuriate him even more. 'I don't need your sense of duty and your pity. I need your love.' He fell into a chair, with his head in his hands, sobbing. She took him in her arms, and they stayed like that for a long time.

For days after their fight, she struggled.

What was she doing? She had to think of Anne, she couldn't be that selfish. And Anne needed and deserved a father and a mother, a loving family. And she had to think of Vincent too. It broke her heart to see how she was hurting him.

The more she thought about it, the more it seemed there was only one mature, responsible option: to try and make things work with Vincent, give her marriage another chance.

They decided they would move to Colmar, to be close to Anne who was starting her first year at La Rolande in the fall. Dominique would take the head curator position at the Unterlinden and Vincent could work on the book he had been talking about for years.

Dominique bought the house from Constance, who reluctantly accepted her money. But Dominique wouldn't have it any other way. She was going home, to the house she loved so much, in the town that meant so much to her, with her husband and their daughter. *This has to be a real chance we're giving our family, no more skeletons in closets, no more baggage, just a fresh start,* she conditioned herself, realizing they wouldn't stand a chance otherwise. Wondering if they stood a chance at all. But they had made a vow; they had made promises to each other. She had to at least try. Really try.

Dominique knew what that meant. Alexander had been gone for over a decade. He was gone. And she had to stop seeing him in every man she met or talked to. Anthony was not Alexander; he was just another man. She had to stop. It was time to say goodbye to Anthony.

But it wasn't easy. She felt despair and emptiness thinking about cutting all ties with him. She couldn't explain it, but he was her hope. Hope in something that couldn't be. The poor man had no idea; he must have wondered why she kept pouring her heart out to him in tens of letters.

With a heavy heart, she wrote one last letter. White lies weaved with hard truths.

Dear Anthony,

Please forgive me for the long letter you're about to read.

Years ago, I lost someone dear, someone I loved more than I thought was possible. After that, I went through hell and back for a long time and never thought I would pick myself up again. But I did, with the help of a kind, caring man who later became my husband. He offered me what I had been missing: a sense of belonging, love and family.

Recently, I came dangerously close to losing my husband. All this will surprise you but the reason I almost broke up my home is you. No, it's not your fault and it's not you – Anthony Peltz. It's you as I perceived you, as I imagined you. You have a lot in common with the man I loved and lost, and I was confused. I missed him so much and I was hanging on to some shred of hope that he wasn't lost. That I could make him come back to me.

I am so sorry to have dragged you into my unfinished

business, but I am writing to tell you I have decided to give my marriage a real chance. To truly do that, I have to give up once and for all this fantasy I have created. I have to let you go; you and everything that you have meant to me – even if it was only in my imagination.

I will hand in my official resignation from the European Restoration Initiative separately.

Dominique

Dominique left the letter to be forwarded by the European Restoration Initiative office at the Louvre as she arrived that morning and did her best not to think about it for the rest of the day. Impossible to do when her heart was filled with doubts and uneasiness.

How could she feel this bad if she'd done the right thing? She'd chosen family over loneliness; she'd chosen reality over a dream. She'd only said goodbye to a stranger, a man she'd never even seen. Why did she feel so heartbroken?

When the post was brought to her later that day, she found a letter from Anthony.

Dear Dominique,

You might not understand this now, but you must trust me. I need to leave for a while, to get my life in order.

I haven't told you a lot about myself but there is a reason for that and while I cannot tell you that reason now, I believe deep down in my heart it is for the best.

For years now I have been the ghost of the man I used to be, and I can't go on like this. I need to take my time to somehow accept everything that's happened to me and, if the stars align, to try and rebuild my life, without regrets and guilt.

I have made many mistakes, some out of fear, some out of good intentions gone wrong. I just hope it's not too late to fix them. I am sorry I cannot say more or give you more right now, but out of respect for you and your family, I feel I am doing the right thing.

Anthony

What that meant, Dominique had a hard time grasping entirely. On the same day, they were both telling each other goodbye. In different ways, with different words and for different reasons but that day was an end. The end of something that never even started, she thought and quickly wiped away her tears.

DOMINIQUE

5 SEPTEMBER 1974

COLMAR

Dominique and Vincent tried to make it work in Colmar. But no matter what they did, nothing seemed to make things better between them. The atmosphere was always tense. He couldn't get past what she had told him about Anthony, despite hearing again and again that they had stopped all communication.

Although, on the surface, she chose Vincent, Alexander was still in her heart. She hadn't let him go. She'd said goodbye to Anthony, yes, but never to the hope. Never to the dream. And Vincent knew it. He felt it. They were never alone. Alexander's ghost was always around.

More late-night fights followed in the next few months and things got much worse after Anne went to school. The gap between them widened. As time went by, their relationship seemed to go from bad to worse, until one day they sat down and had the conversation. With terrible sadness, they both admitted they were unhappy, lonely, and tired and, as painful as it was, it was time to move on. It was time to get a divorce.

Dominique often wondered why she had told her husband about Anthony and with such vivid detail. Subconsciously, she knew she had been looking for a way out. Out of their marriage and out of their perfectly rich and artificial Parisian life.

Vincent was right: she had never loved him like she loved Alexander.

'Was it all a lie then? Your marriage,' Lisa asked her one day.

'No, there are more types of love in this world than we could ever imagine.'

'Are you happy it's over?'

'Happy? I'm not happy, but I am at peace.'

'How is Anne taking it?'

'Better than I thought. She's such a big girl now. She heard us fighting, and she knew we were not happy, and she felt guilty. I think she felt we stayed together in the last year, at least, for her. But she has her school now, which she loves, and her friends, and I will see her every other weekend, when she's not staying with her father.'

'Are you coming back to Paris?'

'No. Vincent is, but I have decided to stay here, in Colmar. This is where home is. Always was. Don't worry. I'll be fine. We'll be fine.'

DOMINIQUE

9 OCTOBER 1974

COLMAR

With Anne away at school, Dominique found herself alone for the first time in years, and feeling lost, but she desperately refused to become a victim of her own decisions.

She didn't know what to do but dedicate all her time and energy to her work, to transforming the Alsatian museum into a veritable art institution. The Unterlinden had been in dire need of repairs ever since she was a child and the art collection needed heavy restoration as well.

Dominique knew it was in her power to make it happen. She used the money from her inheritance to restore the old Unterlinden Museum and its entire art collection. And outside of the work she was already doing with Marmottan and the Louvre, she started helping Unterlinden's big brothers – Moma, Palazzo Reale, and Tate – with their restoration efforts. Anything that prevented her from having time to think. Or be sad. Or imagine impossible scenarios.

On Anne's first weekend back from La Rolande, Dominique took a break from the museum renovation, and they both decided to declutter the study. It was long overdue.

'Why do you need all these books? Nobody's touched them in years,' said Anne.

She wiped the dust off one of them. 'I think we should give some to charity.'

'What books?' asked Dominique absentmindedly.

'Old stuff, adventure novels, a few art books but not like the ones you have in your library. I think it's mostly junk.'

'Sure, give them away.'

'Do you mind putting them in the hallway on your way out, Maman?' she asked.

Dominique nodded, got the books and left the room. The door to the hallway was closed and the pile of books made it impossible for her to open it properly. She tried a balancing act, which failed miserably, all the books landing on the floor. She picked them up, and among them she found some of the books she had read as a teenager. Painting, restoration, Impressionism, books she'd forgotten she had.

Among them, a large envelope.

'Where did this come from?' she asked out loud and opened it.

In it, she found a book covered in yellow paper and a letter.

And on the outside of the letter it said, 'For Zara, from Leon.'

'Are you alright?' asked Anne.

'I'm fine. I just need to go upstairs for a minute,' she said.

In her room, Dominique sat on the bed and opened the letter with trembling hands.

Dear Zara,

Here I am, back in Colmar, for the third time. It's been five years since I met you that evening in the museum. Five years when I couldn't forget about you. I think about you every day, still. I sometimes wonder why you left without a word and worry you might still be upset with me for missing our meeting. I hope I am wrong. I hope you found it in your heart to forgive me. I miss you. So much. I never thought I would feel this way, but here I am. Oh, how I wish I made it to Colmar that day.

I know what happened to your mother. I am so sorry you had to go through that alone. I would've wanted to be there for you. How I wish I had the chance to tell you how much you meant to me. How much you will always mean to me. I don't know what life has in store for me, but I know that because of you, I am better. I want to do better.

I also find myself often thinking about you and wondering if your life in Paris is glamorous and amazing, as you deserve. I hope it is. If I close my eyes, I can see you there, spending your time in museums, making magic happen. I can't wait to hear about you one day and all the amazing things you have done.

I don't know when or if you will ever get this. Know that whenever that happens, nothing will have changed for me. I'll still be the same person I was that first day in Colmar. Even if it's fifty years later.

Zara, I hope that wherever you are and whatever you do, you are happy and please, never ever give up your dreams.

And I hope that one day I will see you again. Or see you for the first time. It's strange, isn't it? I don't even know what you look like, yet I do. How could I not? You're in my heart. You are part of me.

Here's something to remember me by. I know Monet had always been mine, but I've always felt he brought us together and I want to give him to you. My godfather said this book can change lives. It changed mine because it brought me to you. I want you to have it. And perhaps, somehow, someday, it will bring you to me.

Always and forever,

Your Leon

She quietly sobbed. 'Leon,' she whispered.

Slowly, with great care, she held the book in her arms. How much she had loved that book and all that it represented. She hadn't seen it in twenty years.

On the first page, the initials she knew by heart.

A.P.

L.P.

Incredible. It was the exact same copy from the Unterlinden Museum. The one that had disappeared. How did it end up with Leon? How was it his?

The yellow paper covering it was frail and torn at the corners and barely holding on. Such an ugly cover for such a beautiful book. She ripped it, and underneath, untouched, the water lilies cover shone in the sun like an old friend saying hello. On the left inner cover, she found a handwritten note that had been protected all those years by the yellow paper.

June 8, 1954

Dear Leonard,

Give this book to your boy. When the time is right, it will change his life.

Your friend,

Jean Jacques D'Angers

Leon's letter and that inscription. The words floated in front of her eyes, like magic.

My godfather: Jean Jacques D'Angers.

Wait, JJ was Alexander's godfather. Was it possible?

Her conversation with JJ before he died:

'Who's Leonard? I've never heard you talking about him.'

'But you did, a long time ago. Leonard, Alexander's father.'

Leonard, Alexander's father. Leon Price. Alexander Price.

The blood drained from her face. 'Leon. Alexander,' she repeated. Like a robot.

Leonard Price. L.P.

Alexander Price. A.P.

It was never Vincent. It had never been him. No, that couldn't be. Vincent wouldn't have lied to her like that. And for so many years. Why would do such a thing? But he had, hadn't he?

The more she thought about it, the more she realized she had no doubt about it. Deep down in her heart, she knew. And somehow, she'd always known it. She could only truly love one man. And Leon, the boy she fell in love with when she was just a child was Alexander, the man she fell in love with when she grew up.

She'd loved only one man her entire life. How could she have been so oblivious to the signs, so stupid, so blind not to see the similarities? Yes, she had no way of knowing what Leon looked like but what about art? What about Monet? What about restoration? It was all there, finally clear after all those years of wondering. Same personality, same passion, same... so much 'same'. Her heart should've known. And it had, but her mind refused to believe it could happen. Fate did everything it could, but fate can't forcefully open somebody's eyes; people need to open them on their own.

Dominique wondered how it was possible they had both missed recognizing each other. Had neither of them wanted to believe destiny had played such a role in their story?

Yes, she had loved one man for twenty years and at that point she knew she would always love him. Only him.

What she felt for Anthony Peltz could only be explained one way.

'Oh, Mamie. What did you do? Did you run after him? Did you show up at his door?'

I smile. 'No, I didn't. Remember, it was all in my heart.

There was no proof, no certainty. Only what I felt. As always.'

'What then?'

'I wrote him a letter.'

'And what did he say when he wrote back?'

'He never did write.'

DOMINIQUE

12 OCTOBER 1974

PARIS

It had been a couple of months since Dominique had seen Vincent. He went back to Paris while she stayed in Colmar. They promised each other they would stay friends, maybe for Anne's sake, maybe even for themselves, since they had so much history. Just because their marriage hadn't worked didn't mean they would stop being in each other's lives. He said there were no hard feelings; she said the same.

But now, after Dominique had realized the truth about Leon, she wasn't so sure about what kind of feelings she had towards her ex-husband. One thing was clear though. She had to see Vincent right away. She wanted to hear it from him. His side of the story. There had to be an explanation. Because, as things stood then, she didn't know if she could ever forgive him for what he had done.

She called him before leaving Colmar and Vincent, although sounding surprised to hear she was coming over, didn't hesitate to suggest she should stay over at his place for the night. Dominique refused and told him she would instead stay with Constance, which he accepted without insisting.

In Paris, they met at Champ de Mars. He showed up five minutes late. 'We need to talk. Will you walk with me?' she asked.

'Of course. I miss our talks,' he replied and smiled.

'I'm afraid this might not be a very pleasant conversation. But it's all up to you.'

'Why? What's wrong? You sound serious.'

He sounded and looked a bit nervous. Apprehensive.

'It's about Leon,' she said after taking a few steps in silence.

He stopped. 'Leon?'

'It's not you, is it? It's never been you, Vincent. That was funny. The whole "I was brave like a lion". I let myself be fooled by it because I so wanted to believe it was you.'

'You wanted to, but you never did fully believe it,' he said with a sigh. 'I'm sorry.' His voice was shaky and he stopped for a moment. 'I'm sorry I was an idiot and lied to you. I never thought things would get this far. I never thought I would feel as much as I did for you. I was just curious at first and then—'

'You're not helping your cause, Vincent. If you're trying to apologize, let's just leave it at that,' Dominique said. She wanted to be more mad at him. But, from his demeanor, it was clear he already felt bad. He was already hurt. And he had been hurting for a long time.

'Yes, it is an apology. A heartfelt one, Dominique. You have to believe me. It was such a long time ago. At first,

I guess I just wanted to see what all the fuss was about. Who was the girl Leon was so cuckoo over? Besides, I'd promised I would get back at him if given the opportunity. And I guess that opportunity just fell in my lap. I'd never liked the guy. Because of him, my relationship with Nicole failed miserably. I just thought it was ironic she was in love with him, and he was in love with you. And here I was, minding my own business, and you showed up.'

'So you did all this because you wanted to get back at Leon for getting between you and Nicole?'

He shrugged. 'I don't know. Maybe. Initially. But—'

'But what?'

He took a deep breath. 'Then I spent more and more time with you and I fell in love with you, and I just couldn't tell you the truth without risking losing you.'

'So you continued lying to me all those years? Even after Alexander showed up. You knew he was Leon.'

'I was shocked you didn't recognize him, to be honest. I thought Colmar would come up in one of your conversations; I thought maybe Nicole would say something. But time passed, and you seemed oblivious. And I... I couldn't tell you the truth.'

'How could I recognize him? I had never seen him. And I heard his voice for an hour, when we were kids. He was a man when we met again. What you did was cruel,' said Dominique, feeling both angry and disappointed.

'Cruel? I loved you. I really loved you. And if he was the one for you, as you so strongly believe, you would've recognized him. But you didn't. I wasn't about to give you up just for the sake of honesty. I am not a bad man, Dominique, and you know that. All I did was because I loved you. Yes, it was wrong and childish of me – the whole curiosity and revenge thing – but that only lasted for a short while. Remember when I showed up at your house with a big bouquet of flowers and took you out for a picnic? After that day, I knew it wasn't just about revenge. It was about you and how you made me feel. I was falling for you so fast, it surprised me too.'

He looked away, then let his head down. He seemed older, tired. Alone.

'I never meant to hurt you. I just wanted us to be together. And I do regret lying to you. I was tempted to tell you the truth. Many times, actually. But after the accident—'

He stopped walking and looked at her.

'That's when I thought it would truly be cruel to reveal the truth. What was the point? He was dead and there was nothing anyone could have done to change that.'

Dominique's eyes were in tears.

She was about to tell him, 'You're wrong. He's not dead. He was never dead.' But she decided against it. They had both been through enough. He'd lied to her; she loved someone else. It wasn't all black and white. It had never been. And although her first reaction was to be furious with him, now, seeing Vincent and hearing him, she believed him. Maybe she couldn't forgive him. Not right away. But in time…

'I should go,' she said.

He hesitated for a moment. 'Do you think you could give me ten more minutes?'

'What for?'

'I want to show you something. I have it at home.'

'I don't know, Vincent. I really should get going.'

'Just ten minutes,' he insisted.

She agreed and followed Vincent back to his apartment, two streets away.

He led her to his office and invited her to sit.

'What is this about?' she asked as she sat.

He took an envelope out of a drawer and gave it to her. 'This. I think you should read it.'

'What is it?' she asked, opening it.

'A letter from Nicole that she wrote to me a week or so before she died.'

She held the paper in her hand. 'I don't think I should read it then.'

'Trust me,' he said.

Dominique tilted her head to the side. 'Is this the same letter you presented to the court?'

'And they didn't admit it as evidence,' he said sadly. 'Yes.'

Vincent,

I know this is out of the blue. It's been so many years since I wrote you a letter. Not since our days at La Rolande when you left for Paris. Who would've thought then we would end up in this situation? Not me.

I've been thinking a lot about my life lately; what it used to be and what it has become. And about yours too.

We've talked about our guilt over our affair ad nauseam and we'd always refer to it as us cheating on them with each other, but I'm coming to the realization that we were wrong. They cheated on each other with us. And not for a few months, like we did, but for years. They lied to themselves, they lied to us but, ironically, we're responsible for it. We pretended not to see what was happening, not knowing that even though they might not have recognized each other, in a strange, inexplicable way... they did.

We never should've strayed away from our path and into their lives, because these two were like comets. Blinding, burning fast, and destroying everything in their way and on their way to each other. We lost what we had, chasing the impossible. You can't make someone love you, no matter what you do. I think we both know that. Why didn't we realize it sooner? Why didn't we get out when we still had time? We could've been happy together; I think we could've. That night at the charity, when you told me who she was, I should've grabbed your hand and left.

I understand now how similar we are. Maybe too similar, and that has been our doom. Loving people who were never ours to love in the first place.

But now it's too late. For all of us. That's the saddest part of all of this.

Alexander is dead, my father hates me, you hate me, Dominique hates both of us, and an innocent soul has to suffer the consequences of our mistakes.

I look at Anne and know I must do something to spare her from the same fate I had. If she grows up with me, she'll become me. I'm sorry I can't give her to you. I'm really sorry. But I fear that for her sake, you would try to make things work between us. I know you. You are that kind of man. And I couldn't bear seeing the pain in your eyes. I've seen it too many times before... in my father's eyes, in Alexander's eyes when I was there and not someone else.

I think I know what's best for her, and it will not

take me much to make it happen. My father thinks the worst of me anyway; all I have to do is push him to his breaking point and he will ask me for Anne. I will agree immediately, because it is what he expects me to do.

That way... Anne will have what I didn't. She will be raised by him; she will get a chance to redo the life I so sadly failed at.

I want you to know, without a doubt, that I loved you. And, as much as you don't want to hear this, I loved him too. But I didn't love you enough to hold on to you, and I didn't love him enough to let him go.

But I love her enough!

It will break my heart to be parted from her, but I must do this. And I hope you will understand. I hope you will accept it in time.

I don't know why I am telling you all this. I guess I wanted to make sure you would understand when you found out, and you wouldn't be surprised. And don't be sad, whatever happens; know that everything happens for a reason and it's for the best.

Nico

Dominique had tears in her eyes. 'Do you think she—' She couldn't say it. 'Do you think her death wasn't an accident?'

'I don't know.'

'Back then, they were saying so many things about her. I never imagined what happened with Anne was her own planning. I guess I never really knew her.'

'I wonder if anyone truly knew her.'

Dominique sighed. 'She thought I hated her and that

makes me sad, because I didn't hate her. I felt sorry for her and—'

'And you felt sorry for me,' he said sadly.

She looked down.

'Nico was right though. We should have never done what we did. So many lives were changed because of that.'

'Yes, they were.'

'Don't hate me,' he said, almost begging her. 'Please, don't. I don't think I could live with myself knowing you hate me. I know I made a mistake. But I never meant to hurt you, Dominique. Please believe that. I loved you. Yes, I was selfish, but I never had bad intentions.'

She nodded, looked at him one more time, then turned around and left.

So many years she had lost. They both knew. They had known from the beginning. If only they had told them.

So many years she would never get back with Leon. But what about all the years ahead?

ANTHONY

CAMBRIDGE

Anthony had decided he needed a change of scenery, at least for a while. He would travel more so than usual and didn't plan on returning to England for a few months.

It was early December when he came back home for the first time in almost three months, and Mary was waiting for him at the door.

She helped him unpack and poured two glasses of wine for them to celebrate his return.

He had missed her, and he'd missed home too.

She called for him from the other room. 'Before I forget. I have these letters from October and November. Some have been forwarded from the Louvre. What do you want me to do with them?' she asked.

'Old mail? Just throw it,' Anthony said, but a moment

later changed his mind. 'Wait! Better yet, put everything in a box. I'll look at it later.'

She was about to leave for the night, but in the doorway, she stopped.

'On, and one more thing. Isn't JJ the man you told me about? Your godfather?'

'Yes. He was. Why?'

'I was arranging your shelves the other day saw an inscription on one of the books—'

'What book?'

'Not sure, something with flowers on the cover.'

'An inscription?' he repeated.

'It said something like "from JJ to AP". You told me to stack your old books but I didn't know if you meant that one too.'

'Where is it?' he asked, and Mary showed him a pile of boxes in the corner. 'In there, somewhere.'

He searched every single box. The book JJ had given him in the hospital and told him to wait before opening it. He had done as he was asked but when it was time to look at it, he couldn't find it anymore.

'I'll leave you to it then,' she said and quietly closed the door.

'Found it!' he yelped.

Anthony cleaned his desk and moved the box of old mail – that he had no real intention of opening – next to the door, to make room for the book. He opened it and flipped the pages slowly, carefully. A small envelope taped to the inner cover and some notes on different pages.

'Here goes nothing,' said Anthony.

1 December 1969

Dear Mr Jean-Jacques Angers,

Please be informed our agent in Milan has located another painting that matches the given description, and, per your instructions, he has initiated the transaction without delay.

The buy will need to be listed but we took every possible safety measure to ensure your privacy is protected. The transaction will be cataloged as a private sale and the name of the buyer is under private collection/ anonymous so there will not be any associations between your name or your company's name and the painting.

The artwork has been securely transferred to Banque Hottinguer under the name you indicated, alongside the others.

As always, a pleasure doing business with you.
Giuseppe M. Bartolomeo

He browsed the book again, not knowing exactly what to look for. On page 77 he found the initials again, A.P., and a series of numbers written in pencil, in JJ's handwriting: 381209 and on page 144 another set: 120964.

'One or more paintings, A.P., a bank name and two sets of numbers,' said Anthony out loud, trying to make sense of it all. 'I trust you will know how to find what you are looking for. Even if you don't know you're looking for it.' JJ's last words to him echoed.

Was he talking about the writings in the book and the letter? How strange it was that the same book reappeared in his life, twenty years later. True, not the same copy he had as a child. This must've been JJ's copy. And he'd given it to him. Yet again. Anthony closed his eyes and remembered the inscription on the first book, the one he'd gifted Zara.

8 June 1954

Dear Leonard,
    Give this book to your boy. When the time is right, it will change his life.
    Your friend,
    Jean Jacques D'Angers

'JJ was right, the book did change my life,' he said and smiled. 'And now, somehow, it has come back to me. To change my life again? I wonder...'

ANTHONY

ZURICH

The last couple of days had been a whirlwind. Armed with the book, the letter and the codes, Anthony got in his car and drove to Zurich. He got to the bank shortly before closing, and in the most casual tone possible, asked to discuss something confidential with the branch manager.

The manager invited him to his office. 'Could I please have the name on the account?' he asked after closing the door behind him.

Anthony hesitated for a second. What if they asked for ID?

'Alexander Price?'

The man nodded slightly, then asked, 'May I please have the code?'

Anthony took a deep breath.

'I have two actually,' he said, testing the waters.

'You are correct. May I please have the codes?'

'They are 381209 and 120964.'

'Please follow me,' the manager said and took Anthony to a vaulted room.

'Someone will be with you shortly. Thank you for your business, Mr Price. It is truly an honor to finally meet you,' the man said then left the room quietly.

Anthony could hardly believe what was happening. It was all like a passage from one of the adventure books he read as a child.

A young woman followed by a man, twice Anthony's size, brought in three huge flat boxes and laid them on a long metal table. The woman placed a small box on the table as well.

'If you have any questions, we are outside,' said the man, before leaving the room.

Anthony knew what the size and shape of the boxes meant. There were paintings inside, but he didn't dare hope what paintings he might find. When he opened them, he couldn't believe his eyes. The painting he had been looking for, ever since he was a child. Only that there were three of them. One in every box. All seemingly identical. It was incredible!

He'd always known there were four. One, the original, displayed in museums and three gifted to close friends. Never made known to the public. He started laughing. He had all three now, not one. Three incredibly valuable, priceless works of art.

'JJ, you are a clairvoyant,' he said as if talking to him. 'This book keeps changing my life. *You* keep changing my life, old friend.'

Anthony was both sad and happy. Sad because he was

never going to see JJ again, but also happy because he'd gotten to talk to him one last time and hold his hand. They had said their goodbyes.

'The small box,' said Anthony, almost forgetting about it. 'What more could I hope for?'

Inside, there was only an envelope containing a letter.

Dearest friend,

I didn't believe her for the longest time and even as I'm writing this, I still can't bring myself to fully believe she's right. But, when someone feels so strongly about something, despite all the odds, despite everyone and everything, despite death and time and distance, when someone believes in love as much as she believes... how can you not? How can you not at least hope she's right? How can you not hope she knows something you don't? And so, I too started to hope against hope, alongside her. Because love is a magical thing. And if one thing can bring two people together, that is true love, even if to everyone else it seems impossible.

If she's wrong, I don't want to know. Then this letter will never be read and you, you are not out there anymore. But if she's right, it means I too will be reunited with my love: my beloved Demetria. Because in love anything is possible. And I want to believe. For you and for me!

Alas, time is never on our side and it seems I couldn't wait for you any longer, but do not be sad, my friend. If you are reading this it means that – wherever I am – I am a happy man.

As I come to the end of this mortal life, I am convinced,

now more than ever, that nothing is more important than love. In all its shapes and forms, at all ages and no matter what the ending is. Love is the destination, the journey. Love is the reason.

Your friend, always,

JJ

ANTHONY

LONDON

Anthony returned home. It was dark out and he stood by the window, looking out into space and wondering what he should do. He knew what he wanted to do with the paintings, but how could he, without revealing his identity and without interfering in Dominique's life? He had no right. But it was her big day. The Unterlinden reopening. Those paintings would take her career to soaring heights and she deserved everything good in the world.

In the window, besides his reflection, he saw the box of old mail next to the door. 'I thought I got rid of you.' He laughed out loud, realizing he was talking to a box.

Distracted, he emptied the contents on the floor and started going through the impressive pile of – mostly – junk from the last few months.

'Nothing, nothing, nothing. Junk, magazines, flyers,

nothing. Hmm,' he said and turned an envelope on the other side.

Painfully familiar handwriting. The stamp was from 10 October. Two months before. A letter from Dominique.

Dear Anthony,

If what you're about to read sounds crazy, or it offends you or scares you then please tear this paper into pieces and burn it.

You have your life and I have mine, for better or worse. I have hesitated to write this letter to you. I have started it so many times. Why am I writing to you now? The reason is simple. Regrets. No, not plural. Only one regret. The biggest what-if that I've been carrying with me for over twenty years.

Ever since I received your first letter, I have lived with the feeling that we have met before. Not once, not twice, not accidentally on the street but in a more profound way.

I have recently discovered something that eluded me for decades. That the boy I loved when I was just a girl living here in Colmar turned out to be the man I loved when I was a grown woman. Coincidence, some may say; fate, I dare contradict.

Recently, my husband and I have gone our separate ways. It was wrong of me to even pretend I could ever be with another man, because, you see, since I was fifteen, I have only dreamed of one love, one soul, one heart. Whether his name was Leon, Alexander or…

I don't believe my heart is capable of loving another

man but him. Not in the same unconditional, heart-stopping way. Our lives revolved around each other and even when we didn't know it, all our choices eventually led us back to each other.

My question is this: Who are you, Anthony Peltz? You are him, aren't you? You are my Leon. My Alexander. My one. It's always been you. Only you.

Always,

Your Dominique

Anthony read and reread the letter; he couldn't believe what was happening. What he had hoped but never thought was possible. What he always dreamed of. Dominique was Zara; Zara was Dominique. He had loved one woman his whole life. She was the one and she always had been. And his Dominique knew. She knew who he really was, although it defied all logic. She did, she felt it; her heart recognized his. His Dominique was still his Dominique; she had never stopped being his. He might've been dead to the whole world but not to her.

Anthony's eyes were full of tears but, for the first time in many years, they were happy tears: unexpected, miraculous, wonderful tears.

He kissed the letter, put it back in the envelope, and picked up the phone.

'I need to send three packages from Switzerland to France and I need them to get there by tomorrow noon.'

One more thing left on his list. The Marmottan Museum.

DOMINIQUE

COLMAR

Anthony had never answered her letter and now she was feeling all sorts of doubts. She'd imagined it all: it wasn't him; he didn't receive the letter. She called to see if he was still in charge of the European Restoration. He was. Then he must've received it, just like all the other letters. And it had to be him because her heart had never felt as sure as it had when she found the book and the letter.

With the Unterlinden reopening coming up soon, Dominique knew she had to pull herself together. As hard as it was.

Months since she started working on it, the little Alsatian museum was unrecognizable, even to Dominique. So much work, but she'd made it, and just in time. She was pleased with the result and proud of what they had accomplished, but something was missing, something that would make the museum stand out. She had robust collections, but nothing out of the ordinary.

The day before the reopening, Dominique arrived at the museum a little after seven to get a head start and check on the final details.

In front of the main entrance was a black van with Swiss license plates. Dominique wondered if she had missed a delivery or if there was a problem with one of the exhibits. She hoped nothing was wrong. Although she didn't have any big names attending the reopening, even if it was only for the people of Colmar, it still had to be perfect.

'Miss Gardiner,' her assistant said the moment Dominique opened the door. 'I was just about to call. These gentlemen have a delivery for you. The boxes are in your office.'

Two men, in black suits, were just getting back in the van.

'Excuse me,' said Dominique. 'Who is the delivery from and what is it?'

He looked at the yellow pad that was in the passenger seat. 'Couldn't tell you, madame. It says "Anonymous donation" for three of the boxes and there's a note for the fourth one. Let me find it. One moment please,' he said and went to the back of the van.

'Ahem,' he coughed loudly to get Dominique's attention. 'One-year loan from Musée Marmottan as a token of appreciation for your remarkable restoration efforts.'

'That's it?' asked Dominique, intrigued.

He nodded politely. 'Have a good day.'

Dominique cut the ropes and with her assistant's help

slowly opened the cover of the first box. She took a step back. Her eyes were playing tricks on her, certainly.

It was a Monet. A Le Havre. Strikingly similar to *Impression, Sunrise. Soleil Levant*. But not it. Nothing she'd ever seen before, in reality or even in an art book.

With trembling hands, she opened the other two boxes. Three almost identical paintings. Minuscule differences only scholars and experts would notice. Glorious. Magnificent. Three paintings nobody knew existed. But she knew. Leon had told her. Was that possible? Her heart, her heart wasn't wrong.

One more box to open, bearing the stamp of Musée Marmottan.

When she cut the ropes, she didn't expect to see in front of her eyes, in her museum, in all its glory: Monet's *Impression, Sunrise*. The original painting.

'Is this what I think it is?' asked her assistant.

Dominique collapsed on a chair and stared at the paintings. 'Can this be?'

She kept calling the Marmottan Museum but received no information about the loan. She phoned other experts in Impressionism to inquire about the three paintings. According to official documents, they didn't exist. Of course they didn't.

Her colleagues called other colleagues who called other colleagues and in less than twenty-four hours the entire art scene buzzed with rumors about the never-before-seen Monet inside a small provincial museum in Alsace. Which coincidentally had a grand reopening the very next day. She got bombarded with calls from the press, experts, scholars and countless requests to attend the opening of the museum from the biggest names in the art world. Dominique was overwhelmed.

She kept trying to focus on the opening event but all she could do was think about the paintings. Could she dare to hope? Was it all a dream, again? She couldn't go through the disappointment again. But what a beautiful, impossible, magic dream it was.

DOMINIQUE

9 DECEMBER 1974

COLMAR

The night before the opening Dominique had a dream. The same dream she'd had twenty years before, right before meeting Leon for the first time. But now, when she woke up, it all made sense. She looked like the woman in the mirror. She *was* the woman in the mirror. And that night, when all the guests had arrived, the museum would also look exactly as it had in the dream.

Only two things were missing. In the morning, she rushed to the store next to the town square. She had a dress in mind. A specific dress she had been dreaming of her whole life.

A few hours later, everything was set. Colmar had probably never seen such commotion and trepidation as that day. Important people from all over the world showed up. Dominique couldn't have been happier. Critics, buyers, and media, they were all fighting for a better look at the Monet paintings.

'Who is the owner of these paintings?'

'I am. But I have no intention of selling them, if that's what you're looking for,' replied Dominique to the appraisers, who didn't look like they believed her.

'Each of them is worth well over eighty million dollars,' insisted another.

She smiled, nodded and ignored the conversations about money. Those paintings were priceless. How could they know? How could they understand?

She took a deep breath, before stepping into the big gallery where the reception and party were underway. It looked like people were having a wonderful time. The musician was playing something on the piano but there was too much noise in the gallery and you could barely hear. Something classic perhaps. Vivaldi's *Four Seasons*.

Dominique was there physically but her mind and her heart were somewhere else, uncontrollably searching for him, looking for answers.

Someone said something to her, but she didn't understand or maybe she didn't hear. She kept staring at the women and men, all dressed elegantly, sipping their champagne from crystal flutes and admiring the massive paintings on the walls. Especially the Monet. The Monets.

What a powerful sensation of déjà vu. The noises, the light, the people. Like she had lived that night before.

Dominique walked slowly towards the corner of the room and found herself standing in front of a mirror. She took a step back and gasped, looking at herself in that beautiful, long, flowy emerald-green dress. She touched her hair and the tiara-like headband. Yes, she looked exactly like in her dream. That beautiful, impossible dream, from twenty years ago.

She went to the store, thinking that if somehow she recreated everything she saw in her reverie, the dream would come true. But there was still one missing piece. The most important one. The man in her dream.

The musician stopped, then nodded as if she was talking to someone. Moments later the young woman started playing again and the room, as if on a signal, went quiet. Absolutely quiet. Only Dominique found herself humming along. 'Hymne a l'Amour'.

Her heart beat fast; her legs were weak. She held on to a chair, afraid she'd fall.

Across the room, a pair of sapphire-blue eyes. That was all she saw. It was as if a void ate everybody else in the room up and it was just the two of them, alone, staring at each other. Dominique didn't move, barely breathing. She was even afraid to blink and to miss that moment.

She heard a voice, the same voice she heard a long time ago, that night at the charity ball.

'I am here.'

Dominique couldn't control her tears, she couldn't, and she didn't want to. Not anymore.

He walked towards her and she saw his eyes were tearing up as well. He stopped in front of her, not saying a word, and they stared into each other's eyes.

'I know you, we've met before,' he said, his voice shaky.

'We have, haven't we?'

'Maybe in another life, or maybe in my dreams,' he whispered.

'Maybe in another life, or maybe in my dreams,' she whispered simultaneously.

Tears ran down her cheeks.

He smiled. 'We keep seeing each other,' he said, 'just like that day. That wonderful Wednesday at the café.' Their first Wednesday.

'Seems so,' she replied, still crying. 'You know you're standing in my museum?'

He looked around. 'I am? I'm sorry, I didn't know,' he said, trying to sound serious.

'It's okay,' she continued in the same serious tone. 'You can have it today. You know, this is the best museum in the world.'

'Is it?' he said and took her hands in his.

'What do you see? Out there?' she asked, showing him the walls covered in paintings.

'Lilies? A sunrise? Sunset? Colors?'

'Close your eyes,' she said. And she did too.

'Do you see that skinny girl sitting on the floor and holding a lilies book? What about the boy with his eyes closed, trying to imagine what she looks like? Remembering how she makes him feel so he can find her? Again and again? Always?' she asked.

He opened his eyes. His face lit up. 'I get it. This is the best museum in the world.'

'I've wanted to do this for ten years,' he whispered. His hands cupped the sides of her face, gently. His lips stopped for a moment on her eyes. Her cheeks. Dominique felt she was melting away. Disappearing like a dream in the morning. She felt his warm breath and touching his chest with her hand, she felt his heart beating so fast. In tandem with hers. Same rhythm. One heart. One soul. His lips touched hers and the world stopped. Time stopped.

'People say it for a reason. Because it's true. It does happen. The butterflies, the weak knees, the knots in your stomach. When it happens, hold on to it. Hold on to it like your life depends on it. Because it does. Depend on it.'

She held on to him as if she was losing her balance. As if she was afraid it was all a dream, and she would wake up and he'd be gone. He gently caressed her face, her hair.

'I'm sorry it took me so long to come back, to tell you I love you. I love you!'

'I love you! Only you, always,' she said and pressed her lips to his, losing herself in him. In their love.

DOMINIQUE

9 DECEMBER 2019

COLMAR

'And that, my darling girl, is how your Grandfather Anthony and I fell in love with each other, again and again and again. Three months later, we were married in the small church in Colmar. Shortly after, I got pregnant with our first son and the rest is history,' I say, smiling.

'You mean my Grandfather Alexander. Or should I say Leon?'

I chuckle. 'And *Impression, Sunrise*, well, its adventure continued after I returned it to Musée Marmottan. A few years later, it was stolen. This time the original. Although it is said that whoever took it was looking for one of three your grandfather and I have.'

'Did they ever recover it?'

'Five years later, somewhere in Corsica. And ever since, it's been living a quiet life.'

Valerie laughs. 'So far.'

'So far,' I say.

'Mamie, what about Grandpa Vincent? How did you two...?'

'Become close again?'

'Yes.'

'In time, we forgave each other, I think. We had been not only a couple, but also good friends for such a long time and we missed each other. Plus, we were both your Aunt Anne's parents. I was very upset with him but he apologized so many times for pretending to be Leon, that your Grandfather Anthony couldn't take it anymore and forced me to forgive him. That is... after he punched him in the nose.'

I laugh. 'Vincent said he deserved it. Then, slowly, he started visiting again, even stayed weekends with us here in Colmar. He never remarried, but he was happy, writing his books and spending as much time as he could with Anne, and then with his grandchildren.'

Valerie smiles. 'I remember him telling us stories, when we were kids. Wonderful stories. I am surprised he never told me this one.'

'It wasn't his story to tell,' I say, smiling back.

Valerie stares at me, like a child seeing a snow globe for the first time.

'Magical,' she whispers. 'Thank you. For the story. For everything.'

'With all my love, darling,' I say, and she wraps her arms around me.

Valerie looks out the window, at the snow falling on the trees. Slowly, taking its time.

'I never thought I'd say this or feel it. Is it really possible?'

'What?'

'Falling in love without seeing the other person? Without knowing who they are?'

'What do you think?' I say.

Her eyes are teary. 'I think it's possible. If it's true love. If they're your soulmate. Because your soul recognizes their soul; no matter what they look like, no matter how their voice sounds, what color their eyes are.'

I smile, relieved, like a weight has been lifted off my shoulders.

ANTHONY

COLMAR

I haven't been Alexander Leonard Price in fifty-five years. It was bizarre hearing my old name tonight. Like I've stepped into another world for a few hours. Back in time. I wonder how Dominique felt reliving it all. I know it wasn't easy for her. When she told me a few years ago she wanted to write it all down, her part but also my part, I didn't think it was a good idea. Some of the things we went through were painful. Some were still a blur. But now, listening to her, I understand. Dominique always felt it was her duty to warn Valerie of what might happen if she ignores her heart, but also to let her know about the magical power of their dreams. They share a special bond. Just like we do. Different but just as magical.

I looked at Dominique as she was reading tonight, and I loved her more for it. I loved her more after hearing the entire story. I wanted to say I was sorry for what I put her through, but I know she wouldn't want my apologies. She'd say it was meant to be. We wouldn't be here otherwise.

I've loved her for every moment of every day since I was a boy. When I didn't know what she looked like, when I didn't know if I would ever see her again. I loved her when I couldn't remember her or anything else. I loved her when I thought I'd lost her. And each day since. We've been married for forty-five years. We've traveled the world, raised our children, saved art. We've lived a full, happy, wonderful, magical life, Dominique and me.

Valerie has tears in her eyes.

'The song,' she murmurs. 'The first time he and I talked, I heard a song on Spotify. And when I woke up after the dream, I heard it again.'

'What song, dear?' asks Dominique.

'This one,' she says, her face pale, and turns the volume up on the radio. 'Is this like my book with lilies on the cover?'

Dominique smiles and Valerie doesn't wait for an answer. She jumps to her feet, grabs her phone, throws her laptop in a backpack together with a few random T-shirts. She hugs her grandmother, then me, so tight I can't breathe, and runs out the door.

'Where is she going?' I ask.

'Probably to Sydney.'

'Why Sydney?'

'To follow her dreams.'

'Good girl,' I say and can't help but smile.

*

Today is our anniversary. Sixty-five years since the day we met. And, like every year, we have somewhere to be and we can't be late.

I help Dominique put her coat on, take her hand, and look into her eyes.

'I love you,' she whispers, and my heart is full.

'Always, only you,' I say.

People sometimes ask me – perhaps because I'm old and they think I must be wise as well – what makes people fall in love. Truly in love. I don't know the answer to that question, but I know someone who does. And if you listen to her carefully, you will too. All you have to do is follow your heart. It's that simple.

DOMINIQUE

COLMAR

I've passed on to Valerie everything I know. Everything I felt. All my victories and defeats. She can avoid making the same mistakes if she chooses to. She will make her own. And then, maybe, one day, she will tell her story to her daughter or granddaughter. The story of her dreams and her destiny.

My dream and my destiny are here, in front of me. Smiling lovingly at me, in the dark, like he did sixty-five years ago when I didn't even see him. But I recognized his smile. My soul recognized it. And I would recognize it again if sixty-five more years passed.

As soon as Valerie leaves, we put on our coats and walk hand in hand to the museum. Our museum. When we arrive, we sneak into the rare books section, sit on the floor in the dark, and talk. From time to time, he gently pulls me closer and kisses me.

On our way back, we pass the bistro on the corner and wave at the owner who's busy putting on Christmas lights. We stop and listen to the song playing on his turntable.

Hymne a l'Amour. How fitting. How us.

'Dance with me?' he asks, and I have butterflies. I still do, after all this time.

We dance slowly, as we have done so many times before, fitting perfectly in each other's arms. The lights, the music, the universe are all pushing us in the same direction. As they always have. Towards each other.

I don't know how much time we have left here. It might be a day, a month, a year, and it doesn't really matter. What matters is now. Today. Tonight. What we've had and what we'll always have. Love.

The kind of love that survives time, distance. Even death.

The kind of love I wish for you.

Acknowledgements

I started writing *Someday in Paris* on my birthday in 2015. My intention was to give it to my husband as a gift for our wedding anniversary: a magical love story inspired by our own. That happened as expected. What was totally unexpected was his reaction to it and how that powerful and emotional reaction gave my long-forgotten dreams new wings and led to… today.

Writing has always been the dream. Writing stories the ultimate dream. Fresh out of college, I went about it the only way I knew how, and I got a job with a newspaper, then a television network. I was writing and I should've been happy, but it turns out news articles and love stories have little in common. Nothing, really.

It took me a while to fully and truly listen to my heart — moving from Romania, living in France, getting married, having a baby, then moving to the United States. I had a new life to build in a new country, a demanding, high-responsibility full-time job, a small child and a hundred other things happening. Why add more when there was so little time to go around? Because you can only ignore your heart for so long.

I missed writing terribly. I had to do it. Stolen hours at night, early mornings before work, on weekends. Three years later, I finally decided to write the story of my heart, the one that had been dancing in my mind for a long time. And even though the plan had been just for the two of us to see it, fate disagreed. I'm sure glad it did!

Writing *Someday in Paris* has been the most amazing, thrilling, emotional, enlightening and liberating experience of my life. From that very first draft to the last edits, from not knowing how to even find a literary agent to wondering if anyone would ever love my book as much as I did, I lived it all with maximum intensity. And still do.

There were ups and downs these past five years, I'm not going to say it was all smooth sailing. But what kept me going – outside of my stubbornness and my blind faith in this magical love story – were the people I surrounded myself with on this adventure.

I will start with my brilliant agent, Hannah Sheppard. Just like the characters in my book, we had our own missed connections that lasted almost two years. But as it is with everything that's meant to be, we finally came together and I'm happy we did. Hannah, you are wonderful and such a joy to work with. Thank you for all the love, faith and support (and patience). I couldn't have asked for a better partner on this journey.

Rhea Kurien, editor extraordinaire. Thousands of miles and an eight-hour time difference and I can't even feel it. We are so in tune – spooky, I know – and have such an awesome relationship, I am amazed every single day and so very glad we found each other. Your love, enthusiasm and vision for this story from day one fueled me with positive energy and has been truly inspiring. *Someday in Paris* is better because of you and I will always be thankful for that!

My beta readers, the first people outside my family who told me they cried when reading the story and how much they loved it. They also gave me valuable feedback and constructive criticism which I took to heart. You all said you believed one day this will happen and you were right! Thank you for all your help.

On a personal note, love and a huge thank you, as always, to my family, my parents. I wouldn't be here without you (not just literally). I am who I am – a bookworm among many other things – because of you.

And of course, love and thanks, to my friends. No matter where we are in the world, you are all in my heart.

And for the next three: This one's for you. With all my heart!

My mother, who taught me to believe in myself and who, from near or far, has always been so much more than just a great parent, friend and supporter. Mom, you are everywhere in the book, not just in one character.

Chris, who is not only the love of my life, my biggest cheerleader, the voice of reason, the shoulder, the arms, and the heart, but also a wonderful human being, an incredible father and the best husband this girl could've asked for. Only you, always!

Dominique, my beautiful, strong, smart daughter. I know you're too young now to read the story, but one thing you're not too young for is believing in yourself. Remember that anything you want to do, you can. Anything! And I – we – will always be by your side, loving you and cheering you on, unconditionally. As for love, yes... magical, once-in-a-lifetime, heart stopping, stronger than anything... this is the kind of love I wish for you!

About the Author

OLIVIA LARA was born and raised in Bucharest in a family of booklovers and storytellers. Since university she has worked as a journalist and marketer in Romania, France and the United States. She is currently a marketing executive in San Francisco and lives in the Bay Area with her husband, young daughter and four cats. This is her first novel.

For more from Olivia, visit her website at Olivia-Lara.com. You can also follow her on Twitter @olilara_writes, on Instagram @olivialara.writes, or Facebook at facebook.com/olivialaraauthor.

Hello from Aria

We hope you enjoyed this book! If you did let us know, we'd love to hear from you.

We are Aria, a dynamic digital-first fiction imprint from award-winning independent publishers Head of Zeus. At heart, we're committed to publishing fantastic commercial fiction – from romance and sagas to crime, thrillers and historical fiction. Visit us online and discover a community of like-minded fiction fans!

We're also on the look out for tomorrow's superstar authors. So, if you're a budding writer looking for a publisher, we'd love to hear from you. You can submit your book online at ariafiction.com/we-want-read-your-book

You can find us at:
Email: aria@headofzeus.com
Website: www.ariafiction.com
Submissions: www.ariafiction.com/
we-want-read-your-book

@ariafiction

@Aria_Fiction

@ariafiction